AWAKENING

DANCING WARRIORS TRILOGY ~ PART I

∽

*when Those of Grace hear again
the Unwilled One comes*

∽

KEVIN M DENTON

www.kevinmdenton.com

Published by New Generation Publishing in 2021

Copyright © Kevin M Denton 2021

First Edition

The author asserts the moral right under the Copyright, Designs and Patents Act 1988 to be identified as the author of this work.

All Rights reserved. No part of this publication may be reproduced, stored in a retrieval system or transmitted, in any form or by any means without the prior consent of the author, nor be otherwise circulated in any form of binding or cover other than that which it is published and without a similar condition being imposed on the subsequent purchaser.

ISBN
　　Paperback　　978-1-80031-395-8
　　Hardback　　978-1-80031-394-1
　　Ebook　　　978-1-80031-393-4

Cover design by Nicholas Roberts

www.newgeneration-publishing.com

*Reality is the purview of those
who lack imagination.
It is much overrated.*

This book is dedicated to those who
love to sojourn in distant lands,
far away from their daily toils.

It is my fervent desire to transport you there.

ACKNOWLEDGMENTS

Thank you to all those who have supported me during the considerable number of years it has taken to complete this endeavour.
A book such as this is never solely the product of the author, for so many people contribute in so many ways.

Special thanks must go to Alison, Elaine, Debbie, Steve and Praful for their excellent feedback. Their encouragement, as well as their suggestions, have helped make this book a reality.

Glossary

A full list of character names,
geographical references
and miscellaneous terms
may be found at the end of the book.

1

Nikrá slumped back and tossed his reading glass on to the table, narrowly avoiding several delicate parchments littered across its worn leather surface. The near-miss didn't bother him as much as it should have done. A dreadful neck ache had set in, the result of too many hours spent leaning forwards squinting at texts, trying to make out faded words and fathom long-forgotten meanings. As with many an ancient manuscript in the Cymàtagé library, deciphering such material required good eyes, a modicum of discernment and a plentiful supply of hours. Of those, he could muster only two.

Overtaken by an expansive yawn, he glanced round at the nearby bookcases. They seemed forlorn and unloved, languishing in each other's shadows like forgotten sentries, hopeful that some passer-by might notice them. But there was no one else about. A lack of oil in the desk lamp's reservoir was enough to indicate the hour was an ungodly one, the existence of which no sane man would wish to know. So the absence of other patrons was hardly a surprise. He let out a mirthless chuckle at the thought; studying all night had been a lot easier back when he'd been an acolyte, a young man in his prime. Yet those days were long gone. Now, staying awake much beyond supper was a challenge.

Snapping out of his reverie with a resigned huff, he retrieved his discarded reading glass and got back to work. Another hour trailed its forebears before he was able to lay his quill down for the final time. He picked up his scrap of parchment, some old document too faint to be useful, and scanned what he'd written on the back of it:

> *'when Those of Grace hear again,*
> *the Unwilled One comes.*
> *times of great strife are His path.*
> *under the heel of a new Master the Land will reel.*
> *as water divides, so shall the Peoples be,*
> *then by their own hearts will They be betrayed.'*

"So much work, and so little to show for it," he muttered, giving his head a single shake of dismay.

The revelation had come to him some while ago, but as with all his words of knowledge, it had been delivered in his native tongue, Alondrian. The last few hours had seen it translated into First Dialect A'lyavine, which was no small undertaking, given the language's formidable difficulty.

The Tongue of the Ancients hadn't been a widely spoken language in years. More recently, even his fellow mages and the higher scholars were letting it laps into disuse. So much knowledge had already disappeared into the ether; the pronunciations, the inflections, the obscure meaning of colloquial expressions. Such loss made its translation an unenviable task. So contextually sensitive was it that being an expert in history was almost mandatory to wheedle out the meaning of some of its phrases.

If it had simply been a dead and useless language, its decline would probably have gone unlamented. But that was far from the case. A'lyavine was the Taümathic language, possessed of a unique ability to direct the mind and shape desires. Without it, mages wouldn't be able to bind the Taümatha to their will, rendering the very magic that they made their business next to useless. Yet in this day of spells prepared by those who had gone before, of incantations learned by rote, the mages' creative use of A'lyavine had all but expired.

That thought drew his attention to young Akmir, slumped over the far edge of the table, looking very much as though he too had expired. His head rested on folded forearms, with his grey, curly hair sprouting in an unruly manner in every direction known to man. The present acolytes regarded him as approaching fossilisation, so Nikrá was prepared to admit that perhaps the term 'young' was no longer applicable. Yet having thought of him that way for decades, it was a habit hard to break.

"Rise and shine, my friend."

Akmir stirred and peered out from under a nonchalantly half-opened eyelid. "Hmm?"

"I've finished." Nikrá wafted his completed endeavour in the air.

"Humph."

Akmir usually took a while to find his vocal chords having nodded off. Lamentably, there wasn't any tea to assist with his revival; the pot was cold, the last of its contents long since drained. It would be a few minutes before reality regained his attention.

With an aged grunt, Nikrá rose and began putting away the

reference works he'd been using. He left the ancient copy of the Telem-aki beside Akmir. Within its pages were recorded all the principle revelations of the great prophet, Amatt the Blind, Alondria's most revered seer. The book, one of the Cymàtagé's most precious, had its own dedicated cabinet in the vault downstairs, to which it would be returned once the evening's endeavours had been verified.

"What time is it?" Akmir eventually managed.

Nikrá returned to his seat. "Late – early – take your pick."

Akmir's brow was momentarily thrown into confusion, furling and unfurling a couple of times before he thought to squint up at the library's domed skylight. "Well, at least it's still dark outside. Maybe there's a salvageable element to my night's sleep."

Nikrá let out a grunt. "While you've been snoring, *I've* been working."

"And…"

Nikrá slid his translation across the table. Akmir placed it to one side, stifled a yawn, and opened the Telem-aki to a point he had marked earlier. He began comparing the translation with the book's contents.

Nikrá watched with mild amusement as his friend's reaction began with interest, rose through scepticism, then careered full-tilt towards incredulity.

"Your prophecy matches Amatt's word for word," Akmir concluded with a slight tremor.

Nikrá sighed with relief. This prophecy had landed on him weeks ago, but a lack of discernment over its meaning and intended recipient had led to a great deal of deliberation, much whilst burning the midnight oil. Somewhere along the way, a rather insidious thought had sidled in; this prophecy had been delivered before. Such a notion had posed a thorny question all of its own – who, within the whole panoply of history, could have received the original?

Akmir had provided the answer. He was the Adak-rann's most senior representative at the Cymàtagé, a scholar of extraordinary accomplishment. The members of his order were the experts in all things historical. Preserving the past was their calling, a duty to which each brother dedicated himself with the fervour of a religious devotee. With uncanny insight, he had known almost straight away where to look.

Akmir pushed the Telem-aki across the table, giving it a half turn and pointing out the passage. Nikrá scanned through the original.

Scriptorial lettering verses his scruffy handwriting aside, Amatt's ancient prophecy and his recent one were identical.

"Well, there you have it. So the question now is, what does it mean?"

Akmir sucked in a breath between his teeth. "The more intriguing question is, why has this prophecy been repeated? Twelve hundred years have passed since Amatt's day."

Nikrá nodded as he considered the implications of that. "Prophecies usually either come to pass, or they don't. I've never heard of one coming twice before."

"Nor I. Since they're meant to come from the gods, if they're given to the right person at the right time, they shouldn't need to be given more than once."

Nikrá grimaced. He'd never been keen on the idea of random deities mucking about in what he saw as essentially *his* mind. "Yet this one has, so it seems."

"Then there must be a good reason. Assuming it's true, of course."

"And your opinion on that?"

Akmir puffed his cheeks out as he considered his response. "Well, Amatt was the most reliable prophet Alondria has ever known. All his predictions were fulfilled…"

"Except this one."

"Except, as you say, this one. Twenty-one came to pass during his lifetime, and two just after his death. But this one, it was never regarded as being on a par with the others. It became known as the Twenty-fourth Prophecy, though it was, in point of fact, one of his earlier revelations. It caused a lot of consternation in his day, too, I seem to recall reading."

"Can't imagine why."

Akmir grinned. "It doesn't exactly bode well, does it? '*times of great strife*', '*reeling under the heel of a new master*' – hardly sentiments to set minds at ease. But, like you, Amatt didn't know what the prophecy was about or who it was for. Even he expressed reservations about its authenticity."

Nikrá became lost in thought for a moment. "The Twenty-fourth Prophecy," he repeated, reverently rolling the words around as an idea gradually took shape. "I wonder… do you suppose Amatt's uncertainty could have been due to the fact that, for him, the prophecy had come so far in advance of its fulfilment?"

"Possibly. But that would beg the question, is it about to be fulfilled now?"

"Do you think it might be?"

"Ah, now you're asking me to speculate," Akmir chuckled. "You know me better than that. I've been a brother of the Adak-rann far too long to go down that road. We are scholars and historians. Unlike yours, our job begins *after* the event, not before it."

Nikrá grimaced again. A prophet was a watchman of sorts, expected to shout at the first sign of trouble, but not to spawn too much false alarm. So he had to be careful what he said. People expected him to know what he was talking about. Yet it was never easy sifting out the wheat from the chaff when it came to words of knowledge, wherever they came from. Telling the difference between the mere ramblings of a wandering mind and the equally nebulous thought-horses by which prophecies arrived was a conundrum that kept all conscientious seers awake at night. Only the charlatans in their ranks slept soundly.

He began to wish he hadn't asked Akmir to track down the original now. His prophecy's connection to Amatt the Blind, proven beyond all doubt, elevated the importance of the matter far beyond the realms of the comfortable. Yet he'd discovered long ago that prophecy went hand in hand with fate, from which it was impossible to hide indefinitely. It always found a way to have its day.

"I'm beginning to think that this prophecy was never meant for Amatt's people. It has come to me because it is for us, now. The fact that it happens to be Amatt's only unfulfilled prophecy just lends it greater authenticity. People will be less dismissive, knowing it didn't solely originate from a dusty old has-been like me."

Akmir nodded with a kindly smile. "So who else knows about this?"

"I discussed it with Chancellor Gÿldan the other day, though I didn't mention my suspicions about its connections to the past. That's not the sort of thing to go bandying about without proof."

Akmir retrieved the Telem-aki and closed its cover with great care. "You realise, old friend, that I am unable to advise you on your next course of action, not in a matter of such importance as this. The tenets of the Adak-rann prevent me from taking any action that might affect the course of history."

"Lucky you," Nikrá grumbled. Right now, he rather wished that he too belonged to such an order, one that would allow him to sit on the sidelines and watch things unfold.

But that was not to be. He glanced back down at his translation. Though the prophecy was written in First Dialect A'lyavine, with its authenticity confirmed, it still meant no more to him now than it had before. The who's, the why's and the wherefore's, even the when of it, were all still very much shrouded in the minds of the gods.

If indeed that was where the wretched thing had come from.

2

Riagán watched as a lone horseman broke off from a line of carts in the distance and began cantering up the hill. This was good. In his estimation, it would take at least another half hour for the rest of the approaching party to reach the camp, and that was more time than he was prepared to waste just waiting. Possessed of a desk permanently under siege, he wasn't a man given to loitering outside Mitcha's gates without something to show for it.

With hooves pounding the ground, ejecting a wake of mud and gravel, the rider was at full gallop by the time he breached the outer motte. His cloak streamed out behind him as he leaned into the charge, holding nothing back. Storming the battlements could almost have been his intent. It was certainly enough to cause a nervous glance to flash between the guards posted outside the gates; pondering the wisdom of attempting to challenge a fast-moving stallion, no doubt.

It would be better if they didn't, Riagán chuckled to himself. General Padráig Kirshtahll had a reputation for dealing with things in his path in a fairly decisive manner.

"Sir," he called out, snapping off a salute as the general shot past.

Reining in his panting mount, Kirshtahll wasted no time slipping from the saddle. He landed with a weary grunt.

Riagán trotted back through the gate. No small man himself, even he had to look up when addressing the general at close quarters. Kirshtahll was a great bear of a man, entirely without need of breastplate and travelling cloak to promote his proportions into the realms of the formidable.

"Good journey, sir?"

A derisory snort and a dark scowl answered that.

Helmet removed, a bushy clod of predominantly grey hair enjoyed liberation. "The wretched Els-spear's burst its banks from the Kimballi Pass all the way down to Loch Kim. We had to detour back through the Pass of Trombéi."

Riagán studied his superior's age-etched face for a moment. He'd served with the general for fourteen years, so he knew it took more than mere physical hardships to blacken the man's mood. Failure in some personal endeavour was far more likely to be the cause of that.

"And Alondris, sir, was it worth the trip?"

Kirshtahll gave a contrary growl, but didn't elaborate. "What news from up here?" he demanded, passing his reins to a waiting soldier.

Riagán gave a little shrug with his hands. "Well, sir, we've had the usual spate of raids across the border, but other than that, the only thing of note is these Tsnath scouting parties we've started seeing – the ones I messaged you about."

Kirshtahll clasped his hands behind his back and set course for his quarters. The hem of his cloak swirled about his ankles in an effort to keep up.

"Border raids I can understand. But scouts? The bastards are up to something."

The Tsnath were always up to something, Riagán mused. If they weren't harrying defenceless farmers for grain and livestock, they were putting dents in border town commerce. But at least there was an obvious motive behind that. This new reconnoitring activity was something different. Thus far its purpose had eluded him.

He fell in beside the general. "I had a report come in just yesterday that put a bunch of them up in the Mathians."

"That far south?"

"Aye, sir. Doing their damnedest to avoid us, too. Most peculiar." Riagán shook his head. "The Tsnath I'm used to love a good scrap. Sneaking around behind our backs is just downright – odd."

Kirshtahll let out a sigh. "*Odd* isn't enough, I'm afraid. I tried explaining the implications of a change in tactics to those idiots back in Alondris, but I might as well have been pissing windward. They did nothing but bicker amongst themselves. All I came away with was a demand for evidence of what the Tsnath are playing at."

"That's it for the reinforcements, then?"

"We'll be lucky to keep what we've got," Kirshtahll snorted back. He glanced sideways, "The Assembly thinks protecting our northern border is already too expensive. I tell you, Major, the government is shot full of nothing but short-sighted, self-centred, money-grabbing little bureaucrats. The good of the country is always going to come a poor second with that lot in charge."

Riagán hid his grin. Kirshtahll's distain for the political establishment was no secret. As far as he was concerned, the Grand Assembly consisted of nothing more than minor nobles dabbling in politics because their chances of wielding any other form of power were slim to none.

In theory the Assembly answered to the King's Council, which would have been fine had that fractious bunch of lords not been equally stymied by petty squabbles and self-interests. They exerted no effective control whatsoever. As for King Althar, he was too frail to get out of bed unaided, let alone bring his council to heel. So the country resided in the temerarious hands of his eldest daughter, Princess Midana. She didn't yet have the clout to put the King's Council under her thumb, but she did hold sway over the Assembly, whose ministers answered her beck and call like besotted lapdogs. Or so the impression was given.

Kirshtahll came to a rather sudden halt, wrenching Riagán out of his political musings. "Have you been having a crackdown, Major?"

Riagán glanced round. It was the marked improvement in the tidiness and order that had obviously caught the general's eye. With so many troops stationed at Mitcha, until recently the army had struggled to deal with the amenities side of life.

"Ah, that would be our new officer, sir. Torrin-Ashur. I assigned him camp duties."

"A new officer? I didn't know we'd been expecting a fresh intake."

"He's not up from the Academy, sir. He's a local lad, the son of Lord Naman-Ashur."

"Ah, Ashur's march lord has finally sent his son to serve the bond, has he?"

"Not quite, sir. Naman's eldest – Eldris, I think – declined to enlist. I gather Torrin was only too happy to take his place."

"Not an uncommon scenario with younger siblings," Kirshtahll acknowledged with a nod. "So, we have ourselves a northern volunteer, and you gave him camp duties?"

"Didn't have much choice, sir. The lad has no men of his own. I had to give him command of the Pressed."

Kirshtahll's eyes widened. "He took camp duties *and* accepted the Pressed?"

Riagán shrugged. To most young nobles, having to command the Pressed was an insult. Being a motley collection of slaves and debtors, or petty criminals whose sentences had been commuted into military service, they weren't proper soldiers. Most of the time they were treated like scum, something to be kicked about whenever they got underfoot. Yet with Ashur being unsupported, it had been a case of take on the Pressed or loaf around doing nothing.

"It was his choice, sir." Riagán waved an arm around at the camp. "And he seems to be making quite a good show of it."

Kirshtahll made no further comment, though a raised eyebrow suggested an impression had been made. He resumed course, dipping his head down in his customary thinking fashion. He seemed very much preoccupied, so Riagán refrained from filling the silence with prattle. One of the secrets to being a good adjutant was knowing when to keep one's mouth shut.

On reaching his quarters, Kirshtahll unhooked his cloak and slid the garment from his shoulders, draping it over a stand usually reserved for his armour. He didn't bother removing his breastplate before slumping into the chair behind his desk. A sigh of relief escaped him. The journey down to Alondris was a trying endeavour, even for a young man.

Riagán poured some of the tea his orderly brought in and handed over a mug.

"So, this new Tsnath activity, what's your take on how it affects us here?" Kirshtahll asked, nodding thanks.

Riagán let out a pensive *um*. It was a question he'd considered a thousand times already and still wasn't sure of the answer. "Obviously, scouting parties alone pose no direct threat to the camp. But they are affecting the general safety of the region, sir."

Kirshtahll's attention dwelt for a moment on the assortment of keepsakes, quills, ink and other writing paraphernalia spread across his desk. No one was allowed to touch this little part of his domain, so they were just as he'd left them before departing for Alondris months earlier. Only the dust had ignored standing orders.

"I thought you said the Tsnath were trying to avoid us?"

"They are, sir. The trouble is, they fight like banshees when they're cornered. The more of their units in the area, and the more patrols we mount – well, it stands to reason we'll clash sooner or later. That's making the men uneasy, sir."

"The men?"

"Well, our esteemed officers," Riagán qualified, making no attempt to mask his sarcasm.

Most officers spawned by the Royal Military Academy these days seemed to be little more than fops and dandies. With commissions paid for by overindulgent fathers, they arrived in the north knowing how to look pretty on a parade ground and perhaps make a bit of noise in a sparring yard. But not much else.

"We've gone soft," Kirshtahll muttered, mirroring Riagán's thoughts. "Alondria hasn't had to contend with a serious threat to her sovereignty for thirty years, not since the Kilópeé War. It may seem ironic, Major, but half the problem we face up here is that the damned Tsnath keep their intrusions within the realms of the annoying rather than the menacing. Most southerners simply don't take the situation with our northern border seriously."

Kirshtahll heaved his bulk out of the chair and stepped over to a map mounted on the wall. Made of cork, it was sculpted to show the relief of the land it represented, though Mitcha was now more a valley than a peak, having been prodded too often. A line of knobbly lumps denoting the Mathian Mountains divided Alondria right across her breadth, with the majority of the kingdom lying to the south. Just a thin strip of land lay above, known as the Northern Territories, sandwiched between the mountains and the mighty River Ablath. Everything north of that fluvial line was part of the Tsnathsarré Empire.

The Tsnath had their own name for the Territories, the Tep-Mödiss. Meaning *'Below the River'*, the region had once belonged to them, though a deal struck centuries earlier had seen it change hands. That arrangement hadn't lasted long. Tsnathsarré's warlords, angry at having lost part of their empire without a fight, beheaded their own emperor, Callis, and installed the hard-line and far less friendly Ürengarr as his successor. Demands for the return of the region were immediate, as were assurances Alondria would be compensated – assurances that were never met. They'd been fighting over the place ever since.

"The Assembly think I have nine thousand troops at my disposal to keep our border secure," Kirshtahll said, waving his hand across the map. He gave his head a forlorn shake. "If only that were true."

Riagán had to admit, it was easier pushing water uphill with a rake than getting most of the Academy officers out on patrol. There were exceptions, thank the gods. "You've got the Executive, sir," he offered, trying to sound encouraging.

"The Executive," Kirshtahll repeated, turning from the map, "indeed. But of the hundred or so lieutenants at Mitcha right now, how many are in it – ten, perhaps?"

"About that, sir."

"So what does that say about the rest of the men stationed here?"

Kirshtahll heaved a sigh. "In truth, I probably have less than a thousand troops I can actually rely on. The trouble is, I can't tell the Assembly that, can I? They'd replace me, probably with some idiot deluded enough to still believe in Alondrian invincibility. So here I am, pretending I can do the job; a pretend general, at the head of a pretend army."

Riagán was silent for a moment. He was beginning to realise just how hard Kirshtahll had taken the rebuff from Alondris.

"Sir, you're no pretend general. I wouldn't be standing here if that were true."

He wasn't trying to ingratiate himself. Fourteen years the man's adjutant, he was well beyond that. He was simply stating facts.

Kirshtahll rolled his eyes towards the ceiling and let a smirk thin his lips. "And if I had nine thousand Riagáns under me, I'd march into Tsnathsarré and declare myself emperor."

"Damned right, sir!"

They both chuckled. Riagán was relieved to see the general come back on track. If he ever gave up the fight, the north really would be done for.

Kirshtahll returned his attention to the map. "So, the question is, what *are* we going to do about these wretched Tsnath scouts?"

"Shall I send out a recall and assemble the lads, sir?"

"Yes, good idea. We need to knock heads together and come up with a coherent plan to tackle this."

Riagán detached his shoulder from its usual spot against the wall by the door and made to leave.

"Oh, by the way, I almost forgot," Kirshtahll stalled him, "we'll be having a visitor shortly."

"Sir?"

"Princess Elona."

"Oh gods…" Riagán groaned before he could stop himself. His shoulder reconnected with the wall as he slumped back into his former stance.

"Come now, it's not that bad. It could have been Midana. At least Elona has her head screwed on the same way as the rest of us."

Riagán found such an argument less than comforting. "That's all very well, sir, but what's she coming for? What's she going to do while she's here? How big will her entourage be? For that matter, where's she even going to stay?" The ramifications of hosting a royal visit quickly began to snowball in his mind. His desk was already besieged;

this would bury it.

"You worry too much, Major," Kirshtahll mocked, seemingly unsympathetic to such administrative concerns. He returned to his desk and sat down. "Look, we have plenty of young men in the camp who will be more than happy to entertain her when she arrives."

"But why bring her up here, sir?"

"Because Elona is one of our best allies in Alondris. I want her to see first-hand what we're facing."

Riagán remained unimpressed. "She's only second in line to the throne. She has no real power, not with Midana lording it over her."

"Maybe so. But a quiet word here, a little suggestion there, it all helps. She does, after all, have the ear of the king."

"Not that that counts for much these days, sir, what with Althar being bedridden and all."

Kirshtahll seemed momentarily saddened at the reminder of the king's gradual demise. He and Althar had been friends for many years. "Nevertheless, the way I see it, getting Elona up here can't hurt."

Riagán already had a host of arguments with which to counter that. Bandits in the Mathians; Tsnath raiding parties cropping up unexpectedly; unpredictable weather in the passes – and that was only concerned with getting the princess safely to Mitcha. The camp had its own problems.

"So long as nothing happens to her while she's here."

"Such as?"

"Well, sir, a pretty girl amongst a bunch of young nobles – drunken ones, most likely, given the revelry they'll indulge in when she gets here…"

"Hmm. We'll need to build a compound for her party to stay in. Put that new chap on it."

"Ashur?"

Kirshtahll nodded. His attention turned to his desk, from which he wiped away a little dust with a forefinger. His mind was already moving on to other matters, Riagán realised.

Taking that as his cue, he slipped out of the office and closed the door behind him. There was woe written across his face.

The very last thing he needed was a royal visit on his hands.

3

Sàhodd stepped forwards and thumped the side of the wooden stockade. "They may be the Pressed, Torrin, but I've got to hand it to them – they've made a good job of this."

Torrin-Ashur nodded as he admired the latest addition to the camp. 'Build a compound for the princess to stay in', Major Riagán had ordered, as if such things were commonplace.

Finding and felling enough straight pines from the surrounding forest had been the easy part. Digging foundations deep enough that they'd stand upright, *that* had been hard. Where the bedrock was only a foot beneath the topsoil the new stockade was less than firmly rooted. Still, it didn't have to survive a Tsnath horde, it just had to look the part. Which it did. The hewn trunks stood side by side like sentries, their freshly chiselled tips menacing the sky – as good a deterrent as any against mead-fuelled bravado trying its luck.

"Fit for a princess?"

Sàhodd glanced over his shoulder and let out a snort. "It's a poor palace. But then, this is Mitcha, not Alondris. She'll just have to make do, like the rest of us."

Torrin-Ashur allowed a yawn to overtake him. He stretched, rubbing his hands through short-cropped hair. Uncertainty over exactly when the royal party would reach Mitcha's humble gates had imposed a stringent deadline. To boost the chances of success, he'd taken the unusual step of mucking in with his men. Now that the construction was complete, he just wanted to relax and unwind.

His fellow officers thought he was mad. None of them would have got their hands dirty, particularly not if it meant rubbing shoulders with the Pressed. A great deal of gossip had done the rounds within the camp, little of it to the good of his reputation. He'd noticed most of the other nobles tending to shun him of late.

Sàhodd, son of Henndel, Lord of Söurdina, was a welcome exception. He was one of the few betitled nobles at Mitcha prepared to put associations with the Pressed aside and deem their commanding officer worthy of friendship.

"You've met the princess, haven't you?"

"Briefly," Sàhodd nodded. "Elona was a frequent visitor to the Academy while I was there. She did speak to me once, though not for long, I'm sorry to say."

"Still, that's closer than I'll ever get," Torrin-Ashur sighed. He harboured no illusions about what commanding the Pressed did to his chances of being introduced. "I was just wondering, will she appreciate all the hard work we've put in? Or won't it cross her mind?"

"She's a princess, so who knows? If she's anything like my sister, though, she'll be bored to tears and spend the whole time wishing she was back at home."

"Oh."

"Well," Sàhodd smirked, "would you want to trek all the way up here to the middle of nowhere, just to spend a couple of weeks in this – a wooden hut? When you could be in Alondris, living in a palace?"

The Northern Territories weren't the middle of nowhere, Torrin-Ashur objected silently. Still, Sàhodd did have a point.

"I suppose Mitcha hasn't much to offer compared to the capital."

"Ha! You have the right of it there, my friend."

Until a few weeks ago, royalty hadn't featured much in Torrin-Ashur's thinking. The humdrum, day to day business of the Northern Territories was too far removed from the social shenanigans of Alondris for it to seem relevant. All that had changed after the announcement of Elona's visit. Now, the princess was the only topic of conversation in the camp.

"So what's she like? A fair maiden, I presume?"

Sàhodd gave a forlorn sigh and rolled his eyes skywards. "To die for, Torrin, truly." He would have elaborated, but two bell tones booming out across the camp threw him off course. "Gods, it that the time? I've got to go – my men are on next watch. Shall I catch you this evening?"

"A man with a bottle is always welcome," Torrin-Ashur winked.

Sàhodd tutted, but grinned with it. He waved a casual salute and took his leave.

Torrin-Ashur gave the new compound one last inspection, then set off towards the area of the camp given over to the Pressed, a remote and rather soggy spot to which no one else wanted to lay claim. Even the horses had been afforded a better location.

He reached the corral and clambered over the horizontal poles to cut across the pen rather than skirting round it. A number of inquisitive horses pressed towards him, probably hopeful for a nibble of something tasty. They were out of luck.

As he neared the Pressed's billets on the far side, he noticed things seemed rather quiet. His men were supposed to be resting, so he wasn't expecting a raucous din, but it was too quiet even for that. The hairs on the back of his neck began to rise. He ducked beneath the rope cordon that defined the billet area, threaded his way through a row of grubby tents and emerged into the communal area beyond.

His eye was immediately caught by a cluster of men huddled around a figure on the ground. It looked like a fight.

"Oi, break it up!"

The group parted, affording him a better view. His guts tightened.

Botfiár, one of the Pressed's corporals, was kneeling with the downed man's head supported on his thighs. There was a mixture of anger and anguish in his eyes when he looked up.

"It's Tomàss, sir."

One of the slaves under his command, Torrin-Ashur recalled. He rushed over. The poor wretch's uniform was little but bloodied rags. It looked as though the man had been savaged by wild animals. "Gods be merciful! What happened?" He dropped to his haunches and placed a hand on the injured man's shoulder. "Have you called for a surgeon?"

Botfiár shook his head. "We didn't know whether you'd authorise the expenditure, sir. Besides, what surgeon would waste his time on a slave amongst us lot?"

Torrin-Ashur flashed a warning glance. Slavery wasn't a common practice in the Territories and he'd only accepted command of the Pressed on the condition that no distinction be made between slave and freeman. Not that it made much difference – none of the Pressed were really free.

He glanced round to locate his other corporal. "Silfast, take a couple of men and get help."

"Aye, sir."

Silfast seconded the two men nearest him and set off with a purposeful turn of speed.

Botfiár laid a canteen up against Tomàss's lips. Most of the water just dribbled down the man's cheek.

"How did this happen?" Torrin-Ashur demanded.

A young lad nicknamed Tick stepped forwards. "It were that Lord Borádin, sir."

Torrin-Ashur's eyes bulged. "A *man* did this?"

The lad's nervous facial spasm set his cheek to winking several times in quick succession.

"We was just walkin' past his lordship's camp when his men started throwin' stuff at us, sir, demandin' we clear it up an' all. One of 'em even slung a bucket of horse shit. Hit Tom in the guts, it did – knocked the wind out of him. They was playin' rough, sir."

Torrin-Ashur scowled. It wasn't the first time his men had suffered this kind of treatment. It seemed to be the camp sport.

"Anyways, we tried to get away, but just then his lordship came along on his horse and Tom bumped into him. It were accidental, like."

"And Borádin did this to him – just for that?"

"Aye, sir. Started pushin' Tom around, he did, ridin' at him and such like. His lordship's men were all laughin' and jeerin', and he was playin' up to 'em, I reckon. But then it went bad, sir. Tom got cornered. He put his arms up against the horse – only to defend himself, like – but his lordship took offence, sir." The lad fixed the ground with a worried stare. His cheek went into another fit.

"It's alright, Tick. Just tell me what happened."

Torrin-Ashur could guess the rest, but he wanted to hear it told. He found himself having to fight to remain calm.

"Well, sir, his lordship went mad. Started screamin' and shoutin'. He'd been out huntin', I reckon – he had his dogs with him. He ordered 'em free."

A cold fury took hold of Torrin-Ashur. He struggled to comprehend such callousness. Borádin was a nobleman, of the House of Kin-Shísim, one of the highest in Alondria. Even so, that didn't give him the right to be so brutal – certainly not to a man that wasn't even his own.

"And you saw all this?"

Tick paled further and nodded at the ground. "I would have 'elped, sir, honest I would."

Botfiár rallied to his aid. "Don't worry, lad. Nobody's blaming you for what happened."

"Aye, it's not your fault, Tick." Torrin-Ashur flexed his hands against the rising anger that was making him tremble. "There was nothing you could have done – not without getting the same treatment."

Tomàss coughed and his eyes flickered open for a moment.

Torrin-Ashur leaned in close. "How are you feeling?" He knew it was a stupid question, but the injured man gamely managed a weak smile before his eyes slipped closed again. "Don't worry, we've got a surgeon coming. He'll get you mended."

Torrin-Ashur rose and ordered a nearby table cleared so that Tomàss could be lifted on to it.

Silfast wasn't long in returning. His entourage came in running, albeit not at a great pace; the girth of the surgeon they had in tow suggested exercise wasn't part of the man's daily regime.

One glance was all the newcomer needed to assess what kind of mess he was being expected to deal with. "I shall need plenty of clean water, warm, but not too hot."

Torrin-Ashur snapped his fingers at a couple of the men. Their response was instant. One hurried to the canteen area and grabbed a half-full pail of water. The other ran to the camp fire where a large blackened kettle hung above the embers. The simmering water was tempered with cold and the kettle brought over.

The surgeon rummaged in his bag and extracted a variety of items, mostly bandages and pots of salve, laying them out on the table. The purpose of some of the objects was a little obscure, but it was the sheep shears that really made Torrin-Ashur frown.

"Good for cutting clothing," was the explanation given. The surgeon proceeded to demonstrate by making short work of removing what remained of Tomàss's dignity. With his patient unconscious, he was able to peel away the torn and bloodied cloth without eliciting screams.

Torrin-Ashur ordered the rest of the men to find something better to do, allowing just his two corporals and Tick to remain.

As Tomàss's wounds were progressively cleaned a grimace entrenched itself on the surgeon's face. "Gods," he growled more than once, each time giving his head a shake. "I've seen some bloody messes over the years, believe me, but *off* a battlefield – nothing like this. How did it happen?"

"Hunting dogs."

The surgeon shot Torrin-Ashur a sharp frown. "An accident?"

"I don't believe so."

"Gods."

"Will he be alright?" Botfiár asked.

"Hard to say." The surgeon sucked in a breath as he pondered his prognosis. "They may look bad, but the cuts are not the worry. His recovery will depend on what's broken on the inside."

The outside continued to receive attention. Needle and thread took care of the deeper lacerations, and bandages any torn skin that still oozed blood. To the rest of the abrasions a rather foul-smelling ointment was applied.

Torrin-Ashur pointed at the rags littering the ground. They were far beyond the realms of salvage. "Silfast, Tomàss will be needing a new uniform."

The corporal nodded and dispatched himself once more, this time alone.

The surgeon moved on to an examination of the more latent damage Tomàss had suffered. He discerned two cracked ribs, he suspected a third, a broken forearm and four broken fingers. All he could do for the ribs was supply support strapping. The other breaks he reset, immobilising them with splints. Tomàss's right ankle was a large purple welt, though apparently not broken. How it was possible to tell the difference was a mystery Torrin-Ashur let ride.

An hour passed before the surgeon was satisfied he'd done what he could. He gave instructions for further care and ordered that Tomàss be carried to his cot.

"Botfiár, see to it that someone stays with him," Torrin-Ashur added.

Relieved of his patient, the surgeon wiped his hands clean. "A nasty business," he muttered. He sounded angry. He began putting away his equipment. "Still, you've got yourself a strong man there. Provided his gizzards are in good order, he'll pull through. Keep a close eye on him, mind. If he coughs up any blood, or there's signs of it when he pisses, come and get me."

"I'll see to it," Torrin-Ashur nodded. "And thank you – for all you've done."

The surgeon dismissed the gratitude with a shrug. "It's what I'm here for."

"Still, I'm grateful." Torrin-Ashur held out his hand. "I'm afraid I didn't catch your name earlier…"

"Temesh-ai. Major Temesh-ai."

The mention of rank brought Torrin-Ashur to attention. "I wasn't aware surgeons held commissions, sir."

"They don't. I retired years ago, so you can relax." Temesh-ai returned to packing his bag. "I served for twenty-two years. Fixed up a lot of wounded during that time. When they finally put me out to pasture, I took up medicine rather than go home to a nagging wife."

"I see," Torrin-Ashur acknowledged, somewhat guardedly.

"Oh, don't worry, she prefers me out earning money to having me underfoot," Temesh-ai explained with a grin. "Speaking of which, who gets the pleasure of my bill? The miscreant responsible for today's misfortunes, perhaps?" With a raised eyebrow, he left the suggestion hanging.

Torrin-Ashur hadn't given the matter of payment much thought until that moment. He had to admit, though, placing the cost at Borádin's door did hold a certain appeal.

"Well, no rush," Temesh-ai said, seeing the quandary he'd created. "Neither of us are likely to be going anywhere in the next few days, are we? Not with the arrival of this here princess nearly upon us."

He made out his bill and handed it over.

*

Temesh-ai found himself smiling as he walked away. The young lieutenant in charge of the Pressed hadn't the slightest inkling General Kirshtahll's personal physician had just been employed. The urgent manner in which his corporal had demanded a medic had quite simply dispensed with such niceties as introductions.

He made his way to the general's quarters, hoping he wasn't too late to catch the tail end of lunch. His luck was in. Furnished with a meaty platter, he sat down and proceeded to relate the whole episode in quite some detail.

"I keep hearing about this young lad," Kirshtahll commented afterwards. "Riagán seems to regard him quite highly. Odd, don't you think, considering Ashur's the most junior and least experienced officer in the camp?"

"If you want my opinion, Padráig, you'll be hearing a lot more of him, erelong."

"Oh?"

"A storm's brewing, methinks."

"How so?"

"Well," Temesh-ai paused, shoving a chunk of venison into his mouth whilst attempting to look innocent, "I seem to have suggested that my bill be paid for by whoever did the damage. If I'm any judge, Ashur will see that it is. You should have been there, Padráig, the lad was seething. I wouldn't be at all surprised if there's a showdown very shortly."

A scowl creased Kirshtahll's brow. That would have worried most men. Temesh-ai just smirked and carried on.

"And I'll tell you another thing I noticed – Ashur doesn't insist on all this formality crap, like most of the young nobles do these days. Yet his men obeyed him in an instant. All he had to do was snap his fingers."

"Interesting," Kirshtahll murmured, "considering those men aren't even proper soldiers."

"Quite. Anyway, like I said, a storm's brewing, methinks."

*

It took an hour for Torrin-Ashur to track down his quarry, a search that did little to calm the blood boiling in his veins.

He finally ran the callous nobleman to ground in the Miller's Cup, over in the nearby town of Mitcha, whence the army camp had got its name. Many of the Academy graduates had informally adopted the tavern as their mess, though it was not a place Torrin-Ashur frequented much. With the kind of money Borádin's crowd had to throw around, the son of a minor march lord would be bankrupt in days.

He spotted Borádin on the far side of the parlour and excused, squeezed and elbowed his way past many a fellow officer to reach him. He arrived feeling altogether more flustered than he would have liked.

The casual indifference with which Borádin deigned to acknowledge his presence did not improve his mood.

"I want a word with you, Borádin."

"Really?" the nobleman quipped, feigning surprise. "And what could you possibly want with me, my good man?"

"Don't play the idiot with me. You know damned well why I'm here. You almost killed one of my men."

"What of it? The wretch insulted me."

"He was trying to avoid being trampled to death. Since when did that become an insult?"

"Oh – since this morning, I suppose." Borádin made a show of suppressing a yawn and dusted an imaginary speck off the shoulder of his tunic. One of his companions sniggered.

Torrin-Ashur did not smile. With some deliberation he unfurled Temesh-ai's bill and laid it out on the table.

Borádin glanced down, his eyebrows pinching together. The

moment he realised what it was he was looking at, incredulity took over. "You don't seriously expect me to pay that, do you?"

"Major Temesh-ai does."

Borádin clearly neither recognised the name, nor seemed intimidated by the rank that went with it. He simply screwed up the bill and flicked it back across the table.

"Go away, there's a good fellow. You're beginning to spoil my appetite." He lifted his tankard of ale. It was quite obviously a gesture of dismissal.

Mug and lips did not meet. Torrin-Ashur's back-handed swipe saw to that. Pottery shot sideways, disintegrated against the wall and sprayed froth over several bystanders. Borádin was left gripping nothing but a handle.

"You listen to me, you arrogant bastard," Torrin-Ashur growled, leaning in close across the table, "… if you so much as *look* at one of my men again, I'll run you through."

He snatched Temesh-ai's bill from where it had ended up and backed away. What little self-control he still possessed was on the verge of deserting him. More than anything, he just wanted to pulverise the stunned face starring back at him. He needed to leave, now, before he did something he'd regret.

He got precisely three paces before Borádin shot to his feet, tipping the table in front of him into the laps of those seated opposite.

"How dare you speak to me like that!" the nobleman roared, shoving the upset furniture aside to clear a path.

The altercation had already caused an interested dip in the general hubbub. Now, breath-held silence gripped the parlour as all eyes followed Borádin's advance.

The last vestiges of Torrin-Ashur's restraint evaporated. He spun round fast, sending a fist shooting out towards Borádin with fury-driven force. Knuckles slammed into sternum. The punch nearly lifted the young nobleman off his feet, sending him reeling backwards. He crashed into his seat and his head hit the high backrest with a loud crack.

He seemed to totter on the verge of unconsciousness for a moment. Yet he was quick to recover. Shaking his head to clear the daze, he tried getting up again.

The tip of Torrin-Ashur's sword materialised under his chin.

Borádin's gaze travelled along the blade, up outstretched arm and on into fierce, glaring eyes. There was a steeliness there only a fool would ignore.

Torrin-Ashur allowed a moment to pass, then turned on his heels and all but fled. There was no excusing, squeezing or elbowing – a path opened up before him as he stormed towards the tavern door. He was shaking uncontrollably by the time he burst out into the street.

In his wake, Borádin sat staring at his fingers, transfixed by a smear of blood from the tiniest of cuts to his throat.

*

It was, Kirshtahll considered sourly, unseemly for a general to eavesdrop near the door to his own office. But occasionally it paid to be forewarned about matters that were in imminent danger of troubling his desk.

Outside, Riagán listened with practiced patience as Borádin related his version of the events that had just transpired in the Miller's Cup. The young noble's appearance had come as no surprise. Not only had Temesh-ai's prediction been realised with remarkable speed, but Captain Halam, an accomplished member of the Executive, had stopped by only minutes beforehand to warn of the brewing fiasco.

When Borádin finally finished, Riagán knocked on the door and entered.

"Sir, we've got a problem…"

Kirshtahll held up a hand to stall further explanation. "I heard."

Riagán gave a knowing nod. "So what do you want me to do with him?"

"I'd like to tell the arrogant prat to pack up and go home," Kirshtahll grumbled in a low voice. But he knew that wasn't an option. The last thing he could afford was for Alondris to see him dismissing men for what they would undoubtedly consider to be no good reason. "Make him wait. Leave it half an hour or so, then bring him in."

"Right you are, sir."

Riagán withdrew. Kirshtahll returned to his desk and sat brooding for a while, considering his position on the matter.

When Borádin was eventually wheeled in, Kirshtahll listened to the whole spiel again. The sorry saga seemed to be the subject of further embellishment each time it was recounted. Already this version differed quite blatantly from the more objective account Halam had given earlier. By evening it would no doubt be the tale of an epic battle, with Borádin the long-suffering hero.

The young noble eventually concluded his representations with an inevitable plea. "Sir, I respectfully request your permission to call Ashur out. My honour is at stake."

Kirshtahll practically choked. "*Honour*? Do you even know what that word means? You acted like a pig-headed savage this morning. You nearly killed a man, I'm told."

It was clear Borádin had not expected anyone to have prior knowledge of what had prompted Torrin-Ashur to go on the warpath. Thrown off course, he struggled for a reply.

"I – I was offended, sir. The scum tried to push me off my horse. I had every right to do what I did. The wretch needed to be taught a lesson."

Slaves would scarcely dare raise their eyes to a noble, let alone their arms. It was fast becoming clear to Kirshtahll that Borádin embodied nearly everything that he disliked about the officers the Academy sent up these days. He was an arrogant, egocentric, selfish little upstart.

"Lessons have to be survived if they are to be learned," he intoned in a gravelly voice. "You're lucky my personal physician was on hand to attend to the damage you inflicted. As for your request, I do not condone call-outs. Fighting amongst officers adversely affects discipline within the ranks."

"But sir, Ashur attacked me. I have witnesses."

"Only after provocation."

"He drew blood."

"*Hardly*."

"Sir, I must insist. Blood *was* shed. That gives me the right to call him out. I demand that I be allowed to fight him."

Riagán, stationed in his usual spot just inside the door, visibly cringed.

For a moment, Kirshtahll did little but stare Borádin in the eye.

When he did finally rise from behind his desk, it was with great deliberation. He drew himself up to his full, formidable stature and paused, briefly, on the precipice of a calculated response.

Then he exploded.

"You arrogant little brat! Who do you think you are, coming in here and making *demands*?"

Borádin paled. Half of Mitcha must have heard the roar.

"You're not at home now, *boy*, on your father's estate. You're in the army, in the Northern Territories, with the Tsnath breathing down your neck. I don't care who you are down south – up here you're in my world. That means there's the gods, and then there's *me*!"

Borádin's voice seemed to have deserted him. With the mood Kirshtahll was in, that was probably the only thing that saved him from facing a court martial.

"Major, get this man out of my sight."

Riagán saluted and marched Borádin out of the office. He was gone only a moment. By the time he returned, Kirshtahll had resumed his seat.

"So?"

"Well, I rather enjoyed it," Riagán chuckled.

Kirshtahll shook his head in dismay. "They're all the same. Why can't the Academy teach them how to be men, instead of such idiots?"

"Not much hope of that, sir. The Academy is run by the same type these days. Fops and dandies, the lot of them."

Kirshtahll gave a forlorn nod. "So, what to do, what to do?" he breathed, drumming his fingers on the desk.

"The law's on Borádin's side, I'm sorry to say. It wouldn't have been so bad if Ashur hadn't drawn blood. But…"

"What, that tiny little cut? I've had mosquito bites worse than that."

"I know, sir. But it does give Borádin the right to lay down a challenge, I'm afraid."

"I've a good mind to deny him regardless. That's *my* right. I am supposed to be a bloody general, in case anybody has forgotten."

"Then he might appeal to Alondris, sir. Would you want that?"

"Do you really think he'd go that far?"

Riagán didn't answer – he didn't have to.

"Damn," Kirshtahll muttered. "And if I allow a call-out, what are Ashur's chances? Any idea how he would fare?"

Riagán gave a noncommittal shrug. "Borádin has the advantage of having been through the Academy, but whether he's any good in a fight, I have no idea. As for Ashur – no formal training, very little experience…"

"So the odds are not good."

"It doesn't look like it, sir."

"Damn. Damn, damn, damn!"

Kirshtahll sat fuming for a few minutes more, then got up and went to stand in front of the window, shaking his head from time to time as he gazed out across the camp. Eventually he came to a decision, which he delivered without turning.

"Very well. Inform Borádin he can make his challenge. But

regardless of the outcome, when the call-out is over, I want him gone. He can request a transfer, he can resign – frankly, I don't care if he goes absent without leave. I'll not have him under my command a day longer."

*

Chaos reigned for the rest of the afternoon, caused only in part by Kirshtahll's decision to allow a call-out, the first Mitcha had seen in years.

The appearance of Princess Elona at the camp gates was what had really put the fox inside the henhouse. She had beaten even the most optimistic estimates for her arrival, laying waste to a lot of plans for her reception.

Torrin-Ashur appreciated the irony of that. The higher nobles had quite deliberately excluded him from the majority of the preparations for her visit. In constructing the princess's compound, the Pressed had done their part. All they were required to do now was stay out of the way, preferably out of sight. So it was nice to know that their humble contribution was one of the few things actually ready in time.

The small degree of satisfaction he drew from that did little to alleviate the fact that the rest of his world seemed to be sliding towards insanity.

Borádin's nominated second, a haughty lieutenant by the name of Mir, had arrived on horseback, accompanied by six attendants in full parade uniform. The man was dressed like a peacock, with a number of those noble birds having lost plumage to his truly ridiculous hat. Not even deigning to dismount, Mir had handed over Borádin's challenge, a document drawn up on a parchment scroll, all signed and sealed with the Kin-Shísim emblem set in red wax. Were it not for the obvious fact that Borádin was just showing off his prestige, it would have been an honour to be the subject of such ornate attention.

"Hold still," Torrin-Ashur hissed under his breath, hoping Mir couldn't hear him outside the tent.

Sàhodd pinched the ends of a rather sorry looking reply between his finger-tips, squirming as he tried to avoid being singed.

Efforts to seal the scroll with a blob of wax salvaged from Borádin's missive were proving awkward. As the youngest son of a minor northern lord, Torrin-Ashur didn't have a signet ring of his own. His resort was the common man's insignia – the tip of his sword.

Since it was the same tip that had apparently precipitated all the fuss, he felt it quite appropriate.

He finished putting the final touches to the reply and left the confines of his tent, returning to where Mir was waiting. With deliberate pomposity he pronounced, "Here we are, my lord, you may deliver this to Lord Borádin."

Mir handled the grubby-looking document with some disdain, passing it to one of his attendants. It could have been a soiled undergarment for all the attention it received.

Torrin-Ashur didn't reciprocate the noble's retiring salute. It was more than clear that Mir held little or no respect for him; the gesture was merely typical of the double standards he'd come to expect from Borádin's crowd. They made great show of conducting themselves with all proper decorum, but their sincerity could not have been more superficial.

Yngvarr, one of Sàhodd's friends from the south, raised an eyebrow. "What?" he demanded as soon as Mir was out of earshot. "What's so funny?"

Torrin-Ashur managed to keep a straight face and let slip an innocent shrug.

Sàhodd fared less well in hiding his smirk. "I wish I could be there to see the look on Borádin's face when Mir gets back."

"Why?"

"Torrin's acceptance is written on the back of the bill from Temesh-ai."

"It isn't!" Yngvarr grabbed hold of Sàhodd's tunic. "It isn't, is it?"

Sàhodd didn't manage a reply; Yngvarr's endeavours to shake some sense into him were proving quite violent.

"And you let him do this? You bloody idiot!"

"Calm down." Torrin-Ashur landed a placating hand on Yngvarr's shoulder. "I simply don't want to let Borádin think that I'm taking him too seriously."

"But this *is* serious, Torrin."

Torrin-Ashur's expression hardened. "Perhaps. But it's also stupid. Look, I know I lost my temper in the Miller's. I shouldn't have drawn my sword on him, I admit that. But what's done is done. It's Borádin who's making a fool out of himself. All this fuss over a tiny little cut."

"Torrin, you damn nearly slit his throat."

"That's rubbish, and you know it. Borádin's blown it out of all proportion. He probably gets worse cuts being shaved in the morning."

"Oh, for the sake of the gods, Torrin!" Yngvarr flapped his arms about and glanced round, as though searching for someone to back up his argument. "You haven't the slightest idea what's going to happen now, have you?"

"No, but I suspect you're going to tell me."

Torrin-Ashur returned to the log they'd been sitting on before Mir's arrival. The day had been a pleasant one, but there was a chill to the air now that the sun had dipped below the tree-line and the warmth coming off the camp fire was welcome. Sàhodd and Yngvarr joined him.

"Look, Torrin, call-outs are taken very seriously back in Alondris. Careers are made and broken by them."

"This is hardly the capital," Torrin-Ashur countered with a snort. "As Sàhodd loves to remind me, it's the Northern Territories – the middle of nowhere."

"Right. So who's going to be watching when you enter the Forum? Who's going to be there to witness you getting thrashed? And don't fool yourself, Torrin, a thrashing is exactly what's heading your way."

The light dawned. "Oh."

"Exactly. *Oh*. You're going to be humiliated in front of royalty. And Borádin isn't going to give you any quarter, not now that you've insulted him – *again*."

Sàhodd started to have a giggling fit.

"Shut up," Yngvarr snapped, elbowing him off the log.

Sàhodd collapsed in a helpless heap and made no attempt to get up. He lay on his back wailing.

"Look, what's the worst that can happen?" Torrin-Ashur challenged, smiling but otherwise trying to ignore his downed friend. "I get my arse kicked in public. So what? I was born with a far worse handicap than that – I'm a bloody northerner. I'm never going to be hobnobbing with royalty, am I?" Yngvarr had no immediate answer to that, and Torrin-Ashur deliberately didn't allow him time to think of something clever to parry with. "So what have I lost? Nothing. I'm at the bottom of the pile. I can hardly go any lower."

Sàhodd managed to get as far as propping himself up on his elbows. "You can get hurt, though," he said, the seriousness of his observation rather at odds with his grin.

"He's right," Yngvarr agreed, with an expression that was far from jovial. "Borádin won't go lightly with you now. His terms will be First Blood."

That sobering thought prompted the need for a drink. Torrin-Ashur reached for the bottle Sàhodd had furnished them with earlier and replenished his cup.

"So what's Borádin like? As a fighter, I mean."

"I saw him train at the Academy a few times," Sàhodd said, struggling back on to the log. It was an ungraceful manoeuvre, given that it was occurring feet first from a seated position. "He seemed to be able to take care of himself."

"And don't forget, he'll be in armour," Yngvarr added. "It'll be tailor-made. You'll be lucky to get a blade anywhere near him."

"You paint a bleak picture."

"I'm a realist, Torrin. The more you understand the trouble you're in, the more you'll take it seriously."

"Alright, alright," Torrin-Ashur threw up a hand in submission, "you've made your point. But what can I do? I've got no way out of it now, have I?"

"No, you haven't. All I can say is, just try not to get yourself killed. I haven't known you that long, but that doesn't mean I'd enjoy tending your pyre."

"I'll drink to that," Sàhodd seconded, pouring himself a refill.

Torrin-Ashur raised his cup. "Well – to the fight, then."

"To coming home in one piece," Yngvarr corrected, raising his.

4

Rain lanced at Gömalt with a vindictive fury. Driven by buffeting winds, it stung his eyes and pummelled his cheeks. The brim of his hat, clamped firmly in place by a gauntleted hand, offered scant protection against the assault. For hours, cold rivulets had managed to course their way inside his cloak, sending shivers down his back.

He let slip with a contemptuous curse at the gods and their efforts to thwart his return. Glancing up in defiance, he was just in time to catch the serrated silhouette of Castle Brath'daka dance on the horizon, illuminated by a shard of lightning skittering across the sky. He grunted at the irony; disdain for the deities had afforded him a glimpse of his destination. Without the storm's intermittent flashes, his view extended little beyond the ground beneath his stirrups.

He spurred his horse into a trot. The creature was near to collapse and only managed a few sprightly paces before lapsing back into a leaden gait. Having just seen the castle, Gömalt's concern over whether the animal would last receded. The path might have been a quagmire, with a lack of heather underfoot the only real indication he was still on track, but he knew now that another godsforsaken hour would see him home. Even if he had to abandon the horse and walk.

The storm delivered brief hints of his path many more times before he finally reached Brath'daka's forbidding granite walls. Meagre was the welcome. Every torch mounted outside the main gate had succumbed to the torrential rain, leaving just a few inside the wind-besieged barbican struggling to stay alight. No guards stood watch – not that that came as any surprise.

He smacked one of the crossbars of the portcullis with the end of his scabbard. The sound of a stool crashing over inside the gatehouse answered. A moment later a guard erupted into view, hastily donning a helmet.

"Who goes there?"

Gömalt grunted; one day the sluggards might think of a less predictable challenge. He leaned forwards but remained silent, forcing the guard to liberate one of the beleaguered torches from its sconce and hold the flames up against the iron grille.

"*Oh.*"

The guard shrank away, turned on his heels and fled back inside the gatehouse. A dull bell clanked somewhere in the distance, spurring unseen men into action. Footfalls scuffled across wooden walkways overhead, quickly followed by the sound of ropes hidden within dark recesses beginning to creak and groan as they strained to lift the heavy portcullis. As soon as there was sufficient clearance, Gömalt ducked beneath the vicious spikes along the gate's bottom edge and passed the reappeared guard with little more than a scornful glance.

With just the courtyard to cross before his journey was finally at an end, the intensity of the rain somehow managed to increase. Drops hurled themselves against the cobbles with suicidal abandon. Gömalt got the distinct impression the gods had commanded a last-ditch attempt to defeat him.

A small wave of satisfaction at their eventual failure washed over him as he felt the musty warmth of the stables touch his cheeks.

His dismount was stiff and ungainly, long hours in the saddle having moulded his body and riding gear into seated contours. Everything from muscle and sinew to leather and laces objected to being straightened. Yet the moment his feet hit the floor, he tossed his reins at a waiting groom, untied his pack from the saddle and stepped back out into the courtyard. All without a word spoken.

Inside the inner bailey he navigated along dimly lit, draughty passages to his chambers, dumped his sodden belongings in a heap on the floor and lingered there only long enough to regret not being able to collapse into bed, then made his way on to the great hall.

Despite the ungodly hour the place was brightly lit, an abundance of oil lamps portraying its impressive opulence in full splendour. Ornate suits of armour and ancient weapons stood silent sentry, guarding the huge tapestries and extravagant paintings that adorned the walls. They were familiar trappings and he was too tired to pay them much heed. Instead, he fixed his eyes on the lady of the house and strode across the chequered flagstones towards her.

Baroness Alishe Daka sat in solitude at the end of an immense banqueting table, her piercing eyes tracing his approach. It was the only visible reaction she allowed to his entrance, such was her self-control. He'd been away for months on a mission of the utmost importance, the success of which meant everything to her. Others might have spent their days wearing the flagstones smooth with anxious pacing. Not so Daka. Such outward signs of concern were not her way.

As he approached, he allowed himself to admire her beauty. Her dark hair was swept back into a tight chignon, an orderly, controlled style she favoured on most occasions. Though no longer a young woman, her smooth, supple skin belied her years. Yet she made no attempt to hide the flecks of grey that now showed at her temples. Some might have sought to disguise such tell-tale signs. But again, not so Daka. She was a woman to subjugate the world, not conform to its conventions.

He came to a halt and stiffly lowered himself down on one knee, bowing his head to await her customary acknowledgement. She allowed a few seconds to pass before extending a hand for his feudal kiss.

"Gömalt," she greeted, waving towards the nearest vacant chair, "you look dreadful."

He let slip a cynical smile, feeling the truth of those words deep within his bones. His clothes were still dripping and the week-old stubble on his chin was still moist. His matted hair, as black as night, retained the shape into which his discarded hat had moulded it. Fatigue had sunk his eyes into dark wells, giving his angular face a particularly gaunt appearance. The return from the Mathian Mountains, deep within enemy territory, had taken far more out of him than he cared to admit.

He pulled the proffered chair a little closer and let out a grateful sigh as he sank down.

"Well?" the baroness prompted, finally airing a degree of impatience.

"We have located the first Menhir of Ranadar, my lady."

Gömalt noticed a little flash of excitement momentarily widen Daka's eyes. The baroness usually made it her business to hide her feelings, lest they prove a weakness others might exploit. She went to great lengths to cultivate the cold, iron-hard exterior she presented to the rest of the world. Only a trusted few were ever admitted to the inner sanctum of her true emotions.

"Tell me more," she demanded.

"It was hidden up in the Kimballi Pass, in the caves near the headwaters of the River Els-spear."

Daka leaned back in her chair and let out a satisfied sigh. It was as though a great weight had been lifted from her shoulders.

"So, our information was correct. The Menhir of Ranadar truly exist. Hard to believe that such a secret has lain buried all these years." She paused to savour the moment, until interrupted by an unpalatable thought. "You're certain that what you found wasn't simply some old Dwarvish marker stone?"

Gömalt had anticipated that challenge. Withdrawing a leather pouch from inside his shirt, he untied its bindings and extracted a parchment, which he spread out on the end of the banqueting table for the baroness to examine.

"I had some of the relic's inscription copied so that you could confirm its authenticity for yourself, my lady."

He was personally in no doubt that they had uncovered one of the true Menhir of Ranadar. The Dwarves, once dwellers of the Mathian Mountains, had littered the landscape with chiselled monuments. Little had been intentionally hidden, even if much had since been eroded by centuries of neglect. The menhir, by contrast, had been painstakingly disguised to render it nearly indistinguishable from its rock-wall resting place. It had remained unnoticed for more than a millennium. That set it apart, not only in design, but also in purpose.

He watched the baroness closely as she leaned forwards to study the parchment. After a few moments she paused to unclasp her necklace, a piece of jewellery she was rarely without. It didn't have the look of opulence, to Gömalt's eye it wasn't even particularly appealing, but it was ancient. Its design was in some way linked to their quest, though exactly how had never been explained to him. The baroness placed the piece on the table and drew the nearest candelabra a little closer. Her gaze flitted back and forth as necklace and parchment were subjected to meticulous comparison. Several minutes passed before she sat back and sighed once more, this time with a definitive air of triumph.

"And your men are returning with the menhir?"

"Not immediately, my lady." That elicited a stern frown. "The relic is large and heavy," he added quickly, "so transporting it back to the Empire will be dangerous. We must take precautions. Our searching has aroused a great deal of suspicion amongst the Alondrians. They are mounting more and more patrols."

"So…"

"I have instructed three copies of the relic's text be made and brought back here. That should give us something to be going on with. Bringing the menhir back will take much longer."

"What if these copies fall into enemy hands?"

"They won't. Your men will fight to their last breath to protect your interests. Some already have. They fear you more than they fear death, my lady."

The baroness allowed her guard to slip again, permitting a smile to touch her lips. Though she would never admit it, she loved being reminded of her power.

Years of social manoeuvring had seen her marry into the Daka line, an old and powerful Tsnathsarré house. But her beauty hid a cunning and manipulative mind; simply becoming a dutiful wife had never been the extent of her ambitions.

Even with the baroness newlywed, Gömalt had recognised her as the true power of the house. Subtle, scheming, and oftentimes cruel, she had beguiled him from the start. He'd always known where his allegiances should lie.

It had been a wise choice. Not a year after the birth of her first child had she come to him, her proposition simple; help her be rid of her husband. He hadn't hesitated. A few drops of Dimgäl extract, a poison subtle in its tracks but certain in its results, dispatched the baron. It was merely the first in a long line of kills he'd go on to perform for her. The deed had been paid for with a night of passion and a promise of furtherance.

Without the baroness he was nothing. Because of him, she was feared by many.

"Do your scribes understand the significance of what they are working on?" Daka asked.

"I don't believe so, my lady. I selected the men for their artistic and writing abilities, not their knowledge of A'lyavine."

The Tongue of the Ancients was a formidably difficult language to grasp. As such, it remained mostly the purview of the mages of Alondria. Few other than they ever mastered it.

That didn't satisfy the baroness. "Even so, have them disposed of when the copies are safely in our hands. I want no loose ends."

"Of course, my lady. I will see to it myself."

Gömalt felt little concern that the fate of three men had been so easily sealed; there was far too much at stake to take risks.

"Has there been any word from Omnitas?"

Daka's expression soured. "Yes. Our beloved emperor has deigned to sanction our plan. As though I needed his permission, odious cretin that he is."

Gömalt suppressed a smile. In the past, the Tsnathsarré Empire had always depended on heavy-handed leadership to maintain its cohesion. In Daka's opinion, Omnitas lacked the requisite qualities. Yet for all his wants, the current emperor was cunning. The man relied on others to keep him in power; he had dealt rather than smashed his way to the top. Though to Daka, that was just a sign of his weakness, and weakness was despicable, something to be eradicated. Escaping the fetters of such vapid leadership merely fuelled the furnace of her ambition.

"We only need him for his reinforcements when the time comes, my lady," Gömalt reminded her.

Daka let out a very controlled breath. From anyone else it would have been a huff. It was a rebuke of sorts, enough to warn him to tread carefully. Too tired to risk a confrontation, he decided to change tack.

"My lady, if I may make a suggestion – I believe it would be in our interests to curtail our sorties into Alondria."

"What? Why?"

"To throw the Alondrians off the scent. Our activities so deep inside the Tep-Mödiss are out of character. My spies report that General Kirshtahll has even been south to Alondris to secure more men."

Gömalt's view of most Alondrians was low, but for Kirshtahll he made an exception. The man was a capable leader, in command of all the Alondrian forces stationed in the Tep-Mödiss. As such, he was the one and only true obstacle to Daka's designs on the region.

"Kirshtahll mounts patrols, nothing more," the baroness replied with an air of disdain. "Hardly a major threat."

Gömalt did not agree. He phrased his reply with care. "Still, my lady, it makes no sense waving a red flag before the bull when so much is at stake. I'm not suggesting we stop raiding altogether – that in itself would be suspicious. It's just that, the less threat we pose now, the less justification Kirshtahll has for demanding more support. Sooner or later, we are going to have to face him. When that time comes, the fewer troops he has, the better."

A seductive smile replaced Daka's earlier umbrage, kindling a pang of desire within Gömalt that went a considerable way towards dispelling his fatigue. She leaned forwards and cupped his chin in her hand.

"What would I do without you, Gömalt?"

"I live to serve you, my lady."

Daka rose, drawing him to his feet. She moved closer. "Yes," she purred, "you do."

5

Anna couldn't help noticing how much the mood within the castle had changed since Gömalt's return to Brath'daka. Within as little as a day the furtive whispering, unnecessary during his absence, had become rife once more. Casual conversations were a thing of the past. The household now scurried about its business casting nervous glances over its collective shoulder, trying to detect his insidious presence. Subtle uncertainty was the hallmark of his invasive reign. The baroness was strict and exacting, but she was also aloof, remaining far above the world of manservant and chambermaid. She could be avoided with relative ease. Not so Gömalt – *he* was everywhere. His trespass even seemed to extend into the mind, where personal thoughts became subject to scrutiny. The man could make the innocent feel guilty just by his look.

"He's gone to see Kassandra."

Shyla, one of the cook's assistants, added a worried glance to her whispered warning before hurrying away as though fleeing the scene of a heinous crime.

Anna's blood ran cold. Shyla's words heralded the inevitable moment she'd been dreading. She was more than just a maid to the baroness's daughter, she was a friend. Though that relationship bestowed upon her a certain status within the household, it was status that came at a high price. She was the one expected to pick up the pieces in the aftermath of Gömalt's unsolicited attentions. She was supposed to somehow make amends and know what to do. Impossible. The abuses permitted to befall her mistress could not be justified, no matter what words of consolation were offered in their wake. The situation was hideous, and one that only the baroness could prevent. Yet far from intervening, she seemed to condone what happened.

Angry frustration knotted up Anna's insides as she surged down the passageway. She concealed herself behind the thick drapes that closed off an alcove opposite Kassandra's bedchamber door and waited, straining to detect any sign that the unwelcome visitor was about to depart. There was no sound from within, so it probably wouldn't be long. He rarely lingered after inflicting his pleasure.

Minute followed interminable minute, each one stretched out by dreadful anticipation. When the door latch did eventually break the silence, it made her flinch. She didn't even breathe as Gömalt stepped out, convinced that his uncanny abilities would detect her presence. She felt as though his eyes would see right through the curtain that hid her. Too late did she think to pray that her toes weren't visible beneath its hem.

The gods smiled. Gömalt's footsteps petered away without faltering. The relief that flooded through her left her shaking.

She waited a few moments more, then parted the drapes and nimbly tip-toed after him. She dipped her head round the corner of the passage just in time to see him knock on the door to the baroness's bedchamber. There was a pause, then he entered. He would not emerge for some time, perhaps not even until morning.

Abandoning stealth, she scurried back to Kassandra's door, pausing for a moment with her hand on the latch as she steeled herself for the state her mistress would be in.

Kassandra sat atop her bed, arms hugging her knees. Save for the sheets that covered her legs, she was naked, though a cascade of dark-auburn hair provided a little modesty over her pale skin. Rocking gently to and fro as though praying through some silent mantra, she didn't stir as Anna entered the chamber.

Anna's heart sank. She could see tears streaming down Kassandra's cheeks. She hurried across to the bed and draped an arm around her shoulders. Kassandra tensed at the touch, but all too soon the jolting tremble resumed.

"I can't go on like this anymore, Anna."

Anna tightened her embrace. There were no words she could offer that would give solace; there never were. It was far from the first time she had come to comfort her mistress after a visit from Gömalt. Since being back, the tyrant had wasted little time getting round to making one of his demands for satisfaction.

"Did you see where he went?"

Anna sighed inwardly. She wished she hadn't looked now. She didn't want to say.

Kassandra's stare demanded an answer.

"To your mother's chambers."

"Bastard! And *she's* no better."

The momentary flare of anger stemmed some of the tears. Kassandra threw herself back on to the pillows behind her. The sheets did not follow.

"Shall I get your nightdress, my lady?"

Kassandra's attention was drawn to her nakedness, yet she made no attempt to cover herself. "She uses me as though I was nothing but a whore. I'm not a daughter – I'm just a leash she uses to keep that animal in check. A treat for a dog after an act of obedience."

Anna returned from the wardrobe with one of Kassandra's nightdresses and helped her into the flimsy shift. As they sat back down on the bed, she noticed a distant and unfocused look in Kassandra's eyes.

"But what can you do, my lady? You can't stop Gömalt. No one can."

"I could leave."

Anna sighed. They'd been through this before.

"And go where? You know there's nowhere in the Empire that would be beyond your mother's reach. She'd send Gömalt out after you and he would drag you back, kicking and screaming. Then things would be worse than they are now."

"Worse! *How* could they be worse?"

Anna recoiled at the force of the retort, even though she knew it was not aimed at her.

"You have no idea what it's like having that bastard in your bed; having no choice; knowing that you're just a – a *thing* – used to satisfy him. I could almost bear it if I thought he actually cared for me. But he doesn't. He goes straight from my chambers to my mother's without a second thought. And she knows it!"

A fresh stream of tears broke the dam that anger had built to resist them.

"I'm sorry, my lady, truly I am." Anna's own eyes began to well up. "I know I can't begin to imagine what it's like for you," she took Kassandra's hands in hers, "but though it may not seem like it now, things *could* be worse. You mustn't do anything that might cause your mother to punish you."

"She can't punish me if I'm not here," Kassandra mumbled.

"But where could you go?"

"Alondria."

"Alondria?" Anna did not hide her scepticism. "What makes you think you'd be any better off there?"

"I'm a lady of standing. The Alondrians respect their women."

"You're a lady who belongs to a household that's been a sworn enemy of Alondria for centuries. Even if you managed to get there, you couldn't tell them who you really are. And without lineage, you'd end up married to a peasant, scratching out a meagre existence in a hovel somewhere."

"I'd settle for a beggar if he at least loved me. It would be better than living here."

Anna ignored the sullen remark. "So what if the Alondrians discovered your true identity? They'd most likely throw you in gaol."

"I don't care. At least they'd have reason. Which is more than can be said for my mother."

Anna let out another sigh. The gods had surely dealt Kassandra an unfair hand. All she'd done was make the mistake of being born a daughter instead of a son. That was the root of all her woes. The baroness had wanted a male heir above all else, someone to inherit the fruits of her ambition. But the complications of Kassandra's birth had ended any prospects of the baroness bearing more children. So with only a daughter, whatever the House of Daka became, its eventual status would simply pass to another by marriage.

Kassandra would never be forgiven for that.

"The gods know you have good reason to be upset, my lady. Believe me, it hurts to see you so unhappy." Anna raised Kassandra's hand and kissed the backs of her fingers. "But there's nothing that can be done right now, is there? You can't up and leave tonight. Such things would need planning."

Kassandra's shoulders sagged a little.

"Look, it's getting late. We can talk about this again tomorrow," Anna suggested, hoping that by then Kassandra would be feeling less upset, and might therefore be in a more realistic frame of mind.

More of Kassandra's fight drained away. Her gaze drifted towards her lap.

Deep down, Anna knew any notions of running away were just a clutching at straws. It was a fantasy, something on which to pin a glimmer of hope, a means of escaping the loveless torment her mother permitted.

Reality was harsher by far. It would be next to impossible to break free from the baroness's grip. She was simply too powerful. It was doubtful even Alondria could offer Kassandra safe haven.

Anna plumped up the pillows and tucked Kassandra into bed. As though settling down a child of her own, a sudden maternal instinct prompted her to kiss Kassandra on the forehead. A simple gesture, yet one the baroness had never performed. Not even once.

"Don't go."

Anna's eyes widened. She was taken aback, not by an order, but by a plea.

"Tell me some more about Michàss."

A slight quickening of the heart took hold and Anna felt herself blush. She smiled and perched back down on the bed. In some ways it was good that Kassandra was seeking something to take her mind off things. But it was also awkward. Given what Kassandra had just been subjected to, it seemed almost callous to speak of romantic liaisons. Yet Michàss was a new thing as far as both she and Brath'daka were concerned – he'd only been in service a month – and Kassandra had been keen to sit and listen to gossip about him before Gömalt had returned and ruined everything.

"He's been exploring the castle."

Kassandra's eyebrow rose.

"Learning where to hide when Master Halfdanr comes looking for him," Anna giggled.

The head of the house staff had taken it upon himself to see that the new boy wasn't left idle. Self-preservation had seen Michàss find ways not to be found when Halfdanr was on the prowl.

"It's all a game of cat and mouse to him. He got himself lost the other day."

"Lost? I wouldn't have thought Brath'daka big enough for that."

"Not for you, perhaps, my lady. You've lived here all your life. It's all new for Michàss. He even blundered into the kitchens the day before yesterday. By accident. I did warn him. I told him, 'stand at the door, cap in hand, and wait to be bidden'. Oddon had a right go at him – took to him with a pastry pin – you should have seen the bruises!"

Kassandra managed a smile. "Even mother treats the cook with respect."

"Aye, my lady. She's not the only one. Michàss has learnt his lesson. He won't go in there again unless summoned."

Anna stayed for a long while, gently drawing Kassandra's thoughts away to more pleasant things with all her blather about castle life, the kind usually kept hidden from the highborn.

It was late when she eventually headed for the door. From the far side of the bedchamber she glanced back over her shoulder. She was acutely aware her success in diverting Kassandra's attention from her torment would only be temporary. It struck her how Kassandra's face was silhouetted by the lamplight. Hers were hard lines.

A deep sense of foreboding took hold as she closed the door.

6

Just outside Mitcha's gates, Torrin-Ashur sat with his gaze transfixed by the rugged beauty of the distant Mathian Mountains. The warming hues of an early morning sun crept down their majestic white peaks, transforming frigid snow into gleaming lava. The air was crisp and invigorating. Apart from the chirp of birds and the occasional flurry of wings, nothing else stirred in the landscape. It was that tranquil but all too brief part of the day before men rose to begin their machinations with their fellow men, precipitating the inevitable slide towards chaos.

It would normally have been a pleasure simply to sit and absorb such serenity, but an inner turmoil refused to be quelled. The night had been troubled and dawn long in approaching. Instead of sleeping, thoughts of facing Borádin in the call-out due to take place a few hours hence had plagued him, keeping carefree oblivion at bay.

He tried to imagine what his father might have said under the circumstances. The thick ear and long lecture about temper and stupidity, and how one should not lead to the other, he could do without. What he needed right now was his father's solid, level-headed thinking, the kind of pragmatism that defined a path that could be adhered to with conviction.

Time slipped by with no regard to its import. Sounds from within the camp brought him out of his reverie and with a reluctant sigh he tore himself away from the view and made his way back through the main gates.

He found the Pressed were already up and about when he reached their cordoned area. For the most part he tried to ignore them; they knew their duties. He had more immediate concerns to deal with.

He extracted his sword from its scabbard and gently ran his fingers along its smooth surfaces, checking for burrs. It glistened under a thin film of oil, catching the light and refracting it into an array of colours. The weapon had been in the Ashur household for generations and bore the scars of many battles. Its plain leather-wrapped pommel and limited ornamental embellishments – just some words in A'lyavine engraved along the fuller – gave it a relatively pedestrian appearance. Yet it was a striking weapon. The blade was unusually slender, suggesting a certain flimsiness, which was decidedly misleading. The metal had been folded and quenched many times during manufacture to impart great hardness and strength. The workmanship may have lacked an artistic touch, but it represented the very best of the armourers' ancient craft.

"Morning."

Sàhodd's greeting took him by surprise. He spun round, just in time to notice his friend deposit a sack beside one of the tents.

"Up bright and early, I see."

"More a case of still up late," Torrin-Ashur countered.

"Ah. Well, if it's any consolation, Borádin didn't get much sleep either."

"Oh?"

"He spent most of last night drinking. And boasting. Your name's mud, by the way. Still, with any luck, he'll have a head thick with fog this morning."

"Good. I'm going to need all the help I can get."

Sàhodd's eyebrows pinched together as he caught sight of the words engraved on Torrin-Ashur's sword. He cocked his head sideways trying to read them.

Torrin-Ashur flipped the blade over and presented it to him hilt-first. "*siad-ida Sèliccia~Castrà,*" he rattled off.

"Eh?"

"A sort of family motto."

"Ah," Sàhodd nodded sagely. "Which means…?"

"*Hear ye the song of war.*"

Which clearly meant little to Sàhodd. "I see. Nice – lovely balance." He gave the air a few trial slices before examining the weapon again. "Old?"

"Very. It's been handed down from father to son in my family since the gods know when."

"So how did you end up with it? Shouldn't it have gone to Eldris?"

Torrin-Ashur gave a nod. He recalled the day his elder brother had announced he wasn't going to join the army and honour the terms of the Bond that had granted the Ashurs their lands generations earlier. Their father's reaction had been most telling – silence. A bitter blow to a man for whom family honour meant everything.

"When I volunteered to enlist in Eldris's place, father passed the sword to me there and then. He said the least he could do was give me a decent weapon to get me started."

"I bet that pleased your brother."

"Just a little," Torrin-Ashur smirked. "Still, it's his own fault. If he'd done his duty, the sword would have been his and he'd have been here instead of me. Though probably not in the mess I'm in."

Sàhodd gave the air a few more cuts and parries, then handed the blade back. "Being bonded is rather old-fashioned, isn't it? Surely your family doesn't still have to serve these days?"

"Well, no, I suppose not. But father is very traditional. To him, it's more about family honour than observing the letter of the law. We've been serving the Bond for five hundred years – ever since we became the Lords of Ashur. Besides, the Northern Territories are our home. Someone has to defend them against the wretched Tsnath."

Sàhodd nodded. "Speaking of defence, we should start getting you ready." He reached for the sack he'd brought with him. "Yngvarr has managed to find you a breastplate. Standard issue, I'm afraid, but it might just stop your guts seeing the light of day. That sort of thing's very messy, you know."

Torrin-Ashur smiled; Sàhodd's flippancy belied true concern.

The armour proved a snug fit. It moved with him without slopping about as Torrin-Ashur lunged back and forth. Sàhodd sparred with him for a while to give him a chance to become familiar with wearing it. Without the benefit of proper training, it had been advised that his best defence during the fight would be speed and agility. The breastplate was a concession to Yngvarr; it would at least provide a modicum of protection to the more vital regions.

"Where is Yngvarr this morning?" Torrin-Ashur asked.

"He's over at the Forum. Did you hear, they've built a special stand for the princess so that she can watch the fight?"

Torrin-Ashur glanced round at the Pressed; they were normally relied upon to build things in the camp these days. He shrugged. "Well, cheap entertainment, I suppose. Was Elona with Borádin's crowd last night?"

"Need you ask? Although," Sàhodd lowered his voice to a conspiratorial level, "I gather Borádin didn't exactly make a good impression. Elona found all his bravado rather boring and retired early."

"Good for her."

"Come on," Sàhodd chuckled, "we'd better get going. Being late for your own funeral is frowned upon."

"There's just one thing I've got to do first."

Torrin-Ashur trotted over to the tent where Tomàss was recovering and ducked inside. The injured man tried to sit up. A stab of pain quickly put paid to that idea.

"Relax," Torrin-Ashur ordered, throwing out a staying hand, "ribs don't mend that quickly."

Tomàss slumped back down.

"You have everything you need?"

"Yes, sir. The lads have been seeing to me."

"Good. I'll look in on you later. Who knows, I might even be joining you in the next cot if Borádin has his way."

The attempt at humour failed to elicit a smile.

"I'm sorry I caused you all this trouble, sir."

"Nonsense," Torrin-Ashur countered. "This call-out is entirely my fault."

"But you'd not be facing it if only I'd …"

Torrin-Ashur cut Tomàss off with a pat on the arm. "If this, if that, if the other. My father likes to say, 'a life full of *if only* is a life full of regret'. Not worth the bother."

With a parting nod Torrin-Ashur backed out of the tent. He immediately came face to face with a gathering of the Pressed.

"Well, lads, the time's come."

To a man they wore sombre looks. What chances they thought he'd got, he wasn't sure. They held him in high regard, that much was clear. But that was because he was the first officer they'd had who treated them decently. It didn't mean they had any faith in his fighting skills, which thus far hadn't had much of an airing.

"Sir, couldn't some of us come with you?" Botfiár asked.

"I think it best if you stay here, Corporal."

Botfiár's eyes fell downwards. "I understand, sir."

Torrin-Ashur sighed. Botfiár didn't understand. Resigned looks suggested that neither did the rest of the men. Clearly they thought he was reluctant to be seen accompanied by such lowly supporters.

Nothing could have been further from the truth. He didn't give a damn about appearances. What he did care about was the self-esteem of his men. He'd worked hard to lift them out of the gutter. Clearly the word *scum* was still indelibly etched into their souls.

He had a change of heart.

"Alright, come if you wish. But no pomp and ceremony. That's

Borádin's game, not mine."

*

Kirshtahll stepped aside, motioning for Princess Elona to enter the stand ahead of him. Two rows of seats had been constructed, the rear one raised on a foot-high platform. Elona took her place without further guidance – her seat was the only one graced with a cushion. Kirshtahll installed himself beside her, with Riagán flanking him. Various members of the royal staff and other senior officers slotted themselves in wherever they could. Temesh-ai found himself on the back row next to Céline, Elona's lady-in-waiting. He seemed quite happy with his lot, flirting with her like a wanton harlot. Kirshtahll chastised him with a scowl; the man was old enough to be her father – nay, her grandfather!

Elona glanced at the surroundings and then leaned over to murmur in Kirshtahll's ear. "Not quite the Forum in Alondris, is it?"

"My apologies, Your Highness," he chuckled back. "We didn't have a million tons of marble to hand when we built it."

"Pity."

Mitcha's Forum was comparable to the one in Alondris in name only. The capital's arena was a magnificent edifice, the pride of all Alondria and famed well beyond her borders. Made entirely of white marble, it could seat twenty thousand spectators. Mitcha's offering was a rather more modest affair – a roughly level patch of grass with a knee-high wooden fence defining its boundary. Kirshtahll's normal disposition towards call-outs meant that this part of the camp rarely attracted much attention. On this occasion, most either had to bring their own seating arrangements or settle for standing.

Elona leaned over again. "So tell me, Padráig, this hasn't all been put on just for my benefit, has it? Because if it has, I'd much rather they didn't bother."

Kirshtahll allowed a genuine scowl to trouble his brow. "I'm afraid not, Your Highness."

"I see. So what is it really all about? If the story I heard last night is to be believed, we'd be looking at a court martial, not a call-out."

Kirshtahll told her as much as he knew of the altercation that had taken place between Torrin-Ashur and Borádin in the Millar's Cup, and the reasons behind it.

"Is that all? And you allowed a challenge, just for that?"

"The law is on Borádin's side," Kirshtahll replied, flashing Riagán a glance. "And he did make a *demand*."

"It sounds to me as though this Borádin needs to be taught a lesson," Elona muttered.

Kirshtahll scanned the crowd now surrounding the Forum, trying to spot Torrin-Ashur. The young lad didn't appear to have arrived yet.

"That, I'm afraid, is wishful thinking."

*

As Torrin-Ashur and Sàhodd approached the Forum they caught sight of Yngvarr and veered towards a small cordoned area that he'd managed to preserve against the pressure of gathering spectators. A group of the Pressed followed on behind. They were being discreet as ordered, but there was no hiding the rather odd spectacle of Tomàss being pushed along in a handcart. He'd insisted on coming, despite the pain he was in. Torrin-Ashur hadn't the heart to deny him. The call-out was, after all, being fought partly on his behalf.

"How are you feeling?" Yngvarr asked when they arrived.

Torrin-Ashur grimaced. "Nervous."

"Well, that's not a bad thing. It'll keep you on your toes."

Sàhodd twisted him round and punched him in the guts, ostensibly to make sure that the breastplate was doing its job. He grabbed its edges and gave it a few good tugs.

"Remember, this is not a shield; Borádin might still get through it if he thrusts forwards hard enough."

"I'll keep that in mind. Is Borádin here yet?"

"Oh, I think you'll know when he turns up," Yngvarr advised with some candour.

Torrin-Ashur surveyed the busy scene, looking for any sign of his opponent. Several thousand men had already gathered, with more swelling the crowd as each minute passed. It was certainly going to be a well-attended knock-about. The cordoned area at the opposite end of the Forum, obviously reserved for Borádin's party, was still very much vacant.

His eyes alighted on the stand constructed for the guests of honour, mid-way along the right hand side of the field. It was then that he caught his first glimpse of the princess. Her face captivated him in an instant. A chasm opened up in the pit of his stomach. For a few moments he couldn't breathe. He just stood there, rooted to the spot, mouth ajar.

It took a while for it to register that Elona was gazing back at him. His mouth snapped shut. Plunging into his hopelessly inadequate repertoire of social etiquette, he came up with an understated bow. Elona dipped her head ever so slightly in return, a gesture that would have gone unnoticed by anyone not paying her immediate attention.

Which meant it hadn't escaped Sàhodd's notice. Torrin-Ashur caught his eye and prepared to fend off the glib comment that was about come his way. But Sàhodd never got the chance. He was blown off course by a fanfare of trumpets.

Borádin had arrived.

All eyes immediately swung towards the far end of the field.

The nobleman certainly put on an impressive performance. His escort numbered thirty men, half of whom preceded him. He was on a mount bedecked with enough heraldry to keep any self-respecting monarch happy. On his flank was his second, Lord Mir, similarly on horseback and with no less trimmings.

The first rank of footmen, the heralds that had hijacked the crowd's attention, shouldered their instruments. The rest of the men were armed with twenty-foot pikes, each sporting a gilt-edged banner in the deep rich blue of Borádin's personal standard, that of the House of Kin-Shísim. The banners tapered into long golden ribbon-tails that glinted as they wafted playfully in the gentle summer breeze. It was all fantastically resplendent.

By the precision of their steps, it was obvious that Borádin's escort had rehearsed their moves to perfection. At a predetermined point the forward body split left and right, opening up a passage through which the two riders came to the fore. The men bringing up the rear manoeuvred elegantly into position behind the front ranks and by the time the whole platoon had stomped to a halt, Borádin and Mir were at the Forum rail with a squad of impeccably aligned men on either side.

Torrin-Ashur began to realise just how outclassed he really was. Regardless of any other feelings he had towards the man, he couldn't help but admire Borádin's style. "Teeth of the gods," he whispered under his breath.

Sàhodd glanced at him and raised an agreeing eyebrow.

The silence that had temporarily descended was shattered as some of Borádin's supporters began to clap, an outbreak of applause that caught like a spark to dry tinder. The Forum was quickly engulfed.

Torrin-Ashur swallowed hard. "Do you think anyone would notice if I just quietly slipped away?"

Yngvarr slapped him on the back. "Listen, Torrin, don't be put off. I know you're just a country yokel," he ducked to avoid a friendly swipe, "but all this – it's just Borádin playing the game."

"Alright, so what happens next?"

Yngvarr glanced across the field. Borádin was holding up one arm in an informal salute to the crowd, soaking up the attention.

"In a moment he'll go before the umpire, that'll be Kirshtahll, and formally proclaim his challenge. After that, you'll be summoned. When you get there, don't address Borádin directly. You must speak only to the umpire. Be formal and use full titles."

Sàhodd elbowed Torrin-Ashur and pointed out across the Forum. "He's on the move."

Borádin managed a graceful dismount. Given all the armour he was wearing, that was no mean feat. Many a man would have required steps and the assistance of a squire.

A number of buglers entered the Forum and took up station around the perimeter.

"Observers," Yngvarr explained. "Their job is to spot which of you sheds blood first. When that happens, a bugle will sound and they will indicate which of you has won. You must cease fighting immediately. That's very important. If you win and continue, you forfeit. Lose and carry on, and the winner's second will join in and take you down. The restraint of First Blood is removed if that happens, so be warned. Mir would be within his rights to kill you."

"So – I listen out for the bugle, then I try not to bleed to death."

"Something like that," Yngvarr grinned. "But don't expect it to be quick. If I'm any judge, Borádin will want to knock you about for a while rather than go straight for the cut. That might provide a few opportunities. If he thinks he's got the upper hand he could get overconfident. Don't show him your bite straight away – *let* him beat you up. If you're lucky, you might take him by surprise."

Borádin entered the Forum and crossed over to the front of the stand. Torrin-Ashur could tell words were being exchanged, but couldn't quite discern what was being said.

Kirshtahll eventually nodded in their direction.

"Look sharp, that's you," Sàhodd prompted.

Torrin-Ashur stepped over the low boundary fence and started out across the Forum. A few paces later, Yngvarr hissed an urgent recall.

"Quick, your sword — take it off."

"What?"

"You're not allowed to be armed at this stage."

Torrin-Ashur let out a huff. There was altogether too much nonsense attached to this call-out business. He unbuckled his belt and handed the weapon over.

"Remember what I told you," Yngvarr said, taking the sword, "full titles, and speak only to Kirshtahll."

*

Kirshtahll watched as Torrin-Ashur set out across the Forum, did a quick retreat to divest himself of his weapon, and then set out again. Without the guidance of his seconds, clearly the young man would have had little idea what was expected of him. At this stage, that wasn't so critical. Once battle was joined, it would be a different matter. That was a worry.

The lieutenant came to a halt level with Borádin and swung a crisp salute. Kirshtahll noticed his eyes flicker towards Elona for the briefest of moments; at little more than ten paces, she was no doubt a phenomenal distraction.

"Lieutenant Ashur," he began, "welcome to this Field of Honour. You are before us at the request of Lord Lieutenant Borádin, here standing. You have been made aware of his grievance against you, have you not?"

"My Lord General, I have."

"Gentlemen, as your umpire in this matter, I am required to ask whether amicable settlement has been reached?"

The question was nothing more than a formality. The whole of Mitcha knew that no such settlement had been forthcoming. Both men remained silent.

"Lord Lieutenant Borádin, what are your terms of satisfaction?"

"My Lord General, I ask for First Blood."

Kirshtahll grunted to himself; this day had yet to present any surprises. "Lieutenant Ashur, have you anything to say before I call you both to arms?"

The question seemed to catch the lieutenant off guard. His eyes closed for a moment, as though he was in communion with far off counsel.

"My Lord General, I respectfully ask the Lord Lieutenant if he would consider accepting my apology?"

Kirshtahll blinked. An offer of settlement was unheard of at this late stage. Disputes were occasionally settled off the field, but by the time matters had reached the Forum, an impasse had usually been reached from which neither side was prepared to retreat.

Kirshtahll raised an enquiring eyebrow at Borádin.

"My Lord General, the lieutenant knows my terms."

Kirshtahll returned his gaze to Torrin-Ashur. "Unfortunately, Lieutenant, I believe that that is a *'no'*."

There was a moment of total silence, as though the whole of Mitcha held its breath. Gasps of dismay broke it when Torrin-Ashur pushed up the sleeve of his tunic and held out his arm.

"If the Lord Lieutenant wants blood, he may take it."

Borádin's only response was the tightening of the muscles along his jaw-line.

Kirshtahll sighed aloud. "So be it, gentlemen. To arms."

As Kirshtahll watched the two officers return to their positions, Temesh-ai leaned forwards. "Well, you don't see that every day, Padráig."

"I just hope Ashur doesn't get hurt too badly," he murmured back without turning. "I'm beginning to regret having allowed this."

"You didn't have much choice, sir," Riagán reminded him.

"I'm supposed to be a bloody general. I don't like having my hand forced by an arrogant brat shoving the law in my face."

He slumped back into his seat. His knuckles turned white as he gripped the armrest to suppress his annoyance.

Elona placed a silken hand over his. "Don't worry, Padráig. I've got a feeling about this."

Kirshtahll gave her a curious glance.

He was graced with a wistful smile in reply.

*

Torrin-Ashur returned to his cordoned area. Yngvarr handed him his sword. He didn't strap it back on.

"What was going on out there?" Sàhodd demanded.

"I tried to offer Borádin settlement. He wasn't interested – he wants his moment of glory." Torrin-Ashur glanced over his shoulder to where Borádin was getting ready. His face hardened.

The signalman entered the Forum. Dressed in bright green, presumably to distinguish him from the combatants, he bowed to the guests of honour and took up position in front of the stand. He raised two flags on short poles above his head, one a miniature version of Borádin's standard, similar to the ones gracing the pikes his escort held aloft, the other a simple triangle of red cloth.

There was an expectant dip in the crowd's chatter. As the red flag dropped, their attention swung towards the southern end of the field.

Torrin-Ashur didn't need any more instruction to know his moment had come. The etiquette was over; all he had to do now was fight. And hopefully survive.

Thousands watched him as he ventured out across the Forum. It felt like tens of thousands. Their gaze pressed with a force that seemed physical, hemming him in on every side, very much presenting a wall through which escape was impossible. The field suddenly became a very lonely and inhospitable place.

A third of the way across the grass he came to a halt. Gripping his sword's cross-guard with both hands, he jabbed the scabbard chape into the ground and withdrew the blade, leaving the empty sheath protruding from the mud like the stalk of a barren plant. He dropped to one knee for a moment, appearing to all the world as though peace was being made with gods. When he was done, he rose and drew an imaginary line in the ground just in front of his position. Only then did he nod to the signalman.

The blue flag dropped.

Borádin stepped into the Forum, donning his helmet. Mir hooked a large shield on to the lower cannon of his vambrace. Another retainer handed him his sword. Both were heavy. Bedecked in all his armour, and now laden with weapons, his movements did not seem as agile as they had appeared earlier.

Applause went up for him as he strode out. His sword hand went up in recognition of the tribute.

Torrin-Ashur barely registered the crowd's cheers. His world went strangely quiet. The noise seemed displaced by an intense clarity of thought; everything except Borádin slipped from his mind, becoming distant and immaterial. With his nerves becalmed, an inexplicable peace settled upon him.

He felt himself go slightly light-headed. Borádin was still some fifty paces away, but even so, he fought the sensation with all his might. Fainting now would be an ignominy never to be lived down.

The giddiness did not linger. A sudden surge of power blasted it aside. So intense, so unexpected was it that he gasped, staggering forwards a couple of paces as though drunk.

Despite Borádin's advance, he forced his eyes closed, trying to make sense of the extraordinary feelings surging through him. A powerful, emotive beat flowed deep within his veins; not the pounding of blood, but something with a strange cadence, almost musical in nature. It was hard to tell if it was real. But whatever it was, its effect was empowering. He felt vibrant and full of energy. It completely took over inside. Instead of doubt and fear, there was simply an expectation, one that bordered on elation. It made him feel like dancing.

Bizarre. He *never* danced.

Opening his eyes again, he found the world a different place. Borádin's movements were like that of a man wading through tar. It seemed to take forever for the nobleman to close the gap between them. The man's arrogance kept his sword hand aloft in salute to the crowd, from which his attention didn't waver until he came to a halt a few paces short of where Torrin-Ashur stood. Oozing with confidence, he wore a wolfish grin.

Torrin-Ashur remained still, waiting for Borádin to make the first move. As though forewarned, he knew exactly what to expect.

Without the customary combatant's salute, or even a nod, Borádin sprang forwards, bringing his sword arching from behind to strike a downwards blow. Torrin-Ashur side-stepped the attack with graceful economy of effort. In a blur, he pivoted on a heel and swung his blade round, slamming it into Borádin's over-extended reach. The man's sword smashed to the ground. Such was the force, the cross-guard embedded itself in the grassy mud.

In the moment that followed Torrin-Ashur was too stunned to take the advantage and strike again. He replayed his moves, as though a spectator of his own actions, trying to work out what had just happened. It had all occurred in the blink of an eye, without conscious thought. He stepped away.

The crowd clapped their appreciation. Torrin-Ashur grunted; if they thought he was being chivalrous, they were wrong.

Borádin recovered his sword and a modicum of composure. They faced off once more. This time there was hesitation and an adjustment of tactics. The nobleman's grin was nowhere to be seen.

The tense standoff lasted nearly a minute before Borádin launched his next offensive, charging ahead with shield raised. He seemed intent on ramming his opponent with a broadside.

Somehow Torrin-Ashur knew it was a feint. At the last instant, Borádin thrust forwards with his sword. Torrin-Ashur darted back beyond reach and parried with the flat of his blade, deflecting the advance. He spun round and brought the full force of his sword to bear, striking a stunning blow to Borádin's shield. The nobleman reeled away, flexing his arm to dispel the numbing shock.

As if some invisible restraint had just evaporated, Torrin-Ashur unleashed blow after blow, delivered with frightening speed. The ferocious barrage forced Borádin to retreat unsteadily back across the Forum. From every angle Torrin-Ashur smashed his blade into the nobleman's armour, denting and dislodging it with each hit. The ringing clash of steel on steel became an almost constant clamour.

Borádin's shock became visible. His eyes darted this way and that, searching for a way to escape the vicious onslaught. His earlier cocksure confidence had vanished. Now there was only a defence born of desperation.

Nearing the boundary fence, he veered right to avoid getting tangled. The change in direction opened up an unexpected opportunity. He lunged forwards, dropping low to execute a cross-cut swipe. It caught Torrin-Ashur in the midriff, gouging a deep scar in his breastplate.

Torrin-Ashur had no time to offer Yngvarr thanks for the extra protection. The insistent force compelling him on reacted in an instant, sending a wave of anger flooding through him. He kicked Borádin's extended shin sideways, knocking his leg out from under him. Heavily laden, the noble stumbled and fell to one knee amid a clank of armour. Only the bottom edge of his shield digging into the ground prevented him from keeling over.

Torrin-Ashur brought his blade arching down with all his might, smashing Borádin's sword into the mud for a second time.

There was no holding back now; Torrin-Ashur could not have stayed his hand, even if he had wanted to. The power of the mysterious force thundering within him was utterly relentless. He slammed the pommel of his sword into Borádin's cheek-piece, knocking the man nearly senseless. The noble crashed to the ground.

Whatever gods Borádin revered, they must have smiled. Only by divine intervention could he have remained conscious. Groggily, he managed to roll on to his front and struggle up, first to his knees, thence to his feet, all the while fending off blows. He glanced towards his sword, but Torrin-Ashur's attack made its retrieval impossible. As a last resort, he positioned his shield in front of his body and tried to ram Torrin-Ashur back across the Forum.

The tactic failed. Utterly. It was like hitting a solid wall. Torrin-Ashur hammered upon the shield with merciless persistence. It became the sole focal point for his furious storm. Instead of moving forwards, Borádin found himself staggering backwards under a torrential outpouring of wrath, the deluge of a berserker rage.

The battering forced him right across the Forum to the opposite edge of the field. The backs of his knees met the perimeter fence and he tumbled to the ground yet again.

To the right, just a few yards away, Elona and Kirshtahll sat transfixed. Other spectators urgently shrank back in a bid to get beyond the reach of Torrin-Ashur's flailing sword.

Lying in a demolished heap, Borádin struggled to get his legs clear of the fence. There was no chance of him regaining his stance again now.

Torrin-Ashur let out a terrible roar, venting all his fury against Borádin's pulverised armour. Great, two-handed blows brought his sword crashing down again and again. It was only a matter of seconds before the pounding forced Borádin to relinquish his shield. Torrin-Ashur savagely kicked it aside, leaving the noble bereft of defence. All Borádin could do was wrap his arms around his head and await his fate.

A long moment passed.

The expected strike never came.

Torrin-Ashur stood panting, the tip of his blade resting lightly against an exposed part of Borádin's arm where the leather strapping that held vambrace to pauldron had given way.

An eerie silence descended upon the stunned crowd as they awaited the outcome. Borádin, the pummelling now ceased, risked opening his eyes to meet Torrin-Ashur's exhausted stare.

With a sickening wrench, the mysterious force that had driven Torrin-Ashur throughout the fight deserted him. As though his very soul had been torn from him, he was left utterly devoid of strength. Unable even to retain the grip on his sword, it tumbled from his fingers. He swayed for a moment before his legs buckled and he slumped down in a squat across Borádin's stomach.

Calling on his last reserves, he withdrew a small dagger from his waistband. Out the corner of his eye he caught sudden movement; Kirshtahll shooting to his feet. With his vision inexplicably clouding over, he pressed the hilt of the dagger into Borádin's palm. Then, just has he had before the fight, he pushed up the sleeve of his tunic and offered his bared forearm.

"Take it," he gasped, fighting to stay conscious.

Borádin stared at the knife, seemingly unable to grasp this strange turn of events. Torrin-Ashur grabbed his wrist and positioned the blade for him. "Do it!"

Borádin sliced the dagger across exposed flesh.

The last thing Torrin-Ashur heard was the sound of a far-off bugle.

*

Kirshtahll slumped back down into his seat. His mind was a blank; he didn't know what to think. He wasn't even sure what it was he'd just witnessed. He'd seen fights before; *teeth of the gods*, he'd seen wars! But nothing like the one-man storm that had just roared past.

He glanced across at Elona. She seemed as much in shock as he.

"Feminine intuition?"

Elona's head shook slowly.

*

Torrin-Ashur came round to the sight of Sàhodd's concerned face peering down at him. Recent events seemed like distant memories.

"What happened?"

"You're asking me?" Sàhodd scoffed. "The plan was, you were going to get yourself chopped up, and then Yngvarr and I were going to sally forth and look for all the pieces."

Torrin-Ashur murmured something to the contrary and tried sitting up. "I feel like I've been kicked by a mule. A herd of mules."

"You should see Borádin. He's going to have to throw his armour away and have a new set made."

Torrin-Ashur noticed there was no sign of his erstwhile opponent. In fact, the whole area had been cleared of spectators.

"Well, Lieutenant, are you going to lie there all day, or what?" boomed Major Temesh-ai.

Torrin-Ashur's head jerked round to locate the vaguely familiar voice, whereupon he discovered Kirshtahll standing just a few yards away. Struggling to his feet, he attempted to stand to attention. It was difficult, given that he seemed to have the stability of a newborn fawn. Sàhodd offered himself as a crutch.

"How are you feeling?" Temesh-ai asked.

"Err – confused, sir."

Temesh-ai grunted. "That would make two of us, then." He turned to Kirshtahll and shrugged. "Well, I've no idea what just happened, but he seems fine to me."

Kirshtahll nodded. "Lieutenant Ashur, you have some explaining to do."

"Sir, I…"

Kirshtahll cut him off. "Later. You, what's your name?"

"Sàhodd, sir."

"Right, get him cleaned up. I'll summon him to my quarters later. In the meantime, make sure that he speaks to no one."

7

A rapid tattoo of flapping sandals echoed down the corridor outside Heckart's study, heralding the arrival of one of his learned colleagues long before his door burst open.

"Brother," Yisson gasped between laboured breaths, leaning solidly against the doorframe for much needed support, "there's been a disturbance!"

"Yes – it is customary to knock."

"But Br…,"

Heckart held up his hand. As the head of the Adak-rann Brotherhood, pre-eminent amongst the world's scholastic orders, he was generally expected to be calm and unflappable. His ponderous disposition suited him well to the role. He laid down his quill and folded his hands about his ample midriff. "Brother Yisson," he said patiently, "calm yourself. Take a deep breath…"

Yisson obediently heaved an expansive lungful of air. "It's the Taümathakiya, Brother."

Heckart sighed in annoyance. "Do I really need to be interrupted every time that wretched thing decides to wobble?"

"No, Brother, you don't understand. It's tipped over."

That at least caused a furrow to appear on Heckart's brow. "How far?"

"*Right* over. Oh, and young Jorra-hin has been hurt."

"What?" Heckart immediately rose to his feet. The stirrings of the Taümathakiya were one thing, usually an inconvenience, but the welfare of a brother was quite another.

Once more Yisson's sandals flapped against foot and flagstone as he hurried back through the sprawling labyrinth of Jàb-áldis. The monastery was a topsy-turvy mess of inspirations and afterthoughts, adhering not to one architectural convention, but to many. High up in a remote part of the Mathian Mountains, the buildings undulated to the jagged ramblings of the ridge upon which they were precariously perched. The result was an establishment in which very few rooms were on the same level as the ones next door. This in turn led to a great propensity for steps.

As he followed Yisson's puffing progress up yet another short flight, Heckart reflected briefly on what had possessed anyone to choose such a location; it was an improbable place for a shepherd's hut, let alone a monastic retreat. The answer was simple, though – safety. In eight hundred years of Adak-rann residency, not a single unwelcome visitor had breached its walls. Considering the priceless manuscripts and wealth of knowledge accumulated within its archives, that fact was not to be sniffed at. It did also help that the atmosphere so high up in the mountains was actually quite dry, which was good for storing parchment.

They reached the monitoring room where the Taümathakiya was kept and Yisson once again collapsed against the doorframe. Heckart squeezed his way past.

First to catch his eye was the Taümathakiya itself, standing perfectly still and serene in the centre of the room. His attention lingered there only a moment before being drawn away to a dishevelled-looking Jorra-hin. The young man sat propped up against the far wall with his legs splayed out in front of him across the stone floor. Brother Gerard was dabbing a damp cloth over a graze on the young man's forehead.

"Is he alright?"

"I think so," Gerard answered, glancing back over his shoulder. "He's taken a hefty knock, though. He was out cold when I found him."

"I'm feeling better now," Jorra-hin croaked.

The young man's head rested against the wall; his eyes were still shut; the road to recovery was not yet fully trodden, Heckart surmised.

"Can you tell us what happened?"

"I was sweeping the floor, over by the sand, and then..." Jorra-hin shrugged with his hands, "the next thing I know, Brother Gerard is kneeling over me, calling my name."

Heckart frowned as he appraised the distance to the edge of the neatly tamped circle of sand surrounding the Taümathakiya. It was a good ten paces from there to the wall where Jorra-hin was sitting. "Where exactly was he when you came in?"

"Right here, Brother," Gerard answered.

Heckart's frown deepened. "That's a long way from where he says he was."

"Perhaps the Taümathakiya made him jump," Yisson ventured

from the doorway. "If it made a sudden movement, could it not have startled him?"

Heckart considered that possibility for a moment, but only out of politeness to a fellow brother. The distance was too great for so simple an explanation; such a leap would have been impressive even had it been planned. With a run-up.

He gave the Taümathakiya an accusatory stare. The device was standing as solid as a rock now, despite the residual evidence of its reported movement. Roughly the height of a man, it was shaped like an elongated teardrop, as though it had dripped out of an enormous tap. Made of a glass-like material so utterly black, it seemed to suck the light out of the room. People of a Taümathic persuasion reported that it sucked at the mind, too. He'd seen more than one brother succumb to its vertiginous lure and stumble towards it in an unguarded moment.

Despite his twenty-three years at Jàb-áldis, the object still fascinated him, even though its interruptions were more often inconvenient than interesting. Its most curious facet was that it floated upright on its bulbous end, making no physical contact with the ground. That alone served as a reminder that a mysterious purpose lurked behind its usually static facade. Hooked over the tip of the teardrop was a copper ring to which a series of thin wires were attached. These radiated out like the ribbons of a maypole. Tied to the opposite ends were small weights which sat in the circle of sand surrounding the base.

The Taümathakiya's manufacture may have been an unfathomable mystery, but its operation was, by contrast, relatively simple. Measuring disturbances in the Taümathic flux, if nothing of a magical nature was occurring, then the force of the Taümatha was in equilibrium on all sides and the device stood upright and motionless, as it was now.

But if an event of magical significance produced a disturbance, Taümathic energy rippling out from the point of origin caused the Taümathakiya to bend over, rather like a reed in a gust of wind. As the tip of the device moved, the surrounding weights were displaced, their trails being recorded in the sand. These could then be used to determine the direction the disturbance had come from.

He moved closer and examined the trails the indicator weights had made. Some led right up to the base of the Taümathakiya, suggesting that the device had tipped nearly to the horizontal. Yisson had not been exaggerating.

"Jorra, you didn't by any chance see the Taümathakiya move, did you?" he asked.

"I don't recall, Brother."

"Hmm." He glanced round at the others in the room. "Who is on monitor duty this morning?"

"That would be me," Yisson answered from the doorway.

"So when was the Taümathakiya last checked?"

"Not a quarter hour before Brother Gerard discovered Jorra-hin on the floor."

"And there was no sign of any disturbance then, I take it?"

Yisson shook his head.

Heckart let out a murmur. "Well, brothers, at least we know when the disturbance occurred. Someone make a note of that." Something in his guts told him this matter might prove significant, so it was important to record the facts. "Now, we must establish exactly what everyone was doing at the time. There are only a few of our brethren here with a background in the Taümathic arts, so I want someone to find out if any of them could have caused this. We must rule out possible local disturbances before we start looking further afield."

"I'll see to that," Yisson offered.

Heckart nodded his appreciation. "Fortunate timing; the council is convening shortly. We can discuss this matter then." He gave the Taümathakiya one last scowl before glancing over at Jorra-hin. "You had better go and lie down, young man. That's a nasty bump."

*

The council met in a long chamber with a barrel-vaulted ceiling. It was built of stone, as was much of Jàb-áldis, but for some reason it lacked a fireplace. Meetings were therefore short during the colder months, and rather longer during the warmer ones, though with curiously little difference in productivity to distinguish between them.

Whatever the season, with an inexhaustible supply of excuses, Heckart was invariably late. On this occasion, by a mere ten minutes – good by his standards.

"Sorry to keep you, brothers. Busy morning, as I'm sure you've already gathered." He took his seat, depositing a number of items on the table without drawing any particular attention to them for the moment. "Well now, I imagine you've all heard of this morning's incident, so I won't bore you by going over it again. Brother Yisson, have you managed to speak with our wizardly brethren yet?"

"I have."

"And…?"

"A dead end, I'm afraid. None of them felt a thing."

Heckart had expected as much. But at least now they knew the cause of the disturbance lay further afield.

"Old Tobas inspected the Taümathakiya before the indicator weights were reset," Yisson added. "He said that the power needed to cause it to tip over like that was considerable. It could not have been accidental."

"Was he able to offer any explanation?"

Yisson shook his head.

"Did anyone comment on what happened to Jorra-hin?"

Yisson shook his head again. "So far as we know, Jorra-hin is not Taümathically gifted, so there's no reason why he should have been affected. I still say he was just startled, that's all."

Heckart sighed. Even if the Taümathakiya's movement had taken the young man unawares, that alone didn't explain his mighty leap. No, there was only one conclusion he felt was presenting itself; the Taümatha must have somehow caused the accident. But why? As Yisson had just pointed out, Jorra-hin wasn't known to be Taümathically gifted, so a disturbance in the Taümatha should have had no effect on him. No one else at Jàb-áldis had felt anything, former mages included.

Brother Brömin, the eldest member of the council, tapped a couple of fingers on the edge of the table to get attention. He was a quietly spoken man and never interrupted.

"Has the Taümathakiya ever been displaced so dramatically before, does anyone know?" The question was met with shakes of heads and a few shrugs. "Alright, what of the direction the disturbance came from, then?"

"Ah," Heckart responded, thrusting a finger towards the ceiling, "that we do know. Brother Connrad and I were plotting it earlier." He reached out and unrolled a large parchment that he had brought with him. Several council members helped hold its edges down to stop it curling up again. It was a map, though different from the usual ones of the region in that Jàb-áldis was at its centre. It depicted not only the bulk of Alondria, but also the lower regions of the Tsnathsarré Empire, just to the north of the Ablath. Heckart wafted his hand along a line extending northwest from Jàb-áldis. "It came from somewhere along here."

"As I said earlier – not much there," Connrad murmured.

"No indeed. There is little between us and the Tsnathsarré border in that direction. You have Mitcha and Tail-ébeth, here and here," Heckart went on, pointing to the two towns on the map, "but beyond that, only the Stroth Ford – and even that's a bit off track. Nothing noteworthy."

"What about further afield, in Tsnathsarré, for example?" Yisson enquired.

"Brother, please, let us not get into the realms of pure speculation," Connrad objected. "At this point it is clear we simply don't have the facts at hand."

Yisson huffed. "I was only asking."

Heckart moved quickly to smooth any ruffled feathers. "Brothers, as I'm sure you'll agree, this disturbance is something we should look into as a matter of priority. Rather than sitting here ruminating, let us go out and gather the facts. I propose that we declare this matter an official investigation and appoint Recorders."

Even before he had finished, various heads around the table had started bobbing. Like a dog with a bone, the Adak-rann was happiest when it had something tasty to get its teeth into.

Brother Valis, the council's newest member, raised his hand from the table and waited for an invitation to speak. Heckart gave him a nod.

"I agree with appointing Recorders, Brother, but with the origin for this event unknown, where do we start?"

Heckart drew a breath but Connrad pipped him to the post. "Simple. We send out brothers northwest and leave no stone unturned until we find what we're looking for."

Brother Brosspear ummed. He was the only one present whose past included the Taümathic arts. And with a good few years of sitting on the council behind him, he was well past waiting for a nod before chipping in with his opinion. "Since the Taümatha is the purview of the mages, we should consult the Cymàtagé. If anyone knows what's happened, it ought to be them."

"One of the silly sods has probably gone and blown himself up," Yisson muttered.

Most of the council smiled. The idea of a pompous mage having dispatched himself in a puff of smoke was curiously appealing.

"Alondris lies in nearly the opposite direction to our disturbance. Do you really think they'd know anything?"

"We leave no stone unturned, Valis, wherever that takes us," Connrad reiterated. "I agree with Brosspear, someone should go to Alondris. Or we should at least contact our brethren already down at the Cymàtagé to investigate for us."

It always surprised Heckart how a council discussion would often twist and turn, usually well beyond his control, but then somehow manage to present an opportunity for him to introduce a different item on his agenda.

"Brothers, this may be of relevance here." He held up a small scroll that had arrived a few days earlier. "Most of you know Brother Akmir, our most senior representative at the Cymàtagé. As it happens, he is requesting some assistance."

"Assistance?" Brosspear queried, his tone suddenly wary. "What sort of assistance?"

"Akmir says that he has come into possession of an important manuscript – a complete copy of the Legend of Tallümund. He needs help translating it."

"What does he need it translating for? We've got umpteen copies of that up here," Yisson challenged.

"Ah, true," Heckart countered, "but this one is apparently a very early version. Akmir believes it could even be the original."

A few murmurs fluttered around the table. The Legend of Tallümund was one of the most popular stories in Alondria's rich literary heritage, a tale of daring knights, villainous dragons, great chases and dramatic battles. Almost all Alondrian children had at some point been lulled into dream-filled sleep by its sweeping saga. To have discovered the original would be a great coup for the Adakrann.

"What makes him think that?" Brosspear asked.

"Well," Heckart began, drawing in a breath, "the manuscript was discovered in a tomb known to have been sealed in 446 Before Foundation. Furthermore, it is an A'lyavinical text, written not only in the First Dialect, but in a form that suggests it was written before the First Dialect was formalised. On that basis, Akmir estimates the manuscript to be at least fifteen hundred years old."

Valis whistled. "But that predates the supposed origin of the story itself by…" he paused for a spot of mental arithmetic, "some six hundred years."

Brömin chuckled to himself, garnering a degree of unintended attention.

"No one can translate the First Dialect like young Jorra," he said. "Does he know about this?"

Heckart shook his head. "I wanted to bring the matter to the council before mentioning it to him. No point getting the young man's hopes up if we decide to send someone else. But he would, in my opinion, be the most suitable assistance we could provide, given the nature of Akmir's request."

Brother Egall's eyes popped open. He tended to sit though council meetings looking as though he was fast asleep. Far from it. The man stored away every word in his cavernous mind, like a scribe taking notes.

"Brother Heckart, are you proposing that Jorra-hin be appointed as a Recorder?"

Attention switched back to Heckart. He was secretly pleased that someone else had tabled the suggestion.

"Well, I would not presume to instruct the council on this," he replied, his humility laid on perhaps a little too thickly, "but that was going to be my recommendation."

Brosspear let out another um, this one sounding uncertain. "A Recordership, Brother? Do you not think he's a bit young for that? We have brothers more than twice his age with many years of service behind them who ought to be considered."

"But none with his abilities in A'lyavine." Heckart turned to Brömin for backing. The old man had a very paternal relationship with Jorra-hin, and of all those at Jàb-áldis, he was the one who probably knew him best. "Brother, what do you think? Is Jorra-hin up to such a task?"

It took Brömin a few moments to reply. "Jorra-hin has lived here all his life. I remember the day he was born," he began, chuckling at the recollection. Heckart smiled, too. A number of those now on the council had been at Jàb-áldis the day Jorra-hin's mother had arrived, bringing utter chaos in her wake. Appearing without warning, she had given birth to him virtually on the doorstep. A woman – in an exclusively male preserve. And not just ordinary men, but monks with no idea how to deal with her. They were scholars, not midwives. Marauding armies could not have inflicted the terror she had brought with her that day. "So if it's time spent in the Adak-rann you wish to consider," Brömin continued, "then he has been with us some twenty years. He lives and breathes our ways."

"I don't think Brosspear meant to question Jorra-hin's loyalty to the order, Brömin. My question was, do you think he's *ready* to take on the mantle of a Recordership?"

"That's right," Brosspear said. "All of us here, every other member of the order, came to this way of life having been something else. We have seen other paths and chosen this one. Jorra-hin has not. As you said, he was born within these very walls."

"He's been away from the monastery before."

"Yes, I know. But never for very long, and certainly not as far away as Alondris. Nor was he on his own."

Brömin acknowledged each of Brosspear's points with a gracious nod. "I made him his first cassock, you know." This somewhat lateral comment caused a few frowns, Heckart noted. "He had just turned seven years of age. He'd been pestering me about it for months; he wanted to be like everyone else. Truly, I have never seen anyone put on the robes of our order with more reverence and pride. Day by day I have seen him grow in our ways. He has the keenest intellect I have ever encountered, an enquiring mind that thirsts for knowledge. His memory rivals even that of Brother Egall, here." Brömin gestured towards the end of the table, but Egall had closed his eyes again and didn't notice. "And he has tenacity. If you want someone to discover something for you, I can think of none more suited than young Jorra."

"Yes, yes, I accept all that, but still…" Brosspear persisted, "how will he cope out in the real world? Neither his academic ability nor his unique gifting in A'lyavine will help him deal with the pressures. Believe me, Brother, I know what the Cymàtagé is like. I spent eleven years there."

Brömin sighed. "You know I can't answer that with anything other than conjecture. But in my heart, I believe Jorra-hin is up to the task."

"Brosspear, what is it exactly that bothers you?" Heckart probed. "The failure of a Recordership?"

Brosspear shook his head. "No, I fear for Jorra-hin, for the effect an environment like the Cymàtagé could have on him. You do realise that A'lyavine is the cornerstone of the Mages' Path? Jorra-hin's extraordinary ability to read and translate it, even speak it, will attract significant attention from my former brethren. Not to mention that his gift could draw him down that road quite easily."

Heckart gave his head a pensive nod. The Mages' Path was the instruction the Cymàtagé gave to every acolyte accepted for training in the Taümathic arts. Although it encompassed more than just knowledge; it embodied all aspects of a mage's life and values. Much of its teaching was based on the language of A'lyavine, and anyone who had mastered the ancient tongue had a distinct advantage. In fact, a mage's eventual grasp of A'lyavine was often the yardstick by which they were subsequently measured.

"Brosspear's right, we should be aware of the danger to Jorra-hin," Egall concurred from the end of the table, this time without opening his eyes. "But we are not his masters, nor is the Adak-rann the only way open to him. As the gods are my witness, I have no desire to see him seduced by the Mages' Path. But we must not stand in the way of him making his own decisions based upon the opportunities presented to him."

There was a significant pause in the council's deliberations. If his brothers were having similar thoughts to his own, then Heckart knew none of them really wanted to consider the possibility that Jorra-hin's future might lie outside the order.

It was Brömin who broke the silence. "My brothers, you will appreciate how hard it is for me to bring myself to agree with Brother Egall. But agree with him I must. The purpose of the Adak-rann is to preserve the past and faithfully document the present so that our own history may be handed down to our descendants. To this end, we do not shape events ourselves, we do not interfere. We only observe. Fate, therefore, must be allowed to decide Jorra-hin's future, not us. If we shield him from other paths, we could be the very ones who prevent the natural order of things. We must not allow our fears over his future to restrain our decision."

There were nods of agreement from several around the table. Others were clearly less convinced. Heckart decided it was time to draw the matter to a close.

"Brothers, I do not propose that we order Jorra-hin to the Cymàtagé. But given what we have said, given that we should not shield him unnecessarily, do you agree to my offering him the opportunity to go?"

"As a Recorder?" Egall enquired, his eyes opening again.

"Yes." There were some more nods, but Heckart wanted the council to own this matter. Something in his guts told him it was important, that it might prove to be one of their more significant decisions. "May I have a show of hands, please?"

8

"Stay here," Riagán ordered as he entered Kirshtahll's office.

Torrin-Ashur, awash with uncomfortable thoughts, strained to hear muted voices behind the closed door. It seemed reasonable to assume that he was the subject of the conversation going on within, but there was little to indicate what trouble lay ahead. The chaos of the call-out was but a few hours old and already the camp had been turned upside down. The general was unlikely to be in a good mood.

His trepidation was short-lived. Riagán reappeared and snapped summoning fingers.

Torrin-Ashur hadn't been inside Kirshtahll's quarters before. By Mitcha's rather basic standards they were well upholstered. There were even rugs on the floor. Temesh-ai reclined in the far corner, his substantial girth all but obscuring the long chair supporting him, leaving him seemingly afloat. In his hand was a well-filled cup of what looked like Brock, a fortified wine of local origin. He tipped it in greeting.

Opposite the doctor stood a mannequin bedecked in Kirshtahll's armour. Unlike the full-bodied suit Borádin had worn earlier, this set consisted simply of a breastplate and pauldron assembly over a chainmail vest. The decorative detail on the metalwork was exquisite, as was the embossing of the leather, but years of service had taken their toll, the dents and scars of combat at odds with those of the engraving. It didn't compare favourably with the coquettish armour that came up fresh from Alondris these days. Kirshtahll obviously put little store in keeping up with fashion.

Torrin-Ashur came to a halt in front of the general and saluted.

Instead of returning the gesture, Kirshtahll simply leaned forwards and rested his forearms on the desk. With his broad shoulders hunched up and his iron-grey hair only emphasising his imposing presence, the man managed to dominate the room even without standing.

An awkward moment of silence followed, doing little to make

Torrin-Ashur feel at ease.

"Lieutenant, do you know how long I've been in the army?"

Torrin-Ashur blinked at the unexpected question.

"Thirty-one years," Kirshtahll informed him. "My first battle was against the Nmemians in the Kilópeé War. I have that and several other campaigns under my belt, not to mention a good number of skirmishes against the Tsnath."

Torrin-Ashur remained silent. He knew about the Kilópeé War; his grandfather had died during the campaign against Alondria's western neighbour. But that had been three decades ago, so why Kirshtahll felt the need to mention it now, he had no idea.

"So it goes without saying that I've seen some fighting in my time," Kirshtahll continued. "But, in all my days, I have *never* seen a spectacle such as the one I saw this morning."

"I – I'm sorry, sir. I didn't mean to cause trouble."

"Trouble?" Kirshtahll almost scoffed. "I've had to declare the call-out a draw just to avoid the bookmakers being lynched!"

Torrin-Ashur paled.

"You utterly demolished Borádin; there isn't a man in the camp who would deny it. Yet you gave him the victory. Why?"

"I don't know, sir. It seemed like the thing to do at the time, I guess."

"And what about winning, Lieutenant? Did *that* not occur to you?"

Torrin-Ashur again sought safety in silence. He really didn't have a suitable answer.

Kirshtahll allowed a few moments to pass before moving on. "Very well, leaving aside your unusual capitulation, what has me confused is how you managed to pull off such a fight. To my knowledge you've had no training, nor have you any combat experience. Yet you could have run rings round a veteran this morning. How so?"

Torrin-Ashur swallowed. His performance during the call-out was still a mystery to him, let alone anyone else.

"All I can say, sir, is – something came over me."

"*Something* came over you?" Temesh-ai repeated, his tone sarcastic. He shifted his bulk into a more attentive position, causing the nearly invisible furniture beneath him to creak.

"That's how it felt, sir."

Kirshtahll relaxed back into his seat. The tips of his steepled fingers came to rest across his lips. His eyes did not waver from their target, indicating that more by way of explanation was required.

Torrin-Ashur tried to recall exactly what had happened during the call-out; how the strange sense of power had felt; how it had slammed into him so suddenly, so unexpectedly; how it had urged him on, controlling him, leading him in his every move, right up to the moment it had brutally deserted him. Even as the words came tumbling out, he knew his description fell woefully short of conveying what it had really been like.

Kirshtahll picked up on his last point. "When you and Borádin ceased trading blows, you collapsed. What happened there?"

"Whatever this feeling was, sir, when the fighting stopped, it vanished. I was left absolutely drained, so tired I could hardly even think."

Kirshtahll let out a dismayed snort. "And yet, Lieutenant, despite your fuddled frame of mind, you allowed Borádin to retain his honour, without quite giving him the victory." He shook his head. "Under the circumstances, I doubt many would have thought of such a diplomatic gesture."

Diplomacy had not been the driving force, Torrin-Ashur countered silently. He really couldn't explain why he'd done what he'd done.

Temesh-ai heaved himself up to replenish his empty cup. He seemed fairly free with the general's supplies, even offering Torrin-Ashur a shot. But Brock was not brewed for engendering clarity of thought.

"One thing I find curious, Lieutenant," the surgeon said as he settled himself down again, "that business before the fighting started, planting your scabbard in the ground. Care to explain?"

Torrin-Ashur felt on firmer ground answering that. "It's a family tradition, sir. My father taught me that an Ashur should never allow himself to be pushed backwards on a battlefield. *'That's no way to win'*, he would say. The scabbard marks our starting position, that's all."

Temesh-ai was going to ask another question, but Kirshtahll thwarted him by rising to his feet. "Your sword..."

Torrin-Ashur unbuckled the scabbard and passed it, belt and all, across the desk. In another man's quarters, it was a matter of courtesy not to unsheathe the blade.

Kirshtahll first examined the scabbard, which was not the original, then carefully withdrew the sword. His eyes travelled along its length, picking out the details.

"Well, at least you seem to know how to look after it," he observed.

Torrin-Ashur patted himself on the back for having already whetted the blade to remove the burrs and given it a thin coating of oil.

"This is a fine weapon, Lieutenant. And of some antiquity. It has been in the family long?"

"Many generations, sir. It was originally made for one of my ancestors, Gadrick I think his name was."

"I see. And this writing along the fuller – A'lyavine, I do believe."

"*siad-ida Sèliccia~Castrà*" Torrin-Ashur rattled off.

Kirshtahll nodded. "*Hear ye the song of war.*"

Torrin-Ashur's eyes widened. It was unusual to come across anyone outside his own family who knew what the ancient phrase meant.

The general glanced up. "I recognise this weapon. If I'm not mistaken, it was made at the Foundry of Trombéi, around the fall of the Third Dynasty. That would be some two hundred years before the Foundation of Alondria. There are two swords similar to this one at the Military Academy in Alondris – in the Museum of Arms."

At which point Torrin-Ashur found himself speechless.

Kirshtahll grunted as he re-sheathed the weapon. "I suggest you look after this, Lieutenant," he said, handing it back. "Buy yourself a cheap alternative for bashing around with. It would be a shame to ruin such a rare blade in something as trivial as a call-out."

Torrin-Ashur nodded and re-buckled the belt round his waist.

"You haven't spoken to anyone else about what happened to you this morning, have you?"

"Only to my supporters, sir, Lieutenants Sàhodd and Yngvarr."

"Keep it that way. If anyone asks, just tell them you lost your temper or something." Kirshtahll's wry smile made Temesh-ai chuckle. "You've already given the camp quite enough to gossip about."

Kirshtahll's tone suggested that was a dismissal.

"Will there be anything else, sir?"

"Not for the moment. You may return to your duties."

Torrin-Ashur saluted and turned to leave. Riagán, standing beside the door, leaned over and opened it for him.

"Oh, there is one thing, Lieutenant," Kirshtahll called out, stalling the departure. "I'm having a meeting of the Executive this evening. At the sixth bell. Formal dress."

*

Kirshtahll resumed his seat with something of a slump. "Well, gentlemen, what do you make of that?"

Riagán's eyes rose from a pensive scrutiny of the rugs. "Something is definitely afoot with that young man."

"Indeed. We've all seen how being thrown into the fray can bring out the natural fighter in a man. But what we witnessed with young Ashur this morning was more than just that."

"What struck me, Padráig, wasn't so much his speed, but the *way* he moved," Temesh-ai remarked. "He didn't just dart around, he flowed. It gave me the impression of someone…"

Kirshtahll knew precisely the word Temesh-ai was after. "Dancing."

The surgeon nodded. "Yes, dancing. Exactly so."

Kirshtahll glanced across at his adjutant. "Riagán, you told me a few weeks ago that Ashur comes from hereabouts?"

"That's right, sir. His father is Lord Naman-Ashur, from the town of Tail-ébeth."

"Intriguing." Kirshtahll got up and went to examine the map on the wall. He spent a few moments deep in thought, then abruptly waved his hand across the depiction of the Northern Territories. "This region was once home to a people called the Dendricá. They were renowned for being formidable warriors. And I mean *formidable*."

"Never heard of them," Riagán muttered.

"These days, few have. Their time was before the Foundation of Alondria. The odd thing is, despite being very prominent in their day, the Dendricá disappeared from history almost overnight."

"Disappeared?" Temesh-ai queried.

"It seems so. The histories of that period mention them for a time, spanning a few generations, and then suddenly, nothing. No gradual decline, no invasion that wiped them out – well, none that went recorded, at least."

"Fascinating. And the relevance of this to today's events?"

Kirshtahll regarded his adjutant with a look of bemusement. Riagán was a brilliant administrator, and as dependable as a rock in a fight, but in fourteen years of serving together, none of his own appreciation for the historical had rubbed off on the man.

"Well, for a start, plunging their scabbards into the ground before battle was a trait of the Dendricá. I've not come across anyone else following that custom. I also seem to recall that the Foundry of Trombéi was an exclusive establishment, only ever making weapons for these warriors. After their disappearance, I believe the foundry was dismantled."

There was a pause as these revelations sank in.

Temesh-ai cleared his throat. "So, if Ashur's sword was indeed made at Trombéi, then this ancestor of his, Gadrick, was probably a Dendricá himself."

"What, and Torrin-Ashur's supposed to be a long-lost descendant?" Riagán said, sounding wholly sceptical.

Kirshtahll gave his head a pensive nod. Riagán was right, it was a long shot. But if it were true, then Mitcha's newest lieutenant might very well have warrior blood flowing in his veins.

This young man would bear watching.

9

"Stand still," Sàhodd growled. His attempts to put the final touches to Torrin-Ashur's tunic were meeting resistance, the collar being a little on the tight side. Once the recalcitrant button had surrendered, he finished his ministrations with a flourish, slapping both hands on Torrin-Ashur's shoulders. "There we are, you lucky bastard. That should do you."

Sàhodd was still not over his envy, Torrin-Ashur noted with amusement. After having told him about Kirshtahll's invitation to dine with the Executive, the amicable insults had barely ceased. Not that he minded friendly banter. It was the mutterings of the rest of Mitcha that were of greater concern. According to Yngvarr, few in the camp were happy. All bets were off in the light of Kirshtahll's decision to declare the call-out a draw, so not even the bookmakers had made any money.

Snapping back to matters at hand, he squinted at the results of Sàhodd's fussing in a small square of polished tin that served, rather poorly, as his mirror. Considering he'd had to borrow formal attire for the evening from Yngvarr, aside from a slight strangulation, the outfit wasn't a bad fit. It was just a pity that its owner couldn't be here to see to its fitting. Yngvarr's men had drawn guard duty for the evening, so he was indisposed.

Vanity was cut short by a call from outside.

"Excuse me, sir, but there's a sergeant here what's come to see you," Silfast announced, shaking the wall of the tent.

Sàhodd shot Torrin-Ashur a curious glance.

"Thank you, Corporal. Show him in."

The awning was withdrawn to reveal a resplendently dressed soldier; Torrin-Ashur could see his own face reflected in the polished breastplate that now blocked the entrance. It was a little disconcerting that the man was regaled in full armour, though; thoughts of another challenge briefly flooded to mind. They were quickly dismissed as nonsense.

The new arrival ducked inside the tent and advanced.

"Sergeant," Torrin-Ashur acknowledged, returning the man's crisply delivered salute.

"Begging your pardon for the interruption, sir, but I'm here on behalf of Lord Borádin."

"Oh?" Wary suspicion immediately creased Torrin-Ashur's brow.

"He requests that you accept this as a token of his respect." The sergeant extended his arm, slipping a cloth cover from what he was carrying. Borádin's scarred and dented shield appeared.

Torrin-Ashur floundered for something to say. Receiving such an offering from another noble was an honour indeed. Yet seeing the shield again triggered vivid memories of the call-out. Though little of Borádin's armour had escaped a battering, this particular piece had been a focal point for much of the fight.

He reached out and hefted the shield from the sergeant's arm.

"Lord Borádin also wishes you to know that Major Temesh-ai's bill will be settled in full, sir."

Torrin-Ashur acknowledged that with an appreciative grunt.

"Will that be all, sir?" the man asked, stepping back a pace.

"I think so. Oh, except – please convey my thanks to your commanding officer."

"Very good, sir." The sergeant snapped off another crisp salute, did an about-face and departed.

As the tent flap fell back into place, Torrin-Ashur turned to Sàhodd and let out a breath between puffed cheeks, his eyes wide in surprise. His mind hadn't really caught up yet. The brief encounter with Borádin's sergeant seemed somewhat surreal.

"Did that just happen? I feel like I need to pinch myself."

"Borádin must be smarting right now," Sàhodd smirked. "What a come-down, after all that bragging."

Torrin-Ashur murmured something, but wasn't really concentrating. His thoughts were on the shield. It felt strange to behold such a thing as a gift, considering it had been the subject of so much wrath just a few hours earlier. How quickly things could change. Borádin had somehow gone from arrogance to meekness in the space of an afternoon. It was more than just a come-down – it was a complete change of heart.

Sàhodd traced his fingers over the scars on the shield's covering. "Teeth of the gods, Torrin, you didn't half give this thing a hammering."

"Nothing a good smithy couldn't beat out."

"You're not thinking of using it, surely? Not with the Kin-Shísim standard on the front. Somehow, I can't see you fighting under Borádin's colours."

Torrin-Ashur let out a chuckle. "Well, maybe I'll just hang it up, then." He placed his newfound trophy against the wall of the tent; finding a more permanent place for it would have to wait. It was time to go.

Sàhodd escorted him through the camp towards Kirshtahll's quarters. It was a pleasant evening, with just a few wispy clouds speckling the sky. They had turned a shade of pink on the underside as the sun dipped below the horizon. A handful of the brighter stars had come out, but the cool of night had not yet begun to bite.

Anxiety set a brisk pace and they arrived outside Kirshtahll's quarters well before the sixth bell had sounded.

"I wish Yngvarr was here to see you all dressed up like that," Sàhodd teased.

"Thank the gods for small mercies." Sàhodd's mocking was more than enough. Torrin-Ashur glanced down at himself and tutted. "I look like a peacock."

After a wait that seemed like aeons, the toll of the sixth bell eventually rolled across the camp. A number of distant cries followed as guards formally exchanged positions. Yngvarr's men would be strutting their stuff.

"Well, here goes." Torrin-Ashur took a deep breath and twisted his neck in an attempt to ease the collar. "Ye gods, this is worse than the call-out."

Sàhodd laughed and landed a slap on his back. "It's only dinner."

Kirshtahll was hosting the evening in an enormous tent that had been erected to the side of his office. Torrin-Ashur approached the entrance with some trepidation.

When he stepped into the interior, his appearance brought silence to a gathering of some thirty or so officers, all of whom stared as though an unwelcome interloper had blundered into their midst.

From the far side of the tent Kirshtahll's booming voice redressed that illusion. "Ah, Lieutenant Ashur, come in, come in."

The hubbub immediately resumed, casting Torrin-Ashur adrift. He was left to wait while the general navigated his way through the crowd with an excess of convivial footwork.

"Relax, Lieutenant, this is a social occasion, not a parade ground." Kirshtahll's gaze dropped and he picked at Torrin-Ashur's sleeve. "I see you've managed to find yourself suitable attire."

"Err – borrowed, sir."

"Just as well. It would be a trifle embarrassing to be introduced to a princess dressed like a sapper."

Torrin-Ashur gulped and felt the blood drain away from his face.

"I think a stiff drink is called for," Kirshtahll declared with a raucous laugh.

Ever the good doctor, Temesh-ai was on hand to furnish the much needed restorative. Kirshtahll waited until the Brock had taken effect, then steered Torrin-Ashur towards several nearby officers and left him in their company. With the ice broken, many of the gathering came up and made their own introductions, filling the next hour with names that mostly just came and went. Torrin-Ashur recognised a few; the exploits of the Executive were spoken of with a certain amount of awe within the camp. To most of those he met he found himself repeating his account of the call-out, tailored slightly to meet Kirshtahll's order that he refrain from mentioning the strange force that had empowered him during the fight.

All too quickly the seventh bell sounded, galvanising Kirshtahll into action. "Gentlemen," he called out, "Princess Elona will be here shortly."

Tables that had been pushed to the edges of the tent to create more space for the Executive to mingle were repositioned to form three sides of a square ready for the formal part of the evening to begin. With that done, everyone except Kirshtahll stood to the sides in two opposing lines.

They'd just managed to assemble themselves when the entrance awning was withdrawn to admit a brightly dressed page. The lad marched in a few yards and came to attention, though a lack of military training resulted in a manoeuvre that drew a few bemused smiles. Unperturbed, he took a deep breath and nearly managed to announce the princess.

"I think they already know who I am," Elona advised him, her whisper in his ear sweet but deliberately loud. The lad blushed, bowed and retired with considerable fleetness of foot, leaving the princess standing alone in the entrance. A subtle smile appeared as she surveyed her captivated audience.

Torrin-Ashur wasn't just captivated, he was agog; the entire Tsnathsarré Empire could have invaded Mitcha at that moment and still he wouldn't have been able to tear his eyes away.

Elona's ash-blond tresses, looking particularly golden in the lantern-light, were held high at the back of her head, though still with an abundance of curls cascading down past her shoulders. A few wisps left free at the front framed her face. Her eyebrows were a delicate trace, the merest flick of an artist's brush. A flawless, lightly bronzed complexion made it seem she was aglow from within.

Her dress was of a style Torrin-Ashur had never seen before. There was nothing covering her shoulders, so its suspension appeared to involve a dash of magic. The bodice blended into a swirl of emerald silk that danced around her legs with seemingly impossible intricacy. Without doubt it was the most stunning garment he had ever beheld; though not one that could have been comfortable to wear, to his way of thinking.

It was her eyes that caught his breath most of all. Darkened slightly, they had a smouldering look that was utterly entrancing. They held an unmistakable air of authority about them, too. He suddenly felt very inadequate in such sophisticated company.

Kirshtahll broke the spellbound moment, stepping forwards and bowing. He lifted Elona's proffered hand to his lips.

"Your Highness, it is a great pleasure to have you join us this evening."

Elona gave him a heart-stopping smile. "Padráig, you're such a dear."

Torrin-Ashur suppressed a grin as the general fought off a blush.

"Allow me to introduce you to a few of my officers," Kirshtahll replied, moving on quickly to avoid further embarrassment. He motioned for Elona to precede him.

To Torrin-Ashur's sudden alarm, the princess was steered past five others in the line and led straight to him. That morning, if anyone had suggested he'd ever even meet Elona, he would have scoffed. Yet here she was, just a few feet away. And the only thing he knew with certainty was that he'd never felt more nervous in his life.

"May I present to you Lieutenant Ashur, Torrin, youngest son of Naman. His father is Lord of Tail-ébeth and the March of Ashur."

Elona's eyes brightened with genuine interest. "Ah yes, from the call-out. A pleasure, Lieutenant."

In the absence of coherent thought, Torrin-Ashur's instincts had to take over. With only Kirshtahll's example to call upon, he took Elona's hand and kissed the backs of her fingers.

Elona giggled playfully and turned to Kirshtahll. "Oh, Padráig, I like him." Still straightening from his bow, Torrin-Ashur missed the wink she flashed. "Not at all what I thought he'd be. After the way he dealt with Lord Borádin this morning, I was half expecting a barbarian."

Picking up on her playful tenor, Kirshtahll raised an eyebrow. "Careful, now, Your Highness, I don't think you want to insult him. He might call *you* out next."

Elona giggled again, then gave Torrin-Ashur a challenging pout that, quite rightly, suggested he wouldn't dare.

"Tail-ébeth, is that far from here, Lieutenant?"

"Err, n – not really, Your Highness. Perhaps a couple of days' ride, to the northwest."

"The northwest? Closer to the Tsnathsarré border, then?"

"Too close for comfort sometimes, Your Highness."

Elona turned to Kirshtahll again. "That explains his fighting skills. It's obviously tough country up here."

That seemed to conclude the conversation as far as Torrin-Ashur was concerned. Kirshtahll led the princess off to introduce her to other officers, leaving him both disappointed that the brief encounter was over, and yet immensely relieved that attention was now focused elsewhere.

Elona was eventually shown to her seat at the high table, shared with Kirshtahll and his senior officers. The lesser ranks filtered to the sides and found places along the outer tables. No sooner had they seated themselves than a veritable army of stewards poured in, delivering the culinary offerings of the evening.

As each dish arrived, Torrin-Ashur became more and more astounded at the display; in his experience, such a feast was rarely witnessed in the Northern Territories, a fact that was only reinforced when he found himself staring at a most extraordinary dish. He turned to the man on his left, a captain by the name of Marsisma, and enquired what it was.

"Lobster, Lieutenant. A great delicacy, considering how hard it is to get it this far inland."

Torrin-Ashur nodded at what he presumed was meant to be enlightenment and continued to regard the arrival with a dubious eye. It was still whole and, rather disconcertingly, still retained the capacity to reciprocate his stare. He had absolutely no idea how to go about eating it, if indeed it would let him; the armour-plated creature gave every impression of its being ready for battle and quite prepared to defend itself. He skewered a portion of venison instead.

Kirshtahll allowed ample time for indulgences before he called the gathering to order.

"Gentlemen, we should get down to business. Captain Tonché, would you be good enough to start us off with a report on the recent border activity."

"Of course, sir," Tonché acknowledged, rising to his feet. He gave Elona a deferential nod and smoothed both sides of his considerable moustache with a finger. "We've been concentrating our recent efforts on two particular sections of the River Ablath, the first adjacent to Nabor's Gate and the second at the Stroth Ford."

Torrin-Ashur's ears pricked up at the mention of the ford. He knew it well; lying just west of Loch Shëdd, its southern side gave direct access into the March of Ashur. It was a constant threat to the security of his father's lands. He wondered how long the army had been operating in the area, and whether his father knew of it.

"At those two sections at least, the Tsnath have been coming in, but not heading home again," Tonché continued.

"Standard military practice to return by a different route," Kirshtahll noted.

"Indeed, sir. But so far this year we have very little evidence of northerly movements. Naturally, we've had the Network keeping an eye on things."

Kirshtahll leaned sideways to explain the point to Elona. "The Network consists of townsfolk who report any Tsnath sightings. Local information is one of our most useful resources up here." Kirshtahll nodded back at Tonché. "And the size of these incoming movements?"

"Generally quite small, sir; squads rather than platoons."

"Major Halacon, how does this sit with the information you've gathered?"

"It tallies, sir." The major placed his cup on the table and stood up. He didn't bother with deferential nods. He was a rather thin man, but radiated a tough-as-iron aura. "The Tsnath are definitely heading further south than usual this year, which means they're spending longer inside the Territories before heading home. We've had two reports of them in the Mathians now, though it's difficult to corroborate that. They're playing cat and mouse. The closer they get to the mountains, the more difficult it becomes to track them due to the terrain, and as much as I hate to concede anything to the Tsnath, they do put us to shame when it comes to field-craft. If they don't want to be found, the bastards just up and disappear." He suddenly remembered the company he was in and glanced at Elona. "Sorry, ma'am."

Elona waved a dismissive hand. "That's quite alright, Major." She glanced round at the gathering. "Gentlemen, for the rest of the evening just be yourselves. I'm here purely to listen."

Torrin-Ashur couldn't help becoming more and more intrigued by Elona as time went by. No one could have described her as ordinary, but for all her nobility she seemed so straightforward and unassuming. She even seemed genuinely interested in what was being discussed. As a princess, she was turning out to be a far cry from the flighty image Sàhodd and Yngvarr had painted of her over the past few weeks. The only thing they had not been wrong about was her beauty. In that regard, he found it quite hard to stop himself from lapsing into an absentminded gaze.

Pulling himself together, he tried to dismiss such lovely distractions and concentrate. Since being at Mitcha, it had been frustratingly difficult to find out what was going on in the Territories, such was his lowly position. He didn't want to miss this opportunity to grasp something of the bigger picture.

"The problem we face," Halacon continued, "is that by the time we get wind of where the Tsnath are, they've invariably moved on. We cross paths more by chance than intention. In chasing down specific reports, we've made only one actual contact in the last month…"

"That wouldn't happen to be the group you intercepted just south of Taib-hédi?" Kirshtahll interrupted.

"Yes, sir."

"The group, I'm told, you managed to kill, right down to the last man?"

Halacon gave the table a bashful glance. "Yes, sir. Sorry, sir. It's just that they left us no choice. We tried to take them alive for questioning, but they fought like they'd got demons on their backs."

Kirshtahll nodded. "Which supports my theory that they're up to something much bigger than we might suppose. Let's face it, our treatment of prisoners isn't bad enough to make them fear capture above all else." He let out a sigh. "No, in my opinion, someone in Tsnathsarré must have a very important agenda they want kept from us at all costs. Someone their own soldiers fear more than death itself."

Elona leaned over and whispered something in Kirshtahll's ear. He nodded.

"Lieutenant Ashur, as a local lad, what's your opinion on the Tsnath situation?"

Dim lighting, a loosened collar and a rosy glow from a modicum of Brock prevented another sudden desertion of blood from Torrin-Ashur's face being too noticeable. He stood up slowly, searching for something sensible to contribute.

"Sir, I'm more than familiar with Tsnath raids across the border. What I don't understand is why they would be interested in making their way further south. It doesn't make sense."

"Why not?" Elona enquired directly.

"Err – there's nothing in it for them, ma'am. All the Tsnath activity I've ever heard about was up near the Ablath. They come over, steal what they can, and hop back to their own territory before we can do much about it. Going further south? That's just dangerous."

"Indeed, Lieutenant," Kirshtahll said. "But if you had to venture an opinion about what they're up to…?"

There was no *if* about it. From the gleam in the general's eye, Torrin-Ashur realised this was a test of sorts. He knew he'd have to think damned fast if he was to avoid the ignominy of sliding into the bottomless pit of ignorance.

"Well, sir, my guess is they must be looking for something, something specific. If the Tsnath really are in the mountains, I can't see them going all that way unless they believe there's something important or valuable up there."

"Could they be making maps, do you think?" Tonché ventured to no one in particular.

Halacon shook his head. "On the occasions when we have managed to catch up with them, there's been no evidence found to suggest that. Besides, what soldier fights to the death to safeguard a map his enemy already possesses?"

Kirshtahll vented his frustration with a sigh and turned to speak with Elona again. "You can see why it's so difficult convincing the Grand Assembly that we face a new and specific threat up here. We have lots of facts that point to something going on, but we can't nail down what it is."

Elona nodded, then pinned Torrin-Ashur with another bout of nerve-racking attention. "Lieutenant, what would you say is the general opinion of the army up here?"

Torrin-Ashur had only just sat down again on the assumption that he was off the hook. He rose once more. "Your Highness, I joined the army because I believe it can protect the Territories. But I'm afraid my view probably isn't representative of most northerners."

"Oh? And why not?"

Torrin-Ashur hesitated. This was going to be awkward.

"Out with it, Lieutenant," Kirshtahll ordered.

"Well," he began, wondering how this was going to be received, "most people see the army as it is here at Mitcha, that is to say, thousands of men apparently sitting around doing nothing. Yet every summer harvests are plundered, towns and villages are attacked. The people are sick of it. Every time the army does nothing to protect them, they feel let down. They feel that if we aren't here to put a stop to the Tsnath, then what's the point of us being here at all?"

There was silence for a moment, many in the gathering clearly wondering how the general was going to react.

"Lieutenant, our orders are to maintain a significant presence here to stop the Tsnath from mounting a heavy assault. Here at Mitcha we are central to the whole region. We can move the bulk of the army to wherever it is needed if the Tsnath ever do come over in force. That's why we keep most of our troops here – doing nothing, as you so elegantly put it." He paused for a moment, staring at Torrin-Ashur. "If we were to dash off every which way, trying to put out all the bushfires that spring up, we would end up being spread out too thinly. We would cease to be an effective deterrent against an all-out invasion."

Torrin-Ashur swallowed hard, hoping that his nerves weren't too conspicuous. "I apologise if I have given offence, sir. I was just trying to express what many northerners feel about the situation."

"No apology necessary, Lieutenant. I understand such views."

"Sir, if I may…"

Torrin-Ashur noticed a young man opposite him staring intently at the general, waiting for a nod.

"Yes, Lieutenant D'Amada?"

"Sir, the Tsnath believe they can slip into Alondria any time they please. Shouldn't we be concentrating on stopping them at the border, rather than trying to chase them round the countryside once they've moved further south?"

Captain Tonché immediately shook his head. "Lieutenant, it's not as easy as that. Our border with the Tsnathsarré Empire is nearly six hundred miles long. There might only be a few points they could get a whole army across, but in small numbers, they can cross it at almost any point they wish."

"Yes, I realise that," D'Amada conceded. He wanted to say more, but Halacon cut him short.

"Stopping them at the border doesn't help us find out what they're planning, either. For that, we need to *let* them in."

That didn't seem to satisfy D'Amada, but Tonché nodded in agreement. "As the general has already indicated, Alondris needs to know what's going on. For the time being, it's more important to find out what the Tsnath are up to than it is to put a stop to them."

Several other officers wanted to chip in with their opinions, but Kirshtahll held up his hand.

"Gentlemen, hold it there. Captain Tonché is quite correct; finding out what the Tsnath are doing *is* our main priority. However, Lieutenant D'Amada, to address your concerns, Major Riagán and I have a little something up our sleeves for which we need a couple of volunteers. So thank you for putting your hand up. I'm sure that Lieutenant Ashur and you will get along splendidly."

Torrin-Ashur's eyes positively bulged; he hadn't just been invited to dine with the Executive – he'd been invited to join it.

Kirshtahll called upon several more officers for their reports, after which the meeting dissolved back into an informal gathering. Torrin-Ashur introduced himself to D'Amada and they got down to the serious business of speculating about what Kirshtahll might have planned for them.

It felt good to be in the company of men who harboured a genuine desire to see the situation with the Tsnath resolved. Most of the other officers he had met so far resented being posted north of the Mathians, cut off from their beloved social life and southern comforts. The conversation in this crowd was a far cry from the usual posturing so prevalent throughout the rest of the camp. Outside the Executive, the nobles were parade-ground heroes who bragged of their untried metal. Here, amongst men who'd actually met the enemy, no boasts abounded at all.

As the evening wore on, every so often Torrin-Ashur found his attention wandering back towards Elona. She was always deep in conversation with Kirshtahll and the other officers at her table. Though he had no idea what they were talking about, the seriousness of their discussions was evident from their expressions. It was also quite clear that the princess was holding her own amongst such senior military figures.

It was late when she finally decided to depart; protocol prevented anyone else from leaving until she, as guest of honour, had done so. Silence was effortlessly brought to the gathering when she rose to her feet.

"Gentlemen, I have kept you long enough. You have given me much to think about and take back to Alondris." She clasped a fist to her breast. "Alondria salutes you."

Every officer stood and bowed in response.

"And now, gentlemen, if one of you would be kind enough to escort me back to my quarters..."

No one moved, yet it was as if every man stood on tip-toe waving his hand in the air. Inevitably, Elona had to nominate.

"Well, from what I've heard this evening, the Northern Territories can be a dangerous place, so obviously I shall need an escort capable of defending me in such a hostile environment. Lieutenant Ashur, I doubt anyone would be foolish enough to tackle you after your performance this morning. Would you do me the honour?"

Some things defied belief. Torrin-Ashur was just lucky his jaw didn't drop.

"The honour would be mine, Your Highness."

He made his way round the end of the tables to where Elona stood. She linked her arm through his in a manner that was altogether more familiar than he was anticipating. Her close proximity ignited all kinds of feelings he knew he shouldn't have. The incongruity of it all also struck him; there were only two people of higher station than Elona in all of Alondria – Princess Midana and King Althar. And yet here he was, by her side, minor nobility without so much as a title to call his own. Not to mention in borrowed clothes.

Elona started for the exit, bidding goodnight to those on either side of her. The soldier on duty outside was ready for them and withdrew the canvas awning just as they approached. He snapped to attention as they passed.

The sky had clouded over during the evening and little moonlight now penetrated the fleecy covering. By the time they had moved beyond the torchlight of Kirshtahll's compound, had it not been for the whitewashed boulders and sporadic lanterns placed along the path, their way would have been all but invisible.

"Tell me something, Lieutenant. I know I made fun of it earlier, but is it really such a tough country up here?"

"It can be, sometimes, ma'am. But we do manage to live normal lives. We just have to take precautions and remain vigilant, that's all."

"And learn to fight, I presume?"

Torrin-Ashur smiled. "You're thinking of this morning?"

"Hmm. I've never seen anything quite like that before. It was – a shock."

For none more so than himself, Torrin-Ashur mused.

"Your Highness, it may surprise you to know that before today I never had to fight at close quarters, not even against the Tsnath. The truth is, I arrived at the Forum this morning fully expecting to get my ars…" He just managed to stop himself in time.

"Your arse kicked," Elona finished for him.

He let out a bashful chuckle. "Yes, ma'am, that's about the size of it."

"And is it true that the call-out was all because Borádin mistreated one of your slaves?"

"One of my men, ma'am."

Elona conceded the correction with a nod. "Even so, you risked a great deal to defend him. Especially if, as you say, you didn't expect to fare particularly well."

Torrin-Ashur wondered how to answer that. He drew in a breath. "I'm responsible for the Pressed, so I get tarred with the same brush as they do most of the time. That puts my reputation at the bottom of the pile; I really didn't have much to lose."

"Except your blood, perhaps," Elona returned. In a rather more pensive tone she added, "My father taught me that *'The nobility of a man is measured by his actions, not his birthright'*."

Torrin-Ashur had just enough sense left not to try replying to that. He walked on, almost holding his breath.

It wasn't long before they reached the accommodation the Pressed had built for the princess's visit. The compound looked rather imposing, a dark, jagged silhouette against the night sky. A few flickers of torchlight pierced out through the cracks between the logs, indicating the less than palatial nature of the construction.

As they came to the entrance, Elona extracted her arm from his and turned to face him. "An officer needs to know when to relax, Lieutenant."

Torrin-Ashur allowed himself to slump. "Forgive me, Your Highness. I expected today to be full of humiliation and defeat. And yet here I am, still in one piece – thank the gods – having partaken of an amazing feast, *and* been introduced to a princess." He gave his head a disbelieving shake. "Any moment now, I'm going to wake up and discover I'm late for the call-out."

Elona giggled, but robbed it of any offence by touching his cheek with the backs of her fingers.

"You're very sweet, Lieutenant Ashur, Torrin, son of Naman. Don't let them change you too much."

With that Elona turned and disappeared into her compound, leaving the Ashur blush raging.

Fortunately, it was too dark for anyone to see it.

10

Brömin folded his arms into the sleeves of his robe and quietly drew alongside Jorra-hin, content simply to join him in companionable silence. Despite its familiarity, the beauty of the Jàbáldis Gorge never ceased to inspire him, especially when viewed from up on the ramparts of the monastery. The canopy of the forest far below was adorned in the apparel of early summer, displaying every imaginable hue of green. Its vibrancy was corralled by granite greys, mountain slopes stretching as far as the eye could see. Snow, as perpetual as time itself, capped the peaks in the distance and contrasted vividly with an azure sky. Sometimes, when the weather wasn't as clear, the jagged ridges would blend seamlessly with the clouds and the horizon would cease to exist. Then the Mathians shed their worldly bonds and were married to the firmament, hinting at an undiscovered land beyond the travelling of man. Such a place effortlessly beckoned the mind to wander; there it could become wonderfully lost.

"I shall miss taking these moments, Brother," Jorra-hin murmured, eventually acknowledging Brömin's presence.

Brömin nodded. He would miss them too. He would still come up to the parapet to gaze out, it was an essential restorative to his soul, but Jorra-hin wouldn't be there to share the view with him. His departure would leave a void; the young lad was the nearest thing he would ever have to a son of his own.

He regarded Jorra-hin for a moment, smiling fondly at his curly mop of dark hair. It was as unruly as ever, at odds with an otherwise manicured ensemble. His boyish, ruddy cheeks were losing their colour as he matured, but his opaline eyes would always remain the same, radiating an intelligence that was sometimes uncomfortable in its intensity. Less certain was whether his tall, thin frame would ever broaden out; the lad had a tendency to skip meals, usually far too engrossed in some intriguing manuscript to even notice their passing. He never seemed to be hungry, though. It was as if he had found a way to gain corporal sustenance from the words he so voraciously devoured.

"How's the head?"

"Aching," Jorra-hin grimaced. "I have to be careful not to frown, otherwise I get a sharp reminder of my fall."

"It's a nasty graze," Brömin muttered with concern, pulling Jorra-hin round to examine the injury. "You still have no recollection of what happened?"

"None. Besides, I have other matters to contend with now. Bruises are the least of my worries."

Brömin let out a snort. If he'd been the one thrown across a room by some unseen hand, he'd have wanted to know the cause. Not least in case it might happen again. But Jorra-hin had always been single-minded; once he started down a particular track, nothing else could edge in. If he'd moved on to Heckart's proposal, that was that.

"You don't have to go, Jorra. Remember, it's a choice, not an order."

"Brother Heckart has offered me my first Recordership. Should I have declined? Is that not what all the Adak-rann aspire to?"

Brömin raised an eyebrow. "But is it what you aspire to?"

Jorra-hin appeared to ponder the question, but only for a moment. "Yes."

So that was it, then, Brömin mused. The world he'd known for two decades really was about to change.

Jorra-hin returned his gaze to the mountains. "To be honest, though, I hadn't given much thought to such an appointment until now. It's come upon me rather suddenly."

"Indeed. And do you feel ready?"

"Ah," Jorra-hin shrugged, "now that's an altogether different question. Who's to say?"

Brömin smiled; that was just the sort of answer he would have given.

"I have sworn my oath to Brother Heckart that I shall do my best. What will come of that, only time will tell."

"Your best, Jorra? Let me tell you something – half succeed in fulfilling that oath, and you will make an outstanding Recorder."

It occurred to Brömin that it had been a risk to support Heckart's proposal as firmly as he had during the council meeting. Jorra-hin's current predicament wouldn't have come about had he been against the idea. But the fact remained that the lad was more than ready to take on the Adak-rann's most cherished of duties, despite his youth and lack of experience of the outside world.

They lapsed back into silence again. Brömin allowed himself to absorb the stillness of the Mathians, to become a traveller for a moment in time through an ageless landscape. The lives of men came and went, but the Mathians scarcely noticed. In a hundred generations they would change not one jot. For many within the Adak-rann they were a bedrock of constancy, supplying perspective when the chaos of history tried to inflict its worst.

Eventually his gaze drifted back to Jorra-hin.

"I don't know why the hand of fate brought you to us, Jorra. But whatever it was that led your mother to our door, I know it was for a reason. I have always firmly believed that. It was no accident that it fell to us to raise you, to teach you our ways."

Jorra-hin cocked his head to one side, waiting. Brömin sighed. It was difficult articulating what he wanted to say.

"Jorra, over the coming months much will change. Things will be very different for you outside these walls. I can't say what you will encounter in Alondris, but no doubt it will pull you in many directions."

"Brother, if you are worried about my leaving the brotherhood, you needn't be. The Adak-rann isn't just my order, it's my family."

"Good," Brömin nodded. "Then, for what it's worth, my advice is that you should keep your head below the parapet while you're at the Cymàtagé. It will be easier for you if you stay out of the light."

"Will that be possible?"

"I'm not sure," Brömin admitted, his tone grave. Advice was one thing, practicalities were another. "Your abilities, Jorra, your way with A'lyavine – I know you can't hide that, after all, it's what's taking you to the Cymàtagé. But don't flaunt it. Be cautious, that's really what I'm trying to say. The last thing you need to gain is the interest of the Dinac-Mentà."

"They regulate the mages, don't they? Why would they be interested in me?"

This could be complicated, Brömin realised, letting out a sigh. "Come, let us find somewhere to sit. My old bones don't like standing so long these days."

He led the way down from the parapet to the courtyard below. In the middle was a patch of grass, roughly square, surrounded by a gravel path and beds filled with rose bushes that were just coming into bud. Birds frequented a small fountain that had ceased to function years ago, using it as a bath and a watering hole. Many of the benches positioned around the perimeter were already occupied by brothers taking advantage of the peaceful seclusion and the afternoon sunshine. Nods of acknowledgement were exchanged.

Finding a free bench, Brömin sank down, letting out another sigh, this one of gratitude.

"Well, the Dinac-Mentà – where to begin. I suppose the Mages' War would be a good place, around 432 After Foundation."

"A little over five hundred years ago."

"Indeed," Brömin nodded. "Firstly, you understand the difference between a Natural mage and a Follower of the Path, don't you?"

"I have read the Talmathic Dömon, Brother."

"Ssh," Brömin hissed, waving a dampening hand. He glanced round in case anyone had overheard. Satisfied that no one had, he shook his head and chuckled. Jorra-hin had actually enjoyed wading his way through Amatt the Blind's great treatise on the Nature of the Taümatha. Written in First Dialect A'lyavine, some of its tamer passages were used as translation tests for students of the Mages' Path, at the end of their training at the Cymàtagé. To them it was a fearsome hurdle standing between them and graduation. For Jorra-hin, it had been fun. He'd been fascinated.

But in the wrong hands, some of the book's incantations could wreak havoc. Access to the Talmathic Dömon was therefore strictly controlled by those who ran the Cymàtagé. The Adak-rann were only permitted to hold a copy at Jàb-áldis as a safeguard in case anything should happen to the original. If anyone discovered that Jorra-hin had been allowed to read it, there would be trouble. Particularly as he could probably recite whole passages of it from memory.

"You know that's our little secret. Whatever you do, you must *not* let anyone at the Cymàtagé know about that."

Jorra-hin nodded. "Don't worry, Brother, I won't tell."

"Good. So, the difference between Natural mages and Followers…"

Jorra-hin drew a breath. "Amatt said that the power of the Taümatha was like wine stored up in a huge cask. There are those who must climb up the side and can only ladle out small measures from the top. Such mages are known as Followers of the Path. They have to learn how to release the Taümatha using the training they receive under the Mages' Path. Whereas Natural mages are more akin to those who have the ability to open a tap at the bottom of the cask, allowing the Taümatha to pour out of its own accord. This ability usually comes naturally, without training."

"Indeed," Brömin nodded, "and such mages are consequently much more powerful than Followers. Therein lies the problem. As with any power, in the right hands, the Taümatha can be used for good. But it is not always so. At the time of the Mages' War, many of the Natural mages left the path of benevolence and pursued greed, hungry for power and dominance over their fellows."

"Brother, I know the stories. But how does this concern me?"

"Patience, my lad, patience," Brömin smiled. "It was during this time that the Dinac-Mentà came into being. Some of the Natural mages saw the terrible consequences of their power and it became clear to them that they had to put an end to the abuses of their brethren. Seven of these great mages formed a pact, and in so doing they became the first Dinac-Mentà. They swore to bring order back to their ranks. One by one they defeated all the other Natural mages, eventually bringing the Mages' War to an end."

"I thought all the Natural mages died," Jorra-hin said. "Only one was left at the very end, Mage Solautus. He took his own life for the sake of the people, so that his power could not be misused."

Brömin sighed. "That's what history says."

"Is that not how it happened?"

Brömin shook his head. "The truth is darker by far. Few know of it, and there are those who like to keep it that way, the Dinac-Mentà foremost amongst them. But I've made it a personal study of mine." In Brömin's book, mages were never to be trusted; their repeated attempts to mask the truth was merely poof of that. Perverting the accuracy of the historical record was anathema to him, as it was to every brother of the Adak-rann. "As you know, most of recorded history is written from the point of view of the victor. That's why we of the Adak-rann take no sides, so that we may be unbiased in our recordings. We seek the truth, not some twisted propaganda that serves a corrupted cause."

"So what did happen to Solautus?" Jorra-hin asked, his impatience clipping his tone.

Brömin chuckled; the young lad had an insatiable appetite for new information, especially if it concerned something secret or mysterious.

"The question should really be, what happened to all seven of the mages who signed the pact? Throughout the Mages' War the ranks of the Dinac-Mentà had swelled to encompass not just the seven, but other, lesser mages. Followers. They acted as spies, informants, go-betweens, doing the menial tasks that the seven did not have time for themselves. But when the war was over, there came the problem of what the seven should do with themselves. No one else had the power to subdue them, yet it was only fair, having imposed restrictions on all others of their kind, that they too should be restrained."

"So what did they do?"

"The only thing they could. They submitted to something of their own making. They devised a restraint cast that each of them would wear. It locked away their powers, preventing their use."

"Ah – I think I see where this is going. They became vulnerable," Jorra-hin surmised.

"They did indeed. Once they could no longer defend themselves, the rest of the Dinac-Mentà turned on them."

"They were killed?"

"I'm afraid so."

Jorra-hin fell quiet for a while. Brömin allowed him the time to put the pieces together for himself.

"Brother, why does the Dinac-Mentà persist? Why was it not disbanded once there were no more Natural mages?"

"You need to ask yourself, Jorra, *why* there are no Natural mages these days."

Jorra-hin was clearly vexed. "Is being a Natural mage a hereditary thing? If so, and they were all destroyed, presumably there can be no more." He paused, staring at the gravel beside his feet, as though reading something there only he could see. "I don't recall Amatt discussing that point in the Talmathic Dömon."

Brömin sighed. There was one aspect of Jorra-hin's character that was perhaps not yet ready for the world at large, particularly the Cymàtagé. His failure to appreciate that things were often darker than they seemed was a weakness he would have to overcome.

"Being born to a Natural mage does increase the chances that a person will become one themselves. But it isn't limited to lineage."

"Then why aren't there…" Jorra-hin's voice suddenly trailed off. "No, surely not?"

"I'm afraid so," Brömin nodded. "Oh, to be sure, the Dinac-Mentà of today appear to content themselves with regulating matters of a Taümathic nature. They keep their fellow Followers in line and make sure no one oversteps the mark. But in the dark, far from the public eye, they still perform the same duty they always have, seeking out Natural mages and preventing them from becoming a problem."

"By committing murder?"

"Safeguarding the people, they would say."

"By committing murder."

"They would see it as preventing the atrocities of the past from ever being repeated." Jorra-hin opened his mouth, but Brömin cut him off. "I don't condone their actions, Jorra. But to them, the end justifies the means. As far as they are concerned, the Natural mages cannot be allowed to return to plague us as they did before."

Jorra-hin stood up. He looked troubled now. He paced a few feet away and then returned to the same spot, as though on the verge of something momentous. "You still haven't explained why the Dinac-Mentà might show any interest in me. I'm not a Natural mage. I'm not even intending to be a Follower."

"Thank the gods. No, my fear, Jorra, is that your ability with A'lyavine could be regarded with suspicion. The Tongue of the Ancients is, after all, the language of magic. Followers use it to form the spells they cast. Put in Amatt's terms, A'lyavine is the ladle they use to scoop out a measure of the Taümatha from the cask. The trouble is, your ability with A'lyavine already far exceeds that of anyone I know. That's what could attract the Dinac-Mentà's attention."

"So what do you suggest?"

"You will have to go carefully, that's all I'm saying. At best, make it seem your abilities are the result of your unusual upbringing here at Jàb-áldis; you are unique in that respect. Make it look as though your way with A'lyavine is purely academic, the result of hard work and study."

"I cannot lie."

"No, Jorra, but you can imply. Much can be conveyed by what you don't say. Also, the less interested you seem in the practical application of your gift, the less the Dinac-Mentà will be concerned about you. Confining yourself to academic studies and your Recordership will be your best course."

After a moment of reflection, Jorra-hin smiled. "Since I have no desire to follow the Mages' Path, not being interested in the Taümathic side of the Cymàtagé will not be deceitful. All I need do is act as a member of the Adak-rann engaged upon an official investigation."

"Yes." Brömin's mood brightened. "So, the details of your journey – when do you leave?"

Jorra-hin sat back down. "In the next day or so. Brother Heckart advises that the cause of the Taümathakiya's movement should be investigated while the iron is still hot. That said, the journey to Alondris takes weeks."

"It does indeed. How are you going?"

"Brother Heckart is sending a letter to a general called Kirshtahll over in Mitcha, asking him if I can accompany the next party travelling south."

"Kirshtahll," Brömin repeated, trying to place the name. A few moments later it came to him. "Ah, yes, I met him once, many years ago. Not that he was a general back then. Headstrong, as I recall, full of fire and gusto. Can't say he had much time for monks, though."

"I hope he has warmed to us a little, then, because I appear to need his help."

"It was once a capital crime to refuse the Adak-rann," Brömin sighed forlornly. "Gone are those days, I'm afraid. I sometimes think people consider us nothing more than a nuisance and only humour us because it's easier than obstructing us."

"How are we viewed at the Cymàtagé?"

"Ah, well, we make ourselves useful in our academic capacity. The mages do at least appreciate our efforts, which is enough."

"So," Jorra-hin mused, "my reception might not be warm, but it will at least be civil, yes?"

Brömin decided to hedge his bets. "Probably."

"So the question is, will they assist me with my enquiries?"

"That is not something I can answer for you, Jorra. But don't forget, Brother Akmir holds sway down there. He often attends the Cymàtseà, their equivalent of our council. He will be more than happy to help you. After all, you in turn will be there to assist him."

"Ah, yes, the translation work." Jorra-hin's eyes glistened with excitement. "Brother Heckart says Akmir has come into possession of an original copy of the Legend of Tallümund, and that it has parts in it that have never been seen before. That should be fun." The young lad rubbed his hands together enthusiastically.

Brömin laughed and clapped a hand on Jorra-hin's shoulder. He understood the attraction such an opportunity held. But he also knew how odd it would seem to those less accustomed to the order's ways. Young men of Jorra-hin's age usually had far more frivolous pursuits in mind. Especially the young men admitted to the Cymàtagé.

11

"She can't be naive enough to believe that I actually trust her, can she?"

Döshan bowed his head in deference before replying. The emperor had been in a variable mood of late and he knew it would be best to tread with care.

"Sire, I believe Baroness Daka thinks she can outsmart you, whether you trust her or not. Victory over the Alondrians, if she can achieve it, will certainly make her popular. I imagine she is hoping that will be sufficient to enable a challenge to your position."

Omnitas's expression clouded. "Meddlesome bloody woman!"

"Sire, why not remove Daka now? She will only get stronger as time goes on." Döshan held his breath. He had spoken before thinking through the consequences; a dangerous slip for one in his position. He would not normally have given such advice so blatantly.

"I cannot," Omnitas grumbled after a momentary pause. "I have already given her my agreement. Besides, I can't just get rid of her – the House of Daka is of great prominence. The other barons would not permit it. Too many eyes are on this."

Döshan breathed a little easier. Despite the vexing situation with Daka, the emperor was clearly in a better mood than had been the case earlier in the day. Advisor Kremlish had only narrowly avoided a trip to the guardhouse for laughing at an inappropriate moment. The thought caused Döshan to flick a glance at the ever-present guards secreted amongst the shadows around the perimeter of the hall. They remained just out of earshot, but he didn't doubt they'd be upon him in the blink of an eye if they thought intervention was required.

"No, what we need is a way of turning this situation to our advantage," Omnitas went on.

Döshan's attention quickly snapped back from the hall's extremities. "I have been giving that some thought, Sire. If I may suggest…" he waited for a nod, "delay giving your support as long as possible."

"Why?"

"Sire, with the right timing, you could make it look as though your intervention is saving the day. Let Daka do all the hard work, let her bear the brunt of Alondria's resistance, and only send in your reinforcements towards the end of the campaign. If it can be made to look as though you are rescuing Daka's floundering operation, you will steal much of her thunder."

The clouds on Omnitas's brow began to clear, wiped away by a broadening grin. "I like it. But how? Daka is no fool. If she thought she could succeed in her invasion of the Tep-Mödiss without my help, she would not have come to me in the first place."

"Sire, does not all military action require Imperial sanction?"

"Ah, but that's just it, Döshan," Omnitas exclaimed, slapping the gilded armrest of his throne in annoyance, "Daka means to topple me – you have said as much yourself. She loathes me, even though she tries to hide the obvious behind this veil of curtsies." He snatched up the scroll the baroness had sent and shook it. "If she didn't need my help, she would be carrying out her plan without my approval, of that I am certain. But she *has* come to me. She needs me." The emperor huffed. One of the guards stirred, realised he was not required, and settled back into the shadows again. "Besides, it serves me no good to scupper Daka's plan. It is better that she at least attempts to regain the Tep-Mödiss, even if she fails. The question is, how do I show my support, without putting her in a position to harm me later?"

Döshan bowed his head once more. "Sire, perhaps you could tell her you wish to see proof that her operation has a real chance of success before committing your troops."

"And how does that help?"

"In two ways, Sire. It allows you to delay your support without raising her suspicion, forcing her to take the first steps in the campaign in order to prove that she has a chance to succeed."

"And the second…"

"It silences those looking in on this matter. Our history is, after all, replete with failures in respect of the Tep-Mödiss. To insist on Daka providing evidence that her occupation offers something different this time, something lasting, would seem prudent. Not even your opponents could deny the wisdom of that."

"Well said, Döshan," Omnitas smiled, rubbing his hands together. "So, we will allow Daka to launch her attack and, as you say, do all the hard work." He slapped his armrest again, this time enthusiastically. "When Alondria musters her southern army and brings it north, as surely will happen, Daka will already have expended a goodly portion of her resources dealing with Kirshtahll and whatever he throws at her. I will then move in and establish authority over her campaign. I will play the magnanimous emperor, of course, and allow her some credit. Just not too much."

"Indeed, Sire. If Daka succeeds, the Tep-Mödiss will be ours again. Tsnathsarré benefits and much of the glory will be yours. But if she fails, you can easily distance yourself."

The emperor appeared to slip into deep thought. Döshan knew it was best to keep his own counsel and not interrupt. Omnitas had a tendency to swat his advisors like flies when his thoughts were thrown off course by overzealous guidance. It was nearly a minute before he spoke again.

"And what do you suppose all this will cost me?"

"Sire, not being a military man, it is difficult for me to say," Döshan replied, gesturing openly with his hands. "But if I was to hazard a guess, with Daka bearing most of the burden, I think at worst you may lose a few thousand troops. Then again, it might not go so badly. It all depends on how hard the Alondrians are prepared to fight."

He paused, wondering how reliable his information was regarding the state of southern Alondria. He could not afford an error when steering the emperor in a matter of such gravity as this.

"Go on…" Omnitas prompted.

"Sire, the Alondrian response to an invasion may not be as forceful as it has been in the past."

"Why not?"

"I have heard there is dissension amongst their southern lords. I believe this could be enough to dampen their enthusiasm for war."

Döshan felt his insides tighten. Suspending his advice on threads of speculation, especially when matters were of such importance as these, was a dangerous gambit. Unfortunately, it was hard getting reliable information from so far south of the border, particularly from beyond the Mathian Mountains. Delving into the subtleties of feudal allegiances and inter-house courtship required a personal touch. With Alondris a thousand leagues south on an arrow's tack, that wasn't possible.

The information he had managed to glean suggested that the bonds between the great houses of southern Alondria were more fragile now than they had been for many years. King Althar was not long for this world, word had it, and that put his eldest daughter Midana at the helm.

For Döshan, that was a double-edged sword. This Midana was relatively young and headstrong, an unknown entity, which made it difficult to predict her responses. On the other hand, she was the primary cause of the dissension being reported. Her style of leadership was offhanded and rash. She ruled in an absolute manner instead of pursuing a diplomatic course, issuing decrees rather than negotiating settlements. That had a polarising effect on her lords. She might survive if her power continued unquestioned, but the House of Dönn-àbrah wasn't what it once was. This new queen-to-be might learn the hard way that if she angered too many of her lords, they'd remove her. The constitution of Alondria allowed for such things at the passing of a monarch. A convocation could be called. Althar's death, apparently a day Midana yearned for, might yet be her undoing.

For the time being, though, instability amongst the Alondrian nobility only served to benefit Tsnathsarré aspirations in the Tep-Mödiss. It kept the Alondrians' sights closer to home, perhaps making them less inclined to worry about the long-term impact of losing their northern frontier.

"They will respond, though," Omnitas said. "They will not simply allow us to take over unopposed."

"Quite so, Sire. But wars are costly. Their appetite could be weakened by their disunity."

Omnitas slumped back into the cushions behind him and let out a self-satisfied sigh. His round, rather pudgy face once more took on a far-away look, as though he was seeing into the future. There were other matters that needed to be discussed, but it would be best to wait, Döshan decided.

When Omnitas's eyes eventually refocused, his eyebrows rose slightly, as if he was surprised to find his advisor still there.

"Who does Daka have supporting her, do we know?"

"It is difficult to be certain of the full extent, Sire, but from what I have heard, she has Töuslàn and Fidampàss with her."

That was no surprise. Both neighbours of Daka, like the baroness, they had lands running along the Ablath. Between them they covered the whole Tsnathsarré southern border with Alondria.

"They stand to gain the most from any successes in the Tep-Mödiss," Omnitas acknowledged. "Who else? That can't be all. They alone do not have the men to mount an invasion."

"Indeed, Sire. I gather that Minnàk has also agreed to provide his services."

"What, that old mercenary?"

Döshan nodded. Minnàk was still very much a force to be reckoned with. A privateer, famously impartial when it came to who he fought for, he was much in demand, despite being well past his prime. Like vintage wine, age seemed to agree with him.

"The only thing that surprises me is where Daka expects to get the money from to pay him. I've heard he has some six thousand in his employ on this venture. That would put a dent even in your coffers, Sire."

"I am well aware of the Daka fortune," Omnitas agreed with a frown, "but even so, paying for Minnàk's services is not a decision she can have taken lightly. Tell me, does his support give her all she needs?"

"In terms of troops, quite possibly. She will, after all, have your reinforcements when the time comes, Sire." Döshan paused, letting out a sigh. There was something that still worried him, though to mention it meant having to make recourse to speculation once more. He decided to risk it. "Her bigger problem, I feel, is that she lacks a true military leader. Someone who can think this whole invasion through and produce a winning strategy."

"Couldn't Minnàk fulfil that role?"

"He's a good fighter, Sire; he'll win a battle for you. I feel, however, that planning an entire campaign would not be playing to his strengths."

"Töuslàn is no good," Omnitas nodded, murmuring through fingers now steepled over the bridge of his nose, "he has very little military experience. What about Fidampàss?"

"I have my doubts, Sire. My sources tell me that he is the least committed to the venture. I submit, therefore, that he would not be Daka's first choice for planning the operation on her behalf."

"What about Daka herself?"

Döshan smirked, but quickly thought better of it and shook his head. "She's a wily one, Sire, and certainly intelligent enough for the task. But she either seduces her opponents, or assassinates them. Neither tactic would serve her particularly well in this instance."

"Oh, I don't know," Omnitas rumbled with a grin, "from what I've heard of her appetites, she might try bedding the Alondrians into submission."

As the emperor seemed to be in good spirits, Döshan allowed himself a smile at the lewd suggestion before resuming his more usual stoic expression. "Sire, it is my belief that she is still looking for the right man to lead this invasion. Which might provide us with an opportunity."

"An opportunity?"

"Well, Sire, none of those Daka has with her are any great supporters of your leadership. Töuslàn and Fidampàss are clearly behind Daka, though in Fidampàss's case, that might be more through intimidation than personal aspiration. As for Minnàk, well, he supports whoever pays him. No, to my way of thinking, it would be good to get one of our own into Daka's camp."

"I like your thinking, Döshan. I will consider the matter," Omnitas said, suddenly distracted. "All this talk has given me an appetite." He cast about for something to nibble. Only a platter of fruit was within reach and that didn't appear to be satisfactory. "You may go. I will summon you later and we will discuss this further."

Döshan bowed one more time. The emperor was given to such whims; it sometimes made bringing matters to completion a lengthy affair.

There were those who considered Omnitas unfit to be emperor. He was short, plump, and had an unfortunate tendency to sweat profusely in warmer weather, giving him a rather oily countenance. Yet these appearances were deceiving. Unlike previous emperors, who had usually acted on their own judgements, Omnitas recognised his limitations and surrounded himself with advisors. That made him a far more potent force than any battlefield prowess could bestow. Suffering his whims was a small price to pay for not having a despot on the throne.

"As you wish, Sire." Döshan remained bowed as he backed away. When he had successfully negotiated the dais step, he straightened and turned to leave.

He had reached the doors at the far end of the hall before Omnitas called after him.

"Who did you have in mind, Döshan?"

Döshan chuckled to himself, but hid any sign of his reaction before turning to face the emperor again.

"I thought perhaps Lord Özeransk, Sire."

"Ah yes, Özeransk. Naturally."

As he passed into the corridor, Döshan noted that he'd managed to leave a faint smile on the emperor's lips. It was a good sign.

12

Kassandra tried not to allow her clothes to brush up against the inside of the hidden passage that ran between Brath'daka's great hall and its antechamber. The whole place was filthy. Considering what she had come to do, which essentially boiled down to an act of espionage, she realised too late that white had not been the most sensible of colours to wear.

She pressed her eye up against a tiny crack in the wooden panelling, careful not to make any noise that would give her presence away. The thin veneer was all that separated her from Gömalt, her mother and the three men who had arrived at the castle earlier in the day – scribes, she'd since discovered. They'd just returned from the Mathian Mountains, down in Alondria.

"Gömalt, I have matters to attend to," she heard her mother say.

"Of course, my lady. I will conclude our business with these men."

Gömalt gave the baroness a slight bow. Kassandra noticed his conspiratorial smirk, deliberately hidden from the scribes. She frowned when she saw the knowing smile her mother returned before she left the antechamber by the door that led to the great hall.

Kassandra felt a sudden feeling of claustrophobia take hold as she realised she couldn't leave, even if she wanted to. The passage only had two ways out, and with her mother probably in the hall, both exits led to places that were now occupied. The feeling of being trapped left a pit in her stomach.

"So, what do you make of these markings?" Gömalt asked, waving a hand back at an unrolled parchment on the table around which the scribes were standing. His other hand moved behind his back.

The scribes retuned their attention to the table. The parchment under consideration was being held flat by two copper tubes of the type used to transport and store important documents. Each scribe had brought one back with them. Whatever they were discussing, there were clearly three copies of it.

"We are not learned in A'lyavine, sir," one of the scribes replied.

"No indeed."

Gömalt sounded not in the least bit surprised by the answer. He moved in between two of the scribes and stooped slightly for a closer inspection.

In the blink of an eye, his hand flew out from behind his back. The point of his dagger slashed across the throat of the man on his left. His hand didn't stop. Too bewildered to react, the second scribe barely moved before Gömalt spun on the spot and plunged the stiletto blade into the man's back. The weapon disappeared right up to the hilt. Both victims fell to the floor at the same moment.

The third scribe, with a second or two to comprehend his fate, scrambled for the nearest door. Gömalt's arm shot forwards, sending his blade towards the fleeing target. With stupefying accuracy it took the man in the back of the neck. His body sprawled across the floor almost as though he had dived for cover. He twitched. He wasn't dead, just paralysed.

Gömalt walked over to him and pulled the dagger free. He turned the torso over and knelt on the scribe's throat until his rasping breath had ceased.

Kassandra was frozen in shock, her eye still glued to the panel, struggling to comprehend the scene beyond. In just a few seconds Gömalt had turned the antechamber into a charnel-house, a loathsome place she would never again be able to enter without a feeling of revulsion.

He was just standing there with his back to her, a few yards away, his dagger held at his thigh. It dripped fresh blood on to the flagstones at his feet as he calmly surveyed the carnage.

Bile rose to the back of her throat. The urge to retch became excruciating, yet she fought against it with all her might; if Gömalt detected even the slightest hint of her presence, there would be trouble beyond reckoning. Despite every instinct demanding that she flee, she couldn't move. All she could do was clench and unclench her fists in a desperate battle against the trembling that threatened to give her away.

Her stomach churned. With sickening perversity, her mind insisted on replaying the abhorrent images over and over again. The merciless efficiency with which Gömalt had carried out the executions appalled her. It was no secret that he relished serving as the Daka assassin when her mother demanded it. But she had never expected to witness him in action. Nor could anything have prepared her for it.

Managing to pull her face back from the panelling for a moment, she cursed herself for allowing curiosity to win over better judgement. All she had wanted to do was find out what all the recent fuss was about. For the past few weeks her mother had been acting as though she was excited. Anger was normally the only emotion ever displayed; even a simple smile was a tool reserved for the scheming manipulation of others. The uncharacteristic change in demeanour could mean only one thing – something of great importance was afoot.

When the three scribes had arrived at Brath'daka, it had seemed probable that their advent might have something to do with her mother's mood. Slipping into the hidden passage had seemed like the ideal way of finding out what was going on.

But the good idea of half an hour ago had, in an instant, become a nightmare, one from which there was no immediate escape. Gömalt was in the antechamber, and her mother in the great hall. There was nowhere for her to go. It was obvious now that her mother had only vacated the antechamber to allow Gömalt to carry out his vile act unhindered.

Her mind raced. Despite every jangled nerve screaming for her to get out, she knew she had no option but to stay.

*

Gömalt heard a rap on the door. He finished wiping the blade of his dagger as he walked over to readmit the baroness. His eyes were drawn to the tight-laced bodice of the crimson dress she was wearing; a rather appropriate colour, he thought. The garment accentuated her figure to perfection, kindling a flame of desire within him. He smiled, recognising the familiar heightening of his passions that always came after a kill.

The baroness brushed past him and paused to take in the scene. The mess of death littering the floor made her grimace. She had no compunction about ordering other people to do her dirty work, Gömalt mused, so long as it didn't involve getting her own hands dirty.

She made her way over to one of the bodies and peered down. "Swift work as usual, Gömalt. Any complications?"

"None, my lady," he replied, his tone mildly indignant. As if three scribes could possibly have given him any trouble.

"Good. And this…?" The baroness gave the body at her feet a distasteful poke with the toe of her shoe.

"Alber will be here shortly. We'll take them down to the dungeon and leave them there until nightfall. I have already had a hole dug. When it's dark, we'll take them out and bury them."

The baroness nodded, then waved a hand at the rapidly drying blood that had pooled on the floor. "Make sure you have some of your men clean this up, then get the rugs put back."

"Yes, my lady. And the texts?"

The baroness moved over to the table on which the unrolled document was laid out.

"Ah, yes," she murmured with reverence, "the Ranadar texts." One hand went to feel the ever-present necklace at her throat. "A copy will be sent for translation, the others will remain here. I have already sent a summons to Roumin-Lenka."

Gömalt stiffened. The baroness threw him a glance.

"I don't like the Dwarves," he offered. "They don't think like us. It makes them unpredictable, which worries me."

"It's your job to worry other people. You may have to kill him after he has served his purpose. Just remember that."

A dismissive snort escaped his lips before he could intercept it. "My lady, I am honoured that you think so highly of my skills. But even *I* would have trouble dispatching a Dwarve."

"Then you had better hope it won't be necessary. The Dwarves are usually honourable in their dealings with us, limited though they are."

"Their loyalty comes at a high price."

The baroness dismissed that observation with a slight raising of her chest – as near to a shrug as a lady of her standing would permit. Her attention returned to the parchment. Gömalt had studied it earlier, so he knew that the symbols on it offered no clues as to their meaning. The A'lyavinical text was from another time; it might as well have been from another world.

He wondered what mood that put the baroness in. She was not the sort of person with whom impotence sat well. Nor did she like having to rely on outside help, particularly not when the matters concerned were of such importance; the bodies sprawled across the floor were evidence enough of that. The fate of the three scribes had been sealed the day they had first laid eyes on the Menhir of Ranadar.

"My lady, this translation – do you know how much longer we might have to wait? I only ask because the men are getting restless." Months had been spent searching the Mathians to find the Menhir of Ranadar. Yet the men still had no idea what the relic really was, only that it was important to the baroness and her plans. "Speculation is rife. They're full of anticipation and ready for a fight."

"Let them speculate. There's little chance of them arriving at the truth."

Gömalt sighed inwardly. Such dismissive consideration of others was typical of the baroness. She wasn't the one trying to control the situation. He needed something more specific. There were arrangements to be made.

"My lady, we must not forget that our final preparations will take weeks, even after we have committed to this venture."

"I'm well aware of the critical nature of our timing, Gömalt," Daka retorted. "We have waited for centuries for the opportunity that now presents itself. I will not allow impatience to ruin what we have worked so hard to achieve thus far."

Gömalt realised he'd overstepped the mark and adopted a conciliatory tone. "Of course, my lady."

The baroness paused for a moment, staring resolutely at the Ranadar text. "Send word to the barons and our commanders – have them assemble here and I'll outline our progress. They must be made to understand that we cannot go forwards until we are assured the texts can be translated, otherwise this whole thing could be for nought."

That was news to Gömalt. He had taken the translation as a foregone conclusion.

"Is that likely to be a problem, my lady?"

The baroness didn't reply. She looked worried. She reached out and touched one of the sealed copper tubes. Gömalt knew that its contents were valued above all else. The texts were the tools of the baroness's ambition, her path to the reins of the Empire – *if* things went according to plan.

He did not want to contemplate the consequences if they did not.

*

Kassandra listened to the conversation barely breathing. Men, fighting, menhir – she understood the significance of little, but tried to commit as much of it as she could to memory; it was important, that much was obvious.

More than half an hour passed before her mother finally picked up one of the copper tubes and told Gömalt she was going to put it somewhere safe. She left the antechamber through the door by which she had entered.

Kassandra had a fair idea of where her mother was going. If she was correct, then the hall would be empty in a few moments' time – so long as Gömalt remained in the antechamber to await the arrival of his henchmen.

Taking every step like a nervous cat, she felt her way back through the darkness of the passage. She paused at the entrance. After waiting another minute, just in case her mother had lingered for some reason, she pushed the sliding panel aside. With relief, she found the hall was empty. She slipped out, closed the panel and flitted barefoot across the cold stone floor as soundlessly as a ghost.

Safely back in her chambers, she threw herself on the bed, releasing a flood of bottled-up emotions. As tears drenched the pillows, the images of the dead paraded before her. She wished she could erase the sight, the very memory of it from her mind; she knew with certainty that the scene would haunt her for the rest of her days.

It was a long time before she managed to regain her composure. Turning over, she lay staring up at the embroidered picture on the bed's overhead canopy; its scene of cherubs in puffy white clouds was so familiar that it made no impression at all.

Restless agitation suddenly propelled her to her feet. She began pacing up and down the chamber. Her mind was in complete turmoil. So many disparate thoughts vied for attention that it was nearly impossible to bring order to the chaos.

Yet one thought did eventually distil from the rest; she had to get away, now, tonight, before Gömalt decided to make another of his demands for satisfaction. After what she had just seen him do, the thought of him ever touching her again made her shiver with revulsion.

The problem was, escape was easier thought than done. It wasn't as if she could simply walk out of the main gate. Getting out of Brath'daka without anyone realising she had gone – at least, not for a few hours – was the biggest hurdle. She would need help.

She almost pounced on the bell cord that summoned her maid. The wait was brief. Anna must have already been on her way. The moment the door opened, she grasped Anna by the hands and drew her into the bedchamber, kicking the door closed behind them.

"I'm leaving."

Anna's eyes widened in shock. "My lady?"

"I have to get away from here."

Kassandra led the way over to the bed and made Anna sit down.

"W – what has brought this on so suddenly?" Anna stammered.

For a brief moment Kassandra's lip trembled, but she reined in her shattered emotions and plucked up the courage to recall what had happened. She related how she'd seen the arrival of the scribes in the antechamber and the delivery of the copper tubes they'd brought back with them from Alondria. She went on to describe Gömalt's murderous assault, and afterwards, the blood on his dagger – how it had dripped on to the floor as he'd stood surveying his handiwork – a small detail, insignificant in many ways, but one seared into her memory.

Anna paled as the gory details came flooding out. It was a few moments before she could find her voice.

"You'll have to be so careful, my lady. I understand how shaken you are, but leaving Brath'daka – this is something that needs to be thought out properly."

"It has to be now, Anna. My courage might not hold if I wait any longer. Seeing that bastard kill those poor men – if he ever touches me again..." she choked at the thought, "I couldn't, Anna, I just couldn't bear it."

Anna shut her eyes. She was struggling to adjust.

"My lady, rushing into something like this could lead to disaster. You know your mother will send Gömalt out after you as soon as she finds out you've gone."

Kassandra's lips trembled again. The consequences of being caught were too awful to contemplate.

"Think about it," Anna continued, "it's not as though your mother or Gömalt are after you right now. There's no way they could know you were spying on them, is there?"

"I don't think so."

"Well, there you are then. Couldn't you at least wait a day or two? That would give us time to plan."

Kassandra almost wavered; the suggestion sounded so reasonable. Then the thought of Gömalt coming to her again, of him touching her – with those stained, guilt-soiled, murderous hands – made her blood run cold. She shuddered. It steeled her mind and brought an uncommon clarity to her thinking, shoring up her resolve. If she didn't go now, she might never do it.

"No. It has to be tonight."

Anna let out a sigh. After a long pause, she nodded. "Alright, first of all, where are you going to go?"

"Alondria."

Anna huffed. "And supposing you do actually get there, what then? I've told you before, you can't arrive on their doorstep and tell them who you are. They'd either send you back or lock you up."

"They won't."

"You'll be regarded as an enemy of the kingdom, my lady," Anna persisted, exasperation raising her tone. "What do you think is going to happen when they find out you're a Daka?"

"They won't regard me as an enemy. Not after I tell them about the discovery of the Ranadar texts."

Anna gave a blank stare. Kassandra suddenly realised that she had been so absorbed in relating Gömalt's hideous attack that she hadn't mentioned much of the texts from the Menhir of Ranadar.

"But you don't even know what these texts are," Anna pointed out after hearing the rest of the details. "Neither does your mother, by the sounds of it."

"Maybe not. But whatever they are, they belong to the Alondrians. The menhir was found up in the Mathians. And they must be important, Anna. She may be the most callous, cold-hearted bitch that ever walked the Empire, but even my mother doesn't order people killed just for the sake of it. Those three scribes were executed for nothing more than having seen these texts. Besides, Gömalt spoke about men being prepared for a fight and their timing being crucial. It all adds up, Anna – my mother is planning an attack against the Alondrians."

"And if you alert them, you believe that will gain you their trust?"

"Yes. It may only be a vague warning, but it's got to count for something."

Anna seemed unconvinced. She scrabbled around for another argument to wield. "Well, what about money? You'll need lots of that. Even if they do accept you at your word, the Alondrians aren't going to pay for your upkeep."

"I can steal as much as I need from my mother's strongbox. Look, surviving in Alondria is not the problem. Getting out of the castle unseen is what I can't do on my own."

"That's only the first of your hurdles, my lady. You'll need a horse."

Kassandra hadn't got that far in her thinking. Anna was right, though; finding a horse could be difficult. Without one, Gömalt would overhaul her before the next nightfall. He'd probably catch up with her anyway. By whatever means she managed it, the journey to the border would be a race, with the stakes the highest imaginable – probably her life.

"I know I can't take one from the stables – the only way out from there is across the courtyard and through the main gate. I'll have to buy one once I'm away from the castle."

Anna stared Kassandra in the eye, her head tilted slightly to one side. "You're set on this, aren't you? I can't persuade you to leave it a day or so?"

This time Kassandra didn't hesitate. "It has to be now."

The look of concern on Anna's face did not recede, but after a long moment she sighed in resignation.

"Very well. Let me go and speak to Michàss. I think he knows a way out of the castle that isn't guarded."

Kassandra dismissed her concerns about bringing another person into her confidence. Michàss was Anna's sweetheart, and if she thought she needed him, he would have to be trusted. Besides, even if he couldn't help, he'd be unlikely to betray them to Gömalt.

While Anna was away, Kassandra spent the time concocting a plan for getting to the strongbox that her mother kept in her chambers. It contained only a tiny fraction of the Daka fortune, but even so, it would be no trifling amount – more than enough to get her to Alondria and start a new life.

When Anna returned she looked flushed and excited. She crossed the chamber and ejected a bundle of clothes from within the folds of her apron on to the bed.

"Sorry I was so long," she panted. "I made a detour to the laundry and got you something to wear, some riding leathers and a dark coloured tunic. Men's clothes, I'm afraid, and probably too big for you. But better that than looking too much like a lady, my lady." She grinned and bobbed a mock curtsy.

Kassandra smiled as she held some of the styleless garments against her body, appraising them with a dubious eye. "Well, functional perhaps, but hardly fashionable."

Anna giggled. "Believe it or not, Michàss has also worked out a way of getting you a horse. We're in luck. He's been sent on an errand to the town, so he has leave to take one from the stables. He's going to stage an accident on the way back and return on foot. He'll tie the horse to a tree somewhere along the track. He can show you where it is later on."

"He can get me out of the castle too?"

"You'll have to wait until dark, but yes, he thinks so. It means going down the sewers, though." Anna screwed up her nose.

Kassandra snorted. If that was the worst to come, then she would consider herself lucky. "There's one more thing, Anna. I need food, at least enough for a couple of days. It's a long way to Alondria and I can't afford to stop somewhere. The less trail I leave for Gömalt to follow, the better."

"That could be awkward. You know what the cook's like."

"I've been thinking about that," Kassandra nodded. "I need an opportunity to get into my mother's chambers when I can guarantee she won't come barging in. The best time for that will be during supper. So, I'll pretend to be ill and excuse myself from having to dine in the great hall, and you can tell the cook I'm eating in my chambers and that you're going to keep me company. That way you can bring two meals, along with anything else you can pinch."

Over the next few hours Anna attempted to help pack a haversack with a few essentials. Kassandra spent most of the time changing her mind about what she could and couldn't take. It was slowly sinking in that fleeing to a new life in Alondria meant having to leave behind almost everything she possessed. More than anything, that drove home the finality of her decision. There would be no return to normality after tonight, whatever the outcome.

Shortly after dusk, Anna went to the kitchens as planned and Kassandra made her way to her mother's bedchamber. She tucked a satchel out of sight behind the marble bust, one of her ancestors, that stood beside the door, then continued on to the great hall. She chose a route that did not take her through the antechamber. The sight of that place again would be far too unnerving. She needed a measure of composure for what was coming.

The great hall was lit only by a series of candelabra down the centre of the long banqueting table. That was unusual; at this time in the evening, oil lamps normally blazed around the perimeter so that the paintings and tapestries could be admired. Still, whatever the reason for the change in ambience, Kassandra was grateful. Dim lighting meant it would be difficult for her mother to see her clearly. That made lying to her a little less nerve-wracking.

"You're late."

"I'm sorry, mother. I'm not feeling well. I just came to tell you that I wish to eat in my chambers this evening, then retire early."

Hardly an eyelid batted. Her mother's dismissal was a perfunctory wave of the hand, expressing not one iota of concern. Even servants received more consideration.

As Kassandra walked away it occurred to her that, if all went well, she would never see the woman again. A perfunctory wave of the hand said it all, really. The indifference bothered her not – if anything, it was a relief.

With that encounter out of the way, she was surprised to find how alive she felt. The defiance that had blossomed within her imparted a new lease of life. She had a plan, one that offered real hope of freedom, and her soul clung to it like an overboard sailor to a piece of flotsam.

Her mother's bedchamber door looming in front of her jolted her thoughts back to the task at hand. This was the moment of truth. Pausing only to retrieve the satchel from behind the marble bust, with a deep breath she lifted the latch and slipped inside.

The unfamiliarity of the interior was striking. It was a place she rarely had cause, or desire, to visit. This was where her mother slept, sometimes with Gömalt, where she walked about undressed, brushed her hair and selected her perfumes, preparing every facet of her cold, heartless exterior. It was an alien and unnerving place.

Kassandra crossed over to the gilded dressing table and withdrew the shallow front drawer until it was clear of the guide rails. Placing it on the floor, she reached back inside the empty slot and groped for the small shelf on which sat the key to her mother's strongbox. The touch of cold metal against her fingers sent a tingle of excitement coursing through her. It was tinged with relief; the last time she'd even seen the key was when she had been a little girl.

The strongbox was inside a clothes chamber, concealed beneath a rack of shoes. Meticulously, despite her nerves, she began to set the footwear aside in an orderly row so that they could be replaced without leaving any sign of disturbance. With the rack clear, she pressed a hidden catch to release the locking mechanism and swung the rack up out of the way.

The strongbox was just as Kassandra remembered it. Like the key, it had been years since she'd last seen it. She grasped its handles and pulled. It was reassuringly heavy.

With the lid open, her heart skipped a beat. A copper scroll tube lay on top of the other contents. Its presence was not entirely unexpected; the strongbox was the obvious place for something of importance to have been put. Here was the proof she needed to convince the Alondrians her warning was genuine.

She was about to slip the tube into her satchel when an idea stalled her. The container was still sealed; her mother hadn't even bothered to examine the contents. The seal was nothing fancy, just a cloth strip stuck on with wax and signed with an imprint of some sort. After a judicious bit of scraping with a hairpin, she managed to release the wax from the lid without breaking the remainder of the seal. She slid the top off and tipped the document out, wasting no time examining it. Using the flame of the oil lamp, she warmed the copper lid and pressed the cloth strip firmly back into place, holding it there until the wax had re-solidified. The result wasn't perfect, but then it didn't need to be. She giggled; the look on her mother's face when such treachery was discovered would be priceless.

It was a sight she had no intention of being around to witness.

Having carefully placed the text in the satchel, she turned her attention to the remainder of the strongbox's contents. The jewellery she ignored; valuable though it was, it wasn't as useful as the gold and silver coinage. That she was liberal with removing. A few minutes later the strongbox was locked and pushed back inside its hiding place, the rack closed and every pair of shoes carefully placed exactly as they had been before.

With the key back on its little shelf and the dressing table draw re-seated on its rails and closed, Kassandra slung the satchel over her shoulder. It weighed uncomfortably. She took a last look round to make sure no obvious sign of her trespass had been left, then crossed the chamber to the door. She hesitated for a moment before gingerly cracking it ajar. The passageway outside was dark and unoccupied. She stepped out, closed the door and headed back to her own chambers, barely able to believe what she had just done.

If nothing else, she had her passport into Alondria.

All she had to do now was get there.

*

Michàss chose his spot with care, a place where the road to the town was hard and stony and where there was a convenient birch thicket not far away. He led the horse across the open stretch of scrub and around behind the trees, where he tied its reins to a low branch to prevent the creature from wandering off. Back on the track, he checked to make sure that nothing of the horse could be seen.

Satisfied that all was well, he took out a small knife, drew a deep breath and jabbed himself at the back of his scalp. Head wounds usually bled profusely and he hoped this nick would look convincing enough when he got back to the castle. For extra effect, he lay down on the ground and squirmed around to get his clothes dirty.

That done, he got up and took a long look round to ensure that he could recognise the spot again. By the time he returned with Kassandra later it would be much darker and he didn't want to be wasting time blundering around in the wrong bit of undergrowth.

With his preparations complete, he began a leisurely walk back to the castle. It was just after dusk, still light enough to see where the path lay, but too dim to make out subtle details. Not that that mattered – he had less than a mile to go. He felt quite pleased with the way things had gone so far.

A sudden scramble from behind changed that. He didn't even have time to turn. His heart jumped into his mouth. He cried out in fright. Pain shot up his left arm as it was twisted up behind his back. A cold, sharp blade materialised under his chin.

His first thought was that he'd been set upon by bandits, although what they expected to gain from the likes of him he had no idea. He tried to struggle free, but that only brought more pain.

The assailant leaned in close and murmured in his ear, "You'd better have a damned good reason for being here, *friend*."

Michàss's blood ran cold. He recognised the rasping voice. "Oh please, sir, it's only me, Michàss. I work up at the castle."

The knife didn't waver from his throat.

"Hello, Michàss," Gömalt replied, without the slightest hint of cordiality, "and what might you be doing out here at this time of night?"

The low, menacing tones the assassin used sent shivers down Michàss's spine. "I was on me way back from the town, sir. Master Halfdanr sent me to arrange more supplies for the castle."

"And you went on foot?"

Michàss hesitated. "N – no, sir. I had an accident aways back down the road there. Me horse got spooked and I was thrown. I hit me head when I fell. When I came to I couldn't see hide nor hair of the beast, sir. With the light fading, I thought it best to make me way back to the castle and look for it in the morning."

Gömalt held the dagger at his throat a moment longer, then finally seemed satisfied. A great flood of relief swept over Michàss as the blade disappeared by sleight of hand.

"That must have been a nasty knock you gave yourself there," Gömalt observed, rubbing his fingers together having felt the back of Michàss's head. "Still, no permanent damage done, I trust."

It was amazing how Gömalt could switch from hostile to harmless in an instant. But Michàss knew even the man's pleasantries could be anything but.

"The horse will probably wander back of its own accord when it has calmed down. Assuming it makes it through the night, of course."

"Sir?"

"Oh, there's plenty of other nasty things out here besides me, Michàss. Best you get back to the castle as quick as you can. We wouldn't want any further mishaps to befall you, would we?"

"No, sir. Thank you, sir."

Michàss turned to go, but Gömalt stopped him from getting very far. "Oh, by the way, Michàss, best you forget this little encounter. Not the sort of thing that does any good – remembering a meeting like this."

Michàss nodded. "Right you are, sir. Didn't see a soul, sir."

"Good lad. Give my regards to that young lady of yours, what's her name – Anna, is it?"

A deep chasm opened up in Michàss's stomach. He felt physically sick. How the bastard knew about Anna, he couldn't begin to imagine; they'd done their utmost to keep their relationship a secret. The only other person who knew of it was Kassandra, and she wouldn't have mentioned it.

Gömalt vanished as suddenly has he had appeared, leaving Michàss to make his way back to the castle. He was worried beyond belief now. Grave doubts about their plan flooded in. He wondered whether he ought to carry on, or make Anna convince Kassandra to call the whole thing off.

When he arrived at the castle, far more fuss was made of him than he'd expected. Master Halfdanr insisted on tending to his wound personally. The cut had more than served its purpose; in the light, Michàss looked as if he'd just come off a battlefield. It made the job of convincing everyone that he was merely a little shaken rather more difficult.

By the time he managed to get away it was later than he'd planned.

13

Kassandra felt Anna close on her heels as they followed Michàss down the spiral steps beneath the servants' quarters. Descending into such dark, musty depths did little to inspire conversation, leaving her imagination to run riot, populating the shadows with all manner of malevolence. She had never explored this part of the castle before. It had once served as the laundry, but moisture seeping up though the foundations had eventually rendered the place useless. It had lain abandoned for years.

Michàss's torch flared and spluttered, reacting to the damp air. It had been freshly oiled and ought to burn for several hours. Even so, Kassandra eyed it with mistrust. Her already frayed nerves would not be soothed by the crypt-like surroundings being plunged into absolute darkness.

Michàss came to an unexpected stop and she bumped into him.

"We're at the bottom, my lady. Best stay here. It's a bit dangerous 'til you can see where there's no floor."

Kassandra watched as Michàss tentatively made his way across the worn stonework, probing the darkness at his feet with the torch. After about fifteen paces he stopped again. Just beyond him, faintly discernible in the flickering light, was a large drainage gully covered with the remnants of an iron grille.

"Alright, just come straight to me," Michàss called.

Kassandra grasped Anna's hand for reassurance and ventured out across the flagstones to the edge of the gully. Parts of the ironwork had long since rusted away, leaving shards protruding into the middle like sharpened teeth, turning the hole into the gaping maw of some hell-bound fiend. She shivered. Her courage was waning fast. All her doubts flooded back, threatening to strip away her remaining resolve. The only thing that steeled her was the knowledge that she had already burnt her boats. Considering the hour, her mother would be back in her chambers, so neither the Ranadar text nor the stolen gold could be returned to the strongbox now.

There was simply no going back.

Michàss handed Anna the torch and unslung a bag from his shoulder. He pulled out some old clothes, half of which he offered to Kassandra.

"To guard against the filth down there," he said, gesturing towards the opening.

Kassandra struggled into the second set of clothes. It wasn't easy – the ones she was already wearing, made for men, were far from close fitting.

As soon as he was ready, Michàss lowered himself on to the edge of the drain. "Once I'm down, pass the bags to me."

He didn't wait for acknowledgement; he just heaved himself forwards as though he'd done it a thousand times before. He didn't disappear into oblivion as Kassandra had half expected.

Anna used the torch to light the wick of a small oil lamp, which she placed to one side where it would be safe from draughts. Not much more than a candle's worth, it would be her only bastion against the darkness while she awaited Michàss's return.

With the bags and torch passed down, Kassandra turned to Anna.

"You must be careful. My mother will be furious when she finds out what I've done – she'll be bound to take her anger out on someone. Don't do anything that might bring suspicion on you."

"I won't, my lady."

Kassandra leaned forwards and gave Anna a tight hug. "I pray the gods will bless you for this."

"And I pray they may be with you, too, my lady."

Steadied by Anna's hand, Kassandra followed Michàss's example and sat down on the edge of the drain. While the bottom couldn't be that far away, not being able to see it was disconcerting. She hesitated, wondering how she was supposed to avoid the rusty spikes. Michàss had made it seem easy. A whole minute passed before she plucked up the courage to launch herself off the edge. She went with a squeal, and landed with a squelch.

Anna extended her hand down. Kassandra held on to it, feeling a tremendous reluctance to let go. She didn't know when, or even if, she would see Anna again. But time was pressing – Michàss wasn't waiting, he was already forging his way along the tunnel with the torch. Anna's hand slipped from hers and was quickly lost to the darkness.

The smell was not as awful as Kassandra had anticipated; the drain had only ever been used to take waste from the laundry. That didn't mean it was pleasant. The ancient scum, kept moist by the ever present dampness, was as slippery as ice. Every few paces she slithered one way or the other, slamming elbow, shoulder or hip into the tunnel walls. Progress was painful in every way possible. Michàss was faring no better; he cursed nearly every step. The profanity she could accept, just so long as he didn't dowse the torch mid diatribe.

After making yards and yards of tortuous, bone-jarring headway they came to a point where the tunnel curved to the left. Michàss stopped a little way short and turned. "We'll have to leave the torch here, my lady. Can't risk it being seen from outside."

He began prodding the sludgy bottom until he found a crack in the stonework wide enough to wedge the brand upright. Once it was secured, they crept forwards, groping their way along the slimy walls with the flickering glow of the torch receding behind them. It gradually became possible to discern the end of the tunnel, though only as a slight shift in hue from one shade of darkness to another. More than anything, it was the welcome smell of fresh air that drew them onwards.

"We have to be very careful here, my lady," Michàss whispered when they reached the outlet. "Remember, I bumped into Gömalt earlier. I've no idea what he was doing, but he could still be out there."

An icy chill drew its finger down Kassandra's back. She knew exactly what the assassin had been up to – burying the dead. But Michàss had enough to worry about; he didn't need to know about that.

Broken clouds covered the sky, allowing patchy glimpses of the moon to take the edge off the darkness and provide just enough light to see by. Michàss hopped down the three-foot drop to the ground below and reached back to take the bags one by one. Kassandra followed, taking the hand Michàss offered to steady herself. Before moving away from the castle wall, she removed her temporary outer garments and stuffed them back inside the tunnel. She swilled her hands in a puddle.

Michàss set off in the lead, picking his way over the scrub and heather. They steered clear of the main track until they'd rounded a small bluff and were safely out of sight of the castle, then they converged with the path and picked up the pace.

Their lessened caution was almost fatal.

A pebble skittering across the ground suddenly broke the nocturnal silence. Michàss froze instantly, throwing his arm out to stop Kassandra. Someone was coming up the other way. It didn't take a scholar to guess who. He grabbed Kassandra about the midriff and pulled her to the ground. They rolled into the cover of a shallow gully running alongside the track. Michàss gasped in shock as ice-cold water soaked into his clothing.

Two shadowy figures materialised out of the gloom. They were making no attempt to mask their presence as they strode back towards the castle. It seemed they might walk straight past, but the gods weren't about to be that kind. At the last moment, the taller of the two came to a halt. The other carried on for several paces before realising he was on his own.

"Sir?"

"Strange. Can you smell that?" Gömalt surveyed the surrounding area, sniffing the air.

"Smell what, sir?" Alber queried, testing the night air himself.

"I'm not sure…"

Alber sniffed again, then shook his head. "Can't says I smell anything, except maybe the lavender. Plenty of it about just here."

Gömalt bent down and breathed in the fragrance of the shrubs along the trackside. He let out a dubious grunt.

Kassandra screwed her eyes shut. She held her breath, but her body trembled so violently that she wondered how Gömalt could fail to notice her there; he was only a few yards away. She shrank ever further inwards, sealing off the outside world completely.

Gömalt let out a dismissive grunt and began heading back towards the castle. Kassandra only registered that he'd gone when Michàss pushed her up so that he could get out of the gully.

She couldn't stop shaking. She sat half laughing, half crying as relief turned her emotions every which way. Michàss wasn't much comfort. Lying in frigid water had numbed his legs and he was too busy massaging his muscles back into action.

With the risk of bumping into Gömalt gone, they covered the remaining distance at as close to a run as the night allowed. Michàss had no trouble picking out the spot where he had staged his accident earlier. He left Kassandra with the bags and waded out through the undergrowth to retrieve the horse from behind the birch trees. He was back within a couple of minutes.

"Don't try to ride too fast, my lady. Best not to go more than a gentle trot while it's dark. When you get to the first crossroads, go left on the Oakwood Road; that'll bypass the town. After that, just keep to the main track. It'll probably be getting light before you reach Göndd."

Kassandra kissed him on the cheek. "Thank you, Michàss. I will not forget what you've done for me this night."

Michàss gave her a leg-up into the saddle and helped tie down some of the bags.

"Look after Anna. And don't stay here any longer than needs be."

"No, my lady. With you gone, Anna won't be required any more. We'll try to slip away in the next few weeks." Michàss finished tying the last bag to the rear of the saddle and made sure all was secure. "Go careful like. Remember, if you have to stop, or if you sees others coming towards you, best leave the road and stay out of sight. That way people will have nothing to tell Gömalt if he asks."

"I will. The trouble is, there aren't many routes between here and Alondria," Kassandra replied. "It won't take him long to figure out that's where I'm heading. He knows as well as I do there's no place in the Empire where I'd be safe from him."

With a final nod, Kassandra nudged the horse into a trot.

*

Anna did not sleep well, too buoyed up by what had happened and what was still to come. She rose early, but had to bide her time until Kassandra's usual hour for getting up. Then she made a thespian effort of discovering Kassandra missing. First she called at the kitchen to collect breakfast as usual and proceeded up to Kassandra's chambers. After that, she went all over the castle looking for her; those she met were left in no doubt that her mistress was missing.

Eventually, making it seem a last resort, she went and found the baroness in the great hall. Gömalt was with her. The pair were in conference over something, but abruptly cut short their conversation when she interrupted them.

She curtsied. "I'm sorry for disturbing you, my lady, but I can't find Mistress Kassandra this morning. She wasn't in her chambers when I went to wake her."

The baroness didn't seem overly concerned, Anna noted; it probably never crossed her mind that her timid, spineless daughter could possibly have done something defiant.

Gömalt was not so dismissive. He was perpetually suspicious. "With your permission, my lady," he said, bowing slightly to the baroness before turning to face Anna. "When was the last time you saw her?"

"Last night, sir."

"What time?"

Anna hesitated. "I don't know, sir. Not that late. She wasn't feeling well. We ate together in her chambers and then she went to bed."

"Earlier than usual?"

"Yes, I suppose," Anna stammered.

Gömalt demanded to see Kassandra's chambers. Anna led the way, but stood aside when they reached the door. She was beginning to worry about what he might find and hoped that she could hide her anxiety.

The man poked about in the bedchamber but gave little away as to what it was he was looking for. He paid particular attention to Kassandra's bed. He placed a hand inside the sheets and left it there for several moments.

"This bed wasn't slept in last night," he stated with conviction.

Anna frowned, then tried to look surprised. How he could possibly tell, she couldn't fathom. The bed would have cooled by now, even if Kassandra had been in it all night.

After coming to that conclusion, Gömalt seemed to have the bit between his teeth. He called the rest of his men together and ordered a thorough search of the castle. He also instructed Michàss to be found and brought to him. Anna's heart nearly stopped when she heard his name mentioned. She had no idea why Gömalt would want to single him out for special consideration.

The search didn't take long, but Michàss had gone out to make a pretence of looking for the errant horse. It was an hour before he returned. When he did, he was intercepted by the gate guard and summarily escorted to the antechamber.

*

Gömalt surveyed his small gathering. Besides Michàss, there was Anna, ensconced between a couple of his personal men, with Alber standing close by. The head of the serving staff had been summoned, along with Oddon, the chief cook. She was the only one of the castle's denizens for whom he had any respect. There was a woman who knew how to run a kitchen – she stood no nonsense from anybody and ruled her little kingdom with a rod of iron. The fact that it was ladle-shaped made no odds.

With the pieces of his puzzle gathered, he sent word to the baroness. She waltzed in a few minutes later as though she hadn't a care in the world, no doubt still excited by the arrival of the menhir texts and the advancement of their plans. For once she didn't take charge, but took a seat at the side of the chamber and left the proceedings in his hands.

It seemed fairly obvious to him that Kassandra had left the castle the evening before. What he didn't yet know was why. But putting himself in her shoes, he felt he had nonetheless formulated a reasonable idea of what must have happened. All he had to do was prove his suspicions to his own satisfaction.

He turned his attention first to Halfdanr. "I understand you had need to send someone over to the town yesterday?"

"That's right, sir."

"And you chose Michàss here, correct?"

Halfdanr nodded.

"Why him?"

"He had nothing better to do," Halfdanr replied with a shrug.

Gömalt raised an eyebrow. "He didn't volunteer?"

"Michàss isn't known for his volunteering."

The tiniest shadow of a doubt crossed Gömalt's mind, though he was careful not to let it show. "And you gave permission for him to take a horse?"

"Of course. How else would he have gone?"

Gömalt let the brusque reply pass for now. Halfdanr's position occasionally gave rise to a little arrogance. But as he wasn't the real subject of this interrogation, that was a matter that could be dealt with later.

Gömalt turned then to the cook. "My dear lady," he began, making a point of being nice to the woman who fed him, "apparently Mistress Kassandra was not feeling well last night. Were you aware of this?"

"I was told, sir. She sent young Anna there to fetch some food so she could eat in her chambers instead of in the great hall. I didn't see any harm in that."

"No, of course not. Do you recall what time this would have been?"

"Oh, I don't know, about the seventh hour, I suppose. I was busy and didn't take much notice, sir. As far as I'm concerned, Mistress Kassandra can do as she pleases."

Gömalt nodded. "Thank you."

"Will there be anything else? Only I don't like to be away from the kitchen too long at this time in the morning."

"Of course. So let it not be me who keeps you from such important duties."

The cook curtsied to the baroness, a curious manoeuvre, given her substantial girth. Gömalt felt sure that one day she would sink and fail to resurface.

After her departure, he turned his attention towards his two main suspects, though he addressed the baroness as he spoke.

"My lady, your daughter is neither in the castle, nor in its immediate vicinity."

"Not in itself a cause for alarm…"

"No, my lady. Until you consider the fact that wherever Kassandra slept last night, if at all, it was not in her bed."

The baroness said nothing.

"It is my belief that she has run away," Gömalt declared, turning to face Anna. "And, on the assumption that this is true, and leaving aside the why of it for now, I find myself asking, what would I need if I was a young lady wanting to escape Brath'daka? Hmm? The answer is, help. From someone I trust, someone close to me."

All eyes gravitated towards Anna. She paled.

Guilty.

"Yes, and I'd probably need a horse, too, if it was my intent to get away quickly. But therein lies a problem. You see, my lady," Gömalt cast a glance at the baroness before his gaze settled back on Anna, "the only horses hereabouts are kept, quite naturally, in the stables, and the only exit from that part of the castle big enough to pass a horse through is the main gate. Now, I would be the first to admit that our guards can be inattentive sluggards sometimes, but I think even they might manage to notice a girl on horseback passing through the portcullis – whatever the hour."

The baroness smiled, despite herself.

"That set me to thinking – what if I got someone else to take a horse out for me, say, earlier in the day? And then I remembered a little incident that occurred last night. You see, my lady," Gömalt switched his uncomfortable stare to Michàss, "as I was going about my business, I encountered this young man here, walking back to the castle. Walking, mind, not riding. So I had a quiet word with him. Fallen off his horse, he told me, and, oh dear, the beast had run off. Well, I thought no more about it at the time. But looking back on it now, I find myself thinking – how convenient. On the one hand we have ourselves a young lady in need of a horse, and on the other a young man who just *happens* to have lost one."

"Too convenient for your liking?" the baroness suggested.

"My lady, I'm not a believer in coincidence. Especially not when you consider that Michàss here is intimately involved with this wench," Gömalt said, gesturing towards Anna.

"Oh?" An eyebrow rose on the baroness's forehead. Gömalt knew that not much slipped past her in Brath'daka, but she'd evidently missed this little liaison.

"Indeed. And in my estimation, Anna is the most likely person our wayward household member would turn to for help."

Anna was trembling now.

Even more guilty.

Halfdanr coughed to get attention. "What about Michàss's head, sir? He clearly did have an accident. I cleaned his wound myself."

"Ah, yes, thank you for reminding me." Gömalt walked over to Michàss. "How is your head this morning, Michàss?" He clasped the young man amicably by the shoulder and steered him towards one of the windows where there was plenty of light. "Allow me to take a better look. After all, it was getting dark when we met last night, was it not?"

He bent Michàss's head forwards, not quite as amicably, and examined the spot where skull and stone had apparently met. His inspection was brief; he didn't need long to dispel any of the doubts that had crept in earlier. Satisfied, he stepped back several paces and withdrew a dagger from his waist band. He held it up at eye-level and made a show of observing its tip, testing it with his finger. Point made, he moved over to one of the side tables and picked up a rock about the size of his fist, an item he had collected earlier. He weighed both, almost giving the impression he might start juggling.

"Sir, am I still needed?" Halfdanr asked.

The head servant had suddenly become nervous, Gömalt noticed. Good.

"Stay a while."

Halfdanr nodded. He wasn't happy.

Gömalt moved back to where he'd left Michàss standing. "In my line of work, Michàss, I get to know a lot about wounds. What they look like, what causes them – *how* to cause them. If you were to ask me, the cut on the back of your head doesn't look like it was made by one of these," he lightly tossed the rock up and down in his left hand, "it looks to me more like it was made by one of these…"

For the second time in the space of a day, Gömalt pressed his dagger hard up under Michàss's chin. This time it drew blood.

"You see, Michàss, a rock makes a cut like this…" with lightning speed, he lashed upwards with the granite lump, striking a vicious blow to the side of Michàss's head, crushing ear against skull. Bone cracked.

Anna cried out. She lunged forwards, trying to reach Michàss before he fell. She was stopped in her tracks by a savage backhand from Alber. A hard blow, it nearly broke her jaw. She was too stunned even to cry out in pain. The two henchmen grabbed her by the arms, preventing the possibility of another step being taken.

Michàss staggered drunkenly for a moment before crashing to the floor. Struggling to remain conscious, he dry-retched several times.

Gömalt knelt down and carried on in a perfectly reasonable tone of voice, "A knife, on the other hand…" he gripped a handful of Michàss's hair and yanked his head backwards, "well, a knife makes a cut like this…"

The point of the dagger tore a crimson gash across Michàss's throat, slicing deeply through the soft, jowly flesh. Unable to cry out, the young man's body thrashed, emitting a choked gurgle as frothy blood bubbled from his lips. His futile struggle quickly subsided as the fingers of death locked him in their immutable grip, wringing the last few breaths out of him in a rasping hiss.

Gömalt released his grip. Michàss's head slumped to the floor with a dull thud, his sightless eyes locked on Anna's stricken face.

The moment of silence that followed was shattered by a hysterical scream. Possessed of manic strength, Anna unleashed a frenzied struggle against her captors. It was all they could do to keep their grip. Gömalt watched with a bemused smile on his lips. The fight within the maid was soon spent, though. She was left a panting, sobbing wreck suspended between two utterly indifferent pillars.

The baroness rose from her seat and walked over to where Michàss's lifeless body lay in a slowly expanding pool of blood. Gömalt suddenly realised it was the first time she'd ever witnessed him at work, despite being the source of most of his orders. She regarded the corpse with something akin to curiosity, her head cocked to one side. When she looked up, she appeared flushed and excited.

"You do have a certain propensity for making a mess of the floor in here, Gömalt."

"Sorry, my lady," he mumbled, not quite able to hide a smile.

"I trust you had no further questions for him."

"Oh, I think anything useful he could have told us will be just as ably supplied by the wench." Gömalt threw a wolfish grin at Anna. "It shouldn't take long to find out what we need to know."

The baroness nodded. "I'll leave things in your capable hands, then. I trust you'll come and tell me when you're done."

"Of course, my lady."

The baroness made to leave. She passed Anna as she headed for the door but, in what seemed an afterthought, she stopped, retraced her steps and took hold of Anna's smarting chin in a cruel grip.

"A word of advice, girl – tell Gömalt what he wants to know. He has a penchant for making life unpleasant if he doesn't get what he wants."

Once the baroness had left the antechamber, Gömalt turned to Anna. The look on his face was brutish and malevolent. His lecherous anticipation was distracted only by the sound of Halfdanr being violently sick.

Gömalt sneered; perhaps cleaning up the mess of Michàss's demise would be a suitable lesson for failing to kerb his arrogance.

*

Half an hour later, Gömalt ascended the steps that rose from the lower regions of the castle, all his suppositions confirmed.

His face was set in a mask of suppressed annoyance. What he had learned was worrying. Now he faced the task of informing the baroness of exactly what her daughter was doing. And why.

He found Daka in her dayroom, engrossed in weaving a tapestry. He took a moment to watch her before making his presence known. She was an extraordinary woman; strong, iron-willed, capable of pulling together an alliance of feuding lords and giving them a common purpose – and maybe a little something to fear – and yet, almost at the drop of a hat, able to engage in such a delicate endeavour as needlework. Not an hour ago had she calmly watched a man's throat being slit, right there at her feet. Now here she was relaxing in her favourite surroundings, sewing. He shook his head in something that amounted to awe.

The baroness didn't look up from her work when he cleared his throat and entered the chamber.

"What news of my daughter?"

"She is attempting to reach the Alondrians, my lady. She left last night, at about the tenth hour as far as I can make out."

"You can catch her?"

"I would think so. She's heading for the Stroth Ford. There's only one logical route she can take from Brath'daka and I doubt she will have made particularly good progress during the night."

"You'd better get going, then."

"Yes, my lady. There is one more thing, however. I was curious to know why Kassandra should suddenly decide to take flight like this."

"And…?"

"It appears she witnessed the events in the antechamber yesterday afternoon."

The baroness stopped working on the tapestry and gave him a stern look.

"According to the wench, she saw me kill the scribes. Apparently it – *upset* her."

"I see." After a pause, the baroness resumed her sewing. "I don't care what she saw. I do care about what she may have overheard. Did Anna reveal anything of that?"

"She did. Kassandra heard enough to know that we're planning an operation against the Alondrians, though she has none of the details."

"Are you sure about that?"

"There are no certainties, my lady, but I assure you, I did press the wench on that point."

"I have no doubt," the baroness smiled. "Is she still alive?"

"Yes, my lady. What do you want done with her? Should I release her?"

"No." The baroness didn't even hesitate – or miss a stitch. "Leave her with the gaolers. She can serve as a warning to others, lest anyone else in my household has ideas of asserting their independence."

"Very good, my lady. And Kassandra? She will try to warn the Alondrians. I believe she intends to use her information as a bargaining chip. It is crucial that she be stopped."

"Without question."

"What if she does make it into their hands?"

"Stop at nothing. Bring her back if you can, but don't hesitate to kill her if you must. I'll not allow that wretched girl to ruin my destiny."

Gömalt's heart beat a little faster. That was the order he'd been hoping for.

The hunt was on. The hunt for a Daka, no less. It was a quest he could never have dreamed of until today.

14

'when Those of Grace hear again,
the Unwilled One comes.
times of great strife are His path.
under the heel of a new Master the Land will reel.
as water divides, so shall the Peoples be,
then by their own hearts will They be betrayed.'

Chancellor Gÿldan observed the twelve mages of the Cymàtseà for any sign they were ready to continue. A copy the prophecy Nikrá had received a while ago sat before each of them. These had been the subject of intense scrutiny for some time already, but as no one caught his eye, he decided to allow them a little longer before proceeding. The mages' council was not one that appreciated being rushed; he of all people knew that.

With his thoughts wandering, his attention alighted, as it often did, on the translucent table around which they were all seated. One of a kind, it had been grown from a single crystal shard under decades of Taümathic manipulation. Its polished, mirror-like surface presently only reflected the gently swaying flames of the chamber's lamps, but it could, when occasion demanded, be pressed into service as a scrying pool to divine matters far beyond the walls of the Cymàtagé. Though that took the combined effort of a full council to achieve these days, he reminded himself. The mages of old who had created the table had been considerably more able than those who communed around it now.

He felt a pang of regret that so much knowledge, so much ability, had been lost in recent generations, thanks largely to the intrusions of the Dinac-Mentà. Their influence had become too pervasive by far. No one dared to experiment anymore. With such a dangerous sect lurking in the shadows, boundaries were not pushed and radical paths went untrodden. Fear of denunciation as a Natural had suppressed magely creativity almost to the point of extinction. Stick to being a Follower of the Path; learn only what has gone before; don't get too close to the edge – that's how it went these days.

Gÿldan sighed inwardly. He so desired to begin the reversal of that travesty. As the Cymàtagé's chancellor, he was the head of the most prestigious Taümathic establishment in the known world. If anyone was in a position to try, it was him. But he was under no illusions. Clipping the wings of the Dinac-Mentà was a matter that had to be handled with great care.

It occurred to him that the prophecy the council was here to discuss this evening might prove a driving force for change; it was, after all, a matter deeply rooted in history, portending events of a potentially tumultuous nature. The past was reaching out to the present. The disquiet it caused him whenever he thought about it made him sure the earth was going to tremble before the matter was laid to rest. If the odd Dinac-Mentà bastion should happen to crumble in the process, he wouldn't shed a tear.

With another sigh, this one audible, he heaved himself up out of his chair and smoothed his silken robes at the front before addressing the gathering.

"Gentlemen, as I'm sure you'll agree, it is a grave matter that Nikrá has brought before us. I have known of the prophecy for a while, but I felt now was the time to air it more formally amongst the Cymàtseà." He turned to Nikrá. "My friend, would you be kind enough to share with the council what you told me earlier?"

Nikrá rose to his feet. The old mage's robes were rather more shabby than those worn by the rest of the council, but he didn't seem bothered. Nor did he pay any heed to the usual preening ritual most mages conducted when they became the centre of attention.

"Chancellor, my fellow council members," he began, nodding round. "When this prophecy landed on me, I knew it was a little different from my usual revelations."

"In what way?" Mage Lödmick demanded.

"Well, for a start, I had no sense of its meaning. Nor did I know who it was for." Nikrá lapsed back into his seat with a grunt. "Forgive my old bones," he muttered. "Anyway, as I pondered the matter, a nagging feeling began to plague me; this prophecy had been seen before. I have to confess, I struggled for several weeks trying to place it, until eventually I turned to my good friend, Akmir. With his help we discovered that my revelation was already recorded in the writings of the great prophet, Amatt the Blind."

Some of the Cymàtseà were silenced by their surprise. Shocked murmurs escaped from others. Without exception, Nikrá was held with rapt attention.

Gÿldan smiled at the effect. "Amatt's record showed your prophecy word for word, did it not?" he added, to ensure that point was fully understood by all.

"There were minor differences, Chancellor, but only the result of a choice in how to translate certain words. To alleviate any doubt, I asked the Head of Ancient Studies, the esteemed Sömat, to corroborate my findings. He has kindly retranslated my words into A'lyavine, just as I did, and has carried out a comparison with the original. He has arrived at the same conclusion as Akmir and me – Amatt's prophecy and mine are one and the same."

Further murmurs fluttered round the table, accompanied by a few raised eyebrows.

Gÿldan rose to his feet again. "Gentlemen, what you have before you is Amatt's only unfulfilled prophecy. It is less well known amongst his other works…"

"Why's that?" Lödmick interrupted again.

Gÿldan sighed. Lödmick looked to be on his usual tedious form this evening.

"Amatt expressed reservations about it. The reasons for his doubts are not recorded. However, we feel it may have had something to do with the length of time between the coming of the revelation and its intended fulfilment. You must remember, all of Amatt's other prophecies either saw their fulfilment during his lifetime or within a generation of his passing."

Lödmick frowned. "Chancellor, has there been some sign that this prophecy is coming to pass now?"

"Not as far as we know – except that it has returned," Gÿldan answered. "The point is, this prophecy has been in abeyance for more than a thousand years. We think that Amatt might have had a sense of this intended delay, making him less certain about it than he was with his others."

"Equally, he could have been unsure simply because it was incorrect, misled – who knows?" Lödmick proffered with a shrug.

Gÿldan suppressed the huff that wanted to escape. Lödmick always had to be the one to pick holes. He was a great one for arguing and delving into unnecessary detail. It would have been nice to be rid of the man from the council. Sadly, just being annoying wasn't sufficient a reason to give him the boot.

"But, consider the fact that this prophecy has been given twice," Gÿldan went on. "That in itself is unusual. To be false *twice*, too? I believe the fact that Nikrá has received the very same word is a good indication of its probable authenticity."

That silenced Lödmick for the moment, Gÿldan was relieved to note. He just hoped the man didn't pursue the one avenue that could still be a possibility – that Nikrá may have subconsciously regurgitated the ancient revelation having read it at some point in the long-forgotten past. The old prophet had, after all, been in the prediction business for a considerable number of years. He would almost certainly have studied some of Amatt's writings at one time or another during his long career.

Deputy Chancellor Nÿat spoke without rising to his feet. "Nikrá, you are of the opinion that the time draws near for the fulfilment of this prophecy?"

Nikrá nodded. "I do sense that."

"A specific revelation?" Lödmick challenged.

"No. But you must remember, all aspects of prophecy are 'sense and feeling'. Rarely are they delivered on something as definitive as slips of paper – much though I wish they were."

Gÿldan smiled. Nikrá had always been a rather reluctant prophet. "Gentlemen, Nikrá is not known for putting the fox in the henhouse without reason. I am of the opinion that we should trust his judgement on this." It was sometimes dangerous trying to steer the Cymàtseà so directly; expressing an opinion usually precipitated others to express theirs, often to the contrary. He was pleasantly surprised by the lack of dissension at this point, even from Lödmick. Matters of far lesser importance frequently resulted in hours of wrangling before a consensus was reached. "So, let us move on to consider what this prophecy might mean. Nikrá, have you anything further to add?"

The old mage shook his head. "My lack of insight into its meaning has bothered me greatly."

"The trouble with most prophecies," Nÿat grumbled, "is that there always seems to be scope for ambiguity."

Akmir, an oftentimes invited guest to the council's meetings, let out a bemused grunt, drawing a degree of attention to himself that he probably hadn't intended.

"Brother, you have something to share with us?" Gÿldan prompted.

The old monk looked up sharply from the table. "My apologies,

Chancellor. I was merely reminded of the reason why I prefer my job to Nikrá's. We of the Adak-rann are called upon to look back at history, not predict the future."

"Indeed, but with your analytical mind, Brother, if this was a piece of history, how would you go about interpreting it?"

"Ah."

Gÿldan chuckled quietly. The Adak-rann weren't accustomed to being put under pressure; time waits for no man, but history was there to be dipped into at leisure. Rarely was there any need for urgency – though that never seemed to diminish the brotherhood's fervour.

"Well, I suppose I'd start by dividing it up and trying to deal with it piece by piece."

"Go on…"

Akmir ruffled the hair on the back of his head as he read out the whole prophecy once more.

> *'when Those of Grace hear again,*
> *the Unwilled One comes.*
> *times of great strife are His path.*
> *under the heel of a new Master the Land will reel.*
> *as water divides, so shall the Peoples be,*
> *then by their own hearts will They be betrayed.'*

"Well, there seems to be several different sections. For a start, take the first sentence, clearly there are references to two distinct entities here. You've got *those of Grace*, who are going to hear something, suggesting that they don't hear it at the moment, whatever *it* happens to be. Then you've got this *Unwilled One*, whom I'm supposing is going to be unpopular."

"A supposition based on what?" Lödmick asked.

"In light of the next part – strife, reeling under heels and so forth," Akmir replied. "The link between this *Unwilled One* and the coming of this strife seems fairly clear, suggesting that one brings the other. The link between *those of Grace* and the *Unwilled One* is more tenuous – there isn't much to indicate one way or the other whether they are together or opposed."

Akmir reread the whole text again to himself, mumbling under his breath.

"At this point I need to clarify something." He turned to the Head of Ancient Studies. "Mage Sömat, the prophecies Amatt received –

they were mostly warnings, were they not?"

Sömat nodded. He ringed his ample grey beard between thumb and forefinger and drew it down to a point before letting it go again. "Generally speaking, yes."

"Warnings for Amatt and his people?"

"Yes."

"And as Alondrians, we are Amatt's descendants, are we not?"

"If you want to view it in such terms, I suppose you could say that." Sömat paused, stroked his beard again, then added, "But you have to remember, Alondria wasn't Alondria during Amatt's time. He died in 141 Before Foundation. He merely lived in lands that are now part of our country."

Akmir nodded and went back to his thinking. Gÿldan noted that the rest of the Cymàtseà seemed quite happy to leave him centre stage. It was a refreshing change – the usual problem was getting them to hold their tongues.

"Right, well, I'd say we're in trouble, then," Akmir concluded. "Whoever this *Unwilled One* is, he's coming. I'd say that this prophecy is a warning of times ahead, these *times of great strife* it mentions." He paused to glance around the table, only to be met with deepening furrows of concern. "This reference to a *new master* is particularly worrying. It smacks to me of something like an invasion, perhaps the coming of an oppressor, a new ruler maybe. One that the people do not want, hence the title of *Unwilled One*." He paused once more, before adding more hesitantly, "Although, having said that, I find it a curious title in many respects."

"How so?"

Lödmick. Again.

Akmir raised his eyebrows in a kind of shrug. "Well, it's so ambiguous; it could be almost anything. As you know, A'lyavine is a very contextually sensitive language. The only way to interpret this *Unwilled One* reference is in the light of the subsequent text – *times of great strife are His path*. It seems to me he brings this strife with him. That suggests to me that the people aren't going to want him around. One might, therefore, even call him the *Unwanted One*, or the *Undesired One*."

Gÿldan had to admit to his being impressed. He may have put Akmir on the spot, but the Adak-rann blood in the old monk's veins had risen to the challenge admirably.

"And the last part, Brother, this division it speaks of, any thoughts on that?"

Akmir re-read the last line aloud,
> *'as water divides, so shall the Peoples be,*
> *then by their own hearts will They be betrayed.'*

He took a deep breath and let it out though his nose. "Tricky. No real context in which to place it. It could suggest division by way of land being annexed, for example. Or it could be indicative of a division between people, such as between those who might support an invader and those who do not. That might explain this betrayal reference at the end. No way to be sure, I'm afraid."

"What about the water reference?" Nÿat asked. "How does water divide? A flood, perhaps?"

Eyes that had momentarily flicked to Nÿat quickly switched back to Akmir. The old monk shrugged. "No idea."

There was a deflated pause. Gÿldan glanced round the table, but it was clear that no one else was ready to take up the reins.

"Well, thank you for your insight, Brother. So, let me see if I can summarise where we are. It seems to me we have the possibility of an invader, heralded by persons unknown, who are going to hear something, but we don't know what. This invader is going to cause strife and be an unpopular ruler, which is going to cause some sort of division. Is that about the size of it?"

"Don't forget the betrayal," Nÿat added, his tone more than a little morose.

There was another awkward pause, punctuated only by a few fairly non-committal nods. From Gÿldan's point of view, the great thing about an almost transparent table was that he could see who was fidgeting. There were clearly some uncomfortable Cymàtseà members present.

"If this thing *is* a warning, what are we supposed to do about it?" Nikrá asked. "I mean, aren't we supposed to prepare or something?"

Mage Dümarr, Head of Philosophy, raised an eyebrow. "Interesting point, Nikrá. Inevitability. The Mages' Path teaches that a prophecy is merely a foretelling of that which is to come, just as history is a post-telling of that which has already occurred. Now if that be true, then we can no more stop this than we can go into the past and change that. Something prophesied correctly has already come to pass, only it hasn't, if you see what I mean."

Nikrá chuckled. "That's deep thinking, my friend."

"Indeed," Lödmick said, "but Dümarr has made a good point. We can't escape a *true* prophecy. So the question we must ask ourselves is, how true do we believe this prophecy to be?"

Gÿldan's heart momentarily sank. "I thought we'd agreed earlier that there were good grounds for taking this one seriously," he pointed out, trying to mask his annoyance. He didn't want to have to go through the whole justification argument again.

"Alright, so I repeat my earlier question, what do we do?" Nikrá asked.

The flood of suggestions was underwhelming.

Gÿldan sighed. Being the chancellor did have a few drawbacks; by default, he was always the one who had to pick up the pieces when no one else rose to the challenge.

"We do the only thing we can. We remain vigilant. We wait, and we watch for any sign of the prophecy coming to pass."

"We should inform the palace of our concerns, too," Nÿat observed, his tone if anything even more morose than before. "There might not be much we can do about it, but they won't thank us for keeping them in the dark."

Gÿldan's heart sank further, though he hid it well. Nÿat was right. They couldn't keep the Crown out of something that might materially affect the wellbeing of the entire country. Politics and matters of a Taümathic nature didn't mix, the Mages' War centuries earlier had taught that. Inviolate laws now existed to prevent one from encroaching upon the other, precisely to avoid the atrocities of the past. Yet it was sometimes hard to keep them apart. In this instance, it wouldn't be wise even to try.

But such cheery tidings wouldn't go down well in the palace, that much was certain. Princess Midana wasn't renowned for receiving bad news gracefully, and the threat of another ruler coming on the scene was about as bad as news could get. It was guaranteed to put her in a black mood.

Oh for the days when Althar dealt with matters of state, he mused. He decided to change the subject rather than contemplate how to handle the palace just now.

"While we're here, there is one other matter I'd like to raise. Just a small one – the up and coming Trials and Selection ceremony." There were groans round the table. Gÿldan grinned. "You'll be pleased to know that the post of Overseer for the tests will not be chosen by lot this time round."

"It won't? Oh, thank the gods for that," Dümarr muttered with relief.

Gÿldan noticed several members of the Cymàtseà nod in wholehearted agreement. The admission of new acolytes to the Cymàtagé only occurred once every three years, but that was still far too frequently for the likes of most of those present. Having the halls flooded with new blood only led to disruption, not to mention the sufferance of a whole new set of pranks; only they were never really new, the acolytes merely thought they were. It always took a year or so for students to settle down into a more acceptable pace and adopt the sense of propriety and decorum preferred by the older mages.

"Rhonnin has volunteered."

"Volunteered?" Dümarr spluttered. "My hat's off to him. But why did he want to go and do that? Nobody volunteers to be Overseer."

Gÿldan chuckled. "Well, all I can tell you is, he came to me."

Dümarr shook his head. "Well good on him. Saves the rest of us a lot of bother."

"Actually, it's my fault."

Everyone suddenly found themselves looking at Nikrá again.

"I told him he should speak to the Chancellor about offering his services."

This was news even to Gÿldan. "Did you indeed? Why was that, then?"

Nikrá shrugged. "I believe this time round we need someone with his sensibilities to make the choices."

"Is this another prophecy?" Lödmick asked with suspicion.

Nikrá shifted uneasily in his seat. "Possibly, though not in the normal sense."

Amazingly, Lödmick didn't voice another question. His frown did it for him.

"I've got a feeling that someone is coming who might slip through the net unless Rhonnin is there to spot their talents," Nikrá explained.

"Rhonnin is a healer," Sömat observed.

"Indeed. His gifts border on the prophetic. He has an ability to look inside a person. As a physician, he uses it to determine what ails his patients. But I think on this occasion he is meant to spot talents hidden deep within one of those who will be presenting themselves for selection in a few weeks' time."

So, we could have a new healer on the way, Gÿldan mused. Good. Abilities like that were exactly the sort of thing he wanted to promote. It was high time the Cymàtagé started to be useful again, instead of churning out tricksters whose only value was at banquets.

15

Torrin-Ashur threw a twig into the embers of a small camp fire just beyond his feet and idly watched as the heat dried the slither of sapwood. New flames sprang up, bringing a brief flicker of life to the stagnant ashes. Within moments there was nothing left but a few wisps of smoke curling up through the branches of the surrounding trees.

It had come as a surprise to discover that laying ambushes could be really boring. Being sent up to the Stroth Ford with orders to pick up the trail of an enemy patrol had initially sounded exciting. Covertly shadowing the Tsnath to find out what they were doing had seemed a great way to make a real contribution to Kirshtahll's cause. So far, though, the operation had involved little more than digging holes, an activity to which the Pressed were no strangers.

He thought about making the trip forwards to check on the lookouts at the ford. So that the men didn't have to crawl around in a permanent state of stealth, the main camp had been set up some way back from the river. The consequence of that was a regular, and now tedious, quarter-mile jaunt to keep an eye on things.

Spotting his new sergeant threading through the trees stalled his efforts to rise from the patch of soft pine needles that had been his seat for the last hour.

"Change of watch has just gone in, sir," Nash said as he tramped up to the camp fire. Tick handed him a mug of tea. "Nothing else to report."

Torrin-Ashur was still getting used to having Nash around. The man didn't cut a particularly imposing figure; he was of average height and on the leaner side of medium build. Yet a hard, weathered edge to him spoke volumes about his experience in the field.

Nash's assignment to the Pressed had been a surprise. Part of the permanent standing army, he'd been assigned to Borádin until a few weeks ago. More than that, he'd been the very man who'd come to present the nobleman's shield after the call-out. Borádin's departure from Mitcha had put him at a loose end. Then Major Riagán had had the bright idea that he might be useful in helping knock the Pressed into shape for active duty.

"Nothing else to report," Torrin-Ashur repeated. "You know something, Sergeant, I'm beginning to wonder if we're in the right place."

"Six hundred miles of border, sir. Here's as good a place as any."

"That's what's worrying me. The Stroth Ford is an obvious point to cross the river. But I wonder how obvious it is to the Tsnath?"

Nash cocked his head to one side. "They know this region pretty well, sir. I doubt they'd have overlooked it."

"Exactly. Would *you* choose a route that was so obvious to your enemy?"

A frown creased Nash's brow. "Put like that, perhaps not. But where else, sir? If we're going to attempt to pick up one of their patrols, we've got to try somewhere."

"I know, I know." Torrin-Ashur aired his frustration with a huff. He climbed to his feet, flicked some cold tea at a nearby bush and tossed his empty mug at Tick. "I've been thinking of reconnoitring along the river bank."

Nash's frown deepened.

"I just want to look for signs of recent crossings, that's all. I'm an Ashur, don't forget. Knowing my luck, the enemy has probably skirted our position and is laughing at us from behind."

Nash didn't look convinced. But he seemed up for a walk.

"Tick, get a message over to Lieutenant D'Amada. Tell him we've gone downstream. We won't be long, an hour or so perhaps."

"Aye, sir." Tick gave a casual salute that resembled a tugged forelock.

Torrin-Ashur led the way into the trees, heading east on a diagonal course aimed at converging with the river well downstream of the ford. He was losing faith that the Tsnath were ever going to make an appearance, but that didn't mean he was going to ruin all the preparations they'd made by blundering up to the forward observation point and giving the whole game away.

The forest grew ever more dense the further they went, hampering their progress with a mesh of low branchlets that seemed to exist for the sole purpose of knitting the trees together. The mostly dead wood was dry and brittle, and despite best efforts at a modicum of stealth, silence and forward motion were mutually exclusive. They pushed, cracked and snapped their way through half a mile of resisting brush before eventually catching a glimpse of the Ablath through the matted tangle. Nearer the water's edge the forest gave way to a stretch of open scrub.

"What the..." Nash muttered in surprise as he emerged from the tree-line.

"Sergeant?"

Nash pointed forwards with a thrust of his chin.

Standing in the middle of the river, about three hundred yards further downstream, was what seemed to be the end of a castle, just a circular stone tower, squat in appearance, with a short length of wall leading up to it from the downstream side. There wasn't even an island for it to sit on. It simply rose straight up out of the water.

"Oh, that," Torrin-Ashur said, "nobody really knows what it is."

"Who built it?"

"No idea. It's been there for centuries."

"As Lord of the March, not even your father knows?" Nash persisted.

"It's just one of those things – lost to the mists of time."

The odd structure certainly bore the signs of antiquity. Moss covered substantial areas of its stonework and a small tree, clinging on by a few gnarly roots, protruded awkwardly from the north-facing side. The buttresses, green with algae, had clearly withstood many years of the river's abrasive flow. What had probably started out as a pointed water-break at the base of the tower was now a well-rounded promontory.

"Could it be a lookout post, perhaps?"

Torrin-Ashur shrugged. "I've heard people call them Sentinels. But it's not really tall enough to be of any use. If that was its purpose, it would have been better placed on high ground. Why put it in the middle of the Ablath?"

"The river makes a good moat."

"But it still serves no strategic purpose," Torrin-Ashur countered. "You'd be lucky to fit a couple of archers up it. Hardly a threat. An enemy could easily skirt round it."

Nash conceded the point with a nod. "You said *them* – I take it this isn't the only one, sir?"

Nash didn't miss much, Torrin-Ashur noted. He began making his way along the bank. "I'm told there are six in all, strung out along the Ablath, though I've only seen the ones west of here. A few summers ago, my father took my brother and me on a trip upriver to the Great

Inland Mäss. There's one a few miles inland from the mouth of the river, and another in the middle of Loch Masson, on a tiny island. Masson's big – even with a longbow you couldn't get an arrow from the tower to the shore."

From the far side, looking back upstream, it became evident that the short, wedge-shaped section of wall leading up to the tower supported a flight of steps. They rose from the waterline to a thin gap in the tower's parapet. Access was clearly intended, albeit initially by boat.

The strange tower held Nash's attention until it had receded behind them. Torrin-Ashur had given up wondering about it a long time ago. He'd been up it as a boy. As a crow's nest on a buccaneer ship it had been fun. But as a relic from a forgotten past it hadn't been able to retain its enigmatic air for long.

As they continued along the river the tree-line gradually retreated from the bank and the scrub gave way to grassland, making it easier to cover the ground. With hardly a cloud in the sky it was a balmy afternoon, which went some way towards making up for an otherwise disappointing lack of evidence of recent activity. Torrin-Ashur almost wished the Tsnath *had* been through – at least then he could legitimately pack up camp and find something more interesting to do. They continued on until the Ablath sank into a minor ravine, making crossing that much harder.

"Might as well head back," he suggested. "It's doubtful the Tsnath would have tried crossing further downstream."

The strange tower eventually drifted back into view, but Nash didn't mention it again. They'd lapsed into an agreeable silence, allowing Torrin-Ashur's thoughts to wander to the beauty of the landscape. It was satisfying to know that this land was his, or rather, his father's. Not that it was good for much except raising mosquitoes, he mused sourly. The soil wasn't that fertile, so crops didn't fare well. Nor did the timber seem to reach a particularly good stature. In fact, now that he came to think of it, it was a wonder the Tsnath ever bothered with the place. The only thing the March of Ashur could really boast was an abundance of venison on the hoof, something the Tsnath weren't exactly short of themselves. Yet still they came, year after year, as though harrying the hamlets was a duty.

The snap of a branch somewhere ahead yanked his thoughts back to the present with a jolt. They had just passed the Sentinel and were about to head back into the trees. With a quick glance at Nash, he took cover amongst the low shrubs. The sound of more branches being brushed aside filtered out from the undergrowth. Nash quietly withdrew his sword.

It was unnecessary caution. With a sigh of relief Torrin-Ashur stood up – too suddenly for the newcomer's liking.

"Bloody 'ell!" Tick exclaimed, clasping hand to chest to calm a hammering heart.

"Tick, what are you doing here?"

"Corporal Botfiár sent me, sir. Somethink's goin' on back at the ford."

Buoyed by a sense of excitement, Torrin-Ashur led the charge back into the trees, abandoning stealth in favour of speed. The tangle of dead wood did its worst, reducing them to little more than a trot, but they made it back to camp in good time.

After a quick briefing from Botfiár, Nash ordered Silfast to follow on with some of the archers.

"We're not supposed to be engaging the Tsnath," Torrin-Ashur murmured quietly, not wanting to countermand the sergeant in front of the men.

"I know, sir. But things don't always go according to plan. Better safe than sorry." Nash turned to Silfast. "Just make sure you approach the ford quietly and stay out of sight."

Torrin-Ashur let Nash take the lead as they set off towards the forward observation point. They passed a number of manned dugouts along the way. At each one Nash made sure the men were ready to relay alerts back to camp. Using arrows, messages could be passed back from the front in under a minute.

When the river came into view again Torrin-Ashur dropped to his belly, inching his way forwards.

One of the lookouts noticed his approach and held up a hand. The man backed away from the foremost dugout, nestled behind a line of shrubs close to the riverbank. Torrin-Ashur waited.

"Sir, we appear to have activity across the river," Millardis whispered. "There has been some movement through the trees – several horses, I believe."

"Any attempt to cross?"

"Not as yet, sir. We've not actually seen them."

Torrin-Ashur's brow creased as he glanced at Nash. "If the Tsnath intend to cross, wouldn't they wait until nightfall?"

Nash nodded. "Aye, sir. A daylight crossing would be an

unnecessary risk."

Torrin-Ashur smiled. At last, something to pique his interest. "M'Lud, get over to Lieutenant D'Amada's position and appraise him of the situation."

"As you wish, sir."

Torrin-Ashur smiled. Millardis had earned his nickname on account of his aristocratic accent. He'd been head of the serving staff in a noble house until a liberal attitude towards the silverware had landed him in the Pressed. Despite his reduced status, the man just didn't seem able to shake the habits of his former position when addressing his superiors.

"Would you like me to bring the lieutenant back here, sir?"

Torrin-Ashur thought for a moment, then shook his head. "No. Having too many men here might give away our position."

M'Lud nodded and moved off at the crawling equivalent of a fast sprint.

Torrin-Ashur carefully manoeuvred forwards, sliding down the gentle slope on a raft of pine needles, staying below the cover of the riverside shrubs.

When he reached the dugout, he found the hole inexorably filling up with water. The log that had been placed across the bottom for the lookouts to put their feet on was now almost submerged.

He settled into the damp hole and began scanning the opposite side of the river. Many hours over the last week had been spent becoming familiar with its every detail. He stared intently, willing there to be Tsnath hidden beyond the fringe of dense pines, but try as he might, there was nothing visible except vegetation. His concentration eventually drifted to the sizable glade a little to the right of their position.

A full five minutes passed before the sound of a horse whinnying in the trees rolled across the water. A gruff shout and the scrabble of riders pushing unseen through the undergrowth followed. Then things went quiet again. A long minute of frustrating silence ensued.

Suddenly, a shrill scream pierced the air. Torrin-Ashur flinched. A deeper cry, one of pain, came next, followed by a bout of what was almost certainly Tsnathsarré swearing.

A few seconds later, a single horse bolted out of the trees on the far right of the glade. Tearing diagonally across the open stretch of scrub, its rider lashed reins from side to side in a furious bid to gain speed. Two more riders burst into view and took up pursuit. The first rapidly began to pound across the glade. The second fell behind, nursing an injured arm.

It took Torrin-Ashur a few moments to realise that the quarry in this chase was a woman. Her features were too distant to be clear, her clothes perhaps too manly, but only a woman could have had such a cloud of auburn locks billowing out behind her. He watched, confused and fascinated. Whatever was going on, this was no attempt to invade Alondria by stealth.

Another three horses came crashing out of the trees on the left side of the glade, intent on cutting off the woman before she could reach the ford. With a quick glance over her shoulder, she veered away, angling directly towards the riverbank. In a matter of seconds she covered the remaining ground and spurred her horse into the water. She all but disappeared in a maelstrom of spray.

Most of her momentum was lost as her mount began to heave against in the deepening waters of the Ablath. A decent sized horse could cross the Stroth Ford without having to swim. She had entered downstream, where the water was deeper.

The nearest pursuer reached the water's edge and plunged in. Four more men appeared at the edge of the tree line, directly opposite the dugout.

Seeing them sent a shot of fear coursing through Torrin-Ashur. His guts tightened. He felt a slight wave of giddiness wash over him. He dismissed it as excitement.

"Archers!" he hissed.

Whoever this fugitive was, it was obvious the Tsnath were not about to let her reach the Alondrian side of the river.

The rider with the injured arm gave up the chase. The other three reached the bank and ploughed their way into the Ablath. Their progress immediately slowed to a crawl. That clearly wasn't going to matter. The rider who had chased the woman right across the glade was well ahead of them. His expertise in the saddle was obvious. Inexorably the gap between him and the woman narrowed. By mid-river he caught up. He grabbed the bridle of her horse, fending off a hopelessly ineffectual barrage of slaps and blows.

Amidst the mêlée the woman screamed something in Tsnathsarré.

Torrin-Ashur didn't need to understand the words. Terror was terror. Something inside him snapped. Without conscious intention, his legs propelled him upwards out of the dugout and into full view of the oncoming Tsnath.

His appearance distracted the woman's attacker. She lashed out with a small blade, catching her assailant on the jaw, slicing his flesh to the bone. He swore vehemently. Relinquishing her bridle, he peeled away, clutching his face.

He was not out of action for long. Shouting a command to his men on the bank, he made a chopping sign with a blood-soaked hand and pointed at the woman. The Tsnath archers immediately brought their bows to bear.

The world around Torrin-Ashur began to slow to a crawl. His head swam with dizziness. He recognised the symptoms; it was the call-out all over again. The same, elemental beat and sense of unbridled power began coursing through him, bringing with it total clarity of thought. He snatched up a bow belonging to one of the lookouts. In one fluid move, he slung a quiver across his back, rose, nocked an arrow and let loose. The shot went wide of the mark by just a fraction, thudding into the trunk of a tree inches from the face of one of the enemy archers. The man dived for cover the instant his wits had caught up with him.

The other Tsnath riders faltered in their pursuit, looking to their leader for guidance. Ignoring them, he sat in the middle of the river, his face a blood-soaked scowl, staring at Torrin-Ashur.

The lookout next to Nash began laying down a suppressing volley. It was quickly answered. A furious exchange erupted. Arrows crisscrossed the Ablath as three of the Tsnath archers switched their aim. One continued to concentrate on stopping the woman. His first shot missed, going high. The next went wide. His third set an arrow into the exposed flank of the woman's horse. The creature gave out a loud whinny and quickly began to struggle against the Ablath's current.

Torrin-Ashur and the lookout redoubled their efforts, letting loose with arrow after arrow in a desperate bid to make the Tsnath archers take cover. The enemy's reply thudded into the ground all around the dugout and the embankment beyond.

Torrin-Ashur was oblivious to the danger. His ears pounded with an all-encompassing beat. Its intensity grew with each passing moment. Its power overwhelmed him, flooding him with an absolute sense of purpose.

"She'll never make it!" he cried, thrusting his bow at Nash. He charged off towards the river, pounding into the water before the sergeant could object. A string of curses against all things impulsive chased after him.

The woman frantically goaded her horse onwards. Her efforts were increasingly futile. Weakened by the arrow in its flank, the creature was disorientated and rapidly becoming unresponsive.

An Alondrian arrow found a mark, bursting through the neck of a Tsnath archer, throwing him off his feet. He landed in a writhing heap. There was a brief lull in the skirmish as morbid curiosity gripped men on both sides of the river.

It didn't last. The remaining Tsnath archers dived behind the nearest pines. Becoming more and more desperate to bring a halt to the woman's flight, they began to concentrate on her alone, darting out from behind cover to take snap shots. Nash and the lookout continued to send arrows their way, trying to disrupt their aim.

Torrin-Ashur thrashed his way towards the marooned woman, hampered by the increasing drag of his waterlogged clothing. He wasn't wearing much armour, but if he tripped, the breastplate alone would sink him like a stone. Swimming was out of the question. Even though the woman had made it about two thirds of the way across the river, the water was still deep enough to lap at her knees. She was a long way short of the bank and terribly exposed, her horse barely moving while arrows darted all around her.

Torrin-Ashur signalled for her to dismount and use the horse for cover. It was no use; she was so singularly determined to reach the far bank that his shouts and gestures went unheeded.

Still some thirty yards short of her position, his senses stopped him dead in his tracks. As though an unseen hand had grabbed his head and wrenched it sideways, his sight was drawn to the shudder of a Tsnath bow as an arrow leapt from its string. His vision became tunnelled, focused solely on the barbed head streaking towards him, its fletched shaft spiralling behind. He tried to sidestep the oncoming missile, but found himself mired, as though the waters of the Ablath clung to him like tar. A fiery pain exploded in his left arm as the arrow struck home. The force of the blow twisted his torso. He lost his footing and plunged beneath the surface.

A rush of bubbles swirled around his head as he fought the lure of the deep. He choked on inhaled water, fighting desperately not to take another breath. Pain and the Ablath's frigid embrace assailed his senses. A moment of panic gripped him. Only by the grace of some unknown god did his foot hit something solid. In an instant he propelled himself up and his head broke the surface. He sucked in a mighty gulp of air, only to cough it all out again.

Struggling for breath, coughs frustrating intakes, he tried to regain his footing. The flow of the river carried him downstream at an alarming rate. He scrabbled about, digging his feet into the gravelly bottom, but they did little more than gouge furrows, like hopelessly inadequate anchors trying to arrest the passage of a storm-riven ship. His calf slammed into a submerged boulder, sending another sharp pain shooting through his body. But it at least brought him to a stop. In just a few seconds he'd travelled twenty yards.

Still coughing and panting, he managed to steady himself against the boulder and regain his feet, rising out of the chest-high water and the immediate danger of drowning. But his problems weren't over. The barb of the Tsnath arrow had passed through his biceps, leaving the shaft lodged right through him. His whole arm felt like it had been turned into molten lead. Strangely, the pain seemed bearable; the beat, all the while thundering through him, somehow pushed it away. The intense clarity of thought was also still with him. He knew he couldn't stay standing exposed in the middle of the river for long. He had to act fast.

Clenching his teeth, he gripped the protruding arrow and snapped off its fletched end. Before he could think better of it, he ripped the remainder of the shaft free. The jagged end tore through the wound. He yelled, more in rage than agony.

Fighting waves of giddiness, he waded back upstream towards the stricken horse. The rider was no longer upright and struggling, but slumped forwards, her arms loosely draped around the animal's neck. An arrow protruded from her back, just above her hips. Anger flooded through him, fuelling his determination to reach her.

The closer he got, the more the bulk of the horse provided relief from the current's relentless push. He managed to tug the young woman from the saddle, catching her under the arms lest she dip beneath the surface; she didn't need a lungful of river water like he'd just had. More pain exploded in his arm as her body weighed heavily on him. He had no choice but to ignore it; her fingers stubbornly gripped the horse's reins and he had to fight to make her let go.

He became dimly aware of Silfast storming down to the river bank with more men in tow. They began laying down a suppressing bombardment. Their arrival trebled the Alondrian cover, tipping the battle decisively in their favour. The Tsnath riders fled the exposed water for the safety of the trees behind them.

Their archers hadn't given up completely, but with the bulk of the horse affording a small amount of cover, Torrin-Ashur had a moment to take stock. The arrow in the woman's back had to be removed; the risk of it causing her more injury as he wrestled her to the bank was too great to leave it in place. He gripped the shaft, hesitated a heartbeat, then pulled.

There was no scream. The young woman was already too far gone for that. She moaned and slipped the rest of the way into unconsciousness. All Torrin-Ashur could do was pray to the gods that she was strong enough to endure the rough handling she was going to suffer.

With the horse between him and the Tsnath, he staggered back towards the Alondrian bank, doing his best to support the woman with just his good arm.

Nash relinquished his bow and waded out into the river. He relieved Torrin-Ashur of his burden. Silfast splashed in behind and grabbed the horse's reins, hauling the creature back towards the bank.

The enemy action rapidly dwindled to nothing. Their archers melted into the trees and disappeared.

Nash carefully handed the unconscious woman over to several of the men. They carried her to the nearest patch of dry ground and laid her down with the reverence due a holy relic.

"Next time, sir, give me some warning when you're about to dash off like that," Nash admonished. Relief brought a smile to his lips.

Torrin-Ashur chuckled and sank to his knees. The strange beat that had kept him going was deserting him, just as it had after the call-out. Only this time he was left feeling like he was on fire.

"Sergeant," he gasped, gritting his teeth, "we need to get this woman to Tail-ébeth. We have an old mage there – he'll know what to do." He paused for breath, fighting off another wave of giddiness. "Besides, we've blown our cover. There's no point us staying here now."

With that, and before anyone could move to catch him, the edges of his vision folded in and he toppled face-first into the mud.

16

Familiar shapes gradually resolved before Torrin-Ashur's eyes. For some reason, focusing on them was harder than it ought to be. He was in bed, at home in Tail-ébeth, that much was clear, but with no recollection of how he'd come to be there, confusion reigned. He tried chasing the tail of the last thing he could remember. Through the thinning fog the concerned face of Sergeant Nash came to the fore, triggering a flood of memories – cold water, arrows, pain. A large horse.

The young woman!

He sat bolt upright, regretted it instantly and flopped back down again, reeling from a wave of dizziness that sent the room spinning. Several minutes went by before he made another attempt to sit up – this time with no sudden movements.

Fresh clothes had been put out for him. Before donning them an inspection of his arm was in order. All his limbs felt inordinately stiff, yet strangely the arrow wound didn't hurt that much. That didn't allay his fears of there being a gangrenous hole beneath the large wadded bandage.

It came as a shock to discover an injury well on the way to recovery. "How long have I been out?" he murmured to no one.

Dressing was a slow affair, though given a certain urgency by the need to satisfy a rather aggressive hunger. A quick glance at the sun through the window suggested it was about mid-morning; if he was lucky, the tail end of breakfast might still be in the offing.

As he made his way towards the kitchens, the familiarity of the place put a smile on his face. Little things caught his attention the most; pictures hanging where they always had, worn rugs covering foot-smoothed floor boards, the heart-shaped crack above the door at the end of the corridor, along with the cobweb next to it. So much for the diligence of the servants, he mused. Speaking of which, it occurred to him that the house was strangely quiet. He wondered if something was going on.

Appetising aromas wafting up from the kitchens began to

antagonise his hunger. His stomach responded with a rumble. He took the steps down two at a time, a habit since childhood, and appeared at the kitchen entrance rather suddenly. The cook was taken by surprise, her ladle going astray in an urn of stock.

"Oh, Master Torrin!" the woman exclaimed. "Oh, bless me, but it's good to see you up and about again."

Ladle forsaken, the elderly cook wiped her hands on a well-stained apron and waddled towards him, skirting the end of the huge table that took up most of the floor space. With no regard for injuries, she gave him an all-encompassing hug, bringing tears to his eyes – for entirely non-sentimental reasons.

"Where is everybody?" he croaked.

The cook gasped. "O-oh. We've got visitors," she announced proudly.

"Visitors? Who?"

With a conspiratorial grin, the cook herded him out of the kitchen and up the steps that led to the main hall. He didn't even manage to grab a bun from the table.

He wasn't propelled all the way up, just given sufficient momentum to guarantee his arrival. Before he'd reached the top, several distinctive laughs came his way. One was the familiar rumbling of his father, whose chortle was near indistinguishable from a cough that came with too much drawing on the pipe. The other rather took him by surprise. It belonged to Kirshtahll.

The general occupied an armchair to one side of the unlit fireplace, the bulk of the man seemingly as formidable as ever. Torrin-Ashur spotted his father sitting opposite. Eldris was by his side, trying to look important. The hall's other occupants included Major Temesh-ai, perched on a stool near the general, and old Cosmin, the local mage, come doctor, come occasional priest of whatever religion was doing the rounds.

He hardly knew who to acknowledge first.

"Ah, Lieutenant, how are you feeling?" Kirshtahll greeted, taking the lead on that score.

Torrin-Ashur grimaced. "I've been better, sir." In truth, he was still suffering something akin to a severe hangover.

His father caught his eye and smiled warmly. "Well, at least you're back in the land of the living, m'boy. Not knowing how much poison had infected you, we weren't sure when to expect you up."

"Poison?"

"Not the fatal kind," Cosmin reassured him. "The Tsnath tip their arrows with Goa venom. It usually only renders its victims unconscious, though I'm told it does have some unpleasant after-effects."

Torrin-Ashur grunted. That explained the headache.

"How's the arm?" Temesh-ai asked.

Torrin-Ashur prodded the bandaging. "I have you to thank for this? It's healed faster than I would have expected."

Temesh-ai shrugged. "Well, you'd be surprised what remedies you can cook up with a few herbs and spices."

Cosmin nearly choked, though apparently in agreement.

"How long has it been?"

"Nearly three days."

Shock registered on Torrin-Ashur's face. For that to be the case, Cosmin must have given Temesh-ai's cooking a magely stir.

He turned his attention to Kirshtahll. "Sir, my men, are they alright? I presume they're here somewhere."

"Yes, Lieutenant, they're here. Billeted around the town, wherever we could fit them in."

Torrin-Ashur hesitated before asking the more burning question on his mind. He feared what the answer might be. "And the young woman, sir, is she alright? Did she survive?"

His concern was met by several knowing smiles.

"She's fine, Torrin," Naman-Ashur replied. "In fact, she came round sooner than you did."

"Well, she's had a lot of help from Cosmin," Temesh-ai said. "The fact is, we took one look at you and decided you could mend on your own. With the young lady, it was a different story. She'd be dead if it wasn't for this man here." Temesh-ai gave Cosmin a congratulatory pat on the shoulder. "I don't mind admitting, my prejudice against mages mucking about in medicinal matters is under review in light of what I've seen over the last few days."

"Wonders will never cease," Kirshtahll muttered, catching Cosmin's gaze and rolling his eyes towards the ceiling.

Torrin-Ashur felt immensely relieved. "Well then, would anyone mind if I looked in on her?"

"I think there's someone else you ought to say hello to first."

It took Torrin-Ashur a moment to realise that Kirshtahll wasn't gazing at him, but past him. He turned to see who was there. He was not well prepared for the shock that followed.

Princess Elona stood just a few feet behind him. She must have entered the hall on tiptoe for all the sound she'd made, though why she'd deliberately approach by stealth was beyond him. Her ash-blond hair was no longer arranged high and formal, as it had been for the dinner with the Executive. Now it was just gathered back in a simple ponytail. The mesmerising emerald gown had given way to a rather more utilitarian kirtle over a linen shift. Yet she was no less regal. Her soft, dark eyes once again held him captive, the hint of a smile almost mocking him.

A number of thoughts about what to say passed through his head, none of which were particularly intelligent. Finally he managed, "Your, err..." in a discrete sentence.

"Highness?" she proffered, her tone sweetly helpful, suggesting that it was perhaps merely one of a number of possibilities he might consider.

"Your Highness. Yes. Sorry."

He bowed to hide the Ashur blush he could feel coming on.

Elona's eyebrow rose a notch. Finally she let slip one of her disarming giggles – the kind that could melt the resolve of marauding armies.

"I'm glad they haven't changed you too much yet, Lieutenant," she said quietly, barely above a whisper. She turned and headed for an armchair. She slipped her shoes off, descended on to the cushions and tucked her legs up beneath her. It was a relaxed and informal posture that Torrin-Ashur found quite hard to associate with someone of such high station. "I hear you've been rescuing damsels in distress," she continued in a louder voice. "You've got half my staff swooning around thinking it's all very romantic."

Torrin-Ashur laughed, gingerly touching his arm. "It doesn't feel very romantic, ma'am. Maybe I should shoot a few of them, so they'd know what true romance is really like?"

Elona pretended to give the offer serious consideration, before giving her head a brief perhaps-not shake.

Torrin-Ashur positioned himself so that he could face everyone without turning his back on Elona again. He caught a hint of his brother's expression; awe, mixed with a healthy dose of pure jealousy. Eldris was no doubt wondering how his younger brother was already on familiar terms with the princess.

"Sir, if I may ask, how is it you come to be here?" It didn't seem likely to Torrin-Ashur that a general would have journeyed all the way from Mitcha just to enquire about the health of one of his junior lieutenants.

"The princess is on route back to Alondris, via the Akanu Pass over the Mathians," Kirshtahll replied. "She is visiting Nairnkirsh first, though. And as Tail-ébeth was only a minor detour on the way there, we decided to make a port of call. When we heard the news of your little fracas, we decided to stay a while. Since then matters have taken some interesting turns."

"Turns, sir?"

"Hmm. Have you any idea who it is you fished out the Ablath?"

Torrin-Ashur shook his head.

Kirshtahll harrumphed. "Well, her name is Kassandra. She is the daughter of Baroness Alishe Daka."

"Oh," Torrin-Ashur managed. Suddenly he could have done with a chair. Unfortunately, there wasn't one to hand.

"That's one way of putting it," Kirshtahll chuckled. "As far as we've been able to gather, she was attempting to flee her mother's clutches. It's remarkably fortunate that you arrived when you did, otherwise things would have gone very badly for her."

Torrin-Ashur's look of confusion prompted the general to elaborate further.

"The man who almost succeeded in catching her goes by the name of Gömalt. He's Daka's right hand man, and a thoroughly vile specimen by all accounts. Were it not for your timely intervention, Kassandra would have been forcibly returned to Brath'daka. That would probably have resulted in her execution. The baroness is not a woman to be crossed."

"I'll vouch for that," Naman-Ashur concurred wholeheartedly. "The wretched woman has been the bane of my life for decades."

Torrin-Ashur knew that to be true. Daka's lands bordered theirs, just the other side of the Ablath. The times her raiding parties had plagued the march could not easily be numbered.

"So you see, Lieutenant, our curiosity has been piqued. A Tsnathsarré noblewoman in dire need of assistance turning up in Alondria is not your everyday occurrence."

Torrin-Ashur was about to agree when his train of thought was distracted. A young man entered the hall, his clerical status proclaimed by a full-length black cassock with red piping around the collar and cuffs. He stood quietly just inside the doorway, poised with his hands clasped in front of him. He was tall, but really quite thin, had a ruddy, boyish complexion, and dark curly hair, an unruly mass that suggested it had a mind of its own.

Naman-Ashur's face brightened. "Ah, Torrin, allow me to introduce you to another of our guests. This is Brother Jorra-hin. Jorra-hin, my youngest son, Torrin."

Torrin-Ashur advanced across the hall to offer his hand. Before he had made it half way, the young monk bent double in a remarkably formal bow. Surprise stopped Torrin-Ashur in his tracks. He didn't often warrant such homage.

"Jorra-hin is from the Adak-rann," his father explained. "Their monastery is up in the Jàb-áldis Pass, southeast of Mitcha. He is also on his way to Alondris."

"I see. May the hospitality of this house meet your every need," Torrin-Ashur greeted, abandoning the idea of shaking hands.

Jorra-hin smiled but remained silent.

"So, Brother, any progress?" Temesh-ai enquired.

A look of disappointment crossed the young monk's face. "Sadly, no. I'm afraid the document has been too badly stained. All I can tell you is that it was a recent work."

"What makes you say that?" Kirshtahll asked.

"The ink wasn't well set on the parchment. Had it been older, the river water would not have caused it to run so badly."

"That's a pity," Elona said. "Kassandra risked her life to bring it here. That alone makes it important."

Another furrow creased Torrin-Ashur's brow. "What document is this?"

"When we started tending to Kassandra's injury," Temesh-ai explained, "we discovered that she was wearing a leather satchel, hidden under her riding cloak. It bore the brunt of the arrow that hit her. Probably saved her life. When we opened it, we discovered a parchment, but unfortunately river water and blood seem to have leaked in and ruined it."

Torrin-Ashur noticed a scowl cross Jorra-hin's face. He knew that the world of the Adak-rann was one in which all documents, regardless of age, were revered. They felt that if a matter was worth committing to parchment, then it was worth preserving. The brothers of Jorra-hin's order spent their lives piecing together history from fragments left throughout the centuries. Yet with so much already having been lost to carelessness or a lack of foresight, to see a document damaged or destroyed went against the grain of everything they stood for.

"You would not have been able to read it anyway," the young monk mumbled. There was genuine bitterness in his voice. "From the little that I could make out, the document appears to have been written in A'lyavine."

No one in the hall was under any illusions about the limitations that imposed. Even Cosmin declined to comment.

"Is there anything you can tell us about it?" Kirshtahll asked.

"Not from the document itself, my lord. However, over the last few days I have overheard Kassandra say things that have caught my attention. I don't know how reliable this is…"

"Given the circumstances, I don't think we need worry about Kassandra trying to lie to us," Elona declared with some conviction. "Her countrymen did just try to kill her."

"I didn't mean to suggest deceit on her part, Your Highness," Jorra-hin conceded with a gracious nod. "It's just that she has been suffering a fever and could have been delirious."

"Maybe so, but you might as well tell us anyway," Kirshtahll suggested.

Jorra-hin nodded again. "She seems to have had one particular thing on her mind, something she calls the Menhir of Ranadar."

Blank looks made it obvious that this revelation hadn't struck a chord with anyone.

"Well," Jorra-hin continued, "the only Ranadar with whom I am familiar was a Dwarvish king, from a period when the Dwarve Nation lived in this part of the world. In fact, it was under his rule that they left the Mathians and settled further north, beyond the borders of what is now the Tsnathsarré Empire."

"That was a long time ago. Even I know that," Eldris-Ashur declared.

Jorra-hin didn't miss a beat. "Eight hundred and sixty one years before the Foundation of Alondria."

"In other words, just over eighteen hundred years ago," Kirshtahll added. He raised his eyebrows. "And the document, what connection do you suppose there might be to this Ranadar?"

Jorra-hin hesitated before voicing his thoughts. "Well, a menhir is typically a marker stone, quite often bearing inscriptions. Given the known Dwarvish propensity for commemorating events in stone, I find it quite likely that King Ranadar would have wished to leave some memorial of his people's departure from the Mathians. I'm wondering, therefore, whether this document Kassandra has brought us might have been a copy of the text from such a monument. Though I hasten to add, this is pure conjecture."

Torrin-Ashur frowned. "I thought Kassandra was awake now. Can't you just ask her what it is?"

Jorra-hin shook his head. "She doesn't know. She stole this document because she knew it was important to her mother, and that it might therefore also be important to us. But whatever it is, I can tell you that Baroness Daka wishes it to be kept a secret at all costs."

"Oh?" Kirshtahll's eyebrow went up a notch.

"Apparently there are three copies. Kassandra witnessed the scribes that made them being executed – just for having seen this text."

Kirshtahll's eyes widened. He let out a heavy sigh. "What in the name of the gods could Daka know that she'd want to keep so guarded, even from her own people?" As no one seemed to have an answer to that, he went on, "Is Kassandra up to answering some more questions?"

"She needs rest, Padráig," Temesh-ai advised. "You'll have to keep it short."

"Fair enough. Jorra-hin, if you would be so kind, I shall require your assistance again later on. My Tsnathsarré leaves a lot to be desired."

That signalled adjournment, prompting Elona to unfold her legs and stretch, wiggling her toes in mid-air to get the blood flowing again. "I don't think it would do any harm if I introduced our patient to her knight in shining armour."

She stood up and grabbed hold of Torrin-Ashur's sleeve to steady herself while she stepped back into her shoes. Then she slid her arm through his and steered him towards the door.

Out of the corner of his eye, Torrin-Ashur caught a glimpse of his brother. Eldris was in the process of picking his jaw up off the floor.

*

Jorra-hin was about to follow when Kirshtahll beckoned him over for a quiet word.

"Brother, I was wondering whether you might consider doing me a great service when you reach Alondris?"

Jorra-hin's eyes widened with interest.

"I don't mean to detract you from your other duties, but a young man in your position would be ideally placed for what I have in mind. I need someone to look into this Ranadar business for me. Why the Tsnath might be so interested in a piece of ancient history baffles me. Any light you can shed on it would be most helpful."

Jorra-hin kept his expression neutral, though he was secretly pleased to have been asked.

"This investigation needs to be carried out in confidence, though," Kirshtahll added. "Not everyone in Alondris is keen on the army's role up here in the Northern Territories. I'd prefer not to let loose with rumours that might come back to bite me. Not until we know exactly what it is we're dealing with here."

"I understand, my lord. I would be delighted to assist in any way I can." Jorra-hin glanced over his shoulder. "I'd better go – I expect my translation skills will be needed."

Kirshtahll nodded. Jorra-hin gave him a slight bow and turned to leave.

Hurrying towards the room in which Kassandra was being tended, he found it odd that no one in the Ashur household had any real grasp of the Tsnathsarré language. Given the proximity of Tail-ébeth to the Tsnathsarré border, it would have made sense for the people hereabouts to be bilingual. But then, not everyone had his penchant for foreign tongues, he supposed. Besides, any interaction Alondrians had with the Tsnathsarré was rarely on the conversational level these days. Opportunities to learn were probably limited.

He caught up with the princess and Torrin-Ashur just as they'd reached Kassandra's door.

"The Princess and I had better go in first," he advised. "Kassandra is still wary of anyone she doesn't know."

*

Torrin-Ashur stood aside as Jorra-hin opened the door and bid Elona precede him. The pair were inside about a minute before the princess peered round the door and beckoned him in.

The first person he encountered inside was his mother. He gave her a warm, one-armed hug. Only after exchanging a few pleasantries did he turn his attention to the young lady he'd rescued.

Kassandra was staring at him with wide eyes. Clearly she recognised who he was. She looked very tired, bearing the strained, almost haunted look of someone having just come through a high fever. Her dark auburn hair was tangled and ⟨…⟩ the billowing cloud he remembered from her d⟨…⟩ back at the Ablath. Yet for all that, she was undenia⟨…⟩

"*Eck em-hidda,*" she breathed, just above a whisper.

Torrin-Ashur glanced round for assistance.

"Literally, '*him me that saved*'," Jorra-hin translated. "H⟨…⟩ saying, 'my saviour'."

Torrin-Ashur knew damned well his blush had just betrayed he could feel its heat on his cheeks.

"Tell her she's welcome."

Kassandra took hold of his hand and held it to the side of her face. That only made the Ashur blush rage even more.

Elona stepped over to his mother and whispered, "We're going to have to watch this one back in Alondris, my lady."

Torrin-Ashur almost missed the inference. "Alondris?"

His mother smiled. "I think you ought to have a word with your father. He has something to tell you."

7

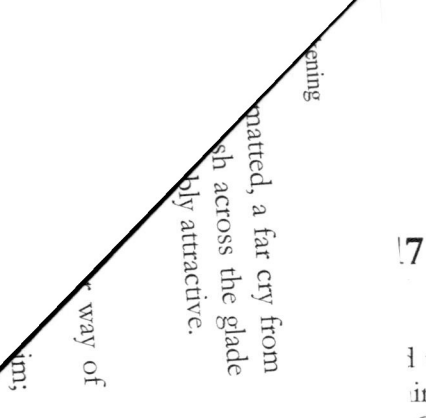

...l taking a leisurely stroll out in the ...im. The sight of the latter brought ... Given that in military circles the ... only just below the gods, it was hard to reconcile that view of the man with one who would take the time to enjoy such simple pleasures as pottering about amongst flowers.

But then the garden was subject to the ceaseless efforts of the lady of the house and thereby kept in a constant state of perfection. So there was much to admire. The meticulous precision of its layout still managed to give the impression of a random medley of flowerbeds, neatly bordered and interspersed with manicured bushes. Marble statues and secluded benches, many ensconced in creeper-entwined trellising, waited to be discovered by the casual wanderer meandering along the winding stone paths.

Torrin-Ashur lingered on the periphery, unsure whether to interrupt. The matter was taken out of his hands as soon as his presence was noticed.

Kirshtahll turned to his host. "Well, Naman, I'll take my leave. No doubt you and your son have some catching up to do."

"Thank you, Padráig."

Kirshtahll beat an unhurried retreat across the garden, stopping to examine several botanical curiosities along the way. He dipped his head at Torrin-Ashur as he passed by.

With the general out of earshot, Torrin-Ashur approached his father. "Padráig? You're on first name terms with my commanding officer, now?"

Naman-Ashur smiled. "A lot has happened these past few days."

"So I'm beginning to suspect."

They found themselves a secluded alcove furnished with comfortable seats and settled down.

"Mother mentioned you had something to tell me – something about Alondris?"

"We'll come to that in a minute. But first, tell me, how have you been? We've heard so little from you since you went to Mitcha. You could at least have sent word."

"I have been rather busy," Torrin-Ashur defended, somewhat weakly.

His father flashed a dubious glance. A young man's natural propensity for things other than writing letters obviously wasn't going to hold water as an excuse.

"Padráig tells me you've been making an impression."

Torrin-Ashur's eyebrow rose slightly. "A favourable one?"

"Perhaps. Though not with everyone, I hear."

"Ah. I have had some differences with one or two, I suppose."

"Differences? Major confrontations, I hear tell."

Torrin-Ashur braced himself. "So you've heard about the call-out?"

His father let out a grunt. "Princess Elona supplied most of the details. You seem to have left an impression there, too, if I'm any judge."

Torrin-Ashur felt a brief flurry of excitement, but suppressed it as quickly as it had arisen. Allowing hope to blossom in that direction was futile. The social gulf that divided him from the princess was as great as the Mathians.

"But that aside, I'm not pleased that you became embroiled in such nonsense. Duelling is for arrogant fools with no better cause than defending their so-called honour. I expect more from you than that."

"Did the princess tell you why the call-out happened?"

Naman-Ashur nodded. "But the fact remains, you let your temper get the better of you. That's what got you into trouble. As usual."

"It wasn't all my fault, father. I did actually try to avoid the fight."

"It *was* your fault. You stormed off straight into a confrontation. And worse still, you drew your weapon. I didn't give you the family sword just so you could go round flaunting it under the noses of other people."

Torrin-Ashur's anger kindled. "You weren't there, father. You didn't see what happened. One of my men was nearly killed. His name is Tomàss…"

"Don't argue with me, young man!" Naman-Ashur glared for a moment, before moderating his tone. "I'm not saying you didn't have provocation, perhaps even just cause. What I am saying is, you should not have acted on the spur of the moment. I'll not have a son of mine allowing himself be led astray by his temper. You are to be more careful how you conduct yourself in future."

Torrin-Ashur sat in stony silence. There was never any winning of this type of argument; he'd learnt that long ago. The only thing to do was to bite his tongue.

Fortunately, his father wasn't one for endlessly repeating himself. Once he'd said his piece, he tended to move on.

"So, how's the arm?"

Torrin-Ashur touched the wound. "Tender. But better than I would have expected. Cosmin must have done more than just let Temesh-ai patch me up."

"Aye, that's a fact. But you know him, he played down his role, as always. Actually, I think he was trying to avoid offending Temesh-ai. The good doctor was quite against any Taümathic meddling when he first arrived." Naman-Ashur paused for a moment, reflecting on something. "You know, you won't always be lucky enough to have the likes of Cosmin to hand. You took a great risk at the ford."

"I know, father. But I am a soldier now. It comes with the job."

"Yes, but being a little less impulsive would be wise."

Torrin-Ashur let out a mild snort. He wanted to mention the strange force that had compelled him into action, both in the call-out and at the river, but his father was nothing if not a practical, worldly man. The details would not be heard with an understanding ear. Besides, he was more than a little confused on the matter himself. He still didn't have an explanation for what had happened.

"There wasn't much else I could have done. If I'd delayed, Kassandra would be dead by now."

"I don't doubt it. But you have to remember, you're not just a soldier, Torrin, you're an officer. You have responsibilities. Your men depend on your leadership. It serves them no good if you're the first to fall on the battlefield."

"No, but – I can't expect them to do things that I'm not prepared to do myself. Lead by example. *You* taught me that."

His father chuckled. "Aye, well, difficult to argue against that, I suppose. The truth is, it's your example to your men, your willingness to get stuck in alongside them, that has brought you to Kirshtahll's attention."

Getting alongside the men wasn't the way it was done amongst the higher nobles, Torrin-Ashur mused. Particularly not if the men in question were the Pressed.

"It hasn't made me very popular with my fellow lieutenants."

"They're not the ones that matter. What the general thinks of you is far more important than this Borádin character and his ilk."

"I know that," Torrin-Ashur replied, feeling a little awkward. "So, seeing as how I have come to Kirshtahll's attention, what's this about Alondris?"

Naman-Ashur sighed with a nod. "The general has decided to send you to the capital to receive a commission."

Torrin-Ashur's eyes widened in shock.

"It will give your career the footing it needs; enable you to progress beyond being a bonded officer."

"But commissions cost a fortune. How are we going to afford it?"

"I did say a lot has happened these past few days."

"We haven't suddenly become rich, have we?"

"Not quite," Naman-Ashur chuckled. "Padráig has offered to act as your sponsor."

Torrin-Ashur's eyebrows shot up.

"He is one of the richest men in Alondria. You do know he's a personal friend of King Althar, don't you?"

Torrin-Ashur slumped forwards, dumping his chin into the palms of his hands. He covered the bridge of his nose with steepled fingers and blew out a long breath as he tried to grasp the enormity of this development. Alondris? That meant the Royal Military Academy. Where Borádin's crowd were schooled. Ye gods, he'd rather be back at the Ablath being shot at by the Tsnath.

"Does Eldris know about this? I can just imagine how this will endear me to him."

"He'll get over it. He will be Lord of Ashur one day, Master of the March and everything that goes with it."

"I'm not the one that needs reminding."

"I know." His father let out a tired sigh. "Eldris will just have to wait a while longer to get what's coming to him. A little practice at patience wouldn't harm him. You, meanwhile, have got to make the best of the hand you're dealt. And from the looks of things, fate is smiling on you at the moment."

Torrin-Ashur shook his head in disbelief. This dramatic change in circumstances was not only a shock, but something that was going to take time to assimilate.

They lapsed into silence for a few minutes, each with his own thoughts. A gentle breeze wafted through the garden, blending scents together into a jumbled fragrance. A lone butterfly punctuated the stillness, lazily navigating through the colourful profusion. It alighted briefly on a trailing azalea before taking off again and bobbing out of sight over the garden wall.

The muted encroachment of everyday sounds from the town drew Torrin-Ashur's thoughts to the wider impact of these developments. It seemed odd how a small change might reorder the lives of some, and yet leave others completely unaffected. For the townsfolk of Tail-ébeth, life would go on just as it always had, untouched by the changing fortunes of their lord's youngest son. Yet for the Pressed there might be significant changes, some perhaps not for the best.

"Is this an order, or an offer?" he asked.

"Should that make a difference? It would be foolish to turn it down."

"So I've got to go."

"You sound reluctant. Had such an opportunity fallen in my lap at your age, I'd have been overjoyed."

"You haven't seen the type of idiot that comes up from the Academy, father. I'll not fit in down there – I'm a northerner. *Teeth of the gods*, I don't even get on with them up here."

"You won't be there long. Only while you await an audience with Princess Midana. It will be worth the inconvenience. A commission from Alondris means infinitely more than simply being an officer serving under bonds. It will open doors that would otherwise be closed to you."

Torrin-Ashur let out a heavy sigh. "Father, I'm proud to be an Ashur, you know that. But with respect, I'm the second son of a minor northern lord, with no title of my own. Just how far do you think I can go?"

"As the second son of a minor northern lord – with no title – perhaps not far. But with the support of the House of Kirshtahll? That changes things significantly."

Torrin-Ashur shook his head again. It felt as though he was drowning in a sea of change. But one thought was refusing to succumb to the waves. "Has the general said anything about what will happen to my men?"

His father patted him on the shoulder. "Thinking of them at a time like this is an admirable thing, Torrin. But you have to look to your own future now."

That didn't ease his concerns. The Pressed were good lads; he'd worked hard to pick them up out of the gutter. The last thing he wanted was to see them kicked back down again, through no fault of their own.

*

Elona wandered into the garden. Just as she'd hoped, she spotted Torrin-Ashur sitting alone. He was perched on a wooden bench tucked inside a trellised alcove. He seemed engrossed.

Deciding not to make her presence known, she stood for a moment and observed him from a distance. He looked very much a soldier, even though he wasn't in uniform. She hadn't quite decided how old he was, just into his twenties perhaps, but his face had already lost the roundness of youth. It was a common trait up here in the Territories, where the outdoors lifestyle lent a weathered, more hardy countenance to its residents. He wasn't what most girls would have considered dashing, but he was handsome enough in a rugged sort of way. His hair needed attention, though. It was too short, practical perhaps, but hardly the style of choice for a nobleman. The fashion-conscious eye of Alondris would not approve. She couldn't help noticing that he was well built, now that he was only wearing a light linen shirt rather than the thick tunics and armour she'd seen him in previously.

Keeping her footsteps soft, she drew near, hoping to take him by surprise for the second time that day.

"May I join you?"

Torrin-Ashur's head snapped up. He shot to his feet.

Elona threw out a staying hand. "Please – no need. This is your house, after all. You must learn when it is necessary to be formal, and when not."

"Your Highness," Torrin-Ashur acknowledged.

She sat down on the cushioned bench next to his. "And it's Elona. I don't suppose it would destroy the fabric of society if you called me by name once in a while."

Torrin-Ashur blinked a couple of times. A country boy he may have been, but apparently even he knew enough etiquette to recognise the privilege he'd just been granted. He smiled, but said nothing. It hadn't escaped her notice that her presence tended to make him trip over his words. Silence was probably his safest haven at such a moment.

She let her gaze rove over the surroundings. The garden really was an exquisite creation, quite unlike anything else she'd seen since being in the north. As incongruous as finding an oasis in a desert, it seemed almost too delicate to exist amid the rugged landscape of the Territories. It even rivalled the pampered grounds of the royal palace.

"It's lovely here," she murmured.

Torrin-Ashur let out a snort of agreement. "I swear, if you disturbed so much as a petal, my mother would know."

Elona smiled, but the gesture hid a pang of regret that unexpectedly surfaced. She had no memory of her own mother; Queen Bernice had been stripped of her title and put away from the royal household for an indiscretion with another man. Elona had only been a year old at the time, far too young to understand what was going on. As with many arranged marriages, there had been a huge gap in years between king and queen. She didn't blame her father for the action he'd taken. In many ways he'd shown great leniency; the crime had been treason against the king and the law decreed death. Yet in another household the infidelity could have been handled in a way that didn't tear the family asunder. In a royal house, politics negated the possibility of forgiveness.

She couldn't help feeling slightly envious of Torrin-Ashur. He was very lucky to have such a close relationship with both his parents. Although, there were signs things were not so amicable between the brothers. She could empathise with that; sibling rivalry blighted them both, it seemed.

"I hope you won't mind my asking, but is Eldris always..."

"Such an idiot?" Torrin-Ashur interrupted. A laugh erupted from him. "Oh, gods, what's he done now?"

Elona threw up her hand. "Nothing improper, I assure you. It's just that – well, he took me for a walk through the town yesterday, which was nice. But he rather spoiled it by strutting about, ordering people around, demanding things be done. Silly things, things that didn't need doing. It was all so – unnecessary."

Torrin-Ashur rolled his eyes skywards. "That sounds like Eldris. I expect he was just trying to impress you, that's all. Though I doubt there's much in Tail-ébeth to bowl you over. For someone used to Alondris, I imagine it's all rather dull up here."

"Have you ever been to the capital?" Elona asked, eyeing him quite directly.

"I've never even been south of the Mathians. I've heard people speak of it, though. I have pictures in my mind's eye of what it must be like."

"Hmm." Elona's murmur was deliberately dubious. Alondris was not a place merely to imagine. It tended to exceed people's expectations on a first visit. "I won't deny there are some wonderful things down there. You'll be seeing them for yourself soon enough. But once you get used to Alondris, you'd be surprised how nice it is to get away from it all. You may think Tail-ébeth hasn't got much to offer, but it's quaint and peaceful – two qualities Alondris has in very short supply."

"Is that why you came up to the Northern Territories – a chance to escape?"

"It was one of the attractions," Elona admitted. "That, and the fact that someone in my position should take opportunities to learn about the kingdom when they are offered. It's rather too easy to become blinkered, ensconced in a palace."

Torrin-Ashur frowned a little. "I'd imagined royalty would get to travel around all the time."

"Far from it. One of the drawbacks of being a princess..." she noticed Torrin-Ashur raise an eyebrow and smiled back at him wistfully, "is that nothing is ever a simple process. Everything manages to turn itself into a state occasion. It all gets rather tedious. That's why I've enjoyed spending a few days here so much. It's been such a pleasure to be treated like a normal person for a change." She paused, then added as an afterthought, "Do you know, I was actually able to go out for a walk by myself this morning. It sounds silly, doesn't it? But even such a small thing like that is a rarity for me."

Torrin-Ashur shook his head in amazement. He'd probably never thought of it like that before; that a position of such privilege could be so restrictive.

"Of course, I caused panic everywhere I went," she continued with a giggle. "People just don't expect a princess to simply stroll in off the street."

Torrin-Ashur laughed at her pout. "That I can understand."

"Strange as it may seem, one of the warmest receptions I received was from the Pressed."

The mention of his men made Torrin-Ashur sit up. "Oh?"

"I happened across them at the old mill. They're mending it, I gather."

"Aye. I really should have been to check up on them myself, but such a lot has happened today."

"I wouldn't worry. Your sergeant had everything under control. I think they'd almost finished. Anyway," she let out another giggle, recalling how the poor dears had reacted on discovering who she was, "they made me feel most welcome. They even shared their lunch with me." It was hard to remember the last time she'd enjoyed the simple pleasure of a picnic, albeit in strange company. But it had been worth it, just to hear what they thought of Torrin-Ashur.

"The lads are a good bunch. They're enjoying being away from Mitcha, I know that much."

Elona nodded. "Their lot has improved considerably since you took command."

"Who told you that?"

"It would be difficult to miss. They think very highly of you."

Torrin-Ashur blushed slightly and found it convenient to inspect his shoes. Elona noted she seemed to have a knack for making him do that, too.

"And your sergeant, he was very charming. He escorted me back to town like a real gentleman. He was very sweet."

"I don't know whether he'd like to be called *sweet*," Torrin-Ashur grinned, "but he's a good soldier. I don't know what I'd have done without him. Come to think of it, I have Borádin to thank on that score."

"Oh?"

"Nash was his sergeant before being assigned to me."

"Really? Borádin didn't have his own man?"

Torrin-Ashur shrugged. "He may have done. But all new officers up here are assigned an experienced sergeant from the standing army to begin with, to show them the ropes."

"But not you?"

"Ah, no – I was assigned to the Pressed. My position didn't warrant one at the time."

"Well, there must have been something about you that made Nash accept the position, Torrin. Oh – you don't mind my calling you that, do you?"

Torrin-Ashur's eyes widened, then softened as he smiled. "Oh, I don't suppose it would destroy the fabric of society if you called me by my name."

Elona gave him a playful kick in the shin. "Careful, *Lieutenant*."

"My apologies, *Your Royal Highness,*" he rejoined, mustering as much sincerity as he could. He tried a mock, postulating bow from his seated position, but it all went to pot when his bench tipped forwards unexpectedly.

Elona laughed freely. "Graceful, very graceful. May I suggest lessons in etiquette when you get to Alondris."

"Aye," Torrin-Ashur nodded, "that and about a thousand other things. To tell you the truth, now that I've had a little time to adjust to the idea, I'm feeling a bit overwhelmed at the prospect of going. I haven't had much experience rubbing shoulders with high society."

"For what it's worth, Torrin, my advice would be to ignore everyone else and just concentrate on being good at what you do. Don't try being someone you're not. You'll soon discover that nine tenths of Alondria's high society, as you so aptly put it, are just people deluding themselves as to their own importance."

Torrin-Ashur frowned.

"This may sound rather arrogant," Elona went on, "but the majority of the people I know are pompous snobs whose real station in life is several rungs down the ladder from where they think they are."

"Oh, well, I'll be alright then. I'm not even *on* the ladder."

It surprised Elona to hear him say that. She was about to reply, but then reconsidered. She wanted to contradict him on two counts; the first was that he clearly hadn't yet grasped the ramifications of being sponsored by the House of Kirshtahll – that alone catapulted him up the hierarchy; the second was that he'd been chatting to a princess for the last few minutes and managing to make her feel quite at ease – no small feat in itself. Unlike the nine tenths, he was one of the few who were a lot further up the ladder than they thought.

But some things people just had to discover for themselves.

Out of the corner of her eye she spotted Riagán stride into the garden and head in their direction. *Not now*, she sighed to herself.

"Ah, Major, what can we do for you?" she greeted when he arrived.

Riagán gave her a slight bow. "Sorry to interrupt, Your Highness, but the general would like a word with this young man."

Torrin-Ashur rose to his feet. Elona wondered whether she'd detected a degree of reluctance on his part. Or perhaps that was just wishful thinking.

"It has been a pleasure, Your Highness, but if you would excuse me."

She watched as Torrin-Ashur returned inside the house with Riagán. It left her feeling oddly disquieted, as though robbed. She had to suppress a certain resentment towards Kirshtahll's adjutant for spoiling her mood; it wasn't as if the man had done anything wrong.

She tried to let the serenity of the garden sooth her, but her heart seemed to quicken as her thoughts kept drifting back towards Torrin-Ashur. He was so very different from the majority of the young noblemen she met. She smiled at the way he'd reacted to being given leave to address her by name. Most would all too readily have assumed the right to informality, some even without permission. Borádin had, she recalled. But Torrin-Ashur's reservation bordered on the bashful. It was a refreshing change from the posturing socialites that tended to hound her at court.

*

Kirshtahll had set up office in a room the Ashur household called the Library. His first impression had been that it was not a use of the word as the Adak-rann would have understood it. But still, it sufficed for his temporary needs.

There was a short rap on the door.

"Come."

Not unexpectedly, it was Torrin-Ashur.

"Ah, Lieutenant, come in, take a seat." He pointed the feathered end of a quill at a chair just in front of the table serving as his desk. "I'll be with you in a moment."

Resuming the letter he was writing, his quill jostled and jolted, the nib scratching across the rough parchment. When he was finished, he slipped the completed missive to one side without bothering to read it through.

"Well, I presume your father has told you of my offer."

"Yes, sir."

"And…?"

Torrin-Ashur drew a breath. "I'm not quite sure what to say, sir. I'm very grateful for the interest you're showing in my career. But if I may ask, sir, why me?"

Kirshtahll cocked his head to one side and considered his response for a moment. "The truth? You're part of my retirement plan." There was a definitive pause, filled with nothing but a look of utter confusion on Torrin-Ashur's part. Kirshtahll chuckled and held up his hand. "Fear not, I have no immediate plans to depart. But the simple fact is, I won't be here forever, and a prudent man plans ahead."

He briefly thought back over his career; he'd been looking out for the security of the Northern Territories for the last fifteen years, nearly half his time in the army. The Tsnath had been kept a bay, but fundamentally nothing had really changed. He wondered if it ever truly would.

"When the time does come for me to move on, I want to have left in place a hierarchy of officers who will continue to take the security of our northern border seriously. From what I've seen of you so far, I'm confident that you are such a one."

"The Territories are my home, sir. Protecting them is my duty."

"Indeed."

If only more of his kinsmen thought the same way. But compared with the south, the north provided so few officers of nobility that their numbers made little impact on the prevailing view.

"The trouble is, Lieutenant, too many in the south think that it would be acceptable for Alondria to dispense with the Northern Territories altogether, in essence, giving them over to the Tsnath. They have no understanding of the region's strategic importance to the security of the country as a whole. To counter that, I've been building a core of men I can trust – you know of them as the Executive – men who, for whatever reason, feel as you do. But, while you've already joined their ranks, you won't amount to much unless you get the right opportunities in your career. Few bonded officers rise above captain. A commission from Alondris can change that for you."

Torrin-Ashur nodded.

"When I'm gone, the north will need senior ranking officers with the military clout to continue what I've done; to be the voice in the south that keeps the focus on what's going on up here. Sadly, it takes more than lieutenants and captains to shake the Grand Assembly." Kirshtahll paused and let out a derisive snort, "Hell, even I have trouble doing that!"

"I understand, sir."

From Torrin-Ashur's tone, there was obviously something troubling him. "Out with it, Lieutenant."

"Sir, what is to happen to the Pressed?"

It was not an unexpected question.

"You will dismiss them back to Mitcha."

He watched Torrin-Ashur closely for his reaction. The lad's eyes slipped closed; clearly not the order he had hoped to hear.

"Lieutenant?"

Torrin-Ashur's eyes flickered open again.

"Sir, I don't want to see them returned to the state they were in when I took command."

There were many things this young man would have to learn, Kirshtahll mused. It was good that he had regard for the men under him, even if they were only the Pressed; it meant he wouldn't throw lives away needlessly when push came to shove. There were too many in positions of leadership who didn't give a damn about anything except their own skins. But there were limits to how far an officer could allow his personal feelings to affect the execution of his duty.

"The thing about military leadership, Lieutenant, is that some decisions you have to take can be tough on your subordinates. You must not allow yourself to get so attached to those under your command that you cannot take those decisions."

Torrin-Ashur nodded, though his reluctance was evident. "May I at least request that they be spared camp duties back at Mitcha?"

"I won't promise anything, Lieutenant, but I'll mention it to Major Riagán."

"Thank you, sir." The lad paused a moment, then asked, "So, when will I be leaving for Alondris?"

"That depends. I have another job for you first. As soon as Kassandra has recovered sufficiently to travel, I want you to take her down to my estate in Kirsh. My wife, Karina, will take care of her there."

Torrin-Ashur seemed surprised. "I don't speak much Tsnathsarré, sir."

"I have considered that. Jorra-hin will accompany you. He was to have travelled with the princess, but it doesn't really matter how he gets to Alondris, so long as he arrives safely."

"Sir, you said this morning that the royal party is going over the Akanu Pass. Isn't Kirsh almost on the way to Alondris from there? Wouldn't Kassandra be more comfortable travelling with the princess?"

"Fair point," Kirshtahll conceded. The lad certainly had no qualms about asking questions. That was good, so as long as he knew where and when to draw the line. "My concern, however, is that Kassandra may still be in danger, so I'd rather not have her too close to Elona. I feel sure that her arrival is of greater importance than we might yet imagine. In rescuing her from the clutches of this Gömalt character, you may have inadvertently delivered us the key to what the Tsnath have been up to these last few months."

Kirshtahll noticed a growing frown on Torrin-Ashur's brow.

"Kassandra has told me that her mother's men have been scouring the Mathians for months looking for this Menhir of Ranadar Jorra-hin spoke of earlier. It appears that they found it some weeks ago. This document Kassandra brought with her *is* a copy of whatever is written on this stone, just as Jorra-hin supposed."

Torrin-Ashur nodded. "And now that they've found it, sir, do you think that's why Tsnath activity seems to have dropped off recently?"

"Very probably, Lieutenant." He was pleased to see that Torrin-Ashur was thinking strategically. It may have been his fighting prowess that had brought him to the fore, but it was reassuring to note that the lad had some brains to go with his brawn. "So the question now is, what does Daka have up her sleeve? Kassandra believes her mother is planning some sort of action against us, but what and when she cannot say. Daka has two other copies of this document and she is taking steps to get a translation made. Kassandra believes that her mother won't make her move until that process is complete. Clearly these texts are key to Daka's plans. Which is why it's very frustrating that the copy Kassandra brought us has been destroyed." He huffed and folded his arms, leaning back in his chair. "The next time you feel like rescuing a damsel in distress, Lieutenant, try to do it *before* she gets shot."

"I'll try, sir." Torrin-Ashur's lips curled slightly.

"Anyway, I have decided to keep Kassandra's arrival a secret for now; the fewer people who know of her existence, her identity, and indeed her location, the better."

"Do you think the Tsnath will try to come after her, sir?"

Kirshtahll sighed. "Hard to say. Your father believes Daka is vindictive enough to consider it. It is a foregone conclusion that she knows her daughter has taken a copy of the text. So she may risk an attempt to retrieve it. Which is why you must travel fast and light. I want you to attract as little attention as possible."

"I know the country as far as the Akanu Pass, sir. Staying out of sight won't be a problem. And once we've delivered Kassandra to Kirsh, Jorra-hin and I are to make our way on to Alondris?"

"Yes. It's important that Jorra-hin reaches the Cymàtagé safely."

"The Cymàtagé? Is he to become a mage, sir?"

"No, Lieutenant. He is undertaking a Recordership. He is considered by his brotherhood to be one of their most gifted scholars.

But I have my own reasons for wanting him down there. I have asked him to conduct an investigation for me. I feel that if anyone can unearth what this Menhir of Ranadar business is all about, it is he."

Kirshtahll was rather counting on it. Without anything else to go on, they were still very much in the dark about what the Tsnath were really up to. The key to the mystery may have been delivered, but they still had to find the door it unlocked.

18

Gömalt arrived back at Castle Brath'daka from the debacle at the Stroth Ford feeling drained beyond belief. He wanted nothing more than to sleep. That was not a course open to him. The baroness would have been informed of his return. She would require a report from him without delay, a report he did not relish the prospect of delivering, given that its primary content concerned his failure.

He placed a mirror on the small shelf above the washbasin and regarded his haggard face. Sunken, bloodshot eyes stared back listlessly, glazed over with exhaustion. He was a mess, and almost beyond caring.

He set about drawing a sharpened razor across a week's worth of stubble, trying to avoid opening up the deep gash that Kassandra had inflicted on him in the middle of the Ablath. Within moments the blade caught the tender scar. Blood quickly began to flow, dripping off his jaw into the basin and turning the water a pinkish hue. He cursed vehemently. If the little bitch was still alive, she would pay dearly.

It seemed probable that Kassandra was dead, though it had not been possible to ascertain that with any degree of certainty. After the Alondrians had left the area of the ford, he'd crossed the river and followed them at a distance, looking for an opportunity to reach Kassandra and complete his mission. But the Alondrians had not stopped. They'd ridden throughout the night, reaching the small town of Tail-ébeth, thereby denying him access to his target. He could not walk the streets with his usual anonymity – not with a bloody scar drawing everyone's attention his way.

Scars healed. If Kassandra was still alive, there would be no safety in Alondria – not from him, not after the humiliation she'd inflicted on him.

Half an hour later, looking slightly more presentable in a fresh set of clothes, he proceeded to the great hall.

The baroness stood with her back to him, facing out of a window that commanded a view of the western approach to the castle. She was wearing an undecorated dress of charcoal-grey material that appeared particularly austere. Her hair was tightly arranged such that not a single strand escaped strict control. It was a bad sign. She didn't even turn to look at him when she eventually acknowledged his presence.

"You let my daughter escape."

It was a statement, not a question. She clearly already knew, and that worried him. The baroness had many spies working for her, that much was certain, but to have been told of his failure even before he'd returned to inform her himself was troubling. He couldn't begin to fathom the route by which word had reached her so quickly.

"I'm sorry, my lady."

He refrained from offering further explanation until it was demanded. That would have seemed self-justifying, an admission of failure bordering on fear, and he wasn't prepared to give her that just yet.

The baroness remained motionless facing the window, her hands clasped behind her back. The stance reminded him of a soldier standing on a parade ground. Her continued silence left a dreadful expectation hanging in the air, an uncomfortable moment full of unpleasant foreboding.

Finally she did turn to face him. The scar and the weariness of his visage, manifestly evident, engendered no sympathy. Her cold eyes simply and silently demanded the explanation he had withheld.

"We caught up with Kassandra as she reached the Ablath. We almost had her, my lady. But just as we set out across the ford in pursuit, an Alondrian unit appeared on the far bank. They must have been waiting for her." To Gömalt's surprise, the baroness didn't even blink. She already knew the details. He persevered with his explanation. "Their archers engaged us and things escalated. They had us significantly outnumbered. We simply weren't able to continue."

He paused to see if the baroness would comment, but her silence continued.

"I gave the order for Kassandra to be shot. She was hit, my lady. She took an arrow directly to her back. I doubt she could have survived it." Despite sounding convincing, something in his guts told him that even he didn't believe that now.

The expression on the baroness's face held only anger at being presented with failure.

Gömalt swallowed. "One of the Alondrians waded out and pulled her to their side of the river. We had to retreat out of the range of their archers. Afterwards, we followed them to Tail-ébeth, my lady. I cannot say what became of Kassandra after that."

"The Alondrians were not waiting for her – they were laying an ambush for one of our search parties," the baroness informed him, dispelling any possible doubt about her foreknowledge. "They were hoping to discover what we've been up to over the last few months. It was simply luck that Kassandra happened to run into them."

Gömalt nodded. That explained a few things that had been nagging him. He had not been able to determine quite how Kassandra could have pre-arranged such a reception. His mind had clung to that notion out of a natural distrust of coincidence. Yet coincidence it had evidently been.

"Kassandra isn't dead," the baroness continued. "There is an old mage at Tail-ébeth who goes by the name of Cosmin. Under his ministrations, she has begun to make a recovery."

Daka moved to a table at the side of the hall. Gömalt hadn't noticed before, but one of the copper tubes that had been used to transport the copies of the Ranadar text was lying on it. The baroness picked it up.

"Considering the nature of her wound, my daughter should have died. Would you like to know why she did not?" The baroness didn't wait for him to answer. She simply tossed the tube over to him.

Despite being nearly dead on his feet, he snatched it out of the air with automatic precision. At her bidding, he removed the top and peered inside, somehow already knowing that it would be empty.

"Kassandra was wearing a dispatch pouch on her back, containing the copy of the Ranadar text that should have been in there. The pouch cushioned the arrow's blow, preventing the wound from being fatal."

Such detailed knowledge. Gömalt's mind raced as he wondered how Daka could possibly know all this. It was becoming increasingly irritating that no obvious candidate for informant came to mind. He did his best not to let his frustration show.

The baroness came and stood in front of him, her close proximity no doubt deliberately intended to be intimidating. He examined her face for any sign of what she would do, bracing himself for a furious lashing. What came took him by surprise.

Daka gently touched the line of the scar on his jaw. He flinched and leaned back slightly.

"Kassandra did this?"

He nodded.

The baroness sighed. "I seem to have underestimated my daughter. I always took her for a spineless, timid wretch, unworthy to be a child of mine. Perhaps I was wrong." She paused for a moment, as if considering something, then went on, "Still, no matter. All those who have helped her will die. When we invade, the first thing you will do is take some of our forces and annihilate Tail-ébeth. No stone will be left standing. You will turn the place into a lasting monument to what happens to all who stand against me."

Gömalt smiled, even though it hurt to do so.

"Then you will find my daughter and you will bring her back to me – *alive*. Only then will she know what it truly means to betray me." Daka's voice was cold and quiet, only just above a whisper. It was enough to send a shiver down Gömalt's back, even though he would be the one to deliver the icy retribution when the time came.

Daka abruptly turned and resumed her earlier stance in front of the window.

"My lady, do you know what the Alondrians will do with Kassandra?"

"I expect she will remain in Tail-ébeth until she has recovered, but after that, Kirshtahll will no doubt wish to move her further from our reach."

Kirshtahll had already heard about her? Gömalt felt yet more of the world slip from his grasp. He tried to hide his surprise, not wanting to reveal any more of his ignorance than was necessary.

"Beyond the Mathians?" he wondered aloud.

"Possibly. Or to one of the larger towns in the Tep-Mödiss, Nairnkirsh maybe, or Halam-Gräth over in Vickrà-döthmore."

"There's no safety there."

"Kirshtahll doesn't know that. Only if he had an inkling of the scale of our plans would he realise that nowhere in the Tep-Mödiss will be safe. But he does not. Kassandra's escape may have put him on edge, roused his curiosity, but he is still in the dark. We have been fortunate in one respect; the stolen copy of the text has been rendered unreadable, so there is no chance of the Alondrians translating it. However, it is still a serious development. I fear Kassandra may have become a catalyst that will set Kirshtahll off on a drive to improve his measures against us. It is important that we deal with him."

Gömalt raised his eyebrows, though it was a gesture the baroness could not see. "I could attend to him, my lady."

The baroness scoffed. "*Not* a good idea. Our plan is to invade Alondria, not provoke them into invading us. Besides, we have another problem."

Gömalt remained silent, anticipating more bad news.

"The Adak-rann."

"The Adak-rann?" That, he would never have anticipated. "How are *they* involved, my lady?"

"Through bad luck. The men retrieving the menhir you found — they have managed to break the stone."

"Break it?" Gömalt's tired mind struggled to remain afloat in a sea of facts that seemed unconnected.

"I'm told it was stuck fast in its hiding place. When they tried to lever it free, the top part of the menhir cracked away, leaving the base behind."

Another failure. That could not have boded well for those involved.

"How has this attracted the attention of the Adak-rann, my lady?"

"Because the menhir was more than just a marker, Gömalt."

"My lady?" he frowned, now at a total loss.

Daka turned back to face him.

"The stone had been greatly imbued with Taümathic power; power which was released when the stone was broken. It caused a disturbance that was felt right across Alondria. It appears that the menhir themselves play a more intrinsic part in our plan than I had anticipated."

This was a new slant on things, but Gömalt's exhausted mind was unable to see the significance. "I thought all we needed was the text upon them?"

"As did I. But this disturbance has shed new light on their role. I have given orders that the broken menhir should be left where it is for now."

"Does this affect our plans?"

"I don't know. I am awaiting an assessment from Alondris on where we stand in light of this new development. However, the fact remains that the disturbance was observed by the Adak-rann, at their monastery in the Jàb-áldis Pass. As a result, they have commissioned a Recorder to investigate the cause."

"One monk, hardly a major threat, my lady. I could dispatch him easily."

Daka pinned him with a piercing stare. "Again, not a good idea. Removing one of them would only invite others to take his place. It would alert them to the fact that they are on to something important, and we can do without their further attention. With their tenacity and knowledge of history, if anyone might determine the truth behind the Menhir of Ranadar, it is they. Besides, I may have a better use for this monk. His name is Jorra-hin, and he is on his way to Alondris. He is a young man, with relatively little experience; he will be easy to manipulate once he reaches the Cymàtagé. And since Kirshtahll will undoubtedly use him in an attempt to find out more about the Ranadar texts, we may be able to turn this to our advantage."

"Misinformation?"

Daka didn't reply, but returned her gaze to the window once more.

Gömalt frowned in concentration behind her back. The baroness obviously had access to information from deep inside Alondria, people at the highest levels. One of them was probably close to Kirshtahll, though how she had orchestrated that was utterly beyond him. Others had to have influence in Alondris, otherwise how was she going to manipulate this young monk when he got down there?

He shook his head and sighed quietly. For someone who prided himself on knowing everything going on, the continued anonymity of the baroness's informants was really starting to grate.

19

Torrin-Ashur heard the clash of battle and frowned. Hugging the wall, he surreptitiously dipped his head round the edge of the stable wall and peered into the courtyard. He was met with the sight of his brother standing between the stalls, attacking the wooden sparring horse.

"Having fun?"

Eldris-Ashur froze mid blow, holding the family sword aloft.

Torrin-Ashur slouched against the wall and folded his arms, holding his brother's gaze. It was no great surprise to discover that Eldris had taken the weapon from his bedchamber. They'd played with the sword all throughout their childhood, bickering constantly over who should wield it for the battle of the day. As the elder, his brother had nearly always won possession, unless their father had intervened to impose a modicum of fairness.

"You could at least have asked before taking it."

Eldris-Ashur tried to sidestep an accusatory stare.

"You've added a few new scars to the blade." He made a show of running a keen eye along its length.

"It's a sword. That tends to happen when you have to fight with it for real."

Eldris-Ashur snorted. "A call-out? That's not a *real* fight."

"Oh, and you know all about such things, do you, o slayer of mighty beasts?"

Torrin-Ashur glanced at his brother's inanimate opponent, a strange contraption with arms and legs, shields and spikes, all of which spun when hit, attempting to return blows of their own.

"Father didn't give you this so you could go and ruin it in some trivial knockabout. It belongs to the family."

Torrin-Ashur's bemused expression quickly soured.

"It belongs to me, now. So I'll use it how I see fit."

He immediately felt churlish. The trouble was, his brother's haughty attitude never failed to get under his skin.

A scowl crossed Eldris-Ashur's face. He retrieved the scabbard from where he'd left it and slammed the blade home. He tossed the sheathed weapon across the forecourt. It fell short. Torrin-Ashur darted forwards to catch it.

"Well the least you could do is act like you cared," Eldris-Ashur muttered. "It's a family heirloom. Or does that mean nothing to you?"

The remainder of Torrin-Ashur's patience snapped.

"You hypocrite! If you gave a damn about what matters to the family, you'd have done your duty and served the Bond."

Eldris-Ashur's scowl turned to daggers. "Shoes you lost no time jumping into." He stormed out of the courtyard.

Torrin-Ashur allowed his brother to get out of earshot before letting rip with a string of expletives.

Since being back he and his brother had only spoken a couple of times. A confrontation had been inevitable at some point. With the two of them getting under each other's feet, it was never long before something of the sort broke out. He'd hoped that the months spent away at Mitcha might have changed things, but they hadn't.

He could have trodden the path more carefully, he had to admit. But that didn't change the fact that the encounter had left him with a feeling of indignation, and that was hard to quell. Eldris acted as though he'd been deprived of his whole birthright, not merely a single heirloom. If he'd just answered the call to join the army and serve under bonds for a couple of years, as every other eldest son had done before him, then their positions would have been reversed. *He* would have been the officer, bearing the family sword and the pride of their father.

It wasn't just the sword that roused his brother's jealousy, though. Eldris hadn't wanted to join the army because he'd seen no benefit in it. If he'd ever had the notion that he might find himself on his way to Alondris, he'd have leapt at the chance. Yet fate would have played out differently, had that been the case. Eldris wouldn't have accepted command of the Pressed, or become embroiled with Borádin. The call-out would never have happened and he wouldn't have come to the attention of Kirshtahll. Or, for that matter, Elona.

Torrin-Ashur sighed. It was true, he *had* jumped into his brother's vacant shoes. But making them fit had been hard work. If Eldris could see past his jealousy for more than a moment, maybe he'd realise that.

Sliding the scabbard off the blade again, he advanced across the forecourt, spun on his heels and took an angry swipe at his brother's former opponent. The hit was hard, splintering one of the wooden arms and sending a shard hurtling into a nearby stall. Its startled occupant gave out a loud bray.

Torrin-Ashur beat a hasty retreat before the equerry came to investigate.

*

The following week dragged by with an interminable lack of urgency. The Pressed had gone, returned to Mitcha and an unknown fate. Dismissing them for the final time had proven to be one of the hardest things Torrin-Ashur had ever faced. It had taken all of his self-control to hide his emotions.

Elona, Kirshtahll and the rest of their party had also departed, resuming their westwards trip to Nairnkirsh in the neighbouring march. Since then Tail-ébeth had become a strangely empty place. Of all those that had descended on the town recently, only Kassandra and Jorra-hin remained.

Looking back on it, he was surprised at how quickly he'd grown used to having so many people around. Their absence left him feeling like a visitor in his own home. It didn't help that he and his brother were now avoiding each other as much as possible.

That wasn't the main cause of his disquiet, though. The real reason, he came to realise, was that he'd grown used to the busyness of leadership, to always being occupied with some task or other. Loitering about with little to do felt wrong now. It wasn't relaxing, it just left him on edge.

On top of all that, Cosmin was being exasperating. With him, there was simply no rushing convalescence. Whenever pressed, the old mage simply said Kassandra could leave when she was well enough to travel, which was vague and unhelpful in the extreme. And that was that.

The only respite from the frustration was teaching Jorra-hin how to ride a horse. Occasionally amusing though that was, it had its limitations as a distraction.

When Cosmin did eventually declare Kassandra fit enough to undertake the journey to Kirsh, Torrin-Ashur lost no time making the final preparations for departure.

Kassandra's horse still hadn't recovered, so she was given a giant but docile mount that was rather more carthorse than stallion. It didn't befit her station, but would at least provide a comfortable ride. The same could not be said for Jorra-hin. Kirshtahll had made provision for him from Mitcha's stables, a rather skittish filly not best suited to a novice rider.

As the day of their departure finally arrived, Torrin-Ashur found himself feeling increasingly detached, as though a spectator on the sidelines of his own story. Something in his guts told him this day was a key juncture in his life, like the day he'd left to join the army. Only back then he'd had a reasonable idea of what to expect. Now the future was nothing but a void into which his imagination poured myriad possibilities.

Part of the unknown was that he was about to head south of the Mathians for the very first time. The mountains had always defined the bottom edge of his world, and in some ways it seemed strange to think that much existed beyond them. Of course, he knew full well that the Northern Territories were only a small part of a much larger country, but it wasn't easy seeing things from that perspective when the north was all he'd ever known. And who knew what lay in store in those distant, southern lands? *There be dragons*, as the old maps used to say.

He grunted to himself; dragons he could handle – it was the thought of an endless supply of arrogant nobility that made him want to desert before reaching the courtyard gate.

"I'm not sure when I'll be back," he said, hugging his mother. "Alondris is a long way, and I've no idea how long I'll have to wait before I get an audience. It might not be until after the winter."

"I know, Torrin. All the more reason for you to write."

There was an admonishing tone in his mother's voice. He smiled. "I'll try."

His father wandered over and grasped him by the shoulders. "Well, lad, this is it – time to go and show these southerners what you're made of."

"Aye, father. I don't think they're going to like it."

There was a hearty laugh. "Just stay out of trouble. No more call-outs."

"That might be easier said than done."

"Promise me," Naman-Ashur insisted, momentarily stern.

"Alright – no more call-outs. I promise."

His father's smile returned. He delivered a brief but fairly crushing bear-hug.

Torrin-Ashur moved over to his horse and climbed into the saddle. He glanced across at his travelling companions. "All set?"

"As much as I'll ever be," Jorra-hin muttered.

The young monk didn't look at all comfortable. Torrin-Ashur hid a smile; ahead lay disagreements regarding who was in charge – man or beast.

Kassandra, by contrast, looked settled atop her mount, albeit putting the mundane creature to shame with her graceful poise. Lady Ashur stepped over to her and reached up to take her hand. "Goodbye, my dear."

Jorra-hin automatically translated.

Kassandra kissed her fingers and said something in Tsnathsarré.

"She says she will never forget you."

Lady Ashur smiled and gave Kassandra's hand a quick squeeze, then withdrew out of the way.

Torrin-Ashur blew his mother a final kiss, then threw Eldris a casual wave. Although they'd not spoken in the last few days, at least his brother had come out to see them off. Whether that was at their father's insistence or not, he wasn't sure.

With that he gently spurred his horse and led the small party out of the courtyard. They passed along the town's narrow streets, sandwiched between jumbled wooden buildings, towards the western gate. Many of the townsfolk nodded or doffed their caps, some calling out to wish him luck; word of his changing fortunes had spread. There was an air of excitement amongst the onlookers, though quite why was hard to fathom. He couldn't shake the feeling that his going would make very little difference to their lives, one way or another. Still, it was a pleasant send-off.

Once they had passed through the town's gate, Tail-ébeth slowly sank away behind them and they settled into an unhurried trot along the same road that Elona and Kirshtahll had taken the week before. Nairnkirsh was three days' ride away, but in light of the general's instructions to conduct Kassandra to his estate as discreetly as possible, they headed on to a southerly tack well before reaching the March of Nairn's principal town, thereby avoiding the more populated areas. They made their way across the lower part of the march, forging their own path over its sparse heathland as they headed towards the start of the Akanu Pass. Only when they came within a day's ride of the pass itself did the gradually narrowing Akanu Valley funnel them back on to the main road again. By that stage other travellers were relatively few and far between. Only those intending to cross the mountains came this far south.

At the town of Hassguard, a thriving little outpost that served as the gateway to the pass, Torrin-Ashur left the others to make enquiries about the crossing.

"There's a party of merchants about to set off," he reported upon his return. "We can join them."

Jorra-hin translated for Kassandra's benefit, then asked, "I thought the general wanted us to travel in secret. Joining another party doesn't seem particularly discreet."

"I think the general would prefer that we get to Kirsh in one piece than not at all. There are bandits up there." Torrin-Ashur pointed up the valley with a nod. It was normal to take the pass in caravans for mutual protection, though that was because most travellers were merchants with something to lose. A trio with no visible goods in tow was probably less of a tempting target. But there was no value in taking chances; unbeknown to anyone else, Kassandra did have a small fortune in coins tucked away in one of her bags. They may have been Tsnathsarré dals, but gold was gold, and rich pickings for any lucky opportunist.

They dawdled for several hours while the caravan was assembled. Nobody seemed in any hurry and it was well past midday before they got underway. It seemed an odd time to be setting off, but a quick chat with one of the merchants revealed that the first campsite lay a mere four leagues up the pass, an easy afternoon's trek. After that, things would get tougher. The distance covered each day would not be great, since the deeper they penetrated the mountains, the slower and more arduous the going would become. Crossing the apex of the pass would be the hardest day, beginning before dawn and ending after nightfall.

Jorra-hin groaned when he heard what was in store.

"Look on the bright side – at least half the journey will be downhill," Torrin-Ashur offered with a wink.

Jorra-hin didn't look encouraged. "It's still riding. Up, down, it's all the same to me."

Apart from the occasional grumble, for the most part Jorra-hin bore his pains stoically. Torrin-Ashur found his respect for the young monk growing. A journey such as this couldn't have been easy on one so unfamiliar with horses. As for Kassandra, she was simply amazing. It was impossible to tell, outwardly at least, that she had been at death's door not long ago. She was either made of iron, or Cosmin's magic had performed miracles. Probably a little of both, he decided.

Over the next few days the merchant's prediction of arduous trekking came true with a vengeance. The path slowly narrowed until it wasn't possible to ride side by side any more. Higher up still, the path turned to loose rock, shale-like in places, with precipitous drops just feet away. Then even riding was simply too dangerous. Reduced to walking their animals for hours at a time, progress became a slow and exhausting slog, the thinning air sapping their energy and giving them headaches. Only Jorra-hin seemed to cope well at that point.

"You must be used to this," Torrin-Ashur said, waving at the surroundings. He stopped to take a swig from his canteen.

"It does remind me of home," Jorra-hin agreed.

Torrin-Ashur glanced round at the stunning scenery. Sharp, snow-capped ridges towered over them, supported by vast swathes of grey mountainside, all granite above the tree line which now lay far below them. From such a height, looking north he imagined he could see all the way to the Ablath and into Tsnathsarré beyond.

"Is your home this high up?"

Jorra-hin paused to consider that. "I would imagine so. The Jàb-áldis pass is much like this one, and our monastery is right at the top of it. Fewer people come our way, though. Our pass isn't a direct route through the mountains, so merchants don't take it unless they're coming to us for some reason. Perhaps that's why we don't have a problem with bandits."

Torrin-Ashur chuckled. It was hard to imagine anyone living so high up, even those of a brigandish nature. The landscape was awe-inspiring in grandeur, a privilege to visit for a brief while, but for all its rugged beauty it was not a hospitable place.

"Must be hard in winter. Cut off for months at a time. And bone-chillingly cold, too, I shouldn't wonder."

Jorra-hin shrugged. "You become accustomed to it. You have to remember, I've never known anything else. I find being able to see trees out of a window quite odd."

Torrin-Ashur shook his head in bemusement. A life not surrounded by trees – now that was truly unusual across most of the Northern Territories.

They reached the apex of the pass on the fourth day and stopped for a short break to observe the tradition of adding more stones to the cairn that marked the summit. The merchants were in the habit of combining that ritual with one of their own, the consumption of *sadura*, a powerfully alcoholic concoction normally served warmed.

While they built a small fire, Torrin-Ashur wandered a little way along the pass to be alone for a while. He found a spot where he could stand straddling the ridge, enabling him to compare the southern view with the northern one. He chuckled to himself; there really was something on the other side, not just a half-expected void. And somewhere in the distance, far beyond the horizon, lay Alondris. In that moment it felt as though his future took a significant step closer.

The descent towards Toutleth, Hassguard's equivalent on the southern side of the mountains, was much faster and only took a further two days. There the travellers had a choice of three routes. The majority of the merchants took the road to Am-còt, heading for the flotilla of river barges that would readily transport them down the Alam-goùrd towards the capital and other southern cities. The remaining merchants mostly took the road through the Dramm-Mastür Forest towards the west country.

Only one merchant's party set off south into the heart of the Kirsh province, along the same road Torrin-Ashur was intending to take. Encumbered with goods, the merchant was slow and was soon left behind. There was very little chance of the Tsnath having any presence this far south, but having no witnesses to where Kassandra was being taken was still desirable as far as Torrin-Ashur was concerned.

As they descended through the remaining undulations of the Mathian foothills, he began to notice the differences between north and south. For one thing, it was considerably warmer. The landscape was less rugged and the further the Mathians receded behind them, the flatter it became. It had been tamed, cultivated rather than left to the wilds of forests. The only place like it in the north, as far as he knew, was the Vale of Caspárr. But that lay to the southeast of Mitcha, just north of the Pass of Trombéi, and was not a region he had visited much.

One of the most striking differences was that cattle were left to roam untended in their fields. Within range of Tsnath raiding parties, that was unheard of. Nor were there any fortifications to the farm buildings.

So much for the dragons, he mused. That just left the aristocracy to worry about.

His thoughts turned to the prospect of meeting Lady Kirshtahll.

He wondered what she would be like. Then there was the question of how well Kassandra would get on with her. After all the girl had been through, it was a lot to expect of her to settle into a new place, surrounded by yet more strangers who probably wouldn't be able to speak her language. Outwardly she seemed to be taking everything in her stride, but it was next to impossible to gauge how she was really adjusting.

Late on the tenth day of the journey the Kirsh estate came into view. It wasn't what Torrin-Ashur had expected at all. He'd anticipated a castle. It turned out to be a great country house with a considerable number of wings, extensions and outbuildings. Being far from the dangers of the Tsnath, it offered none of the defences of its northern counterparts. But what it lacked in protection, it more than made up for in grandeur. Instead of battlements and buttresses, it had balconies and balustrades. Fluted columns supported delicate arches and decorative gables, while huge leaded windows overlooked long terraces broached by sweeping flights of dressed-stone steps. It was truly magnificent, the product of years of endeavour by armies of stonemasons. It was hard to imagine how Kirshtahll put up with his extremely basic quarters at Mitcha knowing all this awaited him at home.

By the time they trotted into the forecourt of the vast residence a formal reception had gathered on the steps in front of the main entrance. It wasn't difficult to guess which of them was Lady Kirshtahll. In the middle of the top step stood a woman dressed in a flowing cream-white gown. Hands loosely clasped at her front, her poise proclaimed her nobility quite without effort.

Torrin-Ashur brought his horse to a standstill and dismounted, suppressing a groan as stiffness asserted itself.

"You must be Torrin-Ashur," Lady Kirshtahll greeted. She descended the splayed steps and paused on the bottom one, allowing him to kiss her proffered hand. "Welcome to Kirsh."

"Thank you, my lady."

There was a grunt as Jorra-hin landed beside his horse. Dismounting was a skill he still hadn't mastered; he simply disengaged his feet from the stirrups and allowed the laws of nature to do the rest.

"My lady, may I present to you Brother Jorra-hin of the Adak-rann."

Jorra-hin took a moment to straighten up; he seemed a little worse for wear. Lady Kirshtahll acknowledged him with a respectful nod.

Kassandra managed to dismount with a grace that put both her travelling companions to shame. Lady Kirshtahll immediately descended the final step and glided towards her. She kissed her lightly on both cheeks and then stood back, holding her at arm's length.

"Welcome, my child. My husband told me that you were pretty, but his description didn't do you justice."

Kassandra's earlier look of apprehension vanished, wiped away by a blossoming smile.

Torrin-Ashur leaned across to Jorra-hin. "I take it that was Tsnathsarré?"

Jorra-hin nodded and whispered a rough translation.

Lady Kirshtahll turned her attention to them. "Gentlemen, Jonash here will show you to your chambers. As it is such a pleasant evening, I was intending to take tea in the garden a little later. Perhaps you would care to join me after you've had an opportunity to refresh yourselves?"

"It would be our pleasure, ma'am," Torrin-Ashur replied with a bow.

Lady Kirshtahll nodded, then slipped her arm through Kassandra's and steered her up the steps towards the main entrance. Clearly the lady of the house was not one to let her station get in the way of her hospitality. As the pair disappeared inside, all Torrin-Ashur could hear was a babble of foreign chatter. He smiled with relief; Kassandra would be in good hands here.

Jonash instructed several of the staff to unload the horses before he led the way inside. He showed Torrin-Ashur and Jorra-hin to separate chambers where they were able to wash and change into clean clothes. It wasn't long before he returned to show them into the garden. He served them tea and then retired.

Lady Kirshtahll was a while in making her appearance. With the surroundings sedate and peaceful, Jorra-hin was almost asleep by the time she eventually joined them. Torrin-Ashur delivered him a wake-up call on the shin before standing to greet her.

"Oh, do sit down," she admonished, waving them both back into their seats. Jonash, who had accompanied her out with another tray, poured her some tea before retiring once more.

Torrin-Ashur produced a number of letters that the general had entrusted to him. He sat and watched as they were eagerly devoured. Lady Kirshtahll was by no means a young woman, but the beauty of her younger days was still much in evidence. Her hair was now entirely grey and had a silvery quality to it that looked rather graceful. Strands had been plaited together into bands that wrapped around her head rather like a crown, the remainder falling gently down her back. Though age etched lines on her brow and around her mouth when she smiled, her eyes still held a sparkle that seemed undiminished by her years. He could see them flitting back and forth as she read her husband's missives. Whatever had been written, it seemed to be eliciting a considerable range of emotions.

When finished, she put the letters to one side and observed Torrin-Ashur with a dubious eye. It was not a comfortable gaze under which to sit, so he sought escape.

"May I ask, my lady, how is it you speak Tsnathsarré?"

"My father was Etáin L'Tembarh, the Alondrian Ambassador to the Empire."

"Ambassador? I didn't know there was such a post."

"There isn't, not now. It was during a brief period when the relationship between our two countries was a little more civil than it is today. I spent much of my childhood in Jèdda-galbráith, as a matter of fact."

"Jèdda-galbráith?"

Lady Kirshtahll shot him a look that suggested he was being deliberately dim. "The Tsnathsarré capital."

"Oh, of course." It had sounded familiar, now that he thought about it. "You'll have to forgive me, but we've been battling the Tsnath all my life. I find it hard to think of them as anything except the enemy. It seems strange to me that any Alondrian would have ever lived there."

Lady Kirshtahll nodded. "My husband would probably agree with you. Yet I can't help but be saddened by the state of affairs between our two countries now. There's so much we could offer one another if only we could put our differences aside and stop fighting."

Torrin-Ashur quickly realised it was going to be difficult seeing eye to eye with his host on this subject. The only thing he wanted to offer the Tsnath was a good kicking. He wondered how the general coped with such attitudes; Kirshtahll seemed as set against the Tsnath as the most ardent northerner. It was safer to change the subject than risk offence.

"Will Kassandra be joining us?"

Lady Kirshtahll shook her head. "I'm afraid you've worn her out. She was fit to drop by the time you arrived. I wouldn't be at all surprised if she's fast asleep."

"I'm not far off myself," Jorra-hin murmured, stifling a yawn.

"You pushed her rather too hard," Lady Kirshtahll chided, not taking her eyes off Torrin-Ashur.

He hadn't given much consideration to just how tough the journey must have been for the others. For the most part, he'd found it quite enjoyable.

"I'm sorry. She should have said something."

"Clearly you know very little about Tsnathsarré culture."

Torrin-Ashur raised an eyebrow.

"Kassandra comes from very different ways to our own. In the Empire, women are generally not permitted to speak freely in public. *Speak when spoken to* is the rule amongst men, particularly if husbands are present. And quite apart from anything else, Kassandra is a little in awe of you. You did, after all, risk your life to save her."

Torrin-Ashur felt his treacherous blush ready itself for a quick fling. He sought solace behind his teacup, the remaining contents of which were not going to sustain a credible degree of camouflage for long.

"In the Empire, according to the old customs, Kassandra would now belong to you because of what you did." At which point, Torrin-Ashur's camouflage went down the wrong way. Lady Kirshtahll's lips twisted in a lopsided smile. "Of course, things are a little different here. She will have some adjusting to do."

"Sorry – I didn't realise," Torrin-Ashur gasped, thumping his chest.

"Besides, she's not a big strapping young lad like yourself. You'll have to learn to be more accommodating of the fairer kind, especially in the light of the company Padráig tells me you've been keeping of late." Lady Kirshtahll gestured towards her husband's letters and her eyebrow rose a notch. Holding his gaze for a moment, she picked up her teacup and took a delicate sip, as if to demonstrate how such things were normally done here in the south. Then, quite abruptly, she switched her attention to Jorra-hin. "So, Brother, I understand you're from the monastery up in the Jàb-áldis Pass. How are you finding your foray into the world?"

"It is a much bigger place than I'd ever imagined, ma'am. Every moment is an adventure. Even riding a horse is new to me."

Torrin-Ashur rolled his eyes skywards. Jorra-hin certainly lacked nothing when it came to intelligence, but in mastering practical skills he wasn't quite as quick on the uptake. Nearly two weeks of riding still hadn't discernibly improved his horsemanship.

"And you are on your way to study at the Cymàtagé, Padráig tells me."

"Well, not quite. I've been invited to assist in a piece of translation work. I have a gift for languages, you see."

"A'lyavine in particular, I understand. And what about your Recordership?"

"You know about that?" Jorra-hin seemed surprised. "Well, yes, I've been appointed Recorder for an event we witnessed at the monastery, a disturbance in the Taümatha. As we have no idea what caused it, the council decided that the mages should be consulted. Brother Heckart, the head of our order, decided it made sense to appoint me to the investigation, to kill two birds with one stone."

"So you're not going to the Hall of Mages with any aspirations towards studying the Taümathic Arts, then?"

"No, ma'am. I shall be there purely in an academic capacity."

Lady Kirshtahll regarded Jorra-hin for a moment. "Interesting. Most of the young men I've ever met would have given their right arm to get into the Cymàtagé and have the opportunity to become a mage. Especially if they had any aptitude for A'lyavine."

Jorra-hin nodded. "The attraction for me is having access to the most extensive library in the known world. As you are probably aware, my order is dedicated to the gathering and preservation of knowledge, especially the histories of our people. The Cymàtagé has some of the oldest books in existence. I'm told that many of them haven't been read in living memory."

Jorra-hin simply couldn't help sounding enthusiastic. His was a passion that didn't take much to ignite. Torrin-Ashur stared at him as though he'd gone mad.

Lady Kirshtahll noticed his bemused expression. "And what about you, Torrin-Ashur? Are you looking forwards to Alondris?"

"Oh, well…" he stuttered, having been caught off guard, "the closer it gets, the more daunting it becomes. To tell you the truth, I'm still having trouble believing that I'm actually going there. Your husband's sponsorship has come as a shock."

"I can imagine."

Torrin-Ashur let out a dismayed chuckle. "A few weeks ago, I was living inside a bush up on the northern border, waiting for a Tsnath raiding party to appear. Now I'm heading for the heart of Alondris and heights of society. I have to admit, that's quite a leap."

Lady Kirshtahll laughed and patted the back of his hand. "Padráig gets these little ideas into his head and forgets how much he shakes up other people's lives sometimes."

"Mine's certainly been shaken," Torrin-Ashur agreed. "But it would seem ungrateful of me if I didn't express my appreciation for the generosity of your house, my lady."

"Yes, well," Lady Kirshtahll waved dismissively, "Padráig has to have something to spend his money on and you seem to be it for the time being."

"Don't you have any children of your own?" The words were out before Torrin-Ashur had considered the wisdom of the question. He noticed a slight stiffening of Lady Kirshtahll's posture.

"No. My husband is the kind of man who has to do things well or not at all. To become a father would have meant him giving up the army, and we both knew he could never do that."

Lady Kirshtahll spoke lightly, but Torrin-Ashur detected the traces of regret in her voice. He decided it would be best not to pursue the matter any further. Being childless was a delicate issue in society; barren women were often treated like outcasts. Deciding not to have children was a very unusual step to take, especially for nobility.

Lady Kirshtahll diverted the conversation herself. "Padráig says in his letter that you are to catch up with Princess Elona's party for the rest of your journey to Alondris."

"Yes, ma'am. He was concerned that Kassandra might be in danger, so he thought it best that we travel separately for the first stage of the journey."

"Elona will be heading for Am-còt once she has crossed the mountains?"

"I believe so. The royal barges should be waiting for her there. We are to meet up with them further down the Alam-goürd, at the northern end of Loch Andür."

Lady Kirshtahll sighed. "It's a pity Elona couldn't have made the same detour as you and come here herself. It would have been so nice to see her again."

"Umm," Torrin-Ashur hesitated, "do you mind my asking, what exactly is the relationship between the House of Kirshtahll and the House of Dönn-àbrah? I mean, the general treats the princess…"

"Like a daughter?" Lady Kirshtahll anticipated, nodding. "Padráig is very fond of Elona. Being a close friend of King Althar, he's like an unofficial uncle, I suppose. He's known Elona all her life."

"And her sister?"

"Ah, with Midana it's rather different. Not everything runs as smoothly as one would like in a royal household. What do you know of the House of Dönn-àbrah?"

"Not much. Royalty hasn't featured much in my thinking – until recently." Torrin-Ashur smiled wistfully at the thought. A few months ago it would have seemed ludicrous to dream of even being introduced to Elona. Now, spending time with her was not only realistic, but something he looked forward to.

"Perhaps I'd better explain, then," Lady Kirshtahll said. "Prince Idris died as a young boy, leaving Althar with no male offspring. As Midana is Elona's elder sister by some years, she is therefore now heir to the throne of Alondria."

"But why does Elona not get on with her?"

"I'm afraid Midana sees her as a threat."

"A threat?"

"You have to understand, Elona isn't anything of the sort. But Midana is suspicious, to the point of paranoia, some would say. There's a degree of envy there, too. She watches Elona like a hawk. Whenever possible, she tries to control her, restrict her activity, anything she can do to assert her authority. And that, as you might imagine, does not sit well with someone like Elona."

"Does the king have nothing to say on the matter?" Jorra-hin enquired.

"Althar dotes on Elona, and always has, since the moment she was born. That's part of the problem. While Althar is still alive, Elona is safe enough. But the king is very frail now and the word from Alondris is that it won't be long before he's gathered to his forebears."

Jorra-hin's eyes widened. "I'd heard the king was not in the best of health, but I had no idea his condition had deteriorated so much."

Lady Kirshtahll shrugged with her hands. "It could just be Midana circulating rumours. She all but runs the country now. Althar lingering on is the only thing standing between her and the absolute power she craves. I doubt she will shed many tears when he finally slips away."

"And Elona?" Torrin-Ashur asked.

"She will be devastated."

"What will happen to her then?"

"I don't know." Lady Kirshtahll was clearly worried. She stared at her teacup for a long moment before taking a sip. "I doubt Midana would go as far as exiling her; it's not as though Elona has actually done anything wrong. But when Midana becomes queen, there will be little to constrain her. I imagine she will marry Elona off to a lord of appropriate standing. One, no doubt, who will keep her out of the way."

"A political marriage that suits Midana, but not necessarily Elona," Jorra-hin surmised.

Torrin-Ashur shook his head. "She could end up being married to some miserable sod for the rest of her life," he muttered, allowing his military vocabulary to assert itself.

Lady Kirshtahll didn't seem to mind the slip; she was probably used to it, having been married to an army man for a considerable number of years.

"Quite. So Elona tries to keep on Midana's good side as much as possible. She's done very little to deserve her sister's disfavour, but that doesn't stop her from suffering it. It also means that I must ask you to be very careful."

"*Me?*"

"From what my husband says," Lady Kirshtahll pointed to the letters on the table again, "it appears Elona has decided to extend her friendship to you. But what you must understand is that she often feels very lonely, which in turn makes her vulnerable."

"Lonely?" Torrin-Ashur frowned.

"Yes. Elona has hundreds of acquaintances, but very few *real* friends. That makes her susceptible to those who might try to take advantage of her. Many court her for their own gain and it's often difficult for her to sort out the genuine from those trying to climb the social ladder. So I'm going to ask you to do something for me that I suspect won't be particularly easy."

Torrin-Ashur steeled himself for what he was about to hear.

"Whatever friendship Elona offers you, play it down in front of others. I shouldn't say this, but *lie* if you have to. Don't ever boast of her favour. It would be all too easy to use such friendship to gain status; please don't do that. It's happened before. I do not want to see her go through such pain again."

Torrin-Ashur sat stock-still for a moment as he considered his response.

"As the gods are my witnesses, my lady, I have no interest in climbing any social ladders. In truth, all I want to do is to get back to the Territories, where I can be of some actual use."

Lady Kirshtahll smiled warmly. "I can see why she likes you," she said. The tiniest of tears had come unbidden to her eye. She stood up to mask it. "Come, let me show you two around. If you like history, Jorra-hin, I'm sure you'll love this place. The Kirshtahlls have been shaping events in Alondria for generations."

20

Torrin-Ashur insisted on an early start the following morning. The rendezvous with the royal party at Loch Andür was a good day's ride east and he didn't want to be responsible for keeping the barges waiting.

"Do you have everything you need?" Lady Kirshtahll enquired from the top of the steps in front of the main entrance. She was standing exactly where she had been the day before when greeting their arrival. Not that she was as regally attired now; her cream gown had given way to a blue broadcloth kirtle.

"I believe so, my lady." Torrin-Ashur threw a glance at Jorra-hin to see how he was getting on. Not well, it appeared; every time the young monk tried to mount up, his horse clip-clopped sideways.

"This would be easier if its feet were nailed to the floor," he huffed.

A large brown head swung round and peered at him. Torrin-Ashur could have sworn the horse had understood.

Jonash stepped in to steady the beast, which was clearly in a recalcitrant mood this morning. Jorra-hin muttered his thanks as he climbed aboard. "And could you remind it *I'm* in charge."

Torrin-Ashur had to smile; his travelling companion's affinity for equestrian pursuits was an unlikely proposition. Ever.

Kassandra appeared through the entrance and joined Lady Kirshtahll. The rigours of the recent journey were already behind her. She looked radiant, particularly with the early morning sun glancing off her long tresses, bringing out the flame of her auburn tint. Torrin-Ashur found it hard to reconcile this beautiful young woman with the bedraggled creature he'd hauled out of the Ablath. It was even harder to think of her as being a Daka, nemesis of the north.

Lady Kirshtahll regarded him with an expectant air.

"Thank you for your hospitality," he said, snapping out of his reverie. "It has been a great pleasure to meet you."

Lady Kirshtahll descended to the bottom step. "Look after yourself, young man. I expect to hear good things of you."

He dipped his head and then turned his attention to Kassandra.

"How does one say goodbye in Tsnathsarré?"

"*Tekem-da.*"

"*Tekem-da*," he repeated, stepping over to the young noblewoman. He kissed her hand.

"Until again each other we see, Torrin-Ashur," she replied. Her speech was a little halting, prompting a bashful glance at the ground.

He smiled. "Yes, until we meet again."

With a final nod to his host, he turned and strode over to his horse, gripped the pommel and mounted up with a graceful swing.

Jorra-hin bowed his head to Lady Kirshtahll before commencing the daily battle of wills. His horse caught up with Torrin-Ashur's at the courtyard gate.

They cleared the outlying buildings of the Kirsh estate and settled into an easy gait. It was another fine day, the early morning dew having already evaporated to leave the road parched and dusty.

By midday they'd reached the Monument to Nabor, an unremarkable settlement whose only claim to fame was a battlefield nearby, where its namesake had died. From Torrin-Ashur's perspective, its one and only redeeming feature was an outpost of the Alondrian Message Corps.

"Gentlemen," the elder of the two corpsmen greeted as Torrin-Ashur led Jorra-hin inside the office. The man seemed pleased to have a new visitor.

Torrin-Ashur explained that they were on route to meet the royal barges at Loch Andür. "I'm expecting a message to have been left for me at Alondris." He produced a document authorising him to make use of the service on behalf of General Kirshtahll.

"Right you are, sir," the corpsman responded, having practically come to attention upon realising he was dealing with a matter of some importance. "If I can just take a few details…"

Torrin-Ashur supplied the particulars of his contact in the capital. The corpsman recorded them in a logbook. "Would you like to come through, sir?" the man offered, jabbing a thumb over his shoulder. "We don't usually allow visitors inside the boardroom, but seeing as how you're an officer…" He glanced up and down at the becassocked Jorra-hin and frowned, but let the invitation stand.

Torrin-Ashur was keen to see the message process for himself. This was the first time he'd ever had a chance to use the corps; rarely was he engaged in matters of sufficient urgency to require it. It would have been beyond his own purse anyway.

They passed behind the counter and followed the corpsman through into the boardroom. It was small, with no windows or decoration to brighten the drab walls. The only furniture was a wooden stool. The illumination was supplied by a single brass oil lamp suspended from the ceiling on a chain.

The message board was nothing more than a square table with seven circular dimples carved directly into its surface. Six of these were arranged in an oval, with the remaining one in the middle. Inside each lay a finger-sized black crystal shard, tapered at one end. The outer circles were surrounded by the letters of the Alondrian alphabet. The central crystal's recess just had the word *send* on one side and *receive* on the other.

Jorra-hin bent over for a closer inspection. "There's a matching set of these crystals in Alondris?"

"That's right," the corpsman nodded, "at our main headquarters. They have many sets down there, with counterparts spread out in a network right across the kingdom."

Torrin-Ashur resisted the urge to peer closely, though it was fascinating to think that such simple-looking objects could be used to communicate over vast distances. The crystals came in pairs, and whatever direction one was pointing in, its twin would always try to do the same. The leagues that might separate them mattered not. To make the message process work, all that was required was for identical message boards to be orientated the same way, and for the crystals in each pair to occupy their corresponding recesses so that they pointed to the same things on each board.

Nobody actually knew why the crystals behaved the way they did. Apparently it had nothing to do with magic, or so the mages claimed. It was like the needle of a compass always knowing which way to point – somehow it worked, and that was that.

The corpsman flashed a yellow-toothed grin at his assistant. "Jimmy, m'lad, signal Alondris and we can show 'em how we do things."

The junior corpsman twisted the middle crystal towards the word *send*. Hundreds of leagues away in Alondris, its twin presumably reciprocated.

They waited almost a minute before the status crystal swung round to the word *receive*, as if pushed by an invisible finger. Torrin-Ashur was spellbound. It was magic – it had to be.

"Alondris is ready."

"Good lad. Get the password cleared."

With the security procedure complete, Jimmy sent more details, requesting word on the progress of Elona's party by twisting each crystal to indicate a letter, spelling out words which he sent by rotating the status crystal, telling the other end to read the current settings. When he was done, he folded his arms and settled back to wait. The reply didn't take long; the crystals soon began to wiggle their mysterious dance, dispensing letters like seeds strewn from a sower's hand. Torrin-Ashur found himself utterly mesmerised.

Jimmy translated his scribbled shorthand. "Royal barges departed Am-còt at first light yesterday. Progress slow due to lack of wind."

Torrin-Ashur thanked the corpsmen for their services and ushered Jorra-hin back out of the office to resume their journey.

A light drizzle set in during the afternoon, taking the edge off the heat. It struck Torrin-Ashur just how different the climate was this side of the Mathians. Such warmth was rare in the north. Yet it didn't create an arid landscape. The surrounding vegetation was lush and abundant. Somehow, though, the gentle roll of the hills didn't really inspire him; it lacked the grandeur and rugged beauty of the north.

With his attention at liberty to wander, his thoughts alighted on Jorra-hin.

"Are you looking forward to being at the Cymàtagé?"

When he didn't get an answer, he glanced round to see why not. The young monk had a troubled look on his brow.

"I find myself more fearful of it than anything."

Torrin-Ashur frowned. "Fearful? Why?"

"It's hard to explain. I think, perhaps, deep down I have this feeling that it's going to change my life. Only, I'm not sure I want it to."

"Do you have to go?"

"Well, I could have stayed at Jàb-áldis, I suppose. But then I would have missed a great opportunity. You see, Brother Akmir, our most senior representative at the Cymàtagé, has recently acquired an ancient text and needs my help translating it. That's the main reason why I was selected. If it hadn't been for that, I think an older, more experienced brother would have been appointed as Recorder."

Torrin-Ashur nodded. "Tell me more about these Recorderships. I've never really heard of them before."

"Well, the Adak-rann is a scholastic order, not a religious one. We see our purpose as being to preserve the history of our people. To that end, we spend much of our time in archives, piecing together ancient texts and making new copies of old documents that might not stand the test of time much longer. But we are also mindful that history is happening all around us. We have a saying, *'Today is the history of tomorrow'*. So we take it upon ourselves to function as chroniclers as well as historians. When we hear of something significant occurring, we appoint brothers to go and make a record of what is taking place. Within the Adak-rann, to be given such an opportunity is a great honour."

"Not something you could turn down, then?"

Jorra-hin let out a scoff. "To my knowledge, no brother has ever done so. In times past, the position of Recorder held the authority of a royal decree. A brother of the Adak-rann could go anywhere, ask anything – even compel others to assist."

"But not anymore?"

A forlorn smile crossed Jorra-hin's lips. "Sadly, those days are gone. Now, we rely on favour and goodwill."

Torrin-Ashur spurred his horse to run up a short but rather steep incline. The track went down again just as steeply on the other side. It could almost have been a humpbacked bridge, had there been a small river to cross. As it was, there wasn't even a gully. He waited for Jorra-hin to catch up, watching him cling on for dear life.

"Are you allowed to tell me what it is you're recording?"

With his balance regained, Jorra-hin managed a shrug. "There's not a lot to tell at the moment." He went on to explain about the Taümathakiya, how it measured levels of Taümathic disturbance, and related how it had been bowled over by an event of strong magical origin. "That's what has got us so interested. Events of sufficient magnitude to cause the Taümathakiya to tip over like that are extraordinary. In fact, it is thought that it has never been recorded before. My brothers feel, therefore, that something of great significance must have occurred. But we don't have much to go on, except when the event occurred."

"Tricky."

Jorra-hin harrumphed. "That's one way of putting it. The Adak-rann council decided that enquiries should be made down at the Cymàtagé, in the hope that they might have some answers."

Jorra-hin certainly had his work cut out for him, Torrin-Ashur decided. "Tell me about this other business, this translation you're going to help with."

"Ah, well, that I *am* looking forward to." Jorra-hin's mood immediately brightened. "Brother Akmir has come into possession of a complete copy of the Legend of Tallümund."

"What so special about that?" Even up in the Northern Territories the Legend was well known. It had been an adored children's tale for centuries. Torrin-Ashur remembered his father regaling him with its sweeping saga when he was a boy. It was far from a rare text.

"Well, as you probably know, the legend tells of the battle between the dragon Bël-samir and Lord Tallümund," Jorra-hin explained. "The interesting thing is, the story was previously thought to have originated between eight and nine hundred years ago. The manuscript Brother Akmir has in his possession now predates that by some six hundred years."

From the rising note of excitement in Jorra-hin's voice, Torrin-Ashur realised this was meant to be impressive. "But why does he need your help translating it?"

"Because it's written in a very early form of A'lyavine."

Jorra-hin's tone suggested even more excitement. Torrin-Ashur couldn't quite see the attraction of being summoned all the way to Alondris just to help translate some old document and said as much.

Jorra-hin smiled. "I'm rather hoping that this manuscript will tell us something of the period in which it was written. Documents from that time are extremely rare."

"I thought the legend was just a bedtime story. Surely its historical value would be limited?"

"Perhaps. But with this recent find being so much older, I can't help but hope we might discover a whole new side to the story. Possibly even the truth of its origins."

"The truth? It's a myth. It has to be. I mean – dragons?"

"You don't believe in such creatures?" Jorra-hin returned, his incredulity laid on to an overt degree. "The Tsnathsarré would be shocked. A large part of their culture is based on dragon mythology."

It was Torrin-Ashur's turn to harrumph.

"Alright, then," Jorra-hin went on, undeterred, "you're familiar with the Mathians. Have you heard of Mount Tatënbau?"

"Old Table Top – of course."

"Well, according to the Legend of Tallümund, it was the dragon Bël-samir who gave the mountain its famous shape. The dragon's fiery breath melted the peak, giving it the flat, glassy finish it has today."

"Of course it did," Torrin-Ashur muttered back, his voice thick with sarcasm. "*And* destroyed an entire army. Everyone except old

Tallümund. Tell me, Jorra, how is it that Tallümund survived, but everything else got incinerated?"

Jorra-hin laughed, only for Torrin-Ashur to realise he should have known the young monk would have an answer to that, too.

"Ah – according to the legend, the dragon's breath could not harm the innocent of heart."

Yes, Torrin-Ashur did remember that bit from his father's bedtime stories. "But why, then, were those with Tallümund destroyed? Wasn't the army supposed to be on his side?"

"It's a good question," Jorra-hin conceded, his manner suddenly more serious. "That's why I believe the original version must have been rather different from the one we're familiar with today. The trouble is, stories that are mostly handed down by word of mouth are always subject to embellishment. Even a simple, innocent exaggeration can skew a plot quite dramatically. Something might start out as a modest little tale, but give it a generation or two, and you have a fully-fledged legend on your hands."

Torrin-Ashur smiled. It was quite obvious that Jorra-hin loved his job; his enthusiasm was infectious.

The drizzle that had set in only lasted an hour before the sun reappeared and baked the landscape dry again. They made good time and reached the shores at the northern end of Loch Andür well before dusk. The royal barges were nowhere to be seen.

The only mistake of the day was in being duped into thinking the loch looked inviting after a warm and dusty day's riding. Its water was shockingly frigid. Their dip was the briefest possible, and required a small camp fire and a cup of tea to chase away the chilly after-effects. The first cup was followed by a second; by the end of the third it was dark, reducing the chances of a royal appearance before morning to nil.

Dawn brought a heavier spell of rain, forcing them to shelter in a fisherman's shack nearby. Fortunately, the clouds hadn't the heart for a sustained attack and by midmorning the shower had fizzled to nothing.

"Ah. Look what I see," Torrin-Ashur said, pointing along the shoreline to the head of the loch.

A vessel drifted into view around the nearest bend in the Alamgoürd and slowly made its way towards the open water. There was no doubting its royal status; rigged correctly, the abundance of heraldry could have rendered its sails quite redundant. Not that the latter were having much effect. There was no wind. The current pushing the craft along was so ponderous that its crew had to row occasionally to maintain steerage. Two more barges wallowed on behind, looking rather mundane by comparison.

It took another quarter hour for the flotilla to glide to a halt at the jetty where Torrin-Ashur and Jorra-hin were waiting. A gangplank was shoved ashore. Before either of them could board, Elona appeared at the bulwark. She was dressed in a simple robe of pale blue cloth, relatively unadorned by pattern or embroidery. Her hair was arranged with equal simplicity, the front strands merely swept back and held with a comb at the rear.

"There isn't enough wind to take us across the loch," she explained as she daintily stepped down the ramp. She jumped the last few feet and landed in front of Torrin-Ashur with a bob. "So we're going to proceed to Suth-còt by horse. The barges can catch up in their own time."

Jorra-hin groaned, earning himself a royal frown.

"May I ask, Your Highness, is there any particular reason for the rush?" Torrin-Ashur asked.

A look of surprise crossed the princess's face. "Why, the Festival of Light, of course. It starts tonight. Didn't you know?"

"Festival of Light?"

"Lieutenant Ashur!" Elona exclaimed, giving full vent to her exasperation. "Don't you know anything? Where have you been all your life?"

"Err – the Territories, Your Highness."

Elona smiled as cultural ignorance came into stark relief against the backdrop of the north-south divide.

"Ah, yes. Well, in that case, you'll just have to wait and see."

"Would you mind if I came along with the barges, Your Highness?" Jorra-hin pleaded.

"What, and miss the festival?"

"If you would permit." The young monk's eyes quickly took on a pathetic, imploring look. "I don't think I could face so much as another mile on horseback. I ache most dreadfully – in places it would be inappropriate to mention."

"We could find you a cushion, perhaps?" Elona offered. But even in her enthusiasm it seemed she couldn't bring herself to insist; Jorra-hin looked just too crestfallen at the prospect of mounting up again. "Oh, very well. But you'll regret it, mark my words."

Jorra-hin bowed in heartfelt gratitude.

Captain Agarma, the head of Elona's personal guard, appeared at the top of the gangplank. He was not in uniform, Torrin-Ashur noted. He was a burly man with thickset neck and broad shoulders, though he descended to the bank with agile movements. No doubt a fearsome man in a fight.

"I'll see to the horses, ma'am," he said, moving off towards one of the other barges.

It didn't take long for those going on to Suth-còt to assemble. It was to be a select band, Torrin-Ashur discovered. Apart from Agarma and a handful of his men, none of whom were in uniform, the reduced retinue consisted of himself, Elona and her lady-in-waiting, Céline, whom he'd met a couple of times while they had been at Tail-ébeth. He shot Elona a questioning glance.

"We're going incognito. Having the whole entourage along would rather give the game away, don't you think?"

"Is anonymity important for this festival?"

"You know how people react when they realise who I am. I want to attend this evening like a normal person; I want to enjoy myself."

"But won't people recognise you?"

Elona didn't answer. There was an impish glint in her eyes. She seemed to take particular delight in keeping him in the dark.

Suth-còt was at the far end of Loch Andür. It wasn't a hard ride, a leisurely lunch ate an hour out of the travelling time, but it did take them most of the remaining daylight hours to get there. Twilight was just descending by the time the town came into view.

The first thing that caught Torrin-Ashur's attention was the smell of burning wood that pervaded the air along the shore of the loch as they approached the outskirts. It seemed to be drifting out from within a forest of trees the likes of which he hadn't seen before. Listless smoke hung between the trunks like fog. Occasionally he caught sight of men tending smouldering fires; whatever was going on, it was clearly deliberate.

Suth-còt was shrouded in darkness. From a distance it seemed a ghost-town, giving no impression at all that it was about to host a festival. That changed as they drew closer. It was far from deserted. Hundreds of people milled around in the streets, apparently waiting for something to happen. There was enough moonlight to prevent them from bumping into each other, but Torrin-Ashur could see why Elona wasn't worried about being recognised; good friends could slip past each other as complete strangers.

"Captain, we'll leave the horses here and proceed on foot," Elona ordered as they came alongside a stretch of fencing that led up to the first of the town's outlying buildings.

"Yes, ma'am."

They dismounted and secured the horses to a fence rail. Agarma detailed a man to stay with them. The princess gathered the remaining members of the party around her.

"Now remember, no one is to address me formally, understand?" A stern royal glance ensured hesitant compliance from the guards. Elona seemed satisfied. "Agarma, you may have the pleasure of accompanying Lady Céline for the evening."

Céline utterly failed to hide her smile. Torrin-Ashur had been watching her flirt with the captain all day. It hadn't been hard to conclude that the pair were very much in love.

Elona swung a shawl round her shoulders and flicked part of it up to act as a hood. "Torrin," she said, slipping easily into an informal address, "would you do me the honour?"

"The honour would be mine."

Elona linked her arm though his and steered him towards the darkened streets. She didn't bother to see if the others were following.

"If I may say so, Your – err, Elona, it seems a little misnamed, this Festival of Light."

"Not for long. Jorra-hin would have liked this, but I really didn't have the heart to insist. The poor dear looked so upset at the prospect of more riding."

Torrin-Ashur grinned. "He's suffered these last few weeks."

"And Kassandra – how did she cope with the journey?"

"Not a grumble." The thought of what his recent host had had to say about that made him chuckle.

"What?"

"I, umm, got my knuckles rapped for pushing her a little too hard. According to Lady Kirshtahll, in future I need to be more considerate in the company of ladies."

"Quite so," Elona agreed, delivering him a teasing prod in the ribs. "Life down here is not as hardy as you're used to. Alondrian society – of the type you'll be immersed in shortly – is rather more pampered."

They came to what appeared to be the town square, though it was actually an extremely wide bridge. The Alam-goürd ran straight through the centre of Suth-còt.

There were already a lot of people crowded into the square, with more pouring in by the minute. The air was thick with excitement; whatever was going to happen, it was clearly going to do so soon.

"Quick, Torrin, you see that stall over there – we need to buy a couple of lumines."

Torrin-Ashur didn't argue, despite having no idea what a lumine was. Elona reached the stall first and bent over to give the merchandise as much an inspection as the moonlight permitted. The lumines looked like un-ripened corn cobs, only smaller and more delicate. She carefully selected two and handed them to him. He paid the asking price without haggling. The general sense of urgency to the occasion suggested there wasn't time for that.

"Alright," he said, regarding his acquisitions somewhat suspiciously, wondering if they were edible, "now what?"

"Just watch me and do what I do."

Elona turned and politely but rather purposefully tunnelled her way through the crowd towards the centre of the square. Torrin-Ashur, whose bows weren't as daintily shaped as Elona's, fought to keep up.

Just as they had attained what Elona deemed to be a suitable position, an official, bedecked like a town crier in a tricorne hat and a long coat with large shiny buttons, strode into view. He stopped and raised a strange kind of trumpet to his lips. It brought the gathered throng close to silence. The note of the unusual instrument started low and resonant, but as it continued it rose in pitch until it disappeared beyond hearing. A number of dogs began to bark in the distance when the latent vibe reached them. The moment the trumpeter ceased his call, denoted only by the lowering of the instrument, the crowd erupted with a cacophony of whistling and began waving their lumine pods above their heads. Elona gave Torrin-Ashur a nudge and started to wave hers too.

He felt more than a little stupid. "What in the gods' names are we doing?"

Elona leaned in close. "You see that circular thing over there that looks like the top of a well?"

"Aye."

"Well, beneath it is a cage full of giant moon-moths. Any moment now, they'll be released."

Elona got no further with her explanation. The first escapee bobbed into sight, its large white wings flickering in the moonlight. As more poured upwards into the night sky, the trumpeter resumed his inaudible note. It whipped the emerging swarm into a frenzy. The flimsy creatures ducked and dived in manic confusion, creating an ethereal haze of shimmers.

The throng in the square calmed considerably, concentration on the diaphanous spectacle taking over. They waved their lumine pods as high as they could, trying to entice the undulating cloud towards them. Infants atop their parent's shoulders squealed in excitement as the fluttering mass boiled out over the crowd. Torrin-Ashur found it quite surprising that being enveloped by moths would be regarded as something to get excited about – his mother would have run clear to the edge of town, screaming. But here, even the adults seemed to be standing on tip-toe, like little children eager to answer a teacher's question. He could almost hear them shouting, *me, me, me!*

Several young men nearby had picked up their consorts and were holding them aloft. He decided to risk a little royal wrath. Thrusting his lumine pod into a pocket, he bent down and hoisted Elona off her feet. Holding her around the legs, he seated her on his shoulder. He was relieved to hear a gasp of delight, followed by gleeful laughter as she stretched her lumine skywards.

What manner of thought as might pass through the mind of a moth, Torrin-Ashur had no idea. But as if by royal decree, two of these loyal subjects, their wing spans a hand's breadth apiece, bobbed towards the princess. He watched as Elona quickly split her lumine pod and peeled the outer leaves back to reveal the intricate flower within. It released a sweet fragrance into the night air, reminding him of a perfume his mother sometimes wore.

In the throes of some strange scented ecstasy, the moths immediately began to flutter around the lumine. As they alighted on the unveiled flower and started to consume its nectar, the stamens began to glow. At first the light was just a very faint green, but it gradually grew in intensity until it had turned almost yellow. Even to Torrin-Ashur, not one normally given to the appreciation of such subtleties, the effect was magical.

Elona began to wave her lumine flower towards those being thrust at her by the surrounding crowd. As it came close to the others it acted as a catalyst and triggered them to begin glowing too. Just as a flame might pass from torch to torch, so a slow ripple of illumination began to emanate outwards from the centre of the square.

It took a few minutes for the gentle wave of light to reach the perimeter, then it rolled out into the surrounding streets, continuing no doubt until the entire town was awash with botanical lanterns.

So this was why the occasion was called the Festival of Light, Torrin-Ashur mused. Elona was right, Jorra-hin ought to have been here. This was not a spectacle to be pictured from some mundane description in a dusty old book.

With lofty purposes achieved, he carefully lowered Elona to the ground. She leaned in close and murmured something in his ear, but whatever she said, it was lost to the noise of the crowd.

Céline came barrelling through the masses, dragging Agarma behind her. "You did it, Lony, you did it! You lucky thing," she babbled, hugging the princess.

Agarma slapped a hand on Torrin-Ashur's shoulder. "Well done. You just made Elona the First Light."

"The what?"

"It's the most sought-after honour of the Festival." He glanced at the princess. "So much for being treated like normal," he added with a shrug.

Elona giggled and put a hand to his cheek.

"You'd better get going," Céline prompted. "The people are looking to you."

Elona grabbed Torrin-Ashur by the arm. "Come on, we're expected to lead the procession down to the loch. We have to launch the lights now."

Torrin-Ashur followed her lead, just glad that she knew what she was doing. In fact, it was difficult to imagine a time or a place in which Elona would ever be at a loss. She always seemed so confident, so very much in control. It was hard to reconcile what he saw of her now with some of the things Lady Kirshtahll had said.

He thrust those thoughts aside, not wanting to spoil the mood.

The route to the loch became self-evident as the crowd opened up before them, forming a pathway. He produced his pocketed lumine pod and opened it so that Elona could work her magic on it as she had with so many others.

As they neared the shore, numerous young boys flocked to line the path. Each carried a small raft or boat, most with some sort of mast arrangement. They were all eager that Elona should choose their creation to be the one to carry the First Light out across the water.

Elona was clearly in her element here. Even shrouded in anonymity, she still moved amongst the crowd with a regal air. She complimented each young shipwright and played the game to its full, being most careful in her selection. The look on the young lad's face when she made her decision was a sight worth a king's ransom. Torrin-Ashur couldn't help smiling at what the boy would have done had he known who Elona really was. It was tempting to tell him.

When they reached the edge of the loch, Torrin-Ashur held the miniature craft while Elona secured the two lumine flowers to its mast. Then the shipwright, with flagrant disregard for the frigid water, waded out and set the lights on their little voyage. They didn't actually go very far, the boat just undulated gently on the ripples. Numerous other craft were launched to join it, forming a substantial flotilla of swaying lanterns, all multiplied by their reflections on the water's dark surface.

Torrin-Ashur stooped to picked up a handful of small stones.

"What are you doing?" Elona murmured in alarm, grabbing his arm.

"Trust me."

Lightly tossing one of the projectiles, there was a plop as he deftly landed one just astern of their boat. The ripple propelled it slightly further out across the water. He followed his first shot with several more, generating a respectable gap.

With little to do now but admire their creations in action, the young shipwrights seized Torrin-Ashur's means of propulsion with great enthusiasm. The flotilla began to suffer a bombardment, occasionally with unfortunate results. It didn't take long for the boys' youthful intentions to overstep the mark, becoming more to sink than to propel. At which point they were shooed away.

With tranquillity restored, Torrin-Ashur noticed there were a lot of couples standing together at the water's edge, including Céline and Agarma, all quietly gazing out over the darkness of the loch. Elona stood close to him, her arm loosely linked though his. It was a moment that he wanted to hold on to for as long as possible. Yet all the while he had to fight to keep Lady Kirshtahll's words at bay. They kept reminding him of the reality of his position. Elona made it too easy to forget who she was.

It was blissful while it lasted, but it soon became apparent that their duties as First Light were not yet over.

Agarma came up alongside and nudged his arm. "Time to lead the way to the banquet."

"Banquet?"

"Oh, yes. Under the lumine trees."

Agarma pointed behind him and when Torrin-Ashur turned round, he spotted a townsman approaching, this one dressed in a kind of coat made entirely of coloured ribbons. He was carrying a flaming torch, the only light in the vicinity that wasn't botanical in nature.

"Come, my friends. I am the Master of the Banquet this evening. Everything is ready."

The colourful townsman led the way along a well-trodden path up a slight rise that began just beyond the shore of the loch. At the crest, the sight that met them brought Torrin-Ashur to a standstill. His jaw fell open. An entire forest of the trees that produced the lumine flowers had erupted in a blaze of yellow light, utterly dwarfing the effect seen in the town square earlier. Moon moths in their countless thousands gorged themselves amongst the glowing canopy. Nothing could have prepared him for such an extraordinary sight.

Elona pulled him back to his senses, pushing up under his gaping jaw with her forefinger. "Time to eat," she giggled.

The Master of the Banquet chaperoned them past a toll and through a wicker arch adorned with summer flowers; evidently most people were expected to pay, but not the First Light. The thousands of other festival attendees were shepherded into a queue behind Céline and Agarma. The captain's men were blending in unobtrusively further back. Apart from the threat of invasion from above, there wasn't much for them to guard against. The fluttering mass in the canopy didn't appear to be in the least bit interested in the goings-on down below.

The Master of the Banquet showed them to the beginning of a long table piled high with a fantastic assortment of edibles, from stuffed boar's head and venison, to quail and snipe. Tarts, pies, flans, and bread of all kinds filled every space not taken up by the main dishes. Filling the smaller gaps there seemed more varieties of eggs than birds to lay them. It was a mind-boggling array, and not the only one. The first table was backed up by row upon row of others, all similarly laden.

"Ye gods, there's enough food here to feed half the kingdom," Torrin-Ashur murmured.

"Yes, well, if you knew anything at all, you'd know that this is the most popular festival in Alondria."

Torrin-Ashur chuckled and shook his head. The Northern Territories had nothing that could even begin to compare with the likes of what he was seeing here.

Having done his duty, the Master of the Banquet excused himself and left them to indulge. A few minutes later, with gluttony overflowing their trenchers, they found a spot some distance away from the tables and settled down, joined soon after by Céline and Agarma.

At Elona's prompting, the captain left them briefly to see to the men and get some food taken to the guard who had been left with the horses. Céline watched him go, wearing a pining look of the totally besotted. When the captain returned, they sat very close to each other. Elona caught Torrin-Ashur's eye and shot him a knowing glance.

"How often does this festival take place?" he asked with his mouth full.

"Once every two years." Elona waved her hand up towards the canopy. "The lumine trees only flower every other year. The people of Suth-còt spend the rest of the time cultivating the trees and nurturing the moon moths."

"But how do they get all this to happen on a given night?"

"Magic," Elona winked.

Torrin-Ashur tutted.

"Lumine pods that remain attached to the trees can open themselves, Lieutenant," Agarma explained, "unlike the picked ones. You noticed the smoke on the way in?"

"I did."

"The townsfolk keep fires smouldering beneath the branches during the flowering season, which only lasts a week or so. The smoke stops the pods from opening and keeps away any stray moths. On the night of the festival, once the First Light has been established, with the fires all dampened down the townsmen climb up the trees and start the whole thing off."

Torrin-Ashur sighed. He almost preferred Elona's explanation. The idea that men could control nature on such a grand scale was, if anything, a little disturbing.

"And how long does the festival go on for?"

"A few nights," Agarma answered. "But the first night is always the most impressive. People come from all over the kingdom to see it."

"Except from the Northern Territories, it seems," Elona chuckled, nudging Torrin-Ashur with her toe.

The corners of his mouth turned up in a sheepish grin.

The evening meandered on at a leisurely pace, except for those serving the food; those poor souls were constantly under siege.

Amongst the revellers, over-indulgence brought a feeling of lethargy and a reluctance towards the idea of going home. Torrin-Ashur noticed that some of the younger attendees had already nodded off. Eventually people did start to saunter away to whatever accommodation they had arranged, leaving an ever thinning crowd. Some, it seemed, fully intended to stay the night.

Torrin-Ashur suggested they stroll back to the shore of the loch to see how the light boats were getting on. When they got there, it became obvious a significant number of the little craft had succumbed to the lure of the deep; whether they'd had help or not wasn't clear. He was pleased to see that one miniature craft still sat apart from the rest, gently undulating on the calm water.

Elona turned from gazing out across the darkness. "It has been a wonderful evening, Torrin. I couldn't have wished for it to have turned out any better."

Torrin-Ashur just ummed in agreement. An attempt at anything else would have left him tongue-tied. He would have been thwarted anyway.

"Good evening," came a familiar voice from a little way up the shore.

Torrin-Ashur frowned. The owner of that voice was supposed to be somewhere up the other end of the loch.

"Jorra?"

"Indeed."

"How did you get here?"

"I walked."

"What, all the way down the loch?"

"No, no. About a mile. That's as close as we dared bring the barges. We didn't want to come charging in with the cavalry."

"I'm glad you didn't," Elona approved.

"How did you get the barges down? I thought there wasn't enough wind," Torrin-Ashur asked.

"The crew rowed."

"So the boats are moored just up the shore?"

Jorra-hin nodded, though it was a gesture barely discernible in the dark. It really didn't help that his cassock was also almost entirely black.

"Well, that's bed catered for, then," Elona murmured. "And there I was thinking we'd have to sleep under the stars tonight."

There was a hint of disappointment in her voice.

*

Elona stood in the prow of the barge with her forearms resting atop the gunwale. She watched the entrance to the Alondris Canal drift into view on the port side. The gentle voyage down the river from Suth-còt had been pleasant, but accompanied by a growing disquiet; the end of the journey was nearing. Alondris lay but three or four leagues down the spur, and there the freedom of the countryside and its uncomplicated life would be crushed by the oppressive weight of conformity and expectation. Outside the city walls, it was almost possible to forget Midana and her domineering ways. Inside, especially within the palace, her sister's grip was suffocating.

She toyed with the idea of instructing the barge captain to bypass the canal and take the longer route. That would involve sailing on down the Alam-goürd all the way to Lake Gosh on the south side of Alondris, then tacking across the upper corner of the lake and making a short trip along the River Els-spear back up into the city. It would add a couple of days to the journey. But in the end she knew it was pointless; it would only delay the inevitable.

"Your Highness."

Elona turned and smiled. Torrin-Ashur was always very careful about using her name when others might hear. He was keeping the privilege she'd granted him a secret. She liked that.

"May I join you?"

She nodded, then turned and allowed her gaze to settle back on the approaching canal entrance.

"I gather we are putting in shortly, rather than pushing on to Alondris," he said, drawing alongside.

"We would not reach the city by nightfall. It is better to arrive at a decent hour of the day than in the dark." That wasn't the real reason; one more night of freedom was not to be denied. She glanced at Torrin-Ashur. He seemed troubled. "Is anything wrong?"

"Your Highness, if I may, I will take my leave first thing in the morning."

"What? Why?"

There was a hesitant pause before he answered. "Well, I had hoped to take the city by stealth, rather than by storm. Arriving aboard a royal barge is not the most discreet of means. I'd prefer to slip in relatively unnoticed, if at all possible."

"You do realise that you won't be able to stay in the shadows forever, Torrin."

"I know. But as I have no idea whether I'm going to sink or swim, I figure it's best to edge out into deep water slowly."

Elona could see his point, but wasn't sure it made much difference. One could drown in very shallow water, especially in Alondris.

"Well, do what you think best. You will have to trust your instincts down here. Do you have accommodation arranged?"

Torrin-Ashur gave a quick shrug. "I'm not sure. Kirshtahll's orders are for me to report to someone called Geirvald."

"Really?" Elona's reply was somewhat theatrical.

"You know him?"

"Geirvald sponsored Padráig when *he* was at the Academy."

Elona grinned, but decided not to elaborate. Some people in the city had to be discovered rather than described; the Duke of Cöbèck was one of them. Padráig had obviously not elaborated, so she wasn't going to spoil the surprise. The thought made her giggle.

"Stay here, I'll be back in a minute." She flitted along the deck and ducked into her cabin. A quick rummage revealed what she was looking for and she returned to the prow. "Here, I want you to have this," she said, thrusting a small leather pouch into Torrin-Ashur's hand.

"What is it?"

"A palace pass. It will allow you access, should you choose to pay me a visit."

Torrin-Ashur's eyebrows rose sharply. But he could not hide his smile.

21

Aolap found the darkness debilitating. It robbed his feet of their surety, turning what ought to have been confident strides into short, timid steps. His other senses attempted to compensate, but served only to make matters worse by stealing away his balance. Even the light touch of the guide's hand on his shoulder had faded into a diaphanous uncertainty.

By the time he was brought to a halt, he had no idea how far they'd come; it seemed like miles. The guide's hand lifted and he sensed the man withdraw. A tickling sensation washed across his face as the blindfold melted away. He blinked, expecting something, anything, even just a glimmer of light, but a stygian void was all that confronted him. It triggered a sudden moment of panic.

"Hello?"

Hello, his own hesitant voice rejoined a few moments later. It sounded disconcertingly hollow. Wherever he was, it was a large and empty place. He turned, hoping to detect the residual presence of his guide, but all he felt was utter isolation. The ethereal usher had slipped away without a sound.

Time passed. It was impossible to judge how long, there was nothing to reference, just the tricks of an increasingly apprehensive mind. He began to wonder if this had been such a good idea.

Now is not the time for doubts.

His heart skipped a beat. Had the words been real? He shuddered. No, it was not possible; he had not spoken aloud for anyone to hear him.

Are you sure?

"Is someone there?"

Aolap turned on the spot, as though this might help; the void revealed nothing except a suffocating, oppressive presence. He felt an urge to lower his hood to unfetter his senses, but resisted. His sponsor's instructions had been quite specific on that point.

Why have you come?

Aolap spun round to face the voice he thought he'd heard. The darkness was impenetrable. He hesitated, still unsure whether his mind was playing tricks.

Well?

"I – to submit my candidacy."

Then step forwards.

"Forwards?" Aolap floundered, turning again as he struggled with the miry darkness.

If you are worthy of our ranks, then you will prevail.

Aolap's mind raced. He'd been warned not to seem eager to use his powers. Now it appeared he had little choice. He raised his hand and summoned a small flame to his fingertips.

As his eyes adjusted to the welcome glow, he discovered he was surrounded by a circle of large candles mounted in stands. The wicks were at eye-height. He lit one, then let the flame he'd summoned wink out and used the first candle to light the rest. Even after the flames had settled into their full stature, their glow managed to illuminate little other than the circle in which he stood. The floor was stone-paved and smooth, but that told him nothing of what lay beyond the candles' reach.

So, Aolap, are you prepared to submit to the Searching?

The bodiless voice seemed to come from a different quarter each time it spoke. With a conscious effort he resisted the desire to track its movement any further.

"I am."

You are aware of the consequences should the Searching reveal something – untoward?

Aolap swallowed nervously. He had nothing to fear. He was not a Natural mage. The Dinac-Mentà would find nothing *untoward* in him.

"Yes."

Good. Then we will begin.

There was no warning, no gentle introduction, no benign questions to break the ice. Just a scream, immediately and savagely wrenched from Aolap's lungs. Its echo returned to him time and time again, as did the searing pain stabbing at his mind. Overwhelmed by a power infinitely greater than anything he possessed, he sank to his knees clutching his head, trying to shield himself from the burning daggers piercing him from every angle.

"Stop!" he wailed.

The pain did not stop. It intensified. It became impossible to hold a coherent thought. He could not have coordinated his efforts to stand, let alone flee. He writhed on the floor, desperate for a way to escape the sudden, excruciating agony of a thousand needles thrusting though his skull.

"No more," he gagged, his appeal choked out between clenched teeth, barely intelligible. He retched as the pain wracked not just his mind, but his whole body. This was not a search; it was a rape, a ransacking of his innermost being.

The brutal plunder continued unabated. He threw up, covering his sleeve with bile-ridden gore.

Memories long since forgotten were dredged up from the deep, their fleeting images cast before him, demanding ownership before being torn away by the fiery pain. From glimpses of childhood misdemeanours, to the lie he had told only yesterday; the wanton act of vandalism he'd committed as a boy, for which his younger brother had been blamed; the web of deceit he'd woven to woo the young woman he had bedded the night before last; even Lydia, the girl whose heart he'd broken years ago when he'd spurned her for another. Nothing was spared, nothing escaped the blazing intrusion of the Searching. It was merciless.

The ordeal went on and on.

"Gods – stop – please," he managed to gasp.

The effort of his plea almost suffocated him. He was exhausted beyond anything he'd ever known. He would eject his own entrails across the floor soon. He would die if this kept going.

Then stop us.

Stop them?

Stop us.

"How?"

Stop us.

"I *can't!*" he screamed with all his might. The effort consumed his last speck of will.

There was a sudden silence. Even the echo of his cry had been arrested. For a second he wondered if death had released him from the stabbing torment. Then he felt the hardness of the cold stone floor and reality flooded back. They'd stopped. Oh, merciful gods, they'd stopped. He'd never been more grateful for anything in his life.

He lay on his side, legs drawn up into a foetal position, heaving huge lungfuls of air as he fought off the urge to be sick again. His mind was swimming, hopelessly drunk yet suffering a thunderous headache. His every nerve was jangled, as though he'd been struck by lightning. His muscles trembled, their strength turned to quivering jelly.

It was a long, long time before he managed to roll on to his front and draw himself into a kneeling position. When he finally looked up, he noticed that the chamber had become illuminated. Not brightly, but enough that its extent was now evident through the haze of his blurred vision. It was vast. It had to be one of the caverns under the Cymàtagé.

Correct.

It was disconcerting that the ones behind the voice could read his every thought. Though perhaps not surprising. It was commonly supposed by those outside its ranks that the Dinac-Mentà used such invasive techniques to carry out their business. It was part of what gave them such a hold over their fellows.

Come, Aolap, you have passed the Searching.

"I hope I never have to undergo anything like that again," he rasped. His throat felt terribly parched, bile still dominating his sense of taste.

You will not. Unless you betray us. In which case you will face worse.

Worse? It was hard to imagine such a thing was possible.

There was a grunt of disdain. *You are alive, are you not?*

Aolap climbed to his feet. Yes, he was alive – just. He grabbed one of the candle stands for support as he swayed back and forth, giddiness trying to send him back to the floor.

There were dark-clad figures standing in loose groups beyond the candle circle. They were little more than spectral silhouettes, their hoods preventing any recognisable features from being discerned in the dim lighting. The Dinac-Mentà seemed secretive of their identities even amongst their own ranks.

A necessary precaution, Aolap. We cannot function if we become known to our brethren on the outside. Therefore we maintain secrecy even amongst ourselves.

"Some of you must know each other," Aolap replied, fighting off another wave of nausea.

Yes. But only within our own septagem.

"Septagem?"

Come, I will explain.

A figure stepped away from one of the groups and beckoned him forwards. Aolap made his way unsteadily out through the ring of candles and fell in beside his new guide. He was led towards a wooden lectern which had become illuminated, though by what means was something of a mystery; it seemed bathed in a shaft of sunlight, yet he knew now that they were deep underground. These depths hadn't seen the sun since the dawn of creation. Perhaps not even then.

"Have all the Dinac-Mentà been through such a Searching?"

They have.

Aolap grunted. Some warning from his sponsor of the ordeal in store would have been nice.

Had you known, would you have come?

Probably not, Aolap had to admit. "Why did it hurt so much? I thought you were able to seek out the thoughts of others without them even knowing."

We can. But that was not our purpose here.

"No?"

Today was a test. To push you to the point of breaking. Had you been a Natural mage, you would have tried to use your power to protect yourself. You would not have been able to prevent it, no matter how well disciplined you were.

"And if I had...?"

We would have destroyed you.

But how? Natural mages were powerful, that was the very reason they were considered a threat. How could they be overcome by those who were merely Followers of the Path?

His new guide waved a hand towards the strangely illuminated lectern, now only a few yards away. When they reached it, he pointed to a leather-bound book of some antiquity perched upon its sloping face.

This is the Septis Dömon, Aolap.

"I've never heard of it."

Few outside our ranks have. It contains the seven Incantations of our founding fathers. When the first members of the Dinac-Mentà came together, they devised a means to destroy other Natural mages, but in order that none of them could ever use this magic against the Order, it was made in seven separate parts – the Incantations. Only when each one is brought together with the others do they combine into a force capable of overcoming a Natural mage. Taken individually, they are harmless.

Aolap nodded. "Even so, there must be other safeguards?"

Of course. No single mage may ever be taught more than one Incantation. That is why the Dinac-Mentà is arranged into septagem, groups of seven. Each member of a septagem supplies one of the Incantations when they come together.

"Will I become part of one of these groups?"

Yes. You will take my place and I will go to complete a new septagem that has been waiting for its final member. And before you ask – you will never know who I am.

"You said earlier that members only know those within their own septagem. But what about me? There are many of the Dinac-Mentà present here now. Will they not know who I am?"

No. We have been communicating with you using the bond. This is done by the collective effort of members from a single septagem working together as one. Of those here now, only they will know your identity. And that it how it must remain.

All this secrecy – it seemed a little excessive. Those outside its ranks ran in fear of the lurking power of the Dinac-Mentà, even though they had little inkling of how the organisation really operated. Only the truly deranged would ever deliberately confront one of its members.

Deranged or not, Aolap, there are those who have tried. Granted, they failed. But the point is, there are some who will stop at nothing to bring us down. By maintaining this secrecy, if one of our members ever comes under attack, only one septagem, two at most, are at risk of exposure. We would be on to them quickly and the damage could be limited.

"May I ask, why is anonymity so important?"

Amongst our Follower brethren outside we must remain hidden. You see, it is possible to thwart the methods we use. We occasionally discover a mage who has found a way to mask his thoughts, or mislead our searches. But these things are hard to accomplish, and most of those we have caught trying knew who they needed to guard against.

With the Dinac-Mentà effectively hidden in plain sight, any potential Natural mages had to be on their guard against everyone. It was an effective stratagem, Aolap realised.

Another wave of nausea momentarily made him feel giddy. He reached out towards the lectern for support.

NO!

The guide's hand shot out and intercepted his arm before he could touch the stand, steadying him and drawing him back a few paces.

You must not touch the Septis Dömon. You would die if you did so.

Aolap felt himself go slightly weak at the knees, which had nothing to do with the giddiness.

"I'm sorry. I just needed to hold on to something."

Here, take my arm.

It was comforting to feel the solidity and warmth of a real person again, even if their identity was unknown. It was no surprise that the world of the Dinac-Mentà was a strange one, but it did seem to hold more than its fair share of dangers.

We cannot have just anybody reading the Incantations, Aolap. Only when joined to a septagem can you open the Septis Dömon without consequence. It takes all seven members to lower the Warding.

"Warding? Is that what this strange light is?"

Yes. It has protected the source of our power for hundreds of years. It has taken many lives.

Aolap shuddered. The Dinac-Mentà didn't fool around; they were lethal. But then they had to be. Theirs, and now his, was a sacred duty. The Natural mages could not be allowed to return and wreak the destruction they once had.

Out of the corner of his eye he noticed that six hooded members of the Dinac-Mentà had gathered in a semicircle behind him. Presumably the others of his new septagem. Even though they were close, he still couldn't tell who they were.

You will know soon enough, Aolap. Now, in a moment I will help them lower the Warding around the Septis Dömon so that you may access it, then I will withdraw. From then on, they will teach you everything you must learn. You will only be permitted to read the Incantation I know, since you will be taking my place and must therefore be able to supply what I take with me.

Aolap watched as the man he was to replace went up to the six other members of the septagem in turn and placed a hand on their shoulder. It was as though words were spoken, but nothing that could be heard.

This was a strange world he had entered, Aolap mused. He could only imagine how much stranger it might become.

22

Never before had Torrin-Ashur encountered quite such zealous street merchants as those of Alondris. The young lads offering to act as guides proved the most troublesome. Smelling fresh blood from streets away, they descended in packs. He soon realised there would be no escape.

"Alright, you horrible lot," he barked, "quit yapping and get into line!"

Being treated like soldiers quickly became a game. He strode along their motley rank, giving each one the opportunity to snap to attention and sell themselves, which they did with a shameless lack of humility. Unfortunately, they all said much the same thing and in the end he picked the only one whose name he'd managed to remember.

"An aldar it is then, Benhin," he agreed, dismissing the remainder of the pack to seek a new mark. Half an aldar bought a decent meal in most places, so the price was steep, but he hadn't the appetite for a hard haggle just now. "So, how long did you say you've been a guide?"

"Two years," Benhin replied, holding up his hand in anticipation of payment.

Torrin-Ashur chuckled. About eleven years old, the young lad had grey-blue eyes and what might have been fair hair if all the grime was washed out. His threadbare clothes were slightly too small. No doubt he had to be wise in the ways of the world in order to survive the streets.

"I may be a northerner, Benhin, but I'm not an idiot. You will receive your fee when I've reached my destination."

"You don't trust me, sir?" A smirk undermined Benhin's attempt to sound affronted.

"Trust is something you earn, young man. Now, can you read?"

"No, sir."

Torrin-Ashur sighed and unfurled a slip of paper with Geirvald's address on it. "I need to be taken to a place called Kilópeé Strass."

Benhin's eyes bulged. "That's in the Holmes, sir. Beyond the New Wall."

Which meant nothing to a stranger to the city. "Is that a problem?"

"N-no, sir. It's just, that's where the nobles live. They don't like ordinary folk there, sir."

An appraising glance from the young guide suggested certain standards were not being met.

"You let me worry about that. Your job is to get me there."

Torrin-Ashur felt an urge to mention that he'd taken breakfast with Princess Elona only a few hours ago. But Lady Kirshtahll would not have approved of such boasting, even to a street urchin.

Benhin shrugged. Clutching the bridle of Torrin-Ashur's horse, he turned and began threading his way through Alondris's packed streets. He quickly proved his worth as a deterrent against others of his ilk. He also proved to be an incessant chatterbox, his persistent prattle fuelled by a fabulous collection of city facts.

By the standards Torrin-Ashur was used to, Alondris was vast. According to Benhin, it was now some two leagues across. The mighty River Els-spear snaked through the middle, dividing it into unequal halves. The Westerhalb was the larger, upmarket side. Benhin seemed to be proud of hailing from the Easterhalb.

Throughout its history, the capital had expanded several times, leaving a number of defensive walls embedded within its geography, like the concentric rings of a tree trunk. The innermost, known as the First Wall, now only encompassed the city centre, which included the Royal Military Academy and the Cymàtagé. These occupied opposite sides of the People's Square. The palace, situated on an island in the middle of the river, dominated the Square's eastern flank.

"Then there's the New Wall," Benhin jabbered on.

"I thought there was a middle wall before that?"

"The New Wall *is* the middle wall." Benhin glanced back over his shoulder and grinned. He had surprisingly good teeth for a lad whose diet probably wasn't that wholesome. "The Outer Wall is the new one. The New Wall is about five hundred years old."

That was just perverse. "It ought to have been renamed."

"Nah. We like it that way. Confuses the visitors."

Torrin-Ashur grunted. It had certainly done that.

Benhin explained that in the Westerhalb, the districts that lay between the First Wall and the New Wall were collectively called the Holmes, where the nobility and some of the more successful merchants had their city residences.

Everybody else lived and worked between the New Wall and the

Outer Wall. This was where the chaos seemed to reign, and where Benhin and his fellows came into their own.

"There's a tradesman's toll we have to go through," Benhin warned about an hour later.

They rounded the end of some timber-framed buildings, which seemed to be leaning rather precariously to one side, and the New Wall came into view. Looking like the outer defences of a castle, it was a massive, granite structure at least forty feet high. The street led up to a portcullis complete with the remnants of some lifting gear for a non-existent drawbridge. Whatever moat there may have been had long since been filled in and built over.

A small detachment of soldiers manned a booth just outside the archway. They were a nonchalant bunch, Torrin-Ashur observed, more tax collectors than fighters. As Benhin drew the horse to a standstill in front of a pole-gate, one of them rose from his seat, displaying a distinct lack of enthusiasm for his job.

"Passage fee, twenty cents apiece," he drawled.

"Corporal," Torrin-Ashur acknowledged with a nod, having noticed the faded insignia on the man's tunic, "The toll is for tradesmen and merchants, is that not so?"

Suspicion replaced the look of boredom on the soldier's face.

"Let me assure you, I do not qualify on that score." Wishing he'd kept his uniform on, Torrin-Ashur rummaged about in his belongings for the leather pouch Elona had given him. He flashed it under the corporal's nose. "My name is Lieutenant Ashur. I take it you recognise what that is?"

The corporal backed away. "Yes, sir. A palace pass."

"Quite."

The corporal nodded to one of his men and the gate was lifted — relatively sharply. He looked worried now. He was probably used to exacting the toll from more citizens than his remit permitted.

Once on the other side of the wall, Benhin could hardly contain himself. "Have you really got business at the palace, sir?"

Torrin-Ashur smiled down at his guide's awestruck face. "Indeed. But not today."

The atmosphere was different inside the New Wall. The streets were wider and less crowded, the buildings older but not so haphazardly positioned — the difference between the tangle of a wild hedgerow and the order of a tended garden. Torrin-Ashur mounted up, reached down and grabbed Benhin, unceremoniously depositing him on the back of the horse. The young lad wriggled uncomfortably.

"Sit still, for goodness' sake, or you'll have us both off."

"First time I've been *on* an 'orse, sir," Benhin defended.

It took a while to find Kilópeé Strass. Benhin finally had to admit that he'd never actually been there. But by a process of deduction and a little guesswork he eventually prevailed. Quick to dismount when they arrived, he looked quite relieved to be back on his own two feet.

"Well, Benhin, you've delivered on your bargain, and so must I." Torrin-Ashur handed down a silver aldar. "You don't have to pay the toll to get back through the New Wall, do you?"

"No, sir. Only to get in."

"Good. If I require a guide again, I shall know who to look for."

Benhin tugged his forelock, flashed his white teeth in another grin, and dashed off back the way they'd come.

Torrin-Ashur took a deep breath and nudged his horse on down Kilópeé Strass. The surroundings made him feel uncomfortable. There was an eerie lack of activity. Barely a sound came from anywhere. The clack of hoof on cobble seem incongruously loud, making him feel the unwelcome interloper shattering the peace.

Kirshtahll's instructions indicated that Geirvald's residence would be distinguished from the rest by a life-sized bronze statue of a prancing horse standing in the middle of a fountain. It was hard to miss.

The statue was surrounded by a gravel path wide enough for a carriage. It was raked absolutely smooth. Torrin-Ashur was horrified at the dimples his horse made crossing it. He prayed, really quite earnestly, that hooves were the only evidence of its passage his horse needed to leave.

On the far side a small flight of steps led up to the main entrance of the residence, a door of the blackest mahogany that was polished to a mirror-like sheen. It beckoned with an ominous lure. He dismounted, tied his reins to a railing and approached with some foreboding. A miniature battle axe resting against a small brass shield, a reassuringly military feature, served as a door knocker. He gave it a couple of taps.

The knock was answered within moments.

"Good day. My name is Lieutenant Torrin-Ashur. I am under orders to report here, to a gentleman by the name of Geirvald." Torrin-Ashur offered his letter of introduction forwards.

The doorman stepped aside and Torrin-Ashur was admitted as far as the vestibule. "If you would wait here a moment, sir, I must check with the head of the house. The Master is not usually disturbed at this time in the afternoon."

The servant who'd opened the door departed, leaving Torrin-Ashur under the watchful eye of a young lad who couldn't have been more than fifteen. The task of his being the last line of defence against a military invasion appeared to be making him nervous. He kept his distance and glanced at the floor every time Torrin-Ashur caught his eye.

After some delay, a tall, thin man dressed in rather austere garments of black approached.

"I apologise that you have been kept waiting, sir. My name is Gad, head of the house staff. We weren't expecting you so soon. We were told that you would be arriving with the royal barges, only the Toning has not yet sounded."

"The Toning?"

"Yes, sir. In Alondris, the arrival or departure of a member of the royal household is marked by the Toning. It's a bell, sir."

"Ah."

"If you would like to step this way."

Torrin-Ashur made to follow, but suddenly thought of something. "Is it alright to leave my horse tied up outside?"

"It will be taken care of, sir." Gad's tone suggested he was above having to consider such mundane matters.

The young lad on guard duty moved closer and hovered expectantly.

"Your sword, sir," Gad explained. "It is customary in Alondris to divest oneself of weapons when entering another man's house, sir. Unless, of course, you intend to use them."

Torrin-Ashur was quick to unfasten the belt buckle and hand over his blade. To that he added the dagger from his waistband. The servant bowed and withdrew, carrying his new charges as though they were precious relics.

"The Master of the house is presently asleep in the garden, sir. I will take you to him but I must ask you to wait until he wakes of his own accord. He is never disturbed during the afternoon."

Torrin-Ashur nodded. Gad led the way through the enormous house. If it had seemed impressive from the outside, that was nothing compared to the interior. The ceilings were as white as the finest bleached silk and artistically moulded with floral arrangements. The floor was of polished oak and gleamed like glass. The walls, divided into panels, were hung with huge ornamental mirrors that gave the rooms an even more spacious aspect, not that that was really necessary. Chandeliers abounded, intricate crystal affairs designed to mesmerise a humble northern visitor.

"I apologise for my ignorance, but, who exactly is your master?"

"No apology necessary, sir. The Master is the Duke of Cöbèck".

Torrin-Ashur felt the blood drain from his face. Kirshtahll was up to his tricks again, dropping him in at the deep end. "More royalty," he muttered under his breath.

"Sir?"

"Oh, nothing."

Gad turned and raised a curious eyebrow, but Torrin-Ashur just shrugged and smiled.

"So how does one address a Duke?"

"'Your Grace' is customary, sir."

Gad pushed his way through a pair of glazed doors that opened out on to a multi-tiered terrace extending to a balustrade. Beyond was a steep embankment down which a cascade of steps splayed to an immaculate lawn. Lady Ashur would have approved.

Some way down the garden, appearing slightly at odds with its surroundings, stood a wooden structure resembling a pagoda. Under it sat what Torrin-Ashur presumed to be the Duke. He noticed his letter of introduction had already been placed beside the old man.

"The Master usually takes tea when he wakes. I will bring some out at the appropriate moment. Until then, please feel free to enjoy the garden."

Gad retired back inside his domain, leaving Torrin-Ashur to while away the time wandering round the garden as suggested. It was certainly as immaculately kept as his mother's pride and joy back in Tail-ébeth.

His attention was captured by the delicate bell-shape of a purple cobaea flower. He dropped to his haunches for a closer inspection, marvelling at its exquisite detail, at how all the tiny elements inside performed amazing functions, yet managed to look as though they existed purely by dint of some artist having let slip with imagination.

There was a thud, the kind an apple hitting a stone wall makes. Said missile had just sailed over his head, Torrin-Ashur realised. It had only narrowly missed.

A chuckle rumbled from the pagoda. "Damn."

Torrin-Ashur rose and turned. "Your Grace?"

"Well," the Duke shrugged, "stop wasting my time, boy. Come here, let me take a look at you."

Torrin-Ashur hurried over to the pagoda and took the seat indicated by the old man.

"So, you're the lad young Padráig has decided to sponsor."

Torrin-Ashur couldn't help but smile.

"Something humours you?"

"I'm sorry, Your Grace. It's just that I never thought of General Kirshtahll as being young before."

"I'm a hundred and two, don't you know," the old Duke grunted, "so compared to me, he's just a kid."

As promised, Gad appeared carrying a tray. With a well-practised flourish, he furnished them both with cups and retired once more with nary a word spoken.

"So, do you know why you're here?" the Duke asked.

"Not really, sir."

The old man took a sip of his tea. His thin, bony hand shook a little as he lifted the cup.

"Getting an audience with Princess Midana can be a lengthy affair. Padráig has therefore arranged for you to spend some time at the Academy. You might as well benefit from some training while you're here. However, he has asked me to give you a little introduction to the ways of this fair city before you report there. He also suggested that I might arrange for the services of a decent tailor." The Duke paused for a quick smirk. "Most people here would put your average peacock to shame, as I'm sure you've noticed."

Torrin-Ashur grimaced. The servants were better dressed than he was. Even the street urchins had discerning eyes.

"So you will be staying here for a couple of days."

"Thank you, Your Grace."

The Duke took another gulp of tea. "I gather this is your first time south of the Mathians? Quite a contrast, I should imagine."

"Just a little, sir. Alondris is quite daunting."

"Still, I hear you can take care of yourself. Padráig has told me all about how you rescued a young lady from our Tsnathsarré friends." The old man prompted for further elaboration with a raised eyebrow.

"It was just a clash across the Ablath, sir." Torrin-Ashur continued with a brief account of the day Kassandra had made her escape into Alondria.

"My, my, that takes me back," the Duke chuckled. "I took an arrow in my thigh, once. Hurt like hell. Of course, that was a long time ago."

"Princess Elona said you were General Kirshtahll's sponsor when he was at the Academy. That must have been more than thirty years ago."

"And I was retired even then," the old man nodded. His eyes took on a distant glaze as ancient memories surfaced. "I remember Padráig back in those days. He was an arrogant brat heading in entirely the wrong direction."

"I beg your pardon, sir?"

"He was well on his way to becoming an idiot – until I got hold of him. You can tell him that from me, when next you see him."

"I'd rather not, sir. The purpose of my being here is to improve my prospects, not bury them."

The Duke began to laugh raucously, until he dissolved into a fit of coughing. There were mirthful tears in his eyes by the time he was done.

"My dear boy," he said, dabbing his eyes with the corner of a napkin, "I shall have to take you in small doses if I'm to live to see my next birthday, don't you know."

Gad appeared at the top of the garden steps, looking rather concerned. The Duke shooed him away with a flick of his fingers before leaning forwards to replenish his tea. Torrin-Ashur intercepted the less than steady effort and poured for him.

"I gather you travelled down from the Northern Territories with Elona?"

"Only part of the way, sir. From Loch Andür onwards."

"I see. And what was it like to spend time in such company?"

Torrin-Ashur answered with a subtle smile.

The Duke reciprocated. "As the Toning has not yet sounded, the princess must still be on her way. So tell me, why didn't you stay with her party all the way into the city? Not many get the opportunity to arrive in that kind of style."

"Exactly, sir. I didn't want the attention."

"Why not?"

Torrin-Ashur shrugged. "I don't wish to sound impertinent, Your Grace, or ungrateful, but the truth is, I don't really want to be here. This business of receiving a royal commission – it's just something I have to endure before I can get back to what really matters. I have no wish to be the talk of the town."

The Duke regarded him pensively for a moment. "Good answer, lad, good answer. Much better than your predecessor would have given."

"Predecessor?"

"Hmm. You're not the first that Padráig has sponsored."

"I didn't know that, sir."

"Well, it was a few years ago now. Padráig picked what seemed a bright young man, one Wisehelm of Campas. Unfortunately, it was not a good choice."

"May I ask why not?"

"He was the son of a minor lord, much like yourself. But he became too arrogant; being sponsored by the House of Kirshtahll went to his head. He even had the audacity to attempt to get on familiar terms with our future queen, Princess Midana. His advances were not welcome and he made an utter fool of himself."

Torrin-Ashur began to see another side to why Lady Kirshtahll had her concerns over any relationship he might have with Elona. She probably didn't want the name of Kirshtahll dragged through the mud again. It did seem odd that she had made no mention of this Wisehelm, though.

"I can assure you, Your Grace, I do not intend to be the cause of any disgrace to the House of Kirshtahll."

The Duke leant forwards and patted him on the knee. "Good lad. For what it's worth, I think Padráig has made a better choice this time around."

Torrin-Ashur gave an appreciative nod.

"Well," the old man announced, rising wobbly to his feet, "I expect you'd like to make a start. Let us go find Gad and begin arranging you a new wardrobe. Now that you bear the name of Kirshtahll, we can't very well have you going round dressed like a turnip farmer, can we?"

Oh, dear gods, was it as bad as that, Torrin-Ashur wondered?

23

Jorra-hin marvelled at the transformation the Alondris Canal had undergone. Outside the city walls it could have passed for a river, albeit one a little straighter than nature usually crafted, but inside it was manifestly manmade. Grassy banks gave way to quayside and, according to one of the bargemen, even the bottom was paved – unfortunately rendering punt-poles useless. A lack of wind did the same for the sails. Oars just clashed with oncoming traffic, so that left draught horses as the only practical means of propulsion.

Not too much of a problem, Jorra-hin had assumed. He soon discovered how ignorant he was of the city's ways. Once the royal barge had been recognised, a messenger was dispatched to have the Toning sounded. Another was sent to fetch a dedicated team of horses from the palace, the animals used for hauling common loads being deemed unsuitable for a royal party. Only the gods knew why. All this resulted in the barge wallowing for hours while arrangements were made.

Such protocol did seem rather pointless. It clearly annoyed Elona. Jorra-hin watched as she slipped into her city persona, her giggly, effervescent nature gradually becoming subdued, liberty surrendering to conformity. Though every now and then he caught a knowing smile that said, *it's just a game we have to play*.

The faff wasn't finished even after docking. An honour guard strutted about welcoming the princess back with a short ceremony. To a wide-eyed first-time visitor it was fascinating, but an ill-suppressed yawn suggested Elona was bored to tears by it all. She wasted no time making her move when the formalities were concluded. Whispering something to Céline, she made an immediate beeline for her carriage before anything else could waylay her.

"Her Highness wondered whether you would care to join us?" Céline relayed. "We'll be passing the Cymàtagé on our way to the palace."

Jorra-hin was quick not to let such an opportunity pass and accepted with a grateful smile. He offered Elona his thanks as he climbed aboard the open-topped carriage.

"Well, we couldn't have you getting lost on your first day here, Brother," the princess said. "Alondris can be an unforgiving place to strangers."

The cortège got underway with a jolt. The docks and their rather functional buildings receded and were replaced by the astounding diversity of Alondris. Scores of people seemed to materialise from every door, street and alleyway along the route. Some were deferential, others presumptuous enough to wave. More than one pointed at Jorra-hin, clearly wondering who he was.

"I can see why Torrin-Ashur wanted to enter the city on his own," Jorra-hin said.

"He's probably still trying to push his way through to the New Wall," Elona giggled, glancing at Céline and rolling her eyes up.

As they approached the centre of the city, the grandeur of the buildings became ever more impressive. That only went part way to preparing Jorra-hin for the moment the carriage surged out into the People's Square. His mind was so besieged by the scale of it that he was left speechless. He found it difficult to comprehend how anyone but the gods could have cobbled such an expanse.

His gaze alighted on the Cymàtagé, dominating the north side of the People's Square. It was without doubt the single most daunting building he had ever laid eyes on. The immense edifice was unashamedly contrived to impress upon the beholder the importance of those who resided within. Crystal columns across its breadth refracted the sunlight into countless hues, a thousand rainbows imprisoned into a mesmerising curtain. From a distance nothing behind the translucent portico could be discerned. It reminded him of a phrase Cosmin back in Tail-ébeth had favoured; *in smoke and mirrors much magic lies.*

The gilded letters on the frieze above the portico caught his eye:

Hëlyath é-Cymàtagé

His mind automatically supplied a translation. *Come have ye to the Hall of Mages.*

He was still pondering what that might mean for him personally when the carriage rolled to a stop alongside the huge flight of white marble steps that ran the full width of the building.

"End of the journey, Brother."

A certain nervousness turned Jorra-hin's throat dry. "I'm extremely grateful, Your Highness. It would have taken me a week to get here on my own."

Elona smiled. "Trust me, you will find that the grandeur of Alondris soon becomes commonplace."

Right now, that concept was a little hard to swallow.

As he stepped down from the carriage, Elona leaned forwards. "I don't know how you will find things over the next few weeks, but if you need anything, please feel free to come to the palace. Just ask for Captain Agarma."

"Thank you. That is a most kind offer."

"There is one more thing," she added, lowering her voice slightly. "I know General Kirshtahll has asked you to look into the matter of the Ranadar text. If you wouldn't consider it a breach of his trust, I'd like to be kept informed of any progress you make."

"I suspect the general places greater trust in you than he does in me, Your Highness. You shall be the first to know."

Elona nodded and sat back. The coachman jiggled his reins and the cortège set sail across the cobbled sea towards the palace.

Jorra-hin suddenly felt very much alone, as though he'd been washed up on the shores of some strange and distant land. Bolstering himself with a deep breath, he began scaling the marble steps.

At the top he discovered the wall of the Cymàtagé was set back from the crystal columns by some distance. It was featureless and uninterrupted along its entire length except for one set of enormous bronze doors directly in the centre. He wandered over, grateful that they were open.

Inside the entrance hall, the floor turned to one of obsidian marble. The hallowed interior was huge but devoid of furnishings or people. There was only an incongruously small doorway on the far side. That might have gone unnoticed were it not for a narrow strip of ruby-coloured carpet running towards it.

The austerity did not extend upwards. An intricately vaulted stone ceiling with fluted ridges and liernes cavernously substituted for the heavens. Between the latticework were paintings depicting ancient mages, vividly adorned in sumptuous robes, reposed like gods amongst billowing clouds in an azure sky. They peered down inquisitively, seemingly alive in their curiosity.

Suspended from the centre of this stonemason's utopia was a gold and crystal chandelier. The candles, too numerous to count, were unlit, yet light still caught the thousands of crystal shards and made them sparkle as they gently twisted in an invisible breeze. Jorra-hin stood, neck craned and mouth agape, captivated by its ethereal magnificence.

"Ahem!" said a voice somewhere closer to the ground.

Jorra-hin's attention snapped back down from the lofty heights.

"May I help you?" the newcomer asked.

The man was dressed in a fine cerulean robe covered with silver filigree, as though a score of spiders had tried to smother it in ivy leaves. Had it not been for the characteristic attire and the present environment, it would have been difficult to surmise that the man was of magely persuasion. He was short, middle aged, and lacked the customary beard and imposing airs one might have expected.

Jorra-hin chastised himself for allowing such prejudice to dim his objectivity. "My apologies. I was just admiring the view."

"Many do," the man acknowledged. His face retained an expectant air.

Jorra-hin rummaged inside his satchel for one of his scrolls. The one he selected bore the marks of many leagues of travelling.

It received but a glance.

"My letter of introduction," Jorra-hin prompted.

After an awkward few moments, the welcomer reluctantly took the letter and skimmed through its contents. For some reason it caused him to chuckle. "Oh, very good. Commendable originality."

Jorra-hin's wrinkled forehead was evidence enough of his confusion.

The little man huffed. "Alright, let us suppose, just for a moment, that you really are a monk from the Adak-rann. You still can't come in. Not today, of all days."

"Why not? What's so special about today?"

"Look, why don't you go home and come back tomorrow?"

The welcomer turned and began walking away.

"It has taken me weeks to get here. I can't just *go home*."

The man's retreat continued uninterrupted.

"Wait! You could at least tell me *why* I can't come in."

This plea, delivered with growing ire, had no effect whatsoever.

"Look, if you won't allow me in, then I insist that you let me speak to someone who will," Jorra-hin called out, his voice now very nearly a shout.

At this the little man did at least stop. But he turned with an ominous lack of concern. "Insist?" he repeated. "You *insist*, do you?"

Jorra-hin held his tongue and scowled. He was normally very

tolerant of other people's ways, but he was nearing his limit on this occasion.

"And how exactly are you going to do that?" the man asked. "Insist, I mean?" With a condescending smile, he turned and resumed course along the ruby carpet.

Jorra-hin was at a complete loss. His brain froze in confusion as he tried to make sense of such extraordinary treatment. He failed. All he could do was place his hopes on the next person he met being a little more cooperative.

He glanced around the hall again, looking for a chair or bench to sit on. The cavernous interior was bereft of anything comfort related. He huffed; the Adak-rann would never dream of treating a visitor with such a lack of hospitality. They wouldn't even treat enemies this way. Not that they had any in particular.

As he moved closer to the walls, something caught his eye. They weren't painted, as he'd first surmised. They were covered with plaques, some brass, others wooden. Moving closer still, he discovered they were either etched or carved with A'lyavinical text. His pulse quickened. Some of the plaques were quite mundane, while flourishing scrollwork turned others into exquisite works of art. As for their subject matter, that varied considerably, as did the dates of their writing. They seemed to span the last thousand years, albeit in a rather haphazard fashion.

A thrill ran though him. It was like discovering a secret library, where the books were pinned to the walls rather than stacked on shelves. Intrigued, he was immediately lost amongst the unusual tomes, his mind wandering back and forth between the centuries as the plaques flitted through history.

The lack of chronological order did begin to irk him after a while; he liked things neat and sensibly organised. It took him some time to realise that they were actually arranged in a hierarchy that represented strands of thought, hypothesis and postulation passed between teacher and student down through the ages. With that fact under his belt, things started making more sense. It became fascinating to follow the development of ideas, from their inception, through various stages of refinement, all the way down to canonisation. Occasionally they diverged, evincing the murky depths of factions within the magely realms.

So it was from a state of total preoccupancy that he was wrenched some time later.

"Ahem."

"Hmm?" Jorra-hin murmured absentmindedly. Pulling himself away from a half read plaque, he realised the welcomer had reappeared.

"I would have thought you'd have gone home by now."

Jorra-hin shrugged. "It's a long way."

"So you said." Without further ado, the man turned and headed back the way he'd come. He paused just short of the small door, glanced over his shoulder and frowned. Then he disappeared.

Not many minutes later he surged back into view with a large book tucked under his arm. Reaching Jorra-hin, he thumbed his way through its pages, scanned several paragraphs and then smiled rather smugly. He had the air of a man about to settle a long running argument.

"Alright," he said, tapping the plaque Jorra-hin had been browsing, "so you think you can read that, do you? So go on, then, tell me what's it about."

Jorra-hin hesitated. He hadn't meant to allow himself to be caught reading such material, written as it was in A'lyavine. Curiosity had lowered his guard. But it was already too late to deny his ability now, so he paraphrased the plaque, adding in stutters and pauses in an attempt to make it seem as though it was a difficult task.

The welcomer's smug smile dissolved into a grimace. Blood retreated from his face, leaving it a rather ghostly pallor.

After a moment to recover, he demanded Jorra-hin's letter of introduction and dashed back towards his door. "Stay there, Brother. Do *not* go home," he called over his shoulder before disappearing again.

Ten minutes passed before he reappeared. This time he had another mage in tow.

Jorra-hin suddenly felt a little nervous as the pair advanced across the ruby carpet. The newcomer certainly looked as if he meant business. His appearance was as magely as any could have expected; long greying beard and flowing robes of luxurious vermillion silk, exquisite jewellery in abundance, a gem-encrusted ring on every finger and a gold medallion dangling at his chest. The latter supported a large diamond that glistened a rose-tinted hue against his robe. He had all the imposing airs the original welcomer seemed to lack.

"I am Deputy Chancellor Nÿat," the man declared. He glanced at the letter of introduction in his hand. "And you are apparently Jorra-hin?"

Jorra-hin bowed.

"I must apologise for the misunderstanding. Brother Heckart sent a message warning us you were coming," Nÿat explained, "but we had no idea when you would arrive. It is just unfortunate that it is today of all days."

Once again Jorra-hin had to ask what was so special about this particular day.

"Why, it is the Day of Admissions, of course."

"I'm sorry?"

Nÿat gave him a smile sympathetic to his ignorance. "It is an event held once every three years – the only day on which new entrants are admitted to the Cymàtagé to become acolytes. Martiss, here, was under the impression you were submitting your candidacy. It's his job to perform the first stage in the selection process. Only those who get past him are allowed to take the Trials."

Things began to make a little more sense. "I see. Well, I am not here to be admitted as an acolyte. As I hope Brother Heckart has explained, I'm here to conduct a Recordership on behalf of the Adak-rann."

"Indeed. Which leaves us with a problem," Nÿat replied with a sigh. "I cannot simply let you in."

"But..."

Nÿat held up his hand. "*Only* those that take the Trials are admitted today. It is a custom we have upheld for centuries. I'm afraid not even I, as Deputy Chancellor, can allow that to be broken."

"But what am I to do?" Jorra-hin protested. "I have nowhere else to go."

Nÿat exchanged glances with Martiss. Some unspoken moment of understanding seemed to pass between them. The latter nodded.

"Only those that *take* the Trials are admitted today," Nÿat repeated. He dipped his head once and retreated back across the ruby carpet.

Martiss beckoned Jorra-hin to follow him and led the way over to a section of one of the walls. There was a subtle click as a panel revealed itself to be a doorway. It swung open without a sound. Martiss stood aside and waved Jorra-hin through.

The chamber beyond was substantially smaller than the hall, with a much lower ceiling; a chandelier here would have been an inconvenience. There were no windows. The oak panelling on the walls had darkened with age and polish to such an extent that even an abundance of oil lamps struggled to lift the ambience from the realms of the subdued.

At least there were people, Jorra-hin was relieved to note. His appearance precipitated a dip in the level of their conversations. Quite a number of the gathering unashamedly gave him a head-to-toe appraisal. He gave them a courteous bow in reply and was summarily dismissed from their attention.

There was a click behind him. He spun round and encountered an unbroken section of wall, with no evidence a doorway had ever existed, or Martiss for that matter.

"This *is* the Cymàtagé, Jorra," he muttered under his breath.

The majority of those present were huddled in small groups amongst which family resemblances abounded; hopeful prodigies supported by parents and other relatives, he presumed. One thing was clear; the Trials were an occasion for being attired in one's finest. The prospective candidates wore garments synonymous with the Cymàtagé, billowing displays of shimmering material with yards to spare, showcasing every hue the rainbow had to offer, and some that it didn't. It was all a stark contrast to his own attire, an austere cassock, entirely black with just a touch of red piping around the collar and cuffs. The one he had on now had a distinctly shabby appearance, having endured the trek all the way down from the Northern Territories. Little wonder the judicial eye the gathering had cast over him had been one of disapproval.

He spotted a couple of young men standing alone at the back of the chamber. With no obvious supporters of their own, he decided to join them.

"I hope you don't mind the intrusion. I am Brother Jorra-hin."

"Not at all. Nice to have someone else to talk to. I'm Pomaltheus, and this is Seth."

Pomaltheus waved a hand towards his companion, a large, rugged looking fellow whose stubbled face put Jorra-hin in mind more of a man of war than of magic. Pomaltheus was, by contrast, a tall, scholarly looking man with long bushy hair gathered tightly through a gold ring behind his neck. He looked much more the part of a prospective mage.

Again, Jorra-hin reminded himself not to judge by looks alone. He'd been quite wrong about Martiss.

His attention was diverted by an outbreak of applause. He glanced round and caught sight of a young lady on the far side of the room being swamped by a sea of smiling faces and deluged with congratulatory pats and handshakes.

"A successful candidate, I take it? Would one of you mind explaining these Trials to me? I've only just been made aware of them."

That earned him a pair of perplexed looks.

"I'm not here to become an acolyte," he added quickly. "I'm from the Adak-rann. I had no idea today was the Day of Admissions. Unfortunate timing, I've been told. I gather the only way I can be allowed in is by taking these Trials, whatever they are."

It was ominous that fate had brought him to the Cymàtagé on this day, the only one in a thousand on which he couldn't simply walk in. He felt a slight shiver course down his back at the thought.

"Well," Pomaltheus began, "to be admitted, everyone has to pass a test. They take you into that cubicle over there," he pointed to a booth made of maroon velvet curtains draped over a freestanding circular frame, "and give you a task to perform. If you succeed, they let you in, and if not, well…"

Nÿat had intimated that passing wasn't strictly necessary. Jorra-hin wondered if that applied to everyone, or just to him.

"If a candidate succeeds," Seth took over, "then they have to wait to be taken on by one of the preceptors."

"Preceptors?"

"The mages responsible for training the acolytes."

A few minutes later, another burst of applause rippled throughout the crowd. Jorra-hin watched and chatted while test after test was taken. There didn't appear to be any limit to how long a candidate was allowed to spend in their attempt, so the day wore on rather slowly. It had been a long one even before he'd reached the Cymàtagé. His stomach had begun to rumble by the time Seth's name was called out.

The big lad smiled nervously and headed for the booth. The curtains were drawn closed behind him.

"And now we wait," Pomaltheus sighed. "I hope he makes it. Seth's desperate for a way out of having to follow in his father's footsteps."

"Which would mean him doing what?"

"Farming."

"Not many people get the chance to change their fate."

"No," Pomaltheus agreed. "But one of the surest ways is to get in here, if you can."

"And how does his father feel about it?"

"He stumped up the money for Seth to be here. Being a mage is a good life. It can be quite lucrative if you're any good."

Jorra-hin recalled the time he'd spent with Cosmin up in Tail-ébeth. The old mage considered himself a servant of the people. He was paid for his services, certainly, but he didn't set a charge; people gave as they saw fit or could afford. He certainly hadn't come across as wealthy. Then again, neither had Lord Ashur. Perhaps Cosmin had merely been acting in a manner befitting his primary benefactor.

The crowd began to clap. Seth emerged from behind the booth curtains with a grin spanning from ear to ear. He was patted on the back several times and a number of people shook his hand as he made his way back.

"Gods, I'm glad that's over."

"Well done," Pomaltheus enthused, punching him lightly on the shoulder. "Which test did they give you?"

"Colour of water. I was so lucky I could remember the words. I panicked for a moment, but then it just came to me."

"Words?" Jorra-hin queried.

"To change the colour of water in a jug. *séthath elèm per-sa*." Seth's effort was halting as he struggled to pronounce the A'lyavine.

Jorra-hin winced and closed his eyes, repeating the words quietly to himself. They sounded familiar, but something wasn't quite right. He rolled them around a few moments more, playing with the sounds, then nodded to himself.

"*seé thantt lèm perăs-sa.*"

Both Seth and Pomaltheus blinked in surprise. Jorra-hin kicked himself for the slip. He hadn't meant to speak the results of his deductive reasoning aloud. The Cymàtagé was proving to be a field of bear-traps when it came to not revealing his abilities. Masking them had never been necessary back at Jàb-áldis and he wasn't used to it.

"Wow," Pomaltheus breathed, almost laughing. "That was amazing. How did you do that?"

"Say those words again," Seth urged.

Jorra-hin frowned. "Why?"

"Please, just humour me."

Jorra-hin hesitated a moment, then complied. Once again the look on their faces was one of surprised wonder.

"Such a clear vision," Pomaltheus said at last. "I've never experienced it quite like that before."

"Nor I," Seth agreed. "Your pronunciation must be perfect, Brother. Are you sure you didn't come here to be a mage?"

Jorra-hin shuddered. "That's the last thing I want, I can assure you. Being a mage is the very antithesis of everything the Adak-rann stands for."

"You make it sound like a crime," Pomaltheus muttered, sounding a little put out.

Jorra-hin smiled, trying to rob his previous words of any offence. "Please don't misunderstand me, being a mage is a noble aspiration – for other people. It's just that the keystone tenet of my order is one of non-intervention in the affairs of man. We observe, we record, we document, but we do *not* interfere. We try our best not to influence what happens around us, so that we may record history objectively. Mages, by contrast, do quite the opposite. It is in the very nature of a mage to use the Taümatha to change things, to influence people and events. So you see, we are at opposite poles."

"But still, I am curious," Seth said, "if you have no desire to become a mage, how is it you are able to speak A'lyavine?"

Recalling the advice Brother Brömin had given him, Jorra-hin replied, "I am a scholar. I've lived my whole life in the Jàb-áldis monastery, which is in essence just a big library. I've been learning to read the Tongue of the Ancients since I was very young." Alongside Alondrian, Nicián, Tsnathsarré and Nmemian, to name a few others. He had a flair for languages. Occasionally, in absentminded moments, he even managed to get them all mixed up, sprouting forth in a tongue that had the capacity to confuse half the known world.

What he didn't explain was how he could master the pronunciation of anything written in A'lyavine. It hadn't been a naturally spoken language for centuries. The only people who even tried these days were the mages. Yet his gift with the language allowed him to understand it if things were articulated correctly. So he just kept testing and twisting the sound of words until they made sense.

"Well, in that case," Pomaltheus hesitated, "could I ask a favour of you? There's one test I've never been able to master. Could you tell me where I'm going wrong?"

"I could try."

"It's the most basic test of them all, really. Lighting a candle. It's meant to be easy, but I just can't seem to get the hang of it."

"And the words…?"

"Oh, yes," Pomaltheus smiled, "*seé iccànciá*."

Jorra-hin could see immediately what was wrong. "It's *séà*. You can't have *seé* before a word beginning with *i* – it creates a hiatus in the pronunciation. And on the second word, you have the accentuation reversed. It's long then short, *iccáncià*."

Pomaltheus experimented with the phrase a couple of times until he received a nod of approval.

"And can you tell me what it means?"

"*be ye enflamed*. Now, can I ask you something? How do *you* know any A'lyavine? Surely, the purpose of coming here to the Cymàtagé is to learn such things?"

Pomaltheus gave him a pensive nod. "But as you've already discovered, you have to be able to get in, first. To do that, you have to demonstrate some pre-existing ability."

"It's a chicken and egg problem," Seth added dryly. "It stops the masses from having a go. You see, to pass the Trials, you really need to have had some prior instruction. That can only come from another mage, which doesn't come cheaply."

"Look around," Pomaltheus prompted, "see anyone who looks poor?"

Jorra-hin reappraised the surrounding crowd with a more fiscal eye. These were clearly the cream of society. A group in which, he suddenly realised, Pomaltheus and Seth didn't quite fit.

"I hope you won't take offence, but you two seem a little out of place in this gathering. For one thing, where are your supporters?"

"Couldn't afford to come," Pomaltheus replied. "Seth and I, well, we're not from wealthy families. We're not peasants," he added quickly, "but we're not of noble birth, either. Sending us here has cost our families dearly."

"Paying for a mage to teach you?"

"Actually," Seth countered, "what really costs is the letter of introduction. Mine cost my father a year's income."

Jorra-hin's eyes bulged. He had no idea how much that equated to, and wasn't inclined to embarrass Seth by asking, but it sounded iniquitously expensive. It put a whole new slant on his view of mages. It was a far cry from the image he had of those he knew at Jàb-áldis, or indeed of Cosmin in Tail-ébeth. He'd always thought of them as fairly altruistic.

Several other applicants were tested before Pomaltheus finally got his turn. When his name was called out, he sighed, rolled his eyes towards the ceiling and began threading his way through the gathering towards the booth.

He was inside for less than a minute. When the curtains were drawn open and he emerged again, he wasn't smiling.

"Oh dear," Seth murmured.

Jorra-hin's heart sank, too. But then something occurred to him; Pomaltheus didn't come across as the type to have abandoned his test so quickly, not with so much at stake. Whatever had happened, he looked to be in shock, his face almost white. He ambled back and stopped just in front of Jorra-hin.

"It was the candle test."

Behind him, someone clapped. The confusion of the gathering over what had just happened soon dissipated and the clapping spread as they realised the test had been a success.

Seth gave his friend a hearty slap on the back. Pomaltheus began to smile, bringing some colour back to his cheeks. He reached out and put a hand on Jorra-hin's shoulder.

"I don't know what gods brought you here today, Brother, but I thank them."

Jorra-hin reacted instinctively and gave Pomaltheus a brief, brotherly embrace. "It is hard to sidestep fate, my friend. It was obviously meant to be."

"Brother Jorra-hin of the Adak-rann."

Jorra-hin almost jumped. They were calling for *him*.

For a moment he couldn't move. Confused thoughts and emotions coursed through him, creating an uneasy feeling in his stomach. He reminded himself that he wasn't here to become an acolyte; he'd been caught up in this whole Trials affair by accident. Yet it felt as though a gaping cavern had opened up before him, drawing him forwards with a vertiginous lure. Was this fate, too, he wondered?

Once more he shivered at the thought.

"Brother," Seth urged, giving him a nudge, "they're calling for you. Are you going or not?"

Jorra-hin came to his senses and handed Seth his satchel. He started towards the booth. His movements had a reluctant inevitability about them; feet methodically trod their path, but every step was questioned.

The gathering parted to let him through. They regarded him with curious glances. He didn't fit their expectations. He certainly wasn't dressed for the occasion; a crow amid peacocks.

He found the booth to contain little but a simple wooden table and a chair. Behind these stood a mage from the Cymàtagé, who beckoned him forwards and bid him be seated. On the table was a sheaf of paper and a quill beside an ink well. Next to these, a candle stood in a plain clay stand. It was already alight; probably the one to which Pomaltheus had just given his brief attention.

The curtain was drawn closed behind him. The overseer didn't say anything for a moment. Like those outside, he was probably trying to assess what manner of candidate he had before him.

Fortunately, the awkward silence did not last too long. "Please extinguish the flame."

Jorra-hin nodded. He'd guessed that that was to be his task. He'd already been working on what might be the correct thing to say. Recalling what he'd taught Pomaltheus, logic dictated that the reverse would be something along the lines of, *be ye un-enflamed; seé susa-iccáncià*.

He was about to utter the results of his deductive reasoning, more out of curiosity than any expectation that something would actually happen, when he caught sight of an A'lyavinical phrase carved into the tabletop. It was easy to miss – the conditions of the test were designed to focus the mind elsewhere.

'Just because one can, does not mean one should.'

He frowned and slumped back in the chair. It was a curious phrase to find within the context of the Trials, yet it seemed unlikely it was there by accident. Having done the translation in his head, he tried saying the sentence aloud. That sometimes helped tease out the meaning of a troublesome piece of A'lyavine.

The overseer shot him a startled glance, though he held his tongue.

After a few minutes, Jorra-hin smiled. He stood up, cupped his hand behind the flame and simply blew it out with a gentle puff. A wisp of smoke curled upwards as the tip of the wick briefly clung to life.

He stood there waiting for the overseer to react. Half of him expected outrage. The other half knew his decision had been the right one. Not that it mattered, he reminded himself.

A smile appeared on the overseer's face and he bowed his head a fraction. By some unseen means, the booth curtains were withdrawn.

Amid sporadic applause, Jorra-hin walked back towards Pomaltheus and Seth. No one attempted to shake his hand or pat him on the back as they had done with most of the other candidates. It was as though their curiosity about him somehow made him unapproachable.

"So which test did you get?" Pomaltheus burst out.

"The other half of yours, I think."

"Extinguishing the flame?"

Jorra-hin nodded.

"It didn't take you long," Seth said, sounding slightly envious. "I bet you just spoke the words and out it went."

"Actually, I didn't say anything. I blew it out."

"You did what?"

"I blew it out."

"That's cheating!" Pomaltheus blustered.

Jorra-hin shrugged. "While everyone expects to be required to use the Taümatha to succeed, no one told me magic is strictly necessary. Besides, I don't think I could have done it any other way. I'm not a mage, nor am I here to become one."

"It's still cheating," Pomaltheus grumbled.

There was a click. The door to the entrance hall had reappeared. It slowly swung open, admitting a welcome draught of cool air. A number of mages streamed through and began to circulate amongst the gathering, designating those who were being invited to stay, and those who were not. It wasn't clear how they knew which was which.

Some of the candidates, assuming their fate, had already begun to make their way out. One caught Jorra-hin's eye. She was one of the handful of young ladies that had taken the Trials. Her raven hair glistened softly in the lamplight. Her eyebrows were a subtle arch that tapered aside to nothing. Dark eyes and an olive-tanned complexion suggested she was native to lands beyond Alondria's southern shores. High cheekbones gave her a rather noble mien.

Her distinctive looks were not all that had caught his attention. She was putting on a brave face, but could not mask her disappointment. She glanced in his direction for a moment and dipped her head in a congratulatory manner, as she had with several others. For some reason, catching her eye like that made him feel a sudden disquiet. Something was wrong; he didn't want her to leave.

Movement from the mage who had acted as the overseer of the Trials distracted him. The man started making his way round the side of the chamber, building up a purposeful turn of speed that fell just shy of an unseemly dash. He intercepted the raven-haired young lady at the door. Placing a hand on her shoulder, he drew her aside. A few moments later there was a gasp of delight. No one present could have missed it.

Jorra-hin felt his disquiet subside. He continued to watch. The young lady conducted a rather hurried series of farewells to those with her, then came and stood a few feet away from him.

"*Hepsa,*" he greeted sideways.

"*Hepsa.*" The young lady's eyes widened in surprise. "How did you know I was Nicián?"

"The attire of the gentleman you were with a moment ago. The formal dress of the Nicián High Council, if I'm not mistaken."

"That was my father," the young lady nodded. "He is our Ambassador to Alondria. I am Soprina Kirin-orrà DelaMorjáy." She glanced bashfully at the floor and added, "But most people here just call me Kirin."

Jorra-hin smiled. The Niciáns had a great love of long names that left most foreigners tongue-tied. It was not uncommon for them to simplify their nomenclature when abroad.

"I am Brother Jorra-hin of the Adak-rann." He placed his hand on his chest, then waved it forwards with his palm facing upwards, observing the traditional Nicián custom upon introduction. "And this is…"

He didn't get as far as being able to introduce Pomaltheus or Seth; the remainder of the gathering suddenly hushed as a rather majestic looking mage took to the floor. The man was dressed in a robe of an iridescent material that was mostly charcoal grey but partially changed colour as he moved. It was the very essence of modesty and yet unashamedly resplendent in equal measures. His piercing blue eyes scanned the gathering, clearly expecting to garner everyone's attention. He was not disappointed.

"The Cymàtagé offers its congratulations to those of you who remain. As Chancellor, I extend to you the invitation to take your places as acolytes within our halls."

"That's Gÿldan," Seth whispered.

"In a few moments you will each be assigned a preceptor. But I solemnly warn you now; becoming an acolyte here is not an easy path. Whatever you may think you know, or have achieved thus far, is nothing when compared to what is to come." Gÿldan's penetrating gaze washed over the rapt faces of the new acolytes. "Consider this – while many of you were apparently successful in your Trials, only one of you actually passed."

And for the briefest of moments, Gÿldan's intense gaze fell on Jorra-hin.

Jorra-hin went stone-cold inside.

*

"What made you want to take up the Mages' Path?" Pomaltheus asked Kirin while they waited for the selection proceedings to get under way.

"When I was little, I broke my leg falling off a horse," she replied. She rolled her eyes up, in a manner that suggested even she had to admit that had not been her finest hour. Niciáns were meant to be fantastic horsemen, practically born in the saddle. "As it happened, we had a visiting mage from Alondria staying with us and he was able to heal me. I think that probably planted the first seeds."

"Do you want to be a healer yourself?" Jorra-hin asked.

Kirin nodded.

"You seemed to be on your way out earlier. If I may ask, did you not succeed in your Trial?"

As far as Jorra-hin was aware, the Taümathic arts were not widely practiced in Niciá. If Kirin had not been invited to stay, she would probably never have been able to pursue her dreams.

"No. I tried, but it was the same as always. I have never yet been able to pass a Taümathic test, even under instruction. I suspect that I have only been invited to stay as a favour to my father."

Jorra-hin frowned. There was disappointment in Kirin's voice, as though she feared her abilities would never live up to her aspirations. But something other than political favours had propelled the overseer round the perimeter of the chamber to stop her from leaving, of that he was certain.

"I'm sure the Cymàtagé sees more in you than that," he said by way of encouragement. "Remember what the chancellor said, your achievements thus far are nothing compared with what is to come."

Kirin seemed to take his words to heart and her smile returned. She reached out and squeezed his hand in thanks. He felt something stir within him, a tingle. It was not an unpleasant feeling.

While they'd been talking, more mages had entered the room. Chancellor Gÿldan took to the floor again and began explaining the selection process. Each mage intending to take on an acolyte had been assembled. Some pre-selection had already taken place. For a handful of acolytes the Trials had been a mere formality. Their names were read out and they were introduced to their preceptors, though clearly not for the first time. One or two mages took on several acolytes, garnering a degree of prestige in doing so. If his instincts were working correctly, Jorra-hin suspected there was a spot of rivalry amongst the upper echelons of the Cymàtagé.

With that out of the way, the selection of the rest progressed apace. The mages passed the candidates' letters of introduction between themselves and called for the ones that took their fancy. The ranks of those still waiting to be chosen thinned quite rapidly.

Jorra-hin could see the inevitability of the situation hurtling towards him. He was going to be the one left standing there in the middle of the room. He didn't need a preceptor, but that wasn't the point. It was going to be embarrassing.

Sure enough, one by one the remaining few acolytes were taken on, Seth being the last. His new preceptor shuffled forwards, muttering something about how he might as well mop up the stragglers. Uplifting words with which to begin a teacher-student relationship, Jorra-hin mused.

"Well, Brother, just you to go," Gÿldan announced at the end, as though he felt some need to make an obvious point even more so.

There was a kerfuffle at the back of the crowd.

"Excuse me, thank you, would you mind, sorry, just squeezing through there, thank you." A thin, frail and relatively ancient looking man managed to bustle his way through the masses. He wore the Adak-rann's customary black cassock with the red piping at the collar and cuffs. His grey curly hair was similar to Jorra-hin's in all but colour, sprouting with abandon in every direction. "Ah, Chancellor, most dreadfully sorry. I hope I haven't kept everybody waiting."

Gÿldan smiled and shook his head in dismay. "No, Brother. Your timing is impeccable."

Jorra-hin didn't need an introduction. He recognised Akmir from the description Heckart had given him. A wave of relief flooded through him.

"Oh, dear boy, it's good to see you at last," Akmir exclaimed enthusiastically, closing the gap between them. "We've been so looking forwards to your arrival." The elderly monk gave him a hearty embrace. "How was your journey?"

"Long, Brother. Very, very long."

"Hmm, quite so, quite so. Well, I'm sorry you had to wait. They didn't tell me you'd arrived until just a few minutes ago. I gather you took the Trials. Fun, was it?" Akmir's tone suggested that he considered such things perfectly trivial. For a moment he seemed oblivious to the fact that Gÿldan was standing with his arms folded and his head cocked to one side, looking at him. But that kind of stance could not go unnoticed for long. "Oh, sorry, Chancellor. Come, dear boy, lots to do. Places to go, people to meet, you know the sort of thing."

Akmir, Jorra-hin decided, lived in a world of his own choosing. The old man headed back the way he'd come. The gathering, aware by now that standing in his path made little difference, parted to let him through. Jorra-hin was sucked along in his wake. He managed to catch Pomaltheus's eye in passing and gave him a sort of helpless shrug.

When they were well down the corridor, Akmir slowed his pace to something a little more reasonable. "Sorry about all that," he said with a sideways glance and a grin. "Blithering idiots! Honestly, you hand them a perfectly valid letter of introduction and *still* they won't let you in. I mean, for goodness' sake. Blinded by their own stupidity, the lot of them."

"It's all right, Brother, I really don't mind. It gave me an opportunity to make a few new acquaintances."

"Good, good, I'm glad to hear it," Akmir responded, as if he'd not heard a single word. "But making you take the Trials – honestly. What were they thinking?"

Jorra-hin considered that for a moment. "Well, I don't think they expected me to pass."

Akmir stopped in his tracks. "What? You passed?"

"In a manner of speaking."

"Don't be evasive, boy, out with it."

Akmir certainly wasn't one for mincing his words. Jorra-hin related how he'd conducted his Trial, explaining the reasoning behind his decision to blow the candle out. By the time he'd finished, the old man was howling with laughter.

"That'll teach 'em," he exclaimed, his mirth still rumbling as he set sail down the corridor once more. "Ironic, though, don't you think?"

"I'm sorry?"

"Well, it seems the only person to actually pass their test today was the one person who didn't want to take it. At least, I assume that's correct?"

"Yes, Brother. I have no interest in following the Mages' Path."

"Good, good." Akmir patted him on the back. "Of course, this changes things slightly."

"Oh?"

"According to the Cymàtagé rules, you belong here now. I've been here what – twenty-five, no, twenty-six years; I'm practically part of the furniture. But technically speaking I'm still a guest. You, on the other hand, have the right to be here."

"Will that make any difference to my investigations?"

"Probably not. It just means you can be a little ruder than the rest of us."

"Not a privilege I wish to exercise, Brother."

Akmir grunted. "Give it time, dear boy, give it time."

They continued marching down corridors, passing doorway after doorway. Most had little to distinguish them, but one caught Jorra-hin's attention. He stopped to peer inside. "Excuse me, Brother, but what is this place?"

The room was oval in shape and dim inside. Like the Trials room, it had no windows. The floor appeared to be made of the same black marble as the Cymàtagé's outer hall, with an oval area in the middle covered with fine sand that had been raked into complex patterns. There was a series of stepping stones across it leading to a larger one that formed a platform of sorts in the centre. Apart from lamp-stands around the periphery, the only other objects in the room were four spheres, each a few feet in diameter, that looked like they were made of dark glass. They reminded Jorra-hin of the Taümathakiya back at Jàb-áldis. They were positioned to form the corners of a rectangle just outside the sanded area.

Akmir backtracked and joined him at the doorway. "Ah, this is one of the places where they muck about with magic." There was a note of disapproval in his voice.

"I beg your pardon?"

"Well, practice, try out new things. Acolytes come here when they are learning to handle the Taümatha."

"Why here, particularly?"

"You see the spheres? They're called *sárccanisáe*. How can I explain it?" Akmir paused to give the matter some thought. "They're like sponges. They absorb any Taümatha that gets released by accident when students fail to keep it under control."

"Is that dangerous?"

"Well," the old man shrugged, "my advice is not to get too close. Nothing's foolproof, not with the grade of fool we have to contend with."

Jorra-hin wondered why Akmir seemed to have such a dim view of those of a Taümathic persuasion.

The old monk resumed course and Jorra-hin continued his attempt at memorising the route as passage after passage came and went. It was an impossible task. From the People's Square the Cymàtagé appeared to be just one enormous building. In reality it was made up of many different buildings, all joined together by corridors and courtyards. Impressive they may have been, but the outer walls were simply a way of fencing off part of the city and turning it into an enclave.

His obedience at Akmir's heel eventually paid dividends. They came to a door that led out into the centre of the Cymàtagé, a large octagonal garden several hundred yards across. Now that evening had arrived, the course of its many paths were illuminated by an array of flaming torches in waist-height bronze stands, each one a statue of some mythological creature. It was a breathtaking sight.

In the middle stood the great glass dome of the Cymàtagé's famous library, glowing with a tallowy hue from hidden illumination below. Like the garden, it was octagonal, though that was merely the simplest of its many aspects. Constructed from more than ten thousand individual panes, it was reckoned to be one of the most complex structures ever conceived by the mind of man.

"What do you think?" Akmir prompted.

"It's magnificent," Jorra-hin croaked. His throat had gone dry again. "Drawings don't do it justice. It really does have to be seen to be appreciated."

Akmir smiled. "Thought you'd like it. Come on, let me take you below."

The old monk led the way back inside. The majority of the library was actually underground, the garden was its roof and the dome, though a wonder in its own right, was merely its skylight.

They came to a rather plain and unimpressive spiral staircase made of cast iron. Considering where they were going, somehow Jorra-hin had expected more. Akmir explained that they were heading for an entrance only the librarians used.

At the bottom of the stairs, the equivalent of several floors down, Akmir came to a halt in front of a mediocre-looking door.

"Are you ready?"

"It's only a library, Brother."

Akmir pushed the door open.

The word 'Ah' froze in Jorra-hin's throat.

There were said to be seven and a half million books, scrolls and other works contained within the Cymàtagé. It was a number that went beyond imagining. Row upon row of shelves, spread over countless levels, extended into the distance, so far so that the books themselves lost their individuality and became one homogeneous mass of knowledge.

Jorra-hin found himself rooted to the spot, his mouth agape.

"Come on," Akmir chuckled, "it's *only* a library."

24

Elona stood in the bay window of her reception room, soaking up the morning sun. A light breeze gently crept through the open windows, lazily animating the long curtains. It was already warm; by midday it would be scorching. Over the last few months she had acclimatised to the cooler climes of the north. Now back in familiar surroundings, the difference seemed more noticeable.

Céline came up and stood beside her, slipping an arm through hers. "Glad to be back?"

Elona let out an unladylike snort. "It was nice to sleep in a proper bed again," she conceded, "but I'd swap that for still being back out there." Her hand waved to encompass everything beyond the palace walls.

A knock at the door forestalled Céline's reply.

"Enter."

Captain Agarma appeared round the door. Céline immediately stood a little straighter. Elona sighed and teased her with a smirk.

"Forgive the intrusion, Your Highness, but Princess Midana bids me summon you at your convenience."

"My convenience? I suspect what you really mean is, 'right now'." Elona's eyes widened to emphasise her point.

Agarma gave a helpless shrug.

"Very well. Please convey to my sister that I shall be there shortly."

"Very good, ma'am."

Agarma bowed and shot Céline a wink as he withdrew. When he was gone, Elona playfully snapped her fingers in front of Céline's face.

Céline blushed and avoided meeting her eye. "What do you suppose Midana wants?"

"An opportunity to put me in my place, I suspect. Can't have me gallivanting off around the kingdom without making sure everyone knows that it was on her behalf."

"What are you going to tell her?"

"Oh, I shall give her a concise report of the trip, nothing more."

"No mention of Torrin-Ashur, then?"

"Ye gods, are you mad?"

"You like him, don't you?"

"Yes, he's nice."

"Just nice?"

Elona didn't reply. But she did smile.

Agarma returned a short while later to escort Elona to her sister's quarters on the other side of the palace. They passed the vacant throne room on the way; Midana wasn't yet queen, even if she acted the part, so it wasn't permitted for her to make use of it.

An aide intercepted them when they arrived outside the entrance to Midana's chambers. They were made to wait. It did not amuse Elona to see how her sister exercised these little displays of power, having everyone at her beck and call. The gods only knew what she would be like when she finally took the throne.

The door came open presently and the aide beckoned Elona inside. She gave Agarma a knowing glance and left him standing in the corridor.

"Ah, Elona, good of you to join us at last."

Midana's greetings always managed to infer servanthood rather than sisterhood.

"Midana," she replied, with a deferential nod. A curtsy from her was not required by protocol; only when Midana acceded would that become necessary.

There were more people present than she had expected. The obligatory gaggle of ministers, Parkos the most prominent of them, littered the place. Notable amongst the other retainers was Lord Tanaséy Vickrà. His lands, the March of Vickrà-dōthmore, were the largest and most easterly of those in the Northern Territories. He had only recently inherited his title, but despite his newfound responsibilities he still spent most of his time down in Alondris, just as he had before his father's passing.

He did have good reason, Elona had to admit. It was no secret that he and Midana were lovers. Less well understood was the fact that Midana was waiting until she was queen before making any formal announcement of their engagement. That was to ensure that Tanaséy would have no automatic right to claim the title of king. His eventual position would be entirely on terms Midana laid down. Typical of her thinking. Even with her husband-to-be, she had to have the upper hand. It didn't bode well for the lesser mortals of the kingdom.

"Please, sit," Midana directed, waving towards the chair usually provided for supplicants. Positioned before but not on the dais, it was rather low and deliberately demeaning.

"Permit me to stand," Elona returned. She caught Midana's eye squint slightly at the defiance. "I've been riding a lot recently, and – well, it is more comfortable than sitting at the moment," she explained, adding a bashful pout.

She knew Midana couldn't very well refuse without seeming churlish. As an excuse, it was utter rubbish. As a minor victory in their ongoing war of attrition, it was mildly satisfying. She had Jorrahin to thank for the inspiration.

"You arrived back yesterday, I'm told. Why did you not bother to report to me sooner?"

"I have been travelling for three months. Surely you would permit me a night's rest, at least?" Elona answered smoothly. She had to hide her kindled anger at such an obvious attempt to put her down.

Midana huffed quietly, though not unnoticed by those around her. "So, now that you are here, perhaps you wouldn't mind us imposing upon you for an account of your trip?"

Elona pursed her lips. "As I recall, Midana, it was you who asked me to go."

She regretted the remark the moment her sister stiffened. For a few seconds it seemed Midana might fly off into one of her rants. Kirshtahll had known full well Midana was not keen on traipsing around the countryside, far away from court, her beloved political hub. Particularly not to go all the way up to the Northern Territories. But to make certain she wouldn't come in person, he had timed his request for a royal visit to clash with several engagements he'd known Midana would not want to miss. It had forced her into sending Elona in her stead, which had been Kirshtahll's plan all along. It had irritated Midana intensely.

With all eyes now on her, Midana managed to suppress her annoyance.

"So, your trip…"

There would be repercussions later, of that Elona was certain; Midana didn't just forget. But for now she breathed a sigh of relief. She gave a brief account of the last three months, attempting to make it sound more like the eye-opening adventure of a young girl than a serious fact-finding mission. Anything that lessened its real importance, and therefore her role in state affairs, went down well as far as Midana was concerned. Elona knew how to play this game.

She neglected to mention anything of Torrin-Ashur or the Festival of Light. That was none of Midana's business. She also omitted details of the stopover in Tail-ébeth and Kassandra's dramatic rescue. Until Kirshtahll knew more about the significance of the Ranadar texts, he wanted to keep that under wraps.

"So how is the northern contingent bearing up?" Lord Vickrà asked when her account was finished.

"My lord, that rather depends on who you speak to."

"Oh?"

"The majority of the ordinary ranks are restless; they hear stories of Tsnath activity in the region, but rarely get the chance to do anything about it. Most of the officers, on the other hand, would rather forsake the chance for action and be back here in the south. Mitcha is hardly the centre of society; the majority of them feel rather exiled up there."

"They're serving officers," Midana stated flatly.

"And I'm sure each one will do his duty. But that doesn't mean they like it."

"They're not there to like it."

"You said most of the officers would prefer to be down here..." Vickrà repeated, tactfully trying to douse Midana's indignation, "but there are exceptions?"

"Yes, my lord. General Kirshtahll has a core of officers whom he calls his Executive. These officers are all keen to engage the Tsnath. They are the ones he relies on most."

"But Kirshtahll is constantly calling for more support. If he's so short, why doesn't he use the others more effectively?"

Elona thought that an odd question, coming from someone who knew full well the true purpose the army served by being stationed at Mitcha. Then it occurred to her that Vickrà might just have been trying to give her an opportunity to explain for the benefit of the others present. He was, after all, a landowner with a vested interest in promoting the security of the region.

But it was a difficult question to answer without doing more damage than good to Kirshtahll's position. She couldn't relay to a gathering such as this that the general didn't consider the bulk of his officers capable of repelling a Tsnath attack. Telling Midana that would be asking for trouble.

"As you know, my lord," Elona replied, "the army's purpose in the north is mainly deterrent in nature. Keeping the bulk of the fighting force at Mitcha means we have a strong contingent to rely on should the Tsnath make an aggressive move. The general feels, therefore, that he is better served by using officers who are keen to do the jobs he has for them, whilst keeping the rest in reserve, fulfilling the deterrent role."

"And what of the Tsnath themselves?" Midana asked.

"Kirshtahll is genuinely concerned over their activities these past few months. Their tactics have changed. They used to concentrate purely on raiding, but now they are conducting their incursions on a more covert level. Rather worryingly, they are coming much further south than they have in the past. The general feels that this can only be indicative of something brewing. It could be that they are spying out the land ahead of a more concerted attack."

Parkos cleared his throat. He was one of Alondria's career politicians and an outspoken opponent of the county's northern policy. Midana gave him a nod.

"If I may," he began, his voice obsequious, "I'd like to point out that Kirshtahll said as much when he was down here himself a little while ago. It's all very well telling us that the Tsnath are up to something, but according to him, the Tsnath are always up to something. We need proof, not just gut feelings. Need I remind everybody here that our military presence in the north costs us all a great deal every year? We all know what Kirshtahll is trying to do; he wants us to commit more troops to his command and he's using you to try to secure them."

Midana allowed a slight smile to appear on her face and nodded to Parkos, as if to congratulate him on a point well made.

Elona sighed inwardly. She only just managed to maintain her composure. Alondria was full of nobility whose primary concern was their pocket.

"Minister, I believe General Kirshtahll has Alondria's best interests at heart. He has dedicated a substantial part of his career to the security of our northern border. He is hardly trying to climb the military ladder, and I can assure you, nine thousand troops are more than enough to look after if they are not all, as you seem to imply, actually needed. So to what purpose would he request more support if it wasn't to counter some genuine threat?"

"He's warmongering. He wants the Tsnath to attack so that he can have justification for a campaign," Parkos answered. He seemed smugly assured of his reasoning.

If Elona had been within arm's length, she would have slapped the idiot. Hard. "Nothing could be further from the truth," she snapped.

Her conviction was evident, the reasons for it she dared not say. Kirshtahll had made it all too clear that if the Tsnath ever made a determined attack, the Northern Territories would be in serious trouble. But it would do no good at all to suggest to a man like Parkos that more troops were needed simply to make up for the heavy losses they'd suffer if the Tsnath came over in strength. Parkos was one of the fools who still believed in Alondrian invincibility after the Kilópeé War three decades ago.

Unfortunately, he was not in the minority on that score. Yet the truth was that after years of resting on their laurels, the army had gone to seed. As Kirshtahll had once put it, placing his forces in the path of a Tsnath attack now would be akin to putting a peacock in front of a bull. Very pretty, but only briefly.

Parkos clearly wanted to defend his position further. Vickrà got there first.

"As the lord of a northern march myself, Your Highness, you may rest assured that I take the protection of the Territories very seriously. So while I do not fully agree with Minister Parkos on his stance over our military policy north of the Mathians, nonetheless I have to agree with him in that so far Kirshtahll has provided very little justification for increasing our expenditure to protect the region."

"There seems little point in us paying to have yet more troops sitting at Mitcha doing nothing," Midana added.

To that Elona had no immediate reply, at least, not one that wouldn't offend those present and ultimately do Kirshtahll a disservice.

*

Nearly an hour later Elona managed to escape the inquisition.

"You look a little beleaguered, Your Highness," Agarma noted with concern.

"The only one in there with any sense is Tanaséy," she huffed, "but that's only because he's got a vested interest in the north."

She took off down the corridor at a fair clip. Agarma had trouble keeping up without breaking into a trot. Elona seemed to glide; her dress belied the truth.

"Back to your quarters, ma'am?"

"No. I want to go and see my father."

At the pace she set, it didn't take long to reach the king's chambers.

"His Majesty is asleep, Your Highness," Althar's manservant explained, defensively holding on to the door.

Elona was in no mood to be thwarted. "Terrance, my father hasn't seen me in three months. He would not thank you for extending that any further, I can assure you." Her glare made it quite clear that neither would she.

Terrance hadn't survived palace life for four decades without learning when to put up a fight and when to concede defeat.

Elona gave Agarma his leave, then slipped into her father's bedchamber. Ushering the fussing Terrance out and closing the door behind him, she stepped softly across to the huge four-poster bed and lowered herself on to the edge of the mattress. She took her father's hand and gave it a gentle squeeze.

Althar's eyes flickered open. It seemed to take him a while to orientate his senses and bring recognition to the fore.

"Little one," he exclaimed groggily.

Elona beamed at him and leaned forwards so that he could kiss her forehead as he always did.

"When did you get back?"

"Yesterday afternoon."

"And you didn't come to see me?"

"It was rather hectic and I was tired. I thought it best to wait until this morning."

Althar grunted and pulled her close to give her a hug.

"How have you been?" she asked, concern in her eyes at how frail he seemed.

"Oh, so-so." Althar made a weak effort at a shrug of indifference. "But I feel all the better for seeing you again, little one."

Elona loved it when he called her that; it had always been his affectionate name for her, ever since she could remember.

He stretched out an arm to pull the bell cord beside the small mountain of pillows crowding the bed-head. Terrance immediately appeared at the door.

"Tea, Terrance. And perhaps some toast."

"Yes, Sire," the manservant answered with a smile. "And will the Princess be taking anything?"

"The same."

Terrance bowed and retired to attend to his duties.

"So how was your trip? Did you enjoy it?"

Elona pulled up a chair and made herself comfortable before launching into another account of the last few months. Only this time she could afford to enjoy telling it without fear of reprisal. She omitted nothing.

"It sounds like Padráig is in a bit of a pickle," her father said when she was finished.

Elona slipped her shoes off and buried her feet into the quilted counterpane on the bed. "I'm worried. Nobody down here seems prepared to take the situation seriously. We both know Padráig wouldn't be rattled unless he honestly believed there was something really wrong."

"I know."

"Is there nothing you can do? You are still the king."

"I wish it were so, little one. But you know Midana; she's got me imprisoned in here. She has my doctors wrapped around her little finger. If I so much as get dressed I am pestered by a fleet of mollycoddling fools who tell me I should be careful not to overdo it. Bah!"

Elona smiled at the familiar defiance, but her concern for her father's health was not diminished. She doubted whether he even had the strength to get up unassisted.

Terrance returned with a tray festooned with tea and toast, along with an assortment of preserves. Althar waited until his man had retired again before continuing.

"The thing that worries me most is the assessment of the quality of our military leadership. Are the officers really as bad as Padráig fears?"

Elona closed her eyes to recall some of those she'd met. "It depends. He does rather tar them all with the same brush. He has the Executive, as I mentioned, and I think there are more that would accept that mantle if given the chance."

"Like this Torrin-Ashur you were telling me about?" Althar's lips slipped into a lopsided grin.

Elona felt herself flush. "Yes, he was one who got an opportunity to prove himself. But there are others. Like him, they're mostly lower nobility."

"Ah, yes, the ones that get overlooked until chaos breaks out. Then they come to the fore, usually to the embarrassment of those who should have known better. And the rest, how do you rate them?"

"Father, I just don't know." Elona paused, shaking her head slowly.

"The whole time I was at Mitcha I saw no evidence of their real military ability. I don't know whether they can fight, or just talk about it."

"What about this lad from the House of Kin-Shísim? Tiam's son."

"Borádin? That was a call-out. That's different."

"It's still fighting."

"Yes, but it's not war, father. To begin with it was all bluster. Then I'm not sure what happened. Borádin started off expecting to win, but when it came to it, he found himself fighting for his life. I don't think he would have been nearly so bold had he known what was going to happen."

"So, if the same is true of the rest, and the Tsnath really did invade, all this bravado might melt away?"

Elona shrugged. "Some of them might discover themselves made of sterner stuff. But I wouldn't like to say how many."

She picked up her teacup and walked over to the window. Standing in silence, looking out over the garden, she knew her father was watching her; she could almost feel the intensity of his gaze. He allowed her the space she needed to sort out her thoughts.

"I have this uneasy feeling in the pit of my stomach. Like everything is about to change and there's nothing I can do about it."

"Welcome to the real world, little one. That's how it is for kings, too."

Elona turned to face her father. "But why do I feel such disquiet, so impotent?"

"Have you tried identifying what it is you cannot do?" The question elicited a frown. "What is it you feel is so beyond you?"

"I don't know," Elona shrugged again, "the politicians, Midana, the Tsnath, the whole situation in the north. What can I do about any of that?"

"Is that really it?"

A curious transformation occurred when the veil slowly fell away from her eyes and she saw through the mist of politics and geography to discover the true source of her disquiet.

"But…" she began.

"These eyes may be old, little one, but they still see."

"But…"

"This Torrin-Ashur, he sounds like a decent young man."

Elona was stunned by the way her father was able to cut through the dross and go straight to the heart of the matter.

"You fear the consequences of consorting with him?"

Elona gave a forlorn nod. "For him as much as for me."

Her father patted the bed and she went and sat beside him once more.

"You melted my heart when you were this big," he said, holding up his hands about a foot apart. "But even then, I remember thinking that one day your heart would belong to another. The thing that struck me most, thinking back on it, was that I was actually envious of him, this imaginary man I hadn't even met. Silly, isn't it?"

Elona smiled.

"But do you know something? Over time I came to realise that I owed this man an immeasurable debt of gratitude."

"Gratitude?"

Althar nodded. "The man who wins your heart is the one who will make you happy. And there is *nothing* more important to me than that."

Elona leaned forwards and hugged her father tightly, burying her face into his chest to hide the tears that were endeavouring to escape down her cheek.

"Midana will never allow it," she mumbled.

Althar kissed the top of her head.

"I am still the king," he whispered quietly.

25

Word of Lord Özeransk's arrival reached Döshan's ears just as he was completing his morning devotions. It took him a moment to draw his thoughts back from the hazy world of incense and incantations.

"Thank you," he murmured. The servant who had brought the news remained standing by the sanctuary door. "Where is Özeransk now?"

"In the arboretum, Advisor."

"Well, we'd best not keep him waiting then, hmm?"

Döshan dismissed the servant with a wave, then heaved himself up from his knees. He placed a brass lid over the altar censer to suppress the curls of fragrant smoke rising from within, hoping that the incense would extinguish itself before it was entirely consumed. The stuff cost a king's ransom these days. There weren't so many in the city who followed the old religions anymore and most of his suppliers, only ever devotees of lining their pockets, had long since converted to more lucrative beliefs.

With a wistful sigh, he bowed to the intricate statue of the ancient dragon lord, Bël-aírnon. Cast in bronze, it was overlaid with gold and encrusted with iridescent chips of hematite that were quite scale-like in appearance. A few small emeralds and aquamarines helped to bias the colour. They sparkled when the candlelight played across their cleaved facets, making the statue seem almost alive sometimes. Occasionally, ruby eyes glared defiantly. It was a poor imitation of the majestic creature it represented, yet even after decades of familiarity he still found it a thing of exquisite beauty. It could always be relied upon to lift his spirits and inspire his thoughts.

But there was no time to dawdle, he reminded himself. He was not in a position to keep a man like Özeransk waiting; such allowances might be made for emperors, but not humble advisors. Slipping his feet back into his sandals, he hurried off towards the arboretum, doing his best to collect his thoughts as he went.

Özeransk was seated on a wooden bench and appeared to be in a meditative state when Döshan found him. He was a well-groomed man, his dark hair neither excessively long nor cropped short, as had become a fashion of late. His precisely trimmed beard was in keeping with the style, more than stubble but not full grown. He was tall, lean and muscular, befitting his reputation as a fearsome warrior on the battlefield. Though his attire on this occasion was rather more courtly than military, a long silken robe of charcoal grey held closed with a rich purple cummerbund. Slightly austere and yet sumptuously expensive. Döshan chuckled quietly to himself. He had always found fashion to be one of life's little mysteries; occasionally to be admired, sometimes ridiculed, but never *quite* understood. Although, if Lord Özeransk was wearing it, then he wondered if it was perhaps safe to lean towards admiration.

The warrior's eyes flickered open the moment he realised someone was coming.

"My lord," Döshan opened, bowing respectfully as he approached, "I hope I have not kept you too long."

"Not at all," Özeransk replied in a smooth baritone voice. "It's so peaceful here, I could spend hours sitting under these trees." His gaze roved unhurriedly over the manicured surroundings of the walled arboretum, dwelling momentarily on the nearest of several ornamental ponds. The only sounds were the chirping of birds and the trickling of water along the miniature streams that flowed from pool to pool. Occasional movement caught the eye, the odd firefish wallowing in the depths that suddenly darted up to snatch an insect from the surface before seeking sanctuary back in the deep. "Still, I don't suppose the emperor has summoned me here just to indulge myself."

Döshan smiled. "No, my lord. His Majesty will be most pleased you have come. I, too, am grateful. I know the journey here to Jèdda-galbráith is a long one for you."

Özeransk waved an uncaring hand. "Anything for the emperor. He knows he can rely on my loyalty."

"Indeed. I was counting on it."

"I see. And there I was thinking His Majesty had bidden me here," Özeransk jibed.

Döshan glanced at the ground and tried to look humble. "Well, I may have – nudged him a little, shall we say."

"Ha!" Özeransk rose to his feet and landed a hearty slap on Döshan's shoulder. "Well, in that case, you'd better tell me what you've got me into – before I find myself neck-deep in something serious."

"Serious, my lord?" Döshan smiled, "Whatever makes you say that?"

"Döshan, the day you're not wading in something portentous will be the day they gather you to your forebears. If you've had anything to do with why I'm here, then it's serious – and probably dangerous."

Özeransk was right. The matter at hand was both those things. Not that the man seemed overly worried. If anything, the prospect had put a sparkle in his eye.

*

Özeransk finished reading the letter Baroness Daka had sent to the emperor and then dropped it on to the low table beside him.

"You have agreed to support her in this venture?"

"I have only agreed to supply the reinforcements she has requested," Omnitas replied.

Özeransk shook his head. "She's playing a dangerous game."

The emperor merely nodded, swallowing another grape.

Özeransk leaned back against his richly embroidered floor cushion. He had removed his cummerbund and Döshan noticed that his robe had fallen open to reveal a silken undershirt. The emperor had decided beforehand to conduct this meeting informally, dispensing with the throne and opting to recline on the dais, suitably festooned with comforts.

"So, let me see if I have this straight," Özeransk said. "The baroness intends to invade the Tep-Mödiss. For support she has her two neighbours, together with a mercenary force under Minnàk's command. And with that she hopes to take on Kirshtahll and hold the entire Alondrian army at bay?"

Omnitas grunted. It sounded like a laugh, except that there was no smile in sight.

"And what in the name of Aírnon's arse makes her think she stands a chance of success?" Özeransk demanded. Döshan winced; he didn't mind profanity as such, he just wasn't keen on blasphemous uses of Aírnon's name. "Every other attempt we've made in the last five hundred years has ended in disaster, so what makes Daka's plan any different?"

There was a momentary pause, then Omnitas looked up at Döshan and raised an expectant eyebrow.

Döshan gave a deferential nod before turning his attention to Özeransk. "It is a very good question, my lord. And one His Majesty is hoping you might help us answer."

"How?"

"We were hoping you would agree to join Daka's venture."

Özeransk's eyes widened briefly, but then he allowed the side of his mouth to curl into a sly smile.

"You want me to be a spy in her camp, is that it?"

"Oh, more than just a spy, my dear Özeransk," Omnitas effused, adding a wolfish grin. "With you forming part of her invasion force, you would be able to keep her in check, maybe even take control if matters get out of hand."

The emperor picked up a tray of his favourite snacks and offered it towards his guest. Döshan's jaw nearly dropped. Omnitas really was trying to ingratiate himself today.

But if Özeransk had noted the uncharacteristically servile efforts, he didn't show it. He declined. "Get out of hand?"

Omnitas withdrew the tray and dithered his fingers over the selection, deciding which one to have. With mouth full, he nodded at Döshan again.

Döshan marshalled his thoughts, wondering how best to put this.

"My lord, you are right to question Daka's chances of success. As you pointed out, our history is replete with failure when it comes to regaining the Tep-Mödiss. Every time we manage to secure the region, the Alondrians seem to wrest it from us. That is why this matter is so intriguing."

"Intriguing?"

"Yes, my lord. You see, whatever else she may be, Daka is no fool. I find it most doubtful that she would be embarking on a venture such as this based solely on optimism."

"She has something up her sleeve?" Özeransk pondered aloud.

"All things being equal," Döshan said, bowing his head, "she wouldn't realistically be able to secure the Tep-Mödiss for long. Even facing Kirshtahll's forces poses her great risk. The Alondrian army is not what it once was, but what it lacks in experience it makes up for in size. Daka could incur heavy losses."

"To say nothing of the cost. This is no small undertaking," the emperor added, raising his eyebrows for emphasis.

"So," Özeransk mused, "the stakes are high. The question is, what is it that makes her think she has a realistic chance of success?"

Döshan sighed, though quietly. The only certainty in this situation was that it was vexing. Too many unknowns. He didn't like unknowns; they necessitated something else he despised – speculation.

"There is another possibility," he replied carefully. "Her aims may not be what they seem on the surface."

Özeransk frowned.

"My lord, with a good tactical plan, and especially if you agree to lend your support, then Daka probably can win the initial confrontation with the Alondrians. It's holding on to her conquests that will be the key issue."

"Which is usually where our endeavours start to fall apart," Özeransk pointed out.

"Indeed. But what if holding on to the Tep-Mödiss is not Daka's ultimate goal? What if merely gaining a temporary foothold is all that she requires?"

Özeransk's frown returned, deeper than before. "To what purpose?"

"That's what we don't yet know, my dear Özeransk," Omnitas jumped in.

Özeransk met the emperor's gaze. "But you must have some idea of what her ultimate aims are, surely?"

Omnitas looked to Döshan again, before indulging in another savoury from his tray. The man really did eat too much, Döshan considered. He'd put on far too much weight in the last few months. His opponents despised him for his lack of physical prowess and he was only making it worse by his indulgences.

Döshan returned his attention to Özeransk. "My lord, it is our belief that Daka isn't really interested in the Tep-Mödiss for its own sake. What she really wants is power. We think she has eyes on His Majesty's throne."

Özeransk didn't seem surprised by that. "But how does invading the Tep-Mödiss help her?"

"If she is successful, she would be very popular. After all, at least two previous emperors came to power on the strength of successes in the region."

"That was a long time ago, Döshan, and in both cases they managed to hang on to their conquests – at least long enough to benefit from their victories." Özeransk paused and shook his head. "I don't see Daka in the same position. As you said, she *might* win an initial confrontation, but it won't last long enough for her to be swept to power on a wave of imperial euphoria. Within a season she'll be kicked back this side of the Ablath with nothing but an empty purse to show for her troubles. No, she has to have another motive for all this, or else something that gives her an advantage we don't yet know about."

"Which is why I need you in her camp, my friend," Omnitas said, holding Özeransk's gaze for a moment.

Once more Döshan had to hide his shock; it seemed as though the emperor was almost pleading. But then the situation was dire enough to warrant it. The political stability in Tsnathsarré was deteriorating, eroding the emperor's position. The barons, their predecessors once kings themselves before their domains were folded into the Empire, were now a brooding collection of malcontents. Omnitas was a compromise. Unlike most of the previous emperors, he'd been given his position rather than taken it by force. His sole purpose was to maintain the status quo. But it was a balancing act, and a delicate one at that. If Daka stirred the waters too much, the scales could very easily tip. That wouldn't just mean the emperor's head on a block; the whole Empire might dissolve into civil war.

"I need to know what she's up to," Omnitas continued. "And I need you there to put a stop to her if she looks like being in a position to threaten me. Döshan has advised that I should hold off with my reinforcements until the latter stages of her campaign. But what if by that stage she has already attained her ulterior goal?"

Özeransk shook his head again. "If she could succeed without your help, then why ask for it in the first place? That doesn't make any sense. If her aim is to topple you, she would be better to undertake this invasion without interference. That way she could claim all the credit." Özeransk paused and regarded his feet for a moment. "What I really don't understand is why you are countenancing her plan. Why not simply have her arrested now and be done with the whole thing?"

That, Döshan recalled, had been the advice he'd first given, only it had been too late even then. The emperor had already committed himself; a decision he'd taken without the counsel of any of his advisors.

"It looks bad," Omnitas replied, tiredness in his voice now. "Imagine what my opponents would think if I deliberately thwarted an attempt to regain the Tep-Mödiss."

"But Daka is guilty of sedition."

"Yes. But could I prove it? I can't arrest her simply for trying to restore our national pride, which is all this appears to be on the surface. The barons would never stand for it. I'd need proof of her ambitions as hard as granite. And *that* I don't have."

Özeransk sighed and went back to regarding his feet. It was a while before he spoke again. "Alright, say I agree to join Daka's forces. I will require compensation…"

A look of relief washed over Omnitas. His concern disappeared in a broad smile.

"Fear not. I will supply you with additional troops and pay all your costs. I cannot expect you to undertake this task for me and expect you to pay for the privilege," he chuckled.

"Naturally," Özeransk returned flatly.

Döshan watched, careful to mask the intensity of his interest. This was where the warrior would move in for the kill. There had never been any doubt in his mind that the man would eventually agree. The only question was, what would it cost the emperor?

"What else, I wonder?" Omnitas mused, apparently enjoying himself now. "I have already relieved you of your tax dues for other services rendered in the past."

Özeransk didn't miss a beat. "I have one condition," he replied. He deliberately held off elaborating until Omnitas had raised an eyebrow. "Give me the Sèdessa Range."

"What?" Döshan blurted out.

The emperor shot him an annoyed look. Döshan bowed and apologised for his lack of restraint.

"Sèdessa belongs to Ginngár," Omnitas muttered, his gaze returning to Özeransk.

"Who has achieved nothing with it since you gave it to him. It is a thorn in his side – he will be glad to be rid of it."

Döshan was careful to keep his face neutral, but his mind raced to understand Özeransk's motives. It was a very strange request. The Sèdessa Range lay close to his lands in the northwestern corner of the empire, though not immediately adjacent to them. Like the Tep-Mödiss, it was another region that caused friction. Ginngár, Baron of Üráld, had only been given it on the condition that he quell its rebellious nature. Not that he'd had any success; the Dwarves who lived there were notoriously stubborn when it came to being told what to do, particularly on land they considered their own. Özeransk would almost be doing the emperor a favour by taking over. So what in the name of the gods was the man angling for?

"It's nothing but trouble," Omnitas replied warily. "Ginngár may not mind being freed of his obligations, but why would you want to step into his troubled shoes?"

"The Range is going to waste."

"And you think you can do better?"

"Ginngár has given up trying. I could hardly do worse."

"How?" Omnitas pressed.

Özeransk smiled. "Are we in agreement?"

The emperor's eyes narrowed with suspicion. He didn't give an immediate answer. Döshan found himself holding his breath, wondering what the emperor would say. The problem was, if he wanted Özeransk's cooperation, he really didn't have much choice.

"Alright," Omnitas replied after a considerable pause, "I'll agree to your condition. But you still haven't answered my question. How do you intend to succeed where Ginngár has failed?"

Özeransk shrugged. "By giving the Range back to the Dwarves."

After a moment of shock, Omnitas sucked in his breath.

Döshan found it hard not to smile; now he understood, even if he hadn't seen it coming. To Özeransk, negotiation was merely a form of warfare, something to be tackled like a battle. He had toyed with his opponent just long enough to manoeuvre him into position, then caught him in a pincer movement, pressing home his attack without flinching.

Attire wasn't the only thing Döshan had to admire about the man. It was clear now that he was after an alliance with the Dwarve Nation. And with no tax burden, he was free to enjoy whatever gains that offered. It was a gamble; the Dwarves weren't the most forgiving of races – they might not be amenable to future trade with anyone from the Empire. But then, if he *could* pull it off, and giving them back their lands would certainly be a good start, Özeransk might very well end up the richest man in the Empire.

26

The Duke of Cöbèck's carriage rumbled across the People's Square towards the Royal Military Academy, iron rims grinding on cobbles. When it stopped, the silence that ensued was most welcome.

"Well, young man, your moment of truth awaits."

Torrin-Ashur glanced towards the Academy's entrance, still a hundred yards off. He let out an apprehensive sigh.

"Shall I accompany you in?"

"You've already done so much for me, Your Grace."

"Understood," the Duke smirked. "I wouldn't want my hand holding on my first day, either."

Torrin-Ashur laughed. "No offence intended, sir."

"None taken. From what I've seen of you so far, young man, you're quite capable of landing on your own two feet."

Torrin-Ashur shook the Duke's outstretched hand and descended from the carriage. His uniform was new and uncomfortable; it was the finest set of clothes he'd ever owned, but wearing it made him feel far too conspicuous.

The Duke handed him his sword. "Gad will be along shortly with the rest of your belongings."

"I am most grateful, Your Grace."

With a parting nod, the Duke flicked fingers at his driver and the carriage rumbled away.

As he turned, Torrin-Ashur caught sight of the Cymàtagé with its ethereal crystal columns and celestial-looking steps. He wondered how Jorra-hin was getting on in such a grand place. The palace, dominating the skyline along the eastern edge of the Square, also caught his eye. The three Gosh Bridges linked its island with the rest of Alondris, the upper and lower bridges spanning the River Els-spear all the way to the Easterhalb. The middle one only extended as far as the wall of the palace, ending at a formidable-looking portcullis. What could be seen of the buildings beyond hinted at a grandeur hitherto unimagined, at least by him anyway. And somewhere in the midst of all that was Elona. He shook his head in dismay; once he'd thought highly of the log enclosure the Pressed had built for her at Mitcha.

Reining in his thoughts, he made a start for the Academy entrance. Its arch extended back some distance beyond the outer gates, its dressed sandstone construction suggesting it was more an aesthetic feature than a defensive one. The far end of the tunnel opened out on to a sizable parade ground called the Quad, according to the Duke. Surrounding that were the principal Academy buildings, beyond which lay the sparring grounds, the paddock and stables, and finally some open areas for field craft training, albeit on a somewhat limited scale. He quickly began to appreciate the Duke's earlier efforts to familiarise him with the lay of the land. The old soldier had enjoyed building a model and walking him through it, as though conducting a briefing before an assault.

The moment Torrin-Ashur stepped on to the Quad he became the subject of the duty sergeant's attention. The man made a beeline for him, his hand shuddering in a crisp salute as he stomped to a halt.

"May I be of assistance, sah," the man cried, loud enough to be drilling a platoon a hundred yards away.

Reeling slightly, Torrin-Ashur cleared his throat. "Yes, Sergeant. If you would be good enough to direct me to Captain Corbett's office."

"The captain's office is this way, sah. If you would follow me, sah."

The one-man tattoo smartly turned about and marched back across the Quad.

Torrin-Ashur was shown into a hallway outside Corbett's office. The sergeant knocked on the door, heard a grunt and proceeded inside. Raised voices suggested that a prior matter was reaching its conclusion. A few moments later, a red-faced young man emerged and fled, sparing Torrin-Ashur not so much as a glance.

The sergeant reappeared. "The captain will see you now, sah."

Torrin-Ashur checked his letter of introduction and straightened his uniform before going in.

Corbett's office was surprisingly sparse. No rugs softened the flagstone floor, the windows were bereft of curtains, and even the bookshelves looked as though they'd suffered a literary famine. The only furniture was a desk and two chairs, one occupied by the captain and the other almost certainly redundant on a permanent basis.

Torrin-Ashur came to attention and announced himself.

Corbett's eyebrows pinched together for a moment. "Kirshtahll's new man?"

"Yes, sir."

The letter of introduction received only brief attention. "Very well," the captain sighed, giving the impression the matter was of some inconvenience. "The general wants you to make use of the training on offer here while you await your audience. There's a new intake assembling, you can join them, I suppose." He paused, but only to huff. "This is all very irregular. You may not be a cadet, Ashur, but we have certain standards. While you're here, I expect them to be maintained. Whenever you leave the Academy, you will be appropriately dressed. There will be no rowdy or drunken behaviour – leave that beyond the New Wall. That goes for your men, too."

"I don't have any men with me, sir."

"Kirshtahll has made arrangements." Corbett glanced at the sergeant. "Show the lieutenant to the cadets' mess, then have his men assemble on the Quad for inspection."

"Sar."

Corbett turned his attention to some paperwork. "Dismissed."

Feeling thoroughly welcomed, Torrin-Ashur followed the sergeant out of the office and back on to the Quad.

"Is he always like that?"

"Been in the job a mite too long, sir," the sergeant replied, his voice thankfully now adjusted to a more conspiratorial level.

The sergeant left him at the entrance to the cadets' mess, an austere affair with little to suggest that it had any intention of becoming home for the next few months. Aside from the sleeping quarters on the upper floor, there were two common rooms either side of an entrance hall, neither of which contained much except a fireplace. The dining hall to the rear was furnished only with long tables and wooden benches. The lack of comforts made him chuckle; such deprivations must have come as a shock to those Academy graduates he'd met at Mitcha. Going without wasn't exactly their way.

After a good look round, during which he met absolutely no one, he stepped back outside on to the Quad. For a moment his mind went blank. Thirty pairs of boots, acting as one, stamped the ground. Hands smacked against pikes in a single crack.

"Ye gods!"

"Good to see you too, sir," Sergeant Nash replied.

"But – how, I mean – what are you doing here?"

Torrin-Ashur advanced towards the platoon assembled on the Quad and came face to face with the Pressed. Not that he believed what he was seeing. Nash withdrew a note from his belt pouch and offered it forwards.

Lt. Ashur,

I once told you that the decisions a commander must take can sometimes be tough on his subordinates. Fortunately, this does not always have to be the case.

Kirshtahll.

"I don't understand…"

"Princess Elona put in a good word on our behalf, sir."

Torrin-Ashur's face broke into a wide grin. "I – I had no idea." The truth was, when he'd ordered the Pressed back to Mitcha, he'd presumed his command of them was over. "Wait, that day I dismissed you, you already knew about this?"

Nash tried to look innocent, but failed. "We were under orders not to say anything, sir. The princess insisted that it be a surprise."

"The little minx," Torrin-Ashur snorted under his breath.

"Perhaps you would care to inspect your men, sir?"

Without waiting for a reply, Nash turned on the spot and barked a series of crisp commands. The men smartly shuffled about as they double-spaced themselves ready for inspection.

"You must have been drilling these lads non-stop since I last saw you."

"Wanted to make a favourable impression, sir. Besides, we've been here nearly two weeks now."

Nash explained that having left Tail-ébeth they'd made their way back to Mitcha and then immediately set out for the Kimballi Pass. At Bythe-Kim, on the south side of the mountains, favourable winds had enabled them to make the remainder of the journey by barge, straight down the Els-spear all the way into Alondris.

Torrin-Ashur followed Nash along the ranks, inspecting his men with a careful eye. Each one had a brand new uniform, made to measure, just like his own. Had Gad organised the tailoring, he wondered? They looked impeccable, especially with the Ashur crest on their tabards. When he came to Tomàss he paused to have a word.

"You're looking well. Fully recovered from your run-in with Borádin?"

"Like it never happened, sir."

Torrin-Ashur nodded. "Glad to hear it. Just try not to pick a fight with any of the nobles hereabouts, though. This is *real* call-out country."

Tomàss grinned.

With the inspection over, Torrin-Ashur turned to face Nash again. "How have they been treating you since you arrived?"

"Better than at Mitcha, sir. Nobody down here knows the lads were in the Pressed."

"Were?"

"Yes, sir. They were given a choice; remain at Mitcha, or enlist as Ashurmen. Not a hard decision for most of them."

"Ashurmen?" Torrin-Ashur repeated. That had a nice ring to it. He turned to face the platoon. "Gentlemen, you bear my family's name, just as I bear the name of Kirshtahll, so it seems we all have a lot to live up to. Now, no doubt being at the Academy will present us with a few challenges while we're here. But keep your noses clean, stay out of trouble, and I dare say we might just survive this ordeal."

There was a discernible swelling of chests as a wave of pride rippled through the ranks.

"Well, I don't know about you, Sergeant, but this damned southern sun is trying to melt me. Dismiss the men and you can show me where they've got you billeted."

"Aye, sir."

Nash barked another series of commands, marched the platoon off the Quad and ordered them to make themselves scarce. Following in their wake, he led the way towards the enlisted men's quarters.

After having made sure the men's needs were adequately catered for, Torrin-Ashur drew Nash to one side. "Sergeant, I need you to do something for me. How well do you know the city?"

"Not overly well, sir. We've not been out much."

"Hmm. No matter. I need you to find me a flower stall."

"A what, sir?" Nash was clearly a little uncertain of himself in this particular arena.

Torrin-Ashur had a pensive look on his face. A thank you gesture was required; one fit for a princess.

*

When Torrin-Ashur arrived back at the cadets' mess, he found a corporal waiting for him just outside the door, guarding a pile of belongings. Gad had made his delivery, but had not been able to stay. He dismissed the corporal, picked up his first load and went to find a room.

His mind returned to figuring out how he was going to deliver the thank you gesture he had in mind. It needed to be achieved discreetly. Using the palace pass Elona had given him would lead to rumour and speculation, both of which were to be avoided if he was to honour his word to Lady Kirshtahll. Anonymity was required. Problematic, given that the palace was no doubt one of the most guarded establishments in the kingdom.

Engrossed in plotting, he negotiated the stairs successfully, but failed to spot a cadet coming the other way. They cannoned into each other, sending pieces of equipment clattering to the floor in a raucous din.

There was no denying the fault was his, yet it was the cadet who apologised profusely, standing to attention as though he'd bumped into a general.

After a moment to recover from his surprise, Torrin-Ashur burst out laughing.

"Oh, thank the gods for that," the other lad muttered in relief. "I thought for a moment you might be one for calling me out or something. You never know in this place. There's already been one challenge."

"Really? You've met some of the intake, then?"

"Unfortunately, yes. I'm Timerra by the way. But just call me Tim."

"Torrin, Torrin-Ashur. Where're you from, Tim?"

"Colòtt. Father's the Governor over there. And you?"

"I've just come down from the Northern Territories. My father is lord of the March of Ashur."

Timerra nodded towards Torrin-Ashur's insignia. "You have rank already. How so?"

"I'm a bonded officer. I was serving up at Mitcha until General Kirshtahll decided to post me here."

Timerra's eyes bulged. "Kirshtahll! *The* Kirshtahll?"

Torrin-Ashur smiled. "I'm here under his sponsorship, to collect a commission. What about you? If you'll forgive me for noticing, your uniform doesn't exactly look new."

"It isn't. I've been serving for nearly two years."

"And you're only just coming to the Academy now?"

Timerra shrugged. "My father isn't one for wasting money on fads. It's taken me this long to convince him soldiering is my calling."

"Well, if it's any consolation, I wouldn't be here at all if Kirshtahll hadn't sent me. My family could never afford a commission." Torrin-

Ashur glanced around at the various belongings strewn across the floor. Not all of them were his. "You were on your way somewhere?"

"Just finding myself a new room. It's too noisy down that end." Timerra flicked a glance along the corridor.

"Rowdy lot, are they?"

Timerra let out a grunt. "I haven't had a decent night's sleep since I got here. And the intake hasn't even fully assembled yet."

They collected up their respective belongings and Torrin-Ashur found himself a nearby room that happened to have a window facing east towards the palace. From a higher vantage point than the People's Square, more of the palace buildings could be seen, their grandeur only increasing the lower down they went.

He was still gazing out of the window when Timerra stopped by his door. "Spotted something interesting?"

Torrin-Ashur shrugged. "Just hatching a plan to get myself into Captain Corbett's bad books."

"Not difficult, but sounds like fun."

"What sounds like fun?"

Torrin-Ashur turned. Another young man had appeared. He recognised the newcomer as the lad he'd seen fleeing Corbett's office earlier.

"Oh, Torrin, this is Guyass."

"We've met," Torrin-Ashur replied with a nod. Guyass frowned. "Well, passed each other briefly." Guyass was still not enlightened. "You were in Corbett's office earlier. Corbett didn't sound happy…"

"Oh. You heard that?" Guyass glanced peevishly at the floor. "A slight misunderstanding."

"Actually, a major infraction of one of Corbett's cardinal rules," Timerra supplied with a grin. "Smuggled a girl into the barracks. The captain was furious."

Timerra seemed to enjoy revelling in Guyass's embarrassment, Torrin-Ashur noted. "I didn't realise the Academy was that strict about visitors."

"They're not, when they come and go by way of the main gate, signed in and out and all that. This visit was a little more – clandestine."

"My grandfather is head of the Architect's Guild," Guyass explained, "and a keen historian. I know some of the city's better kept secrets, including a few about the Academy's hidden entrances."

"Really." Torrin-Ashur suddenly found his interest growing.

"Know much about the palace?" He noticed a gleam in Guyass's eye and beckoned him over to the window. "Well, now, my friend, how would you like to get yourself into trouble twice in one day?"

"Err..."

"Good man, good man." He clapped Guyass on the back before the lad had a chance to object. He nodded out of the window. "I need to get inside there. Tonight."

"Oh dear..."

*

The barman of the Wicked Cat glanced up from the mug he was pouring as a new customer appeared at the bar.

"Evenin', Jackam. You're looking rather pleased with yourself. Good day?"

"You could say that."

The barman placed a brimming pot in front of one of his other customers and then gave Jackam his full attention.

"Strangest thing. A bunch of soldiers came calling earlier."

The barman had heard many things, but this was something new. "What happened?"

"Bought my entire stock. Every single flower I 'ad."

"Oh. Well, time to celebrate then," the barman replied, hoping that the army had been generous in its payment.

*

Captain Agarma gave the door to the king's chambers a gentle knock. He almost didn't want to be heard in case the king was asleep, but he needed to extract Elona from within.

Terrance answered a few moments later. Agarma outlined the situation and the king's manservant went to fetch her.

"I'm sorry to disturb you, Your Highness, but there's something I need to show you," Agarma explained when she appeared at the door.

"What?"

"I think it best that you see for yourself."

Elona made him wait while she popped back to say goodnight to her father.

On arrival at her quarters, Agarma paused and gave her a look that suggested she should prepare herself.

Elona gasped as the door swung open. Her shock was gradually replaced by a smile. She covered her lips with the tips of her fingers, clearly not quite able to believe what she was seeing.

Her reception room had been transformed into a floral arrangement.

"We appear to have had a security breach," Agarma observed, rather missing the point. "Whoever brought them did not enter the palace by the usual means."

"Oh, come now, Captain. You know very well who brought them."

"Yes," he conceded, "I have a pretty good idea. I'm just not sure how."

27

"Get in there, you stupid book," Jorra-hin muttered.

The last of the three leather-bound manuscripts he'd spent the evening perusing did not want to return to its proper place. He very nearly lost his temper, but just managed to take a deep breath and restrain himself; the book was considerably older than he was and deserved respect. He reordered the rest of the shelf to create more room, whereupon the offending article slotted into place, allowing him to step down off the mobile ladder.

An expansive yawn overtook him. It was well past midnight and he really needed to get to bed. He was about to head off when a nagging sensation clawed at the edge of his consciousness. It suggested that all was not as it should be; the sort of feeling that would induce insomnia if he didn't investigate before calling it a night.

The library was normally bereft of patrons by this hour, so he decided to wander towards the hub, the large doughnut-shaped desk at the very centre of the library. It was always manned by at least one brother of the Adak-rann.

"Brother Jorra, I didn't know you were still here."

Jorra-hin smiled at Brother Joss. "I was about to be on my way."

"Is anything wrong?"

Jorra-hin shrugged. "I was going to ask you that. Is anyone else in the library at the moment?"

Joss shook his head. "No one has been past the hub since I came on duty an hour ago. If there is anyone here, they're being awfully quiet."

Hardly a conclusive argument, Jorra-hin mused; it was a library, after all.

"I think I'll take a quick look round on my way out," he said, nodding goodnight.

He began to stroll along the rows of shelves, lightly dragging his fingers over the spines of the books thereon. Centuries of knowledge slipped beneath his gentle caress, the offerings of long-forgotten authors making brief appearances at the periphery of his mind. With his eyes closed, guided only by his fingertips, he let the sense of history wash over him. Even in the short time that he'd been at the Cymàtagé, he'd come to love having the library virtually to himself last thing at night.

When the shelves slipped out of reach he opened his eyes again to find that he'd come to one of the reading areas. His eyes were drawn to a figure hunched in the far corner, a girl from what he could make out in the dim lighting. She was leaning forwards on her elbows, head hung disconsolately between palms. He caught a hint of sobbing.

"Are you alright?"

The figure sat bolt upright.

"Kirin?"

Kirin wiped the backs of her hands over her eyes, trying to rub away tears.

Jorra-hin threaded his way between the reading tables and sat down opposite her. The trimmed-down oil lamp didn't shed much light, but it was enough to reveal that her raven hair was tousled, her eyes puffy and her cheeks streaked. His stomach fluttered; she was still pretty.

"Whatever's the matter?"

The reply he got was a deep sigh. He waited for some composure to be regained.

"I'm thinking of leaving the Cymàtagé, Jorra. I'm just not suited to all this…" Kirin plucked at her robes to indicate all things magely.

Jorra-hin was taken aback. He'd come to regard Kirin as a fount of enthusiasm, as passionate about her calling as anyone he'd met. "You can't mean that, surely?"

Kirin let out another deep sigh. "Preceptor Tutt-tus has practically given up with me. I'm useless. Completely incapable of achieving even the smallest of tasks."

"Tutt-tus told you that?"

"Well, no, not in so many words. But it's not hard to tell what he's thinking. Since I've been here, I haven't been able to complete a single exercise he's set me."

"It's early days, yet, Kirin. Give it time. You can't give up now – you've wanted to come here since you were a child."

That was perhaps the wrong thing to have said, Jorra-hin realised too late. Kirin's face took on a deeply pained expression.

"What I *want* won't change the facts. I can't even get the hang of the simplest bits of A'lyavine. I'll just have to face up to the truth, Jorra – I have no Taümathic ability."

"Do you really believe that?" he asked gently.

Kirin's disappointment boiled over and tears rolled down her cheeks again. He reached across the table and took her hand.

"Do you honestly think they'd have let you stay if they thought you had no potential?"

"You know why they let me stay. Because of my father, as a favour."

"Really," Jorra-hin grunted. Her father may have been the Nicián Ambassador, but it had not been politics that had propelled the overseer of the Trials across the room to stop her from leaving on the Day of Admissions. Of that he was certain. "Stay here, I'll be back in a moment."

Without further explanation, he got up and returned to the hub.

"I thought you were going to bed."

"I was, but something's come up. Brother Joss, could I ask a very great favour of you?"

Joss raised his eyebrows.

"I need to borrow the Talmathic Dömon."

Joss's eyes widened in alarm. "Err – Brother, mages are not allowed access to it without prior agreement from the chancellor, you know that."

"I'm not a mage."

"No, but…"

"Look, I only need to borrow it for a few minutes. A friend of mine is upset and needs a little encouragement, and I think I know just the thing. I only want to read a short passage from it."

Joss swallowed as though his throat had gone dry. "I really shouldn't."

"No one will be any the wiser. It'll be back before you know it."

Joss hesitated a moment or two longer, then gave a conspiratorial grin. "Alright, just this once. But if anyone finds out, you held a dagger to my throat, alright?"

Not very plausible, Jorra-hin mused, but he nodded all the same. He moved inside the centre of the hub and followed Joss down a cast-iron spiral staircase to the vault situated directly below. It was where all the really important, valuable or dangerous books were stored.

Joss pulled out a set of keys from his cassock pocket. They were on a chain attached to his belt. Holding a lantern ahead of him, he unlocked the metal-clad door and led the way inside.

The Talmathic Dömon sat on a dedicated lectern in the middle of the vault. It was already open. Jorra-hin made a note of which page was showing so that it could be returned without leaving any sign of its brief sojourn.

As he made to pick up the ancient book, a sudden tingling sensation coursed up his arm. His hand shot back as though bitten. Joss was looking the other way and didn't notice.

"Something wrong?" Joss enquired when he turned a few moments later.

"No, no," Jorra-hin mumbled, "it's just that I've heard so much about the Talmathic Dömon. This is the real thing." He sounded suitably reverent. That he had already read the book from cover to cover made no odds – that had been at Jàb-áldis, from a mere copy. This was the original, written by the hand of Amatt the Blind. The tingling sensation was proof of that. Though he'd never before experienced a sense of connection with an author quite as strongly as he had just now.

"Yes, it is the real thing," Joss affirmed, "so for the sake of the gods, be careful with it. If it gets damaged, you couldn't imagine the trouble we'll be in."

Jorra-hin silently disagreed; he had a fairly vivid imagination where trouble was concerned.

The mages revered the Talmathic Dömon so much that they were exceedingly strict about who could study it. Access was limited partly for the sake of preservation; the manuscript was well over a thousand years old and had to be handled with great care. But the real reason was that the mages were afraid of its power falling into nefarious hands. Some of the incantations it contained could be extremely dangerous.

Jorra-hin made a second attempt to pick up the ancient tome, ready this time for whatever he might experience. The tingling came again, though to a lesser extent, and dissipated altogether not long after, leaving the book simply feeling unnaturally heavy.

With it tucked under his arm, he thanked Joss, ascended the spiral staircase and threaded his way back through the library to where he'd left Kirin. Her head was once more ensconced between hands, more tears having flowed while he'd been gone. He sat back down, gently placing the book on the table between them, and turned up the wick of the lamp.

"What's this?"

"Never mind that," he said, not wanting to scare her unduly before he'd had a chance to explain. Opening the Talmathic Dömon, he leafed through its delicate pages. It was one of the few books of its era that had been bound rather than produced as a scroll. He found the passage he was after and gave it a brief scan. "I want you to close your eyes and just listen. I'm going to read you a short passage. Don't try to analyse the words you hear, or translate them – just let them into your mind."

Kirin frowned, but at his insistence she nodded and closed her eyes.

He allowed her a moment to settle and then began to read. At first, her forehead screwed up in concentration, suggesting that she was ignoring his instructions. She had little hope of translating what she was hearing; the words were in A'lyavine of the First Dialect, the most difficult to understand of all the A'lyavinical forms. But as the reading progressed, he saw her gradually relax. Her face slipped into a serene pose as her mind was caressed by the smooth rhythm of the ancient tongue.

A short while later, a smile spread across her lips. As the passage continued her joy blossomed further, first a sigh of contentment, then a giggle. By the end she was laughing. When the last word rolled off his tongue, Jorra-hin left her hanging on to a final moment of bliss.

Kirin blinked in surprise as she came back to her senses.

"I don't imagine you've experienced A'lyavine quite like that before," Jorra-hin commented, a bemused smile giving his lips a lopsided twist.

"Never. It was wonderful. What was it?"

"A passage from the Talmathic Dömon."

Kirin gasped.

"So you mustn't tell anyone about this, otherwise I'll be in serious trouble."

"The Talmathic Dömon," she said, her whisper reverent. She gingerly reached out to touch the book's pages. "I never dreamed I'd ever see it, let alone hear it read to me. What was the passage?"

"One of Amatt the Blind's examples of the different usages of A'lyavine. It's called *An Ode to Joy*. The point is, if you were to attempt to translate it word for word, you'd miss the purpose of the exercise. You would have felt nothing."

"I'm not sure I follow you, Jorra."

"You said to me earlier that you were having trouble with even the most basic A'lyavinical exercises. Well, you're hardly alone. A'lyavine doesn't lend itself to academic study. It's a Taümathic language. With a lot of hard work you *can* eventually master it by conventional means. But approached like that, it will only ever be a long-forgotten, dead and boring language.'

"The mistake I see most people making, especially here in the Cymàtagé, is that they try too hard. They get out their reference works, their notes and their dictionaries, and use them like surgeons' scalpels, dissecting passages of A'lyavine into sentence fragments, as though tackling them in small enough pieces will make them easier to understand. But with A'lyavine, that's like buying yourself a ladder, removing the sides and then trying to get off the ground using only the rungs."

"I don't see how else you're supposed to do it."

"Don't you?" Jorra-hin challenged with a grin. "So why, then, did you burst out laughing a few minutes ago?"

That elicited a curious frown.

"I'll tell you why – you gave up trying to work it all out and just let the words speak to you. Don't look so surprised, that's the point – it's a *Taümathic* language. It can make itself understood without you getting in the way."

Kirin sat deep in thought for a moment. "But Tutt-tus sets me these exercises to do," she said. "I've tried reading A'lyavine, believe me, and it never makes any sense."

Jorra-hin nodded. "I tell you what, next time he sets you something, bring it to me. I won't do the work for you, but I will help."

Kirin took hold of his hand and kissed his fingers. "And what about my inability to achieve anything with the Taümatha? Can you help me there, too?"

Kirin's touch sent a pleasant tingle though him. "Not directly," he replied, gazing into her eyes. "But for what it's worth, I suspect I know what the root cause of the problem is."

"Oh?"

"Desire."

"Desire?"

Jorra-hin nodded.

"I don't understand," Kirin returned with a frown. "As you said, I've wanted to come here since I was a child. Desire is just about the only thing I can supply."

"I know. You want to be a healer. But how passionate do you feel about turning water a different hue, or lighting a candle, or any of the other silly tasks they expect of you?"

Kirin looked confused. "But it's part of the training. You've got to start somewhere, with the little things."

"So start with a headache."

"What, practice on people?" Kirin recoiled, clearly shocked at the idea. "I couldn't. What if it went wrong? What if I hurt someone, or worse?"

"Not likely."

"Why not?"

"Because everybody who has the Taümatha within them has their own route to releasing it. I think yours is your compassion. For you to hurt someone, you would have to want to do it. So you tell me, is that likely?"

Jorra-hin carefully closed the Talmathic Dömon and stood up.

"I'd better take this back before anyone discovers I've had it out of the vault."

Kirin let him get half way back across the reading area before she called after him. "How do you know so much about the Taümatha, Jorra?"

He stopped and smiled back at her. "I read a lot. It's all in here." He tapped the book under his arm and then broadly indicated the surrounding shelves. "You'd be amazed at what there is."

He turned to go, but Kirin stopped him again. "Why aren't you taking the Mages' Path? You'd make a good mage."

Jorra-hin shrugged. "Like I said, it's all about desire, Kirin. I don't *want* to be one."

28

"My lady, excuse the interruption, but I thought you would like to know – Roumin-Lenka is approaching the castle."

Daka looked up in surprise. "Already?"

Gömalt nodded.

"Very well. Bring him to the great hall when he arrives."

"Yes, my lady. There's just one thing – Roumin-Lenka appears to be a woman."

Shock momentarily registered on the baroness's face. It was quickly replaced by a frown.

"Does that change things?"

The baroness paused a moment. "No, I suppose not."

*

Roumin-Lenka turned heads as she emerged from the barbican, her six-foot frame challenging the notion that all Dwarves were short in stature. From the neck down she was dressed like a clan warrior, but above that line there was little similarity to the usually bearded fighters of her race. Gömalt found her strikingly attractive, in a stern sort of way. Her dark hair was plaitted into multiple strands which were then wound into a single plait extending most of the way down her back. Her people usually adopted the style for battle. Everything about her, from the wary, distrusting glances, to her leather doublet and weaponry, suggested she would make a formidable opponent.

Gömalt watched with growing interest as she steered her horse across the courtyard. Only when she turned towards him did he notice the long scar down her right cheek. It was not a recent affliction. Nor did it detract from her looks; in fact, he found it quite alluring. He traced a finger along his own jaw where Kassandra's knife had left its mark.

Roumin-Lenka drew her horse to a standstill but made no move to dismount. Her hand came to rest on the hilt of a double-edged axe. She glanced about the courtyard, her glare seemingly a challenge to the guards, daring them to advance.

Gömalt stepped forwards. "On behalf of the baroness, may I welcome you to Castle Brath'daka."

Green eyes snapped to him, pinning him with an intense stare. "Daka is here, yes?"

"She is. I will take you to her as soon as you are ready."

"First, show me the stables."

"I will have someone take care of your mount."

Gömalt snapped his fingers at one of the guards. The man approached and reached out to take the reins, but before his fingers even made contact the horse reared on its hind legs, emitting a loud screech. The guard dived aside barely an instant before hooves slammed down on the cobbles, right where he'd been standing.

Roumin-Lenka struggled to regain control. She murmured to the creature in the low, guttural sounds of her native tongue, stroking its neck. As the beast calmed, she turned in the saddle and fixed Gömalt with a scowl. "I said you will show *me* the stables. Cyrèmar does not like men."

Long had there been distrust between man and Dwarve, Gömalt mused. He'd no idea that had rubbed off on their animals. The question on his mind was, how much was still harboured by the rider? Her very presence here was a sign that she was at least prepared to deal with outsiders. But that didn't necessarily mean her visit would be productive.

Roumin-Lenka dismounted. Under Gömalt's direction, she led Cyrèmar to the stables. Everyone else kept their distance. Once inside, she stalled the horse, removed the bridle and saddle and deposited them on the racks above the hay trough, then groomed the beast with meticulous care. She seemed not in the least bit concerned that others were waiting. She even spent a few moments murmuring in the animal's ear whilst stroking its nose. Such affection seemed very much at odds with the rest of her demeanour.

Finally, she picked up her axe and slotted the hilt back into a loop on her belt, allowing it to dangle at her side. She strode across the stable to where Gömalt was waiting, holding out her hand in greeting.

Such contact was not customary in Tsnathsarré. Gömalt reciprocated somewhat warily, hiding a wince as the strength of her grip nearly crushed the life out of his fingers. Once more she bore into him with her penetrating gaze.

"You kill people," she said, as if she had somehow seen inside his head. Her tone was matter-of-fact, conveying not an iota of concern. She reached out and ran a finger along his jaw. His eyes widened; few would have dared such a thing. "And the one who gave you this…?"

He relaxed slightly and smiled. "An outstanding matter."

Roumin-Lenka tutted and flicked a finger towards her own cheek. "My husband. It is settled."

That didn't sound like it had boded well for the other party. Gömalt realised that for the first time in his life he had probably met someone at least as dangerous as himself. The thought was intoxicating.

He led the way to the great hall where the baroness was waiting. As they entered, he noticed Daka looked a little tense. Clearly Roumin-Lenka's womanhood had unnerved her. Not that it would have shown to a stranger.

"Welcome," she greeted. "We did not expect you so soon."

"I have a good horse," was all Roumin-Lenka offered by way of explanation. She showed no sign of deference.

"You will have to forgive my curiosity, but I was told to expect the head of the Lenka Clan."

"That I am."

The baroness's eyebrows rose slightly. "But you are clearly not of Dwarvish descent. How is it that you hold such a position?"

"I fought for it."

That wasn't sufficient for the baroness and her eyebrows prompted for more.

Roumin-Lenka huffed. "Many years ago, my family became indentured to the Akarish Clan to redeem a debt. We lived amongst the Dwarves for five generations before gaining their acceptance. I was the first of my family to be taken in wedlock into another household."

"That's how you came to be part of the Lenka Clan?"

"My husband was its leader. But he thought to treat me like a servant, as with the rest of my family. He was wrong to do this, and I told him so."

"I imagine that was well received," the baroness said with a slight scoff.

"He gave me this," Roumin-Lenka said, drawing a finger down her cheek. "Yet upon marriage I became a full member of the Dwarve Nation, with the same rights as any other. So I appeared before the Sönnatt…"

"The Dwarvish High Council?"

"Yes – to challenge the wrong. I was granted the right to face my husband in combat."

The baroness nodded. "A bout you obviously won, otherwise you wouldn't be standing here."

"All that was my husband's is now mine, including his position as clan leader. Now, enough of my past. I have come a long way and I wish to know whether it was worth the effort. Why did you send for me?"

The baroness motioned towards a chair and invited Roumin-Lenka to sit.

"What I'm about to tell you is in the strictest confidence. What we discuss here must not go beyond these walls."

"Understood."

Gömalt found himself a chair just off to one side. The likelihood of Roumin-Lenka posing a danger to the baroness was slight, but then Dwarves, even strange and alluring ones, were something of an unknown quantity to him and he didn't want to take any chances.

"You have heard of the name Ranadar?" the baroness asked.

"There are many called Ranadar. To which one are you referring?"

"I'm talking about *the* Ranadar. King Ranadar."

A glint of interest appeared in Roumin-Lenka's eyes. "Every man, woman and child of my people has heard of King Ranadar. His story is legend."

"He is more than just a legend."

"But his time was eighteen hundred years ago. What is your interest in him now?"

The baroness motioned for Gömalt to bring one of the copies of the Ranadar text to the table. He crossed to the side of the hall and slid the scroll out of its protective copper tube, then returned to where the two women were seated. He unrolled the document out in front of Roumin-Lenka, orientating it so that she could study it without having to turn.

She leaned forwards. Her initial curiosity was replaced by a frown. "I am no expert in ancient writing."

"Nor do you need to be," Daka replied. "I haven't asked you here as a translator. That is the task of another. What I need from you is the knowledge you possess of your people. You come highly recommended."

"By whom?" Roumin-Lenka retorted, her curt tone stating that flattery was not a tool that could be used to manipulate her.

"I wish that to remain confidential for the time being," Daka answered. "Suffice it to say that I am told your knowledge of the Old Homeland has few equals." The baroness's voice now had an edge to it that made it clear flattery was not her intent.

The two women stared into each other's eyes, a battle of wills ensuing over who would blink first. Gömalt had rarely seen the baroness so blatantly defensive.

Eventually, perhaps because curiosity was beginning to get the better of her, Roumin-Lenka lowered her gaze back to the text on the table. "So what is this document?"

"Gömalt, explain to her how we came by it."

He nodded. "Its source was found in a cave up in the Mathian Mountains, deep inside Alondria. We searched for many months to find it, following information the baroness had acquired."

"But this document is recent. Where is the original? *What* is the original?"

Gömalt smiled, sensing that Roumin-Lenka was becoming intrigued. "This text is a copy of something carved on to a stone tablet, one of the Menhir of Ranadar." He paused for a moment to let that revelation sink in. He noted with satisfaction that their Dwarvish visitor was holding her breath; clearly she understood the significance.

"The Menhir of Ranadar?" she eventually breathed out. "You have found one of the entrance stones?"

"Yes. But only one," Gömalt nodded, holding up a finger. "There are others, which is why we have asked you to come here. Your husband's family has in its possession the only known maps of the Old Homeland."

"You want my help to locate the remaining entrance markers?"

Daka took over. "Our understanding is that there are five more. The problem is, it has taken us months just to find the first, and our operations have roused much suspicion amongst the Alondrians. We no longer have the luxury of searching to our heart's content."

Roumin-Lenka was silent for a long time, staring at the parchment in front of her. It was clear much was running through her mind. At length she asked, "You are after Ranadar's treasure, are you not?"

Daka cast a brief glance at Gömalt. "Does that bother you?"

"Yes."

Daka stole another quick glance, this one hinting that Gömalt should ready himself. He tensed slightly. Very slowly, he shifted into a position from which he could better react.

"I see," Daka murmured. "Does that mean you are unwilling to help us?"

"I did not say that."

Gömalt relaxed a little. His expression changed from one of concern to one of curiosity.

"What troubles you?"

Roumin-Lenka shrugged. "You are chasing a myth."

"A myth? I thought all your people believed in Ranadar's treasure."

For the first time since she had arrived, Roumin-Lenka smiled. Gömalt's stomach knotted with desire.

"They do – as children. Ranadar's treasure is a story we tell our young ones at the coming of shadows. We send them to sleep with thoughts of gold and wealth beyond all counting. In their dreams they search. But when we become adults, such fanciful notions are put aside. Gold is teased out of rock by hard work; it does not sit in piles waiting for someone to discover it. I wish I could say otherwise, but there is no treasure. Believe me, it is a legend, a myth, nothing more."

"Then how do you explain the existence of the menhir?"

"I cannot. Which is the only reason why I am still sitting here."

The baroness seemed pleased with this answer. "I see. Then, just to ensure we share a common understanding, perhaps you would be good enough to tell us the story as you know it."

Roumin-Lenka flicked her head, swinging her long plait of hair forwards over her shoulder so that it wasn't trapped when she leaned back in her chair. Gömalt noticed her *hirack*, a leaf-shaped piece of razor-sharp metal woven into the ends of her braids. To one trained in its use, the *hirack* was as deadly as a dagger. The ease with which she had adjusted its position suggested she was no novice.

"As I said, much of the story is just legend. King Ranadar decided that the time had come for our people to leave the Old Homeland. However, he did not want to leave it open for others to take up residence. So he devised a way of sealing the entrances such that only he or his descendants could return. According to the legend, the magic that was used to achieve this required something of value to be left inside the mountains, something that needed protecting. The greater the value to his people, the stronger the seals would be. Ranadar therefore ordered every male of the Dwarve Nation to contribute one sixth of his wealth. It is said that the treasure was so vast that it would take ten lifetimes to count." Roumin-Lenka paused for a wistful smile. "A slight exaggeration, you will agree."

"And the menhir?" Daka prompted.

"Markers left at each entrance to help our people find their way back inside again if ever they returned. Ranadar meant to pass to his son the secret of how to reopen the Old Homeland, but he is said to have died before doing so. The mountains have remained sealed ever since."

The baroness concurred by dipping her head slightly. "But why, then, do you refuse to believe that the treasure actually exists?"

"It is too fanciful a story upon which to base hope. It is no secret that among my people gold is valued more highly than blood. When a male is faced with a choice between his wealth and his wife, the wife always comes second. This is why I do not believe."

"I don't follow."

"If you knew my people, Daka, you would understand that it is not in our nature to leave our valuables behind for someone else to claim, even if they were thought to be safely guarded. Trust me, all that was Ranadar's would have been taken with him."

"But what about the menhir? Does our discovery not cause you to think again?"

"Daka, I would like nothing more than to believe there is gold sitting under the Mathians. But it is foolish to nurture such hopes."

Daka regarded Gömalt again, silently asking him whether she should reveal more. He nodded. At the end of the day, it was important to get Roumin-Lenka's cooperation, and she clearly needed more convincing.

"What if I were to tell you that actually finding Ranadar's treasure is not my primary objective?"

Roumin-Lenka looked confused. "Explain…"

"I intend to invade the Tep-Mödiss. To do that, I need my supporters to believe in the treasure. The wealth it offers is one of the incentives for their committing to my plan."

Roumin-Lenka frowned and leaned forwards. "Then what part am I in such a plan?"

"Credibility. I need someone who can convince them that the treasure exists, and that we have a real chance of being able to obtain it. You may not believe in it, but the question is, could you convince others that you do?"

"If your terms are good enough, I could convince them that

Ranadar himself will return from the grave and hand it to them."

Daka smiled. Gömalt noted it was genuine. "Then I'm sure we can come to some arrangement that is agreeable to both of us."

Roumin-Lenka nodded. "So what exactly is it you wish from me?"

"Firstly, we need the maps of the Old Homeland so that we can locate the remaining menhir. And then we will need you to act as an adviser in all matters concerning the mines. You must make it appear as if we really are looking for the treasure."

"And what if I succeed in finding it?"

Gömalt laughed. "I thought we'd failed to convince you that it is real."

"I was raised a Dwarve," Roumin-Lenka said, a gleam in her eye. "Dreaming of gold is in my blood."

*

Gömalt awoke to the sight of Roumin-Lenka's intense green eyes boring into him. Lying beside him, her head was propped up on a crooked arm. Her free hand gently stroked his chin.

"Morning," she said.

He sat up, only to discover that he ached all over. Never in his life had he experienced such a night of passion. Roumin-Lenka simply didn't know her own strength when she was in the throes of ecstasy. How different she was to Kassandra, in whose bed they now lay.

As he thumped a pillow to make himself more comfortable, the bed sheets slipped further from Roumin-Lenka's shoulder. Her skin was smooth and lightly tanned, suggestive of a life spent more above ground than below it. Her body was well toned, muscular, but retaining a distinct femininity. Fighting the desires that surfaced again, a smile appeared as an amusing thought occurred to him.

"What?" she demanded.

"I was just recalling the moment you first arrived. You seemed rather frosty, atop that great horse of yours."

"And now you are thinking I have thawed a little?" She let out a throaty laugh.

"Just don't thaw any more – I don't think I'd survive it."

She punched him on the chest, playfully, but harder than he felt was necessary.

They lay in silence for a while, her thumb repeatedly tracing the scar on his jaw. She seemed fascinated by it.

"Who gave you this?"

"The baroness's daughter."

Roumin-Lenka sat up with interest. "Kassandra? Tell me more."

"She ran away, to the Alondrians, stealing a copy of the Ranadar text in the process."

"Like the one I saw yesterday?"

"Yes. I was sent to chase her down and bring her back. Unfortunately, she had a good lead on us and we only caught up with her at the River Ablath."

"What happened?"

"We were ambushed by some Alondrians waiting on the far bank. There was a fight across the river and in the confusion Kassandra managed to escape. But not before giving me this," he gestured to the scar, " – a reminder of my failure."

"So that is the end of it?" Roumin-Lenka asked, her tone suggesting she wouldn't believe it, even if he said as much.

"We shall see. She has been taken beyond my reach, beyond the Mathians, and the baroness will not allow me to go that far south to get her. Not yet, anyway. Perhaps after our plans are under way..." He shrugged. "But for now, I must wait. There are more important matters to deal with."

Roumin-Lenka regarded him thoughtfully. "Your loyalty to Daka is strong. How long have you served her?"

"I was thirteen when I was originally brought into the service of Baron Daka. But my loyalty was always to the baroness; I saw her as the strong one. It proved a good choice in the end."

"How so?"

Gömalt sighed as he dredged up the memories. "The baron was petty. He enjoyed exercising power over the people around him, but he had no ambition. He thought in small ways, and the baroness despised him for it." He wondered whether to tell her about how the baroness had enlisted his help to be rid of her husband, but decided against it. There was no point giving the Dwarve ammunition she might one day use against them. "After the baron died, I became the baroness's right hand and have acted in that capacity ever since."

It occurred to him that both the women with whom he was currently intimate had dispatched their male counterparts for one reason or another. Anyone else might have found that disturbing. He found it mildly amusing.

"Did Daka order you to kill her daughter when you went after her?"

"In a manner of speaking. She gave me leave to do whatever was necessary to stop her getting away."

Roumin-Lenka shook her head and lay back on the pillow, staring up at the overhead canopy. "Daka must have a lot riding on this plan."

Gömalt made no comment.

"Why is she willing to risk so much? If she isn't trying to find Ranadar's treasure, what does she hope to gain?"

"An empire."

Roumin-Lenka's eyebrows clearly didn't know whether to go up in curiosity or knit together in a frown.

Gömalt smiled. Daka had given him permission to divulge some of their plan as a means of garnering the Dwarve's loyalty. To be wholly committed, Roumin-Lenka needed to understand the feasibility of their aims. It would help if she believed they'd admitted her to their confidence. But that only went so far. The real goal was still a closely guarded secret, and would remain so until the very last minute. Then it would be too late – for everyone. "The baroness isn't interested in the Tep-Mödiss for its own sake. She wants to be the one to secure its return to the Tsnathsarré Empire. The popularity she will garner will put her in a powerful position."

"Ha. And what does Omnitas have to say about that?"

"The emperor is weak. Tsnathsarré needs a new and more powerful leader. The baroness simply intends to emerge as the obvious choice."

Roumin-Lenka whistled softly. "She sets her sights high, does she not? If she fails, she will be damned."

Gömalt didn't comment on that, either.

The truth was, they could not afford to fail.

The story continues with

Discovery

DANCING WARRIORS TRILOGY ~ PART II

∽

when Those of Grace hear again
the Unwilled One comes
times of great strife are His path
under the heel of a new Master the Land
will reel

∽

KEVIN M DENTON

www.kevinmdenton.com

Glossary

Alondrian and Nicián Characters

Abiatha – the name of Jorra-hin's mother.

Captain **Agarma** – in charge of Princess Elona's personal bodyguard.

Brother **Akmir** – the Adak-rann's most senior representative at the Cymàtagé.

King **Althar** – King of Alondria.

Secretary **Anton** – a mage at the Cymàtagé.

Mage **Aolap** – a confidant of Chancellor Gÿldan and infiltrator of the Dinac-Mentà.

Benhin – a young guide working the streets of Alondris.

Queen **Bernice** – Princess Elona's mother. Bernice is no longer queen, having been put away from the royal household for an indiscretion with a younger man.

Lord (heir apparent) **Borádin** – young nobleman of Alondria of the House of Kin-Shísim.

Corporal **Botfiár** – one of the Pressed's non-commissioned officers under Torrin-Ashur's command.

Brother **Brömin** – a member of the Adak-rann council.

Brother **Brosspear** – a member of the Adak-rann council, and former mage.

Lady **Céline** – Princess Elona's lady-in-waiting.

Brother **Connrad** – a member of the Adak-rann council.

Captain **Corbett** – the officer in charge of cadets at the Royal Military Academy in Alondris.

Mage **Cosmin** – the local mage in Torrin-Ashur's home town of Tailébeth.

Lieutenant **D'Amada** – an Alondrian officer in Kirshtahll's Executive.

Mage **Dümarr** – Head of Philosophy at the Cymàtagé.

Brother **Egall** – a member of the Adak-rann council.

Elam – a freelance Alondrian mercenary.

Eldris-Ashur – Torrin-Ashur's elder brother and Lord (heir apparent) to the March of Ashur.

Princess **Elona** – second daughter of the House of Dönn-àbrah; younger sister to Princess Midana.

Mage **Emmett** – one of the healers at the Cymàtagé.

Emmy – the little girl Kirin is called to heal.

Etáin L'Tembarh – Lady Karina Kirshtahll's father and former ambassador to the Tsnathsarré Empire.

Mage **Flassmidd** – one of the healers at the Cymàtagé.

Fylmar – a henchman employed by Minister Gëorgas.

Gad – the head of the serving staff at the residence of the Duke of Cöbèck.

Gadrick-Ashur – one of Torrin-Ashur's ancestors.

Duke **Geirvald** – the Duke of Cöbèck.

Minister **Gëorgas** – one of Alondria's career politicians.

Brother **Gerard** – a brother of the Adak-rann.

Gil – a nocturnal opportunist.

Golan – one of the Pressed under Torrin-Ashur's command.

Guyass – a friend of Torrin-Ashur at the Royal Military Academy.

Chancellor **Gÿldan** – the Chancellor of the Cymàtagé, and thereby Alondria's most senior mage.

Major **Halacon** – an Alondrian officer in Kirshtahll's Executive.

Captain **Halam** – an Alondrian officer in Kirshtahll's Executive.

Hallvor – a young Alondrian girl – survivor from Tail-ébeth.

Brother **Heckart** – the head of the Adak-rann and leader of the brotherhood's council.

Minister **Hekdama** – an Alondrian politician and Speaker of the Assembly.

Lord **Henndel** – Lord of Söurdina.

Lord **Huron** – an Alondrian commander under Kirshtahll when he faces the Nmemians.

Ida – Mac's wife.

Prince **Idris** – King Althar's firstborn son. The boy died in infancy.

Jacks – proper name **Jàckrin-àsethàsám** – a Nicián resident of Alondris, curator of the archives at the stonemasons' guildhall.

Brigadier **Jàcos** – the commandant in charge of the Royal Military Academy in Alondris.

Jess – Mac's eldest son.

Jonash – the head of the serving staff at the residence of the Kirshtahll household.

Brother **Jorra-hin** – a brother of the Adak-rann and friend of Torrin-Ashur.

Brother **Joss** – a brother of the Adak-rann at the Cymàtagé.

Lady **Karina** – the wife of General Kirshtahll.

Katla – the daughter of the mayor of Mitcha.

Soprina **Kirin-orrà DelaMorjáy** – more usually called **Kirin**. Daughter of the Nicián ambassador in Alondris, and friend to Jorra-hin at the Cymàtagé.

Mage **Lödmick** – a mage at the Cymàtagé with a seat on the Cymàtseà.

Mac – a freelance Alondrian mercenary.

Marro – Mac's middle son.

Captain **Marsisma** – an Alondrian officer in Kirshtahll's Executive.

Mage **Martiss** – a mage at the Cymàtagé, with particular responsibility for controlling who is admitted.

Massim – a lost Alondrian soldier found on the way to Mitcha.

Mage **Mattohr** – Pomaltheus's preceptor.

Princess **Midana** – first daughter of the House of Dönn-àbrah, Elona's elder sister and heir to the throne of Alondria.

Millardis (nicknamed **M'Lud**) – one of the Pressed under Torrin-Ashur's command.

Lord (heir apparent) **Mir** – an Alondrian noble and Borádin's second in the call-out with Torrin-Ashur.

Myle – the wife of Willoam.

Lord **Naman-Ashur** – Torrin-Ashur's father, Lord of Tail-ébeth and the March of Ashur.

Sergeant **Nash** – Torrin-Ashur's assigned sergeant.

Mage **Nikrá** – an ancient mage at the Cymàtagé, and one of Alondria's most respected present-day seers.

Deputy Chancellor **Nÿat** – the Deputy Chancellor of the Cymàtagé.

General **Padráig Kirshtahll** – Alondria's most senior military figure and commander of the Alondrian army stationed in the Northern Territories, with responsibility for keeping the Tsnathsarré at bay.

Minister **Parkos** – one of Alondria's career politicians and a staunch opponent of Alondria's military policies in the Northern Territories.

Paulus – a young Alondrian boy – survivor from Tail-ébeth.

Acolyte **Pomaltheus** – one of the acolytes Jorra-hin becomes friends with at the Cymàtagé.

Governor **Rakmar** – Timerra's father and Governor of Colòtt.

Mage **Rhonnin** – one of the healers at the Cymàtagé.

Major **Riagán** – the adjutant to General Kirshtahll.

Rogett – one of the mercenaries under Elam's command.

Lord **Ruther** – an Alondrian commander under Kirshtahll when he faces the Nmemians.

Sàhodd – a friend of Torrin-Ashur at Mitcha.

Lord **Saldir** – an Alondrian commander under Kirshtahll when he faces the Nmemians.

Master **Salsar** – Master of the Alondris docks.

Acolyte **Seth** – one of the acolytes Jorra-hin becomes friends with at the Cymàtagé.

Corporal **Silfast** – one of the Pressed's non-commissioned officers under Torrin-Ashur's command.

Mage **Sömat** – head of Ancient Studies at the Cymàtagé.

Symon – one of the Pressed under Torrin-Ashur's command.

Lord **Tanaséy Vickrà** – Lord of Vickrà-döthmore and cohort to Princess Mattrice.

Major **Temesh-ai** – Kirshtahll's personal physician.

Terrance – King Althar's manservant of many years.

Lord **Tiam** – Borádin's father, formally known as Lord Kin-Shísim.

Tick – one of the Pressed under Torrin-Ashur's command.

Lieutenant **Timerra** – a friend of Torrin-Ashur at the Royal Military Academy.

Brother **Tobas** – a brother of the Adak-rann.

Tomàss – one of the Pressed under Torrin-Ashur's command.

Captain **Tonché** – an Alondrian officer in Kirshtahll's Executive.

Corpsman **Tork** – part of the Alondrian Messaging Corps.

Torrin-Ashur – the second son of Naman-Ashur. His father is Lord of Tail-ébeth and the March of Ashur.

Mage **Tutt-tus** – one of the mages at the Cymàtagé, assigned as preceptor to Kirin when she is admitted for training.

Brother **Valis** – a member of the Adak-rann council.

Willoam – the man who accused Golan of attempting to have his way with his wife.

Wisehelm of Campas – a young noble Kirshtahll once chose to sponsor.

Minister **Yeddir** – the politics tutor at the Royal Military Academy in Alondris.

Brother **Yisson** – a member of the Adak-rann council.

Yngvarr – a friend of Torrin-Ashur at Mitcha.

Minister **Zimm** – the Alondrian Finance Minister.

Tsnathsarré Characters

Alber – Gömalt's right hand man.

Baroness **Alishe Daka** – a powerful Tsnathsarré noblewoman. Her lands lie just north of the River Ablath, adjacent to the Marches of Nairn, Ashur and Ràbinth.

Anna – the handmaid to Kassandra.

Bressnar – a Tsnathsarré mercenary.

Emperor **Callis** – the Tsnathsarré emperor at the time when Alondria purchased the Northern Territories.

Advisor **Döshan** – a Tsnathsarré advisor to Emperor Omnitas.

Baron **Fidampàss** – a Tsnathsarré baron and western neighbour to Baroness Daka's lands. His lands lie just north of the River Ablath, adjacent to the March of Léddürland.

Baron **Ginngár** – the Baron of Ürald, a northern province of the Tsnathsarré Empire.

Gömalt – Baroness Daka's right hand man and assassin.

Halfdanr – the head of the serving staff in Baroness Daka's household.

Jonatárn – a spy working on behalf of Baroness Daka.

Kassandra – daughter of Baroness Daka.

Commander **Këddir** – a Tsnathsarré officer under Lord Özeransk.

Advisor **Kremlish** – a Tsnathsarré advisor to Emperor Omnitas.

Michàss – the sweetheart of Kassandra's handmaid, Anna.

Minnàk – a Tsnathsarré mercenary.

Oddon – the chief cook in Baroness Daka's household.

Emperor **Omnitas** – the present Emperor of Tsnathsarré.

Lord **Özeransk** – a respected Tsnathsarré lord and military commander.

Rasmin – a Tsnathsarré fisherman, and part of the advanced party that lands in the Bay of Shallow Graves.

Commander **Scarlis** – a Tsnathsarré commander – part of Töuslàn's landing party.

Shyla – one of the cook's assistants in Baroness Daka's household.

Sörrell – one of Minnàk's mercenary commanders, left to occupy Mitcha.

Commander **Streàck** – a Tsnathsarré commander.

Commander **Tass** – a Tsnathsarré commander – part of Töuslàn's landing party.

Lord **Töuslàn** – a Tsnathsarré baron and eastern neighbour to Baroness Daka's lands. His lands lie just north of the Ablath, adjacent to the March of Vickrà-döthmore.

Baron **Ürengarr** – the Tsnathsarré emperor that succeeded Callis at the time when Alondria purchased the Northern Territories.

Dwarvish, Nmemian and Historical Characters

Amatt the Blind – Alondria's most famous and reliable prophet, who lived about twelve hundred years prior to the present day.

Mage **Cormàcc** – an ancient mage – inventor of Mages' Fire.

Superintendent **Gil-kott** – the district commander of the Nmemian border force.

Gorrack-na-tek – a Dwarvish acquaintance of Advisor Döshan, living in Jèdda-galbráith.

Mage **Holôidees** – an ancient mage – one of those involved in the creation of the Dànis~Lutárn and who stood against Lornadus.

Mad **Iffan** – Alondria's most infamous pirate of old, mentioned in the Legend of Tallümund.

Mage **Joseph** – an ancient mage – one of those involved in the creation of the Dànis~Lutárn and who stood against Lornadus.

Prince **Kassem** – the Eldest son of the King of Nmemia.

Mage **Lornadus** – an ancient mage – leader of those who tried to ensnare the Sèliccia~Castrà.

General **Márcucious** – the general in charge of the Custodians, otherwise known as the Dancing Warriors or the Dendricá.

Mage **Nickölaus** – an ancient mage – one of those involved in the creation of the Dànis~Lutárn and who stood against Lornadus.

Papanos Meiter – Master Stonemason from 232BF to 201BF

King **Ranadar** – the Dwarvish king at the time of the departure of the Dwarve Nation from the Old Homeland.

Commissar **Rolarn** – a Nmemian military commander.

Seya **Roumin-Lenka** – the Dwarvish clan leader summoned by Baroness Daka to assist with finding the Menhir of Ranadar.

Silas – an ancient mage – one of those involved in the creation of the Dànis~Lutárn.

Mage **Solautus** – one of the original Natural mages who founded the Dinac-Mentà in order to bring the Mages' War to an end, some five hundred years prior to the present day.

Mage **Yazcöp D'Bless** – an ancient mage – one of those involved in the creation of the Dànis~Lutárn and who stood against Lornadus.

Country and Regional References

Alondria – the principal country in which the story is set.

The **Great Inland Mäss** – a vast lake, almost a sea, sitting just north of Nmemia. Its northern and eastern coasts are Tsnathsarré lands. Alondria only has a very small exposure to this sea, adjacent to the Am-gött.

Höarst – an island nation lying off the coast of the Tsnathsarré Empire, with whom Alondria has limited relations.

The **Mäss of Súmari** – the sea lying south of Alondria.

Niciá – a country lying south of Alondria, beyond the Mäss of Súmari. Kirin's homeland.

Nmemia – Alondria's western neighbour. There have been wars between the two in the past, but relations between them have been relatively peaceful in recent times.

Söbria – a land lying to the south of Alondria, famed for its spicy meat dishes and other culinary delights.

The **Tsnathsarré Empire** – the country that lies to the north of Alondria. They share a six hundred mile long border with each other, defined by the River Ablath.

The **Vickrà-mäss** – the sea to the east of Vickrà-döthmore.

Alondrian Geographical References

River **Ablath** – the river that marks the border between the Northern Territories of Alondria and the Tsnathsarré Empire.

Akanu Pass – one of the principal passes through the Mathian Mountains.

River **Alam-goürd** – one of Alondria's principal rivers running south from the Mathians.

Alondris – the capital of Alondria.

Am-còt – a trading town on the southern side of the Mathian Mountains near the headwaters of the Alam-goürd.

Am-gött – a short and inhospitable strip of land at the far western end of the Mathian Mountains.

Loch **Andür** – a loch situated part way down the Alam-goürd, between Am-còt and Suth-còt.

Mount **Àthái** – part of the Mathian Mountain range.

Bay of Shallow Graves – a bay off the east coast of the Northern Territories named for its infamous toll on shipping.

Bosün-béck – a town mentioned in the Legend of Tallümund – formerly known as Sag-herron before the Hür Tribe Siege.

Bythe-Kim – a trading town on the southern side of the Mathian Mountains near the headwaters of the Els-spear.

Colòtt – the westernmost region of Alondria, neighbouring Nmemia.

Dórine Basin – a region of Alondria near the Nmemian border. Dispute over its sovereignty led to the Kilópeé War between Alondria and Nmemia some thirty years prior to the present day.

Dramm-Mastür Forest – a large forested region of Alondria lying south of the Mathian Mountains between Colòtt and Kirsh.

Dubré Marsh – a region to the south of the Dumássay Gorge.

Dumássay Gorge – the gorge formed by the Dumássay River, strategically significant because it restricts passage south from Vickrà-dòthmore to the rest of Alondria. It can only be crossed via a handful of suspended bridges.

The **Easterhalb** – the name given to the smaller half of the city of Alondris, lying to the east of the River Els-spear.

River **Ébeth** – a river in the Northern Territories.

River **Els-spear** – one of the principal rivers flowing south from the Mathian mountains down through Alondria. The Els-spear flows through the middle of the city of Alondris.

Lake **Gosh** – a large lake just to the south of Alondris through which the Els-spear flows.

Halam-Gräth – the principal town of the March of Vickrà-döthmore.

Hassguard – a trading town at the northern start point of the Akanu Pass.

Hébott – the principal town of the March of Léddürland.

The **Holmes** – a district within the city of Alondris, between the First Wall and the New Wall, where many of Alondria's nobility have their city residences.

Jàb-áldis – the Adak-rann's monastery up in the Jàb-áldis Pass, high in the Mathian Mountains.

Loch **Kim** – a loch on the south side of the Mathian Mountains, not far from the headwaters of the River Els-spear.

Kimballi Pass – one of the easternmost passes through the Mathian Mountains, and the usual route for most traffic from Alondris travelling north through the Vale of Caspárr to reach Mitcha.

Kirsh – General Kirshtahll's home province.

Lamàst – a border town in Colòtt, not far from the Great West Wall.

Léddürland – the westernmost march of the Northern Territories.

Loch **Masson** – one of the larger lochs along the River Ablath, straddling the border between the March of Nairn and the March of Léddürland.

Mathian Mountains – the principal mountain range that divides Alondria across her breadth, cutting off the Northern Territories from much of the rest of the country.

Mitcha – the name of both the military camp and the local town in the heart of the March of Ràbinth. Kirshtahll's military stronghold.

Monument to Nabor – a small town on route from Kirsh to Loch Andür.

Nabor's Gate – one of the easier places to cross the otherwise treacherous River Ablath.

Nairn – one of the marches of the Northern Territories.

Nairnkirsh – the principal town of the March of Nairn.

Northern Territories – the strip of land that lies between the northern slopes of the Mathian Mountains and the River Ablath. The Tsnathsarré call it the Tep-Mödiss.

Parars Hove – a small town a few miles inland from the mouth of the Dumássay River.

Pass of Trombéi – one of the main eastern passes through the Mathian Mountains.

The **People's Square** – the centre of the city of Alondris.

Ràbinth – one of the marches in the Northern Territories.

River **Sam-hédi** – a river in the Northern Territories.

Shinn-còtt – an arid, almost desert-like region of Alondria.

Sound of Goàtt – a large inlet on the coast of Vickrà-döthmore, just north of the town of Halam-Gräth.

Stroth Ford – one of the easier places to cross the otherwise treacherous River Ablath.

Suth-còt – an Alondrian town at the southern end of Loch Andür, famed for hosting the popular Festival of Light.

Taib-hédi – a strategic town situated in the March of Ràbinth. 'Taib' is a northern term meaning 'across' or 'straddling'. The Sam-hédi runs through the town.

Tail-ébeth – Torrin-Ashur's home town, and principal town of the March of Ashur. 'Tail' is a northern term meaning 'near'. Tail-ébeth means Near (the) Ébeth.

Mount **Tatënbau** – an unusual mountain said to have been shaped by the dragon Bël-samir during the Legend of Tallümund.

Toutleth – a trading town at the southern start point of the Akanu Pass.

Vale of Caspárr – one of the few really fertile regions of the Northern Territories.

Vickrà-döthmore – the easternmost march of the Northern Territories. Lord Tanaséy Vickrà's march.

The **Westerhalb** – the name given to the larger half of the city of Alondris lying to the west of the River Els-spear.

Tsnathsarré Geological References

Brath'daka – the name of the castle Baroness Daka calls home.

Göndd – a small town in southern Tsnathsarré, not far from the Alondrian border.

Jèdda-galbráith – the capital city of the Tsnathsarré Empire.

Sèdessa Range – a region of mountainous country lying north of the Tsnathsarré Empire. Current home to the majority of the Dwarvish clans.

Tep-Mödiss – the Tsnathsarré name for the Northern Territories. It means 'below the river' (the Ablath denotes the border).

Nmemian and Dwarvish Geographical References

Dikàthi – one of the entrances to the Mathian Mines (also known as the Old Homeland).

Dörgànk – the gorge outside the city of Üzsspeck.

Hamm-tak – a border town just inside Nmemia.

Hàttàmoréy – one of the entrances to the Mathian Mines (also known as the Old Homeland).

Niliàthái – one of the entrances to the Mathian Mines (also known as the Old Homeland).

Trombéi – one of the entrances to the Mathian Mines (also known as the Old Homeland).

Üzsspeck – the principal city of the Dwarve Nation when they lived in the Old Homeland under the Mathian Mountains.

Zèet-ársh – a town about seventy miles inside Nmemia.

Miscellaneous References

Adak-rann – a scholastic brotherhood dedicated to the preservation of historical knowledge.

After Foundation (AF) – Alondrian calendar dating system – referring to years after the foundation of Alondria, 947 years prior to the present day.

Akarish – one of the Dwarvish clans.

aldar – the main coinage of Alondria.

A'lyavine – the name of the language used to control magic. Also referred to as the Tongue of the Ancients.

Before Foundation (BF) – Alondrian calendar dating system – referring to years before the foundation of Alondria, 947 years prior to the present day.

Bël-aírnon – dragon god in the old religions of Tsnathsarré, which centre around belief in a number of great dragons, the chief of whom is Bël-aírnon.

Bël-samir – the famous dragon at the centre of one of Alondria's most beloved of fables, The Legend of Tallümund.

Blacksmith of Orea – a folklore character famed for being the best armourer in the world.

Blood – a sharp tasting alcoholic concoction popular with the Dwarves.

Brock – a powerful alcoholic concoction commonly brewed in northern Alondria.

Cymàtagé – the main seat of learning for all mages in Alondria. Cymàtagé is an old A'lyavinical word meaning Hall of Mages.

Cymàtseà – the name given to the mages' council at the Cymàtagé.

Dànis~Lutárn – an ancient magic conceived in part to ensnare the Sèliccia~Castrà.

Dendricá – an ancient tribe of formidable warriors who used to live in the lands now known as the Northern Territories. Also known as the Dancing Warriors.

Dinac-Mentà – a secretive and ruthless sect of mages who see it as their duty to regulate the activity of their fellow mages and eliminate Natural mages, thereby preventing a recurrence of past atrocities.

House of **Dönn-àbrah** – the present royal house of Alondria.

The **Executive** – the group of Alondrian officers Kirshtahll relies on to get things done.

Followers of the Path – a term given to ordinary mages who take up the study of the Mages' Path at the Cymàtagé.

Grand Assembly – Alondria's main legislative body.

Great West Wall – the wall erected between Alondria and Nmemia after the Kilópeé War.

Kilópeé War – the name given to the war between Alondria and Nmemia over the sovereignty of the Dórine Basin, concluded some thirty years prior to the present day.

House of **Kin-Shísim** – one of the high noble houses of Alondria. Borádin's household.

Legend of Tallümund – a beloved tale in Alondrian literature.

Lenka – a Dwarvish clan name. Roumin-Lenka is the clan leader. Most Dwarves use their clan name as the second part of their familiar name.

lumines – a rather special flower, pod-like in appearance when closed, which glows when visited by certain insects, most notably the Giant Moon Moth.

Mages' Path – the name given to the curriculum taught to acolytes at the Cymàtagé, embodying all aspects of a mage's life. Ordinary mages are those who take the Mages' Path, which has led to them being called Followers of the Path.

Menhir of Ranadar – stone tablets, inscribed with A'lyavinical texts, thought to have been left by King Ranadar when he led the Dwarve Nation out of the Mathian Mountains some eighteen hundred years prior to the present day.

Natural mage – the term used to refer to a mage whose powers do not stem from a study of the Mages' Path. They are able to draw power from their surroundings, and are in consequence much more powerful than Followers of the Path. They are therefore targeted by the Dinac-Mentà for supposedly being dangerous.

Old Homeland – the name the Dwarves gave to the system of tunnels and caves that they excavated under the Mathian Mountains.

The **Pressed** – a term used to refer to units of men in the army assembled from slaves, debtors and petty criminals whose sentences have been commuted to military service.

sadura – a rather potent liqueur usually served warm.

Sai-raska – a Tsnathsarré toast – akin to 'cheers' – but reserved for use between warriors who have shared the battlefield.

sárccanisáe – special spherical glass-like objects used to absorb stray magic, known as Taümatha, when it is accidentally released by mages undertaking training at the Cymàtagé.

Sèliccia~Castrà – a First Dialect A'lyavinical reference, meaning War Song.

Sentinels – strange tower-like structures situated along the River Ablath.

Septagem – the name given to groups of seven mages forming the cells within the Dinac-Mentà.

Septis Dömon – the Dinac-Mentà's most sacred book, containing the seven incantations that give them their powers to overcome Natural mages.

Seya – a Dwarvish title, meaning Clan Leader (female).

Sölass~Hésporra – a Wandering Whisper – a kind of magically imbued rumour that can erase the truth and replace it with belief in a falsehood.

Sönnatt – the Dwarvish High Council.

Soprina – a Nicián title, meaning Daughter Of, reserved for unmarried ladies of noble houses.

Talmathic Dömon – Amatt the Blind's great treatise on the Nature of the Taümatha. Written in First Dialect A'lyavine. Guarded most closely by the mages of the Cymàtagé.

Taümatha – the proper name for magic.

Taümathakiya – a device, glass-like in appearance and shaped like a giant teardrop, that resides in the Adak-rann monastery at Jàb-áldis. It is used to detect significant events of Taümathic origin.

Telem-aki – a most treasured historical reference and one of the Cymàtagé's most valuable books, charting the history of the lands that eventually became Alondria. Attributed to many authors, including Amatt the Blind.

Tongue of the Ancients – alternative name for the ancient language of A'lyavine.

Torvàstos – a flat plate-shaped mushroom that tastes a little like bread if dried out.

Tsnath – a common abbreviation used by the Alondrians to refer to the Tsnathsarré.

Printed in Great Britain
by Amazon